SHADOW BEAST SHIFTERS

RECLAIMED

JAYMIN EVE

Jaymin Eve

Reclaimed: Shadow Beast Shifters #2

Have you sold your soul to the Shadow Bastard yet?
What are you waiting for?

JAYMIN'S NERD HERD

Join the group. You know you want to ;)

The best way to stay up to date with the Shadow Beast Shifters world and all new releases, is to join my Facebook group here:

www.facebook/groups/jayminevenerdherd

We share lots of book releases, fun posts, sexy dudes, and generally it's a happy place to exist.

Library of Knowledge — Shadow Beast Shifters

SHADOW BEAST LAIR

FROZEN TUNDRA

DINING HALL

DESERT LANDS

FAERIE

WATCHERS

KARN

SHADOW REALM

VALDOR

HONOR MEADOWS

TUNDERA

BROLDER

DIRECTORY

Frozen Tundra

Desert Lands

Faerie

Watchers

Karn

Shadow Realm

Valdor

Honor Meadows

Tundera

Brolder

Grey lands
Shadow
Holister
Isle of Rechaste
Glistin
Ashan
Samsan Grove
Dety

alm

Chasm

ordes

The Depths

Danker

Trinity

Fraple

Green isle

Rodan

Outher islands

Chapter One

Grief was a debilitating and destructive emotion. Tearing through my soul, shredding it into unrecognizable pieces.

I had experienced a true grief with the death of my father, and back then I'd likened it to a temperamental ocean. One minute, I'd been calmly accepting the news of his demise, and the next, a cacophony of fear, anger and pain had engulfed me, until my emotions were a hurricane crashing against the sand.

Eventually, the storm of his betrayal and death had subsided, and I'd been able to mostly drift along. As more time passed, I'd even believed that I'd finally found my peace, only for some event to trigger another storm and send me back into the crashing waves of pain.

Dannie's death was so new to me that I should have been in stage one: calm denial. But I appeared to have skipped that altogether, and we were in stage two: hurricane season.

I couldn't bear to feel the pain, so I embraced the anger. Anger I was directing squarely at one person: Shadow Beast.

He stood before me, eight feet plus of ripped and gorgeous god...or more accurately, demon. His dark curls were a little tousled, like

1

he'd been through hell to get to me. In all honesty, the disheveled look only made him sexier.

But that wasn't going to save him today.

He had betrayed me in the worst kind of way—false promises that had gotten my friend killed. Or even worse, he'd had a direct hand in her death, explaining why he was always brushing off my concerns about her. Shadow hadn't wanted to piss me off before he'd gotten what he needed from me. He'd kept me prisoner, forced me to touch the Shadow Realm, and stopped me from returning to Torma when I'd known Dannie had been in trouble.

Dannie The Wanderer, who had been more of a mother to me than my own in the last ten years. Ironic in a way that on the same day I'd learned Lucinda Callahan, my actual birth mother, was dead, I'd also found out about Dannie.

One I had mixed feelings about—*my mom*—and the other was the cause of my current raging state.

The pack had killed her *because of me.* Because of Shadow. Both of us really, and she had been our responsibility to save.

"You promised me!" I seethed, and the flames that had inexplicably sprung to life across my skin rose higher. My hair followed suit, flying around me in a wave just as red as the flames themselves, power seeping from my pores.

All of the shifters around us slammed into the ground, and I heard the breaking of bones. A pleasant sound in my current state of being.

If this was what rising from the ashes meant for a phoenix, then I was embracing it to the fullest degree. This power... it was mine, and I would destroy any who stood in my way.

Shadow seemed to be almost spellbound by my current appearance, his gold and fire-touched eyes locked on me in their usual manner of complete and total focus. He dissected me with a mere glance, and even though he didn't speak, we were definitely communicating.

Both of us furious.

Both of us shocked as hell about this new development.

Neither willing to give an inch.

If an outsider was watching me now, they'd never believe that just a mere year ago, I'd been a normal wolf shifter. A year ago I'd never opened a doorway into the locked-away Shadow Realm. Or produced flames across my skin. Or controlled the creatures that I somehow drew from that realm into my world.

The last year had demonstrated that there was more to me than I'd ever known, and while most of the time it freaked me out, today... today I was embracing this change.

A change that had hopefully made me powerful enough to take on Shadow.

At this point the heat was almost pleasant, and I fanned the fire with more pain and anger. He reached out for me, and I waited to see if my flames would burn him.

His arm shot straight through, completely unscathed, and he wrapped one of his big hands around my throat. No doubt he thought that he had me in a vulnerable position, and even as the air was cut off in my lungs, I didn't struggle. I just smiled, my eyes detailing in no uncertain terms exactly what I had planned.

His demise.

"Sunshine," he rumbled, warning in his voice.

What the fuck was he warning me about? Losing my shit? Guess he should have thought of that before he got my friend killed.

His hand flexed against my throat, but I had a sense that he knew the fire power I channeled was preventing him from actually hurting me. This reaction was merely a warning to match the rebuke in his voice, but still... His negotiation skills needed as much work as his people skills.

"Mera. Control your power. You can do it." Reece tried to placate from the side, but neither Shadow nor I turned toward him. Nothing could have broken our gazes.

"What has upset her?" Shadow bellowed into the air. The shifters who had just been climbing to their feet around us hit the deck again. From what I could see anyway; I assumed all of them went down, and not just the ones in my peripherals.

"Dannie The Wanderer is dead."

I was almost certain those words had choked out of Dean Heathcliffe, former beta, and a shifter *high* on my murder list. A murder list was a normal twenty-three-year-old chick thing, right? The other names on there was my oldest *friend*—Jaxson Heathcliffe—and my true mate—Torin Wolfe. I hated them as much as Shadow. Actually, more.

And unlike Shadow, they couldn't counter my power or fight the fire, and that meant this attack was a wasted opportunity. I should have taken those motherfuckers out first, and then paused for a moment to figure out how to best Shadow.

Although... Torin had said he knew about Shadow's weakness. They'd used an incapacitating powder on him. A powder Dannie had lost her life to produce, and maybe that meant I could learn some important information before I stole their useless lives from them.

Shadow's eyes softened. It happened so rarely, but I'd seen it a time or two before. I refused to let it get to me as I would have yesterday. Before I'd found out about his betrayal.

"Mera, listen to me. Dannie is—"

The moment he said her name, my flaming fury surged up, and I embraced it full bodily. With no regard for personal safety or consequences of my actions, I catapulted myself out of his hold. A feat I'd never achieved before, but I was too far gone to even understand the significance of that.

Tilting my head back, my howling scream was deafening, and around us, the already knocked-down wolves cried out. Between Shadow and me, we were breaking these shifters, which was barely the tip of what I was going to do to them.

I let the fire and my wolf rise, and like an inferno hit with a ton of fuel, there was nothing that could have stemmed my pain. My eyes were closed, but I felt the connection to the Shadow Realm. I'd touched it enough times now that when I figured out how to open my link, I could follow the path.

To my vengeance.

Today I needed to assuage the pain in the only way I knew how.

Come to me...

I called them, every shadow creature I could reach, and... whatever else decided to tag along. My arms rose like I could embrace the darkness in this manner, and it was akin to the time I'd touched the spell blocking the doorway to the realm. I opened myself up to a shadowy entity, and it came right home.

My power spun webs around me, and when I finished releasing this new energy that had taken hold of me, my eyes shot open.

It took me a moment to understand what I was seeing.

To understand what I'd just done.

What have I done?

There was no fire now. It had been replaced by a literal wall of smoky darkness, and the sight of that was almost enough to shock me back into my right mind. In my fury I'd called a dark entity filled with synapsing lights, like those I'd often seen in Inky, Shadow's companion.

Speaking of, Shadow was the only being to remain in my line of sight. His flames a visible light in the otherwise endless darkness, as he attempted to break through *whatever the fuck I'd done.* For the first time, a new emotion bisected the relentless pain and anger inside me.

Fear.

I tried to backpedal and close the connection I'd carelessly thrown wide open. But it was like stopping a flood with a paper towel. There wasn't a hope in hell of me reversing what I'd put into place; it was already moving of its own volition.

Despite my current hatred for him, I had to turn to Shadow, hoping he held some answers. From what I could tell, I was truly about to end the world—or multiple worlds—with my selfish actions, and that was not okay. If Dannie knew what I'd set forth tonight in her name, she'd have kicked my ass until I couldn't sit down for a year. This was not what she would have wanted.

Shadow's power finally penetrated through the dark wall, and I hurried toward him while keeping a close eye on the synapsing smoke raging like a tropical storm around me.

"Shadow!" I screamed, throwing myself into the darkness. To my surprise, it didn't block me as it was blocking him, and I fell through like it had no substance at all, right into his arms.

He hauled me up, holding on almost desperately. "What do I do?" I sobbed. "I didn't mean to bring about the apocalypse."

As he held me closer than ever, I could have sworn he breathed me in as if he'd never expected to hold me like this again. It was over so fast, though, that maybe I'd misread the moment.

"Sunshine," he snapped, sounding like his typical asshole of a being, "you have called the mists from the Shadow Realm. You need to send them back before they bring with them every creature that has ever existed in my world."

I choked down my fear and worry. "I don't know how to! I'm useless, Shadow. Fucking useless. I couldn't save my friend. I couldn't stop the creatures. I couldn't open the door."

He shook me, and as my head snapped back, it actually helped to clear my thoughts. Still a bastard move, though.

"Listen to me," he rumbled, and there was so much command in his voice, I had no choice but to obey. "You're the least useless being I've ever met. The way you adapted to the Solaris System, making friends, helping and learning, is nothing short of admirable. You went to the top of my *never to be underestimated* list, and I promise, that's a small list."

His eyes were just red swirls of lava now, the gold faded out completely. And I could see the truth deep inside them. He meant every word he was saying, and I had no choice but to embrace his confidence in me.

I could do this. I had called them. I knew the pathway, and there had to be a way to return the mists.

"Let your pain go," he said softly, pulling me even closer. "I promise that it's not what you think about Dannie. You don't know everything, and I ask that you wait to hear me out before you try to kill me again."

The pain—gods, the pain was so intense as he said her name that I wished for death. Just for a brief moment so I could escape the stabbing force of knowing that she had been tortured and murdered because of me. All along, my anger had really been with myself, and while Shadow's words should have given me hope, I was too far gone for that.

He placed me on my feet, and I returned my focus to the spark-filled smoke. When I reached out and ran my hands over it, it responded almost immediately, curling around me just like... "Is this what Inky is?" I breathed.

"Yes," Shadow said, still pressed to my side.

Through the dark mists, I couldn't see any other person in the underground theater room, and I was seriously hoping I hadn't hurt my best friend, Simone, or Shadow's best friends, Reece and Lucien. The rest could go to hell, but those three were important.

"You must know how to control it," I said, a real punch of hope making itself known in my gut. Inky was a part of the mists that created the shadow creatures, and this thing I'd called was a hulked-out Inky. Stood to reason, right?

"No one controls the mists," Shadow informed me, dashing that hope in an instant, "but a few select beings have been known to bond with a sliver of them. As you've seen with Inky and me. A symbiotic relationship—at this point, we can't live without the other."

"So, is this one bonded to me?"

I could feel it, but not in a way that made me think we had any sort of *freaking symbiotic relationship.*

Shadow shook his head. "You could not handle the power of a mist this size. You have to return it, or I have no idea what the worlds will become."

We both eyed the insanely huge smoke show. "I have to send them back." A whispered truth. "And I have to do it now."

I felt the mists building in intensity, and soon they would escape my tenuous hold and wreak havoc across the lands. I could not let that happen, even if it destroyed me to return what I'd brought into this world.

Closing my eyes, I opened the pathway, and with not a freaking clue what I was doing, touched the smoke again, focusing on the tingling energy under my hands. *Return home,* I begged. *Back to the Shadow Realm.*

I'd never been bonded with Inky, so I hadn't truly understood what it was until this moment. The mists were energy like that of pure creation. A living brain with power beyond anything that had ever existed before. All of the Shadow Realm had been formed using this energy... this power blanket that covered their realm.

I might have only brought a small blob of the power to me, but it was still enough to throw all the worlds off-kilter.

Or worse.

The mists resisted, wanting to stay with me, but I persisted in my quest to return them. Their power threaded through my own, and just as I was about to panic, a disembodied, gender-neutral voice sounded in my head. *We'll see each other again soon.*

Just as I was about to lose my shit and start panic screaming, the resistance faded, and the mists returned through the path I had opened to the realm, leaving me with a mild sense of dread, and the age-old question that had plagued me more often than not lately: What was I?

Chapter Two

"Mera."

Shadow's murmur of my name brought me back to reality. Back to a room that was free of smoke but was filled with a lot of other shit that hadn't been there before I'd let my rage consume me.

Shadow creatures, to be more accurate, and they were spread out as far as I could see. Literally hundreds of them, clearly trying to figure out *what in the freaking shit they were doing here.*

"Fuck," Shadow breathed near my ear, and I had to agree.

"Didn't I send the mists back?" I asked, my heart pounding hard as air frantically sucked in and out of my mouth, while my lungs never seemed to fill.

Shadow shot me a sardonic stare. "You did, Sunshine, but you didn't return what it was hiding."

And the pathway was closed now.

I frantically tried to open it again, but either I was too exhausted, or it literally couldn't be done unless I was angry enough, because no connection sprung to life.

"They're going to kill everyone," I breathed.

Shadow nodded. "Yep."

Narrowing my eyes, I punched him. In the chest. And it fucking hurt... me. Damn his muscles and their rock-like structure. "Ouch and fuck," I cursed, shaking out my fist before flexing my fingers to help the healing process. "But at least you're still not setting my nerve endings on fire when I touch you. Silver lining."

Shadow wasn't smiling, but he also didn't smack me back, so that was a second bonus. "You've managed to do what I thought was impossible," he admitted. "My inbuilt security system no longer considers you... Well, let's just say that there might be six now who are free to touch me without consequences."

If it weren't for the fact that I might have just ended the world—and I still wasn't sure if I needed to be pissed at him over Dannie's death—I'd have shed a tear at that confession.

"Shadowshine," I murmured.

He grimaced, which almost got a smile out of me. His exasperation with our couple nickname was just like the good old days.

Before I could congratulate myself on annoying him once more, the creatures broke free from whatever confused state they'd been in and started rampaging around the room.

"Can you pull the fire from the lair?" I asked, lifting my voice to be heard over the ruckus. "Use it to round them up like you did last time."

He shook his head. "Since I have no idea what else you released, I can't risk the Solaris System. The fire will guard the knowledge."

I didn't even argue about that. The Library of Knowledge and Shadow's lair were two priceless libraries, filled with vast quantities of books about the universe. They had to be protected at all costs. Not to mention all the beings who either resided there or visited daily could be in danger because of me, and I'd never forgive myself if any of them got hurt.

"So what now?" I asked, my heart pounding in my chest at the reality of what we were facing. Hundreds of creatures. More than we'd ever seen or taken down before, and I had not a single clue how to fix this.

Shadow didn't answer, but he did shift me behind him so he could immobilize two creatures who were ready to attack. He moved so quickly that I only just caught sight of the beasts with their *Addams Family* look—long, dark brown hair completely over their faces—before they went down under Shadow's power. He trussed them up with some dark smoke energy, just as a large sprecker pounced from the side.

"Stop!" I commanded, without thought. It had been an instinctive move, and despite the somewhat defective nature of my instincts these days, this time it was right on the money.

Not only did the sprecker stop, but the other creatures did as well. The silence that followed was near deafening, after the noise from before.

Shadow straightened, his face impassive as he stared around the theater basement. He wasn't the only one, as I took a good look at what I'd done.

I was controlling the entire room of creatures, and as I had that realization, the energy strain on my body almost knocked me to my knees. "Shadow, I can't hold them," I bit out through gritted teeth.

"You have to hold them, Mera," he snapped. "If they're restrained in this way, I might be able to move them into the prison rooms."

He looked around, and as if they'd been waiting for his call, Reece and Lucien appeared in front of us. "Is her friend safe?" Shadow asked them.

Reece nodded, his cobalt blue eyes filled with dark emotions, near turning them black. "Yep. We got her out of here and back into their main pack house."

Lucien chuckled, flashing some fang, his blond hair more tousled than usual. "Simone cursed us out the entire way and made us promise that Mera would be safe when this was all done. She has fire, and I have to say... why have we not spent more time with humans?"

Simone was safe. The relief I felt at hearing this almost sent me to my knees, which were already weak and shaky. Reece smiled at me, and as he dropped a heavy hand on my shoulder, I crumpled forward. Shadow caught me before I faceplanted. "Careful," he warned, a growl in his chest. I wasn't sure which one of us he was warning, but Reece's hand lightened, and I was able to stand on my own again.

"I left extra safeguards around the pack house for tonight," Reece told me as he shuffled back a step, running a hand over his shaved head. "No creature will get in there."

Lucien flashed more fang as he looked around, semi-amused by the chaos. "Your overcautious approach was a waste of god-juice. Shadow's little Sunshine has managed to lock the realm creatures down with her particular brand of magic."

Shadow didn't correct him on me being "his sunshine." Instead, he focused on the way I was clearly slumping forward, all but resting against him.

"She's weakening," he said. "We need to get the creatures into a prison room, and hope it's strong enough to contain this many of them."

"Why did you save Simone?" I asked randomly, my head fuzzy. It had been the first question he asked his friends, and that was odd... right?

Shadow let out a low, suffering sigh. "Because she's important to you."

Such a simple answer, but he meant it. The truth was in his voice and eyes. "You didn't kill Dannie, did you?" In my rage, I hadn't given him a chance to admit or deny his guilt. I'd heard his name uttered by Dogshit Dean, and I'd stupidly jumped to conclusions. But logically, if he cared about Simone because of me, it stood to reason he wouldn't have taken part in Dannie's death, either.

Please say no. Please say no.

"No. I did not kill Dannie."

Thank fuck. It legitimately felt like a ten-ton weight had been lifted from my soul in that moment.

"I had nothing to do with her disappearance, Mera, and I will explain everything as soon as we deal with the creatures."

Right, that little issue.

"I have an idea," I said wearily, "and like most of my ideas, it'll probably be a lesson in disaster, but fuck, what other options do we have with this many of them here?"

Three sets of ancient, powerful, perfectly unique eyes locked on me. Red and gold, deep blue, and a forest green so striking it was almost mesmerizing. Fancy fuckers.

"What's your idea?" Shadow asked, reminding me that we were running out of time here.

"For some reason, I'm able to command these creatures," I said. "If I open a path again, I can send them back through to the realm."

I stumbled forward, a cough bursting from me as I struggled to catch my breath.

"You're tapped out with energy," Reece said softly, and he nudged Lucien out of the way so he could scoop me up into his arms. I wanted to protest, but he caught me just as my legs were about to give way. "Let Shadow do his thing. He can work with the hold you already have."

"This hold is going to kill her if she keeps it up," Shadow muttered. "How the fuck is she even doing this? I've not heard of any able to control creatures like this, except maybe a *Danamain*, the true Mist Born. Which is a damn myth."

Reece and Lucien shook their heads. "I have no idea," the vampire breathed, his eyes on me.

Exhausted, I had to close my own eyes, and as I rested my head against Reece's firm chest, I struggled to keep control of the creatures.

"Give her to me," Shadow demanded, and I was fairly certain I'd missed parts of the conversation, fatigue sending my hearing all wonky. Exhaustion could shut down regular bodily functions, apparently. Who knew?

"You're the only one with a shot at getting these creatures out of here before Earth becomes their hunting ground," Reece bit back. "You can handle me holding her for ten fucking minutes."

Shadow's familiar rumbling growl was actually comforting. It was nice that I didn't have to murder him when this was all over. Not fighting every battle alone made a big difference, and I wasn't sure I could ever go back to doing it all by myself.

That would be another death. One of the soul.

Chapter Three

Holding on to the control of the creatures as we left Torma was almost the end of me. I'd just about reached my limit by the time we arrived at the long, white hallway that connected Earth to the Library of Knowledge.

Between the three musketeers and me, we dragged the hundreds along the hall, while Shadow spent what felt like forever, searching the rooms until he found one he was satisfied would hold them.

"It'll have to do for now, until Mera gets her strength back," he said. "Then we can try her plan of returning them through whatever path connects her to the realm."

At this point, I had all but passed out, my brain only coming back online when Shadow growled at Reece.

"Give her to me." Those words were low and dark. "I need to warm her up and get some energy flowing into her again."

Reece let out a low chuckle, and since my eyes were all but glued shut, I couldn't see their expressions. I hated that, but for now, their words would have to tell me everything.

"*I* can warm her up," Lucien said from the side. "It's my specialty."

There was movement and a heavy thud, followed by Lucien's groan. "Just kidding, brother. You know how I roll."

I didn't know how he rolled, but it really didn't matter because I was now in Shadow's arms, and it was here that I felt far too fucking comfortable. "Walk," I managed to choke out. I couldn't lose myself to the beast. At least not until I knew more about him. I might believe he didn't have anything to do with Dannie's death, but he still knew way more than he was letting on. Until I knew it as well, it was best to be cautious.

He just held me closer, his arms strong bands under my ass and across my back. "Release them, Mera," he said, the mild Scottish burr in his voice deepening for a moment. "You need to let go, or they'll take you into the mists with them."

That was too terrifying an idea after everything I'd seen tonight.

"They're definitely contained in the prison?" I managed to choke out, my exhaustion complete.

"They are," he confirmed.

I hesitated and Shadow sighed. "You have no choice but to trust me. Release them or die; those are your options."

Dammit. The big fucker had me there.

You are free.

Instinct took over in my near-dead state, and I didn't fight it like I might have normally. The moment my hold on them faded out, a literal boost of energy cleared my head, and I jerked upright, my eyes open.

"Let me down," I demanded, the blinding white of the hallway making me blink watery eyes as I glared up at the beast.

"Shut up," Shadow snapped, not even glancing at my A-Game resting bitch face. An epic look wasted once again.

"Just like old times," I grumbled, trying to dredge up enough energy to fight him.

Pretty sure he said something about *annoying shifters*, which was drowned out by Reece's laughter.

"Give up, Mera," the desert deity said, and I wasn't sure when we'd become such good friends, but at some point, he'd thawed toward me, acting nothing like the original asshole I'd met in the lair. "Shadow cannot be bested when he sets his mind to a task. Let him take care of you."

I snorted and then groaned, pressing a hand to my forehead. "I don't need a Shadow nurse. I can sort my own shit out, thanks very much."

Digging my elbows into his chest, I tried to leverage myself away, but his hold didn't give an inch. Not. One. Fucking. Inch.

Did he have to be powerful in all ways? It was overkill.

"Sunshine, just... I need to do this, okay?"

He almost sounded sad, and it halted my struggle as I tilted my head back to see him. "Did you kill Dannie? Or in any way contribute to her death?"

Now that I wasn't distracted with hundreds of creatures, my head much clearer, I needed to ask again.

His steps slowed. "She's not dead."

I just blinked at him, trying to figure out if my ears had malfunctioned.

"Don't—" I broke off as my throat got tight. "Please don't lie to make me feel better... Her blood was everywhere. And the pack used her knowledge or energy or *something* to get into the library and shut it all down."

"Those bastards took her blood," he confirmed, "and since she was born in the Shadow Realm, they used it to concoct the potion that knocked me and the library out for a few minutes. It was also powerful enough to block the doorway because it reacted to anything that was connected to me. It wasn't until your power called me that I could break through the blocking spell."

I was blinking at him. Over and over. "Dannie is from the Shadow Realm?" I whispered.

What in the fuck? How in the fuck?

Shadow nodded. "Yes. I don't know the finer details of it, but I recognized her power."

I shook my head like that would clear the jumble of thoughts in there. It didn't help.

Maybe it was best to focus on the part that was even more important. "You promise she's not dead?" I was crying. I tried hard not to cry these days, and especially not in front of Shadow, but the sobs just burst up from my chest and didn't stop coming.

"Fuck," Shadow said softly, and then he was shifting my position so he could hug me. My legs wrapped around his waist as he held me tightly.

"She's not dead? You promise?" I repeated, sobbing into the spot between his neck and shoulder. The heat of his power wrapped around me, but I didn't even care in my distraught state.

His chest shook as an annoyed rumble escaped him. "She's not dead, Sunshine. I don't know who she is or how she made it into your world, but once I smelled her blood, I knew she was from the Shadow Realm. I've been trying to track her ever since, but there's no sign of where she ended up."

"How much blood?" I asked, sniffling. "And how can you be sure she's—"

He cut me off. "I've told you before, no Shadow Realm being can be killed by shifters, even if they believe they had the power to do it. She's out there somewhere, reforming, to one day be your Dannie again."

My tears had started to dry now, but I kept my head buried against Shadow's shoulder. He strode forward again, and it should have been weird and uncomfortable for him to keep holding me this way, but I was an emotional wreck, weak and mentally shaken, so I let it happen. For a few minutes, I soaked up his comfort, but that all came to an end.

"I can walk."

He didn't argue, setting me on my feet. I wobbled for a beat, but he allowed me to find my own strength, and as I wiped away the tears on my face, I noticed Reece and Lucien hovering just behind their friend.

"Thank fuck," Lucien said, his hands held in tight fists at his side. "I never know what to do when women cry. I'm glad Shadow was here."

I narrowed my eyes just as Reece barked out a laugh. "I had no idea Shadow knew what to do with a crying woman, either. Usually, he just silences them with his power so he can't hear their sobs any longer."

The beast himself crossed his arms, staring both of his friends down, and their laughter died off, even if the smiles remained. They didn't fear him, but they respected him. Shadow was lucky to have friends like his. Speaking of...

"I will need to see Simone very soon," I warned him. "Whenever you explain to me exactly what just happened on Earth, I want her to be part of it."

Reece and Lucien were already shaking their heads. "Shadow will never allow another human—"

The desert deity was cut off when Shadow said, "I will make it happen."

All three of us were shocked into silence, and I tried to clear my dry throat. "Thank you," I told Shadow, feeling as if we'd reached a place of mutual respect that we hadn't visited before.

Maybe it was my power matching his for a brief moment on Earth, or how I'd apparently called him when I'd lost my shit. Or maybe it was another secret that I wasn't aware of yet. Only time would tell, and it appeared that I was finally going to learn more about the Shadow Realm, the mists, and these creatures I continued to call into my world.

Had Dannie known what I was all along? She'd definitely taken an interest in me from her first arrival in Torma, and it hurt to think that maybe it had all been a ruse. She'd been a mother figure, but maybe like my real mom, she really hadn't given a fuck about me.

What had her endgame been, though? In the ten or so years we'd known each other, she'd never asked me for anything. She'd given me a job, paid me well, protected me, and cared for me when life had been knocking me down. I found it hard to believe that was all just an act.

Hopefully one day, I'd get a chance to ask her.

"You need to rest," Shadow told me, and he wasn't wrong since I'd once again just drifted off in my fuzzy brain.

"Yes. Right."

We started to walk along the hall, and I was getting more than one concerned look from the three dudes around me, but before anyone could bring it up, a figure burst from the veil connected to the library and flew toward us.

"Angel!" I exclaimed, and if I'd had the energy to run, I would have met her halfway. As it was, I barely managed to hobble a few steps before I wanted to curl up and take a nap.

She must have seen me stumble, and using her wings and preternatural speed, she was at my side in less than a second. Wrapping her arms around me, she steadied me before I fell. "What happened?" she demanded, looking fierce in her battle armor. It reminded me of how she'd fought Shadow for me, right before the library had been attacked by a few dickhead shifters.

Angel was the sort of friend every woman deserved.

"After the battle with Shadow, I went into the dining hall to calm down," she continued, "only to learn upon my return that the library had been attacked and you were taken. The barrier wouldn't allow me to leave and track you on Earth. I've been trying ever since."

Over her shoulder, I found Shadow's eyes. "The barrier was blocked?"

He nodded, completely unsurprised. "I shut it all down until I knew what we were dealing with. An extra protection against any new threats while I was busy getting the current situation under control."

Simmering anger brewed in his eyes, and his jaw was so rigid that I wouldn't have been surprised to hear his teeth crack. The reminder that shifters had managed to sneak in under his watch was sending him into a dark place. And when Shadow went dark, bad things happened.

I turned back to Angel, hoping for a distraction. "Were you planning on heading to Earth to help? Once you got through the barrier?" She'd all but torn into the hall in a frenzy when Shadow had finally released it.

She shook her head. "No. Well, yes and no. I was coming to find you, but I also needed to see Shadow." She stepped away, keeping one hand on me like she knew her energy was helping regulate mine. "The door is open," she said.

It was at this moment my distracted mind snapped into gear. I froze as the absolute truth of what she'd just said penetrated my brain. There was only one door that anyone would speak about with such a combination of fear and distaste.

"Shadow Realm?" Shadow bit out, and he was as focused as me.

Angel nodded. "I don't know how it happened, but the spell on the door is broken. It happened not long ago."

Shadow looked at me, but it wasn't necessary. I'd already done the math, and it was growing obvious that when I'd brought the mists and creatures from the realm to Earth, I'd done more than put my world in peril.

I'd finally opened the door that had been barred for nearly two thousand years.

The door to Shadow's destiny.

Chapter Four

I'd known Shadow for an indeterminate amount of time, but it was at least a year in Earth days, and I'd never seen him move as fast as he did in that moment.

He was literally here one second and gone the next, leaving behind nothing much more than a puff of smoke. If I had to guess, the shadows he controlled had absorbed him and were about to spit him out in the Library of Knowledge.

Lucien and Reece disappeared as well, and almost as quickly, while I was still staring open-jawed at the spot they had all been standing a micro-second earlier.

Angel didn't leave me, tightening her hold around my body as I began hobbling toward the door. "Go," I said, waving my hand forward. "Go and help them. I'll get there in a minute."

"No." Her reply was short and not-that-sweet.

"Angel," I said, forcing my legs to move faster. "You're a warrior. Go battle or whatever you do. I'm holding you back."

She snorted, some of the tension in her tight shoulders easing. "Side by side, girl. We fight side by side, remember? I would never leave a friend behind. And you don't have to worry. The spell on the door has been broken for more than a few minutes, and so far nothing has walked through. They're quite possibly not even aware in the realm that they're free."

One person would be aware, though. The one who'd cast the spell.

"I did this," I admitted, needing her to know that I probably wasn't worthy of her epic-as-fuck friendship. "I thought they'd killed Dannie, the woman who half-raised me, and I lost my shit. I might have possibly *calledthemistsandabillionshadowcreatures*." In shame, I ran all the words together, but Angel's quick mind followed along with ease.

"You did nothing wrong, Mera. Your life has been controlled by forces beyond you for a long time now. You're reacting to the pressure cooker you've been placed under. No one should be surprised when you finally burst into flames."

Wait? Did she know about that?

"Uh, so yeah. I kind of *did* burst into flames," I admitted. "Fire raced across my skin, the same way Shadow's power often reacts."

She blinked at me, and it was clear that her previous comment hadn't actually been a literal reference to the events on Earth.

"You and Shadow have a similar energy," she finally said, her surprise fading as she thought it through. "Not like you're related," she added quickly, knowing me well enough by now to know that my mind immediately went there. "Your powers are compatible. It's interesting, and... it makes sense that you ended up calling the shadows and the flames."

I stumbled. "Seriously? You don't think my reaction was a little excessive? I'm full on kicking my own ass at the moment over how I acted."

She shrugged. "When my family was destroyed, I went on a destructive campaign that lasted sixty years. You got yourself together pretty fast, in my opinion."

Sixty. Years.

Yeah, okay, so maybe she did get it and wasn't judging me at all. It was actually nice to have someone in my corner, and maybe when we got to the bottom of the mystery of *what the actual fuck I was*, Angel and I could spend some time working on our bond. I'd like to see it step up to the next level, just in case she ever needed me for the same support she always offered me.

For now, though, we had far greater concerns to *overthink and unnecessarily stress about.*

"What do you expect will happen now that the Shadow Realm door is no longer barred?" I asked when we reached the veil leading into the library.

Angel didn't answer until we'd stepped through to the other side. "No one has any idea. It's been barred longer than most have lived, and for the rest of us, only time will tell what has changed in that realm."

Well, damn. That was legitimately not even a tiny bit reassuring.

Just as she walked toward the crowds gathered near the Shadow Realm door, I had a sudden thought. Turning to the magical white button, I slapped my hand against it. "Directory."

When the blueprint of the library appeared, I wasted no time pressing the Shadow Realm door. Angel returned to my side, and if her expression was any indication, she was as curious as I was to see if it said the same thing as last time: *Shadow Realm: Information unknown. Critical error.*

There was a ding, and we both stared in silence.

"That's new," she breathed.

Shadow Realm: Built on the ancient mists of yin and yang energy. The royals are the supreme rulers, keeping under their control the creatures, except those that roam in The Grey Lands.

"Holy shit," I said, eyeballing the directory like it held all the answers. "The doorway is really open."

The truth of that had finally hit me. *The realm was freaking open.* Shadow would have no more use for me. He could finally get his revenge, and... what would become of me and my life here?

Why did I suddenly feel like I was about to be homeless? Even worse, kicked out of my favorite places in the world: the libraries. My heart squeezed tightly, and my hands started to sweat as I wrung them together.

I could give up a lot, but I wasn't sure I could stop living among the knowledge and beauty and ancient history so prevalent in the Library of Knowledge and the lair. This place had burrowed its way into my soul, and I couldn't let it go.

It would destroy me.

"Let us go see what has transpired with this new development," Angel said, nudging me toward the main section of the library.

Feeling like *I* was the ancient, thousand-year-old being, I sighed. "Formal talk, hey? Must be serious."

She managed not to roll her eyes at me, but I knew she wanted to. She was just too mature and badass to bother with such a human gesture. "I'm just worried about what we might walk into, and whether or not I can protect you. We need all the information we can gather because eventually something will exit from the realm, and right now you're vulnerable."

I snorted, hobbling after her like I was eighty years older than my current age of... Twenty-three. At some point, I'd had a birthday, but no one cared when most of my friends were in their thousands. "You know I'm the one who broke through the lock on the door"—*with zero idea of how I did it*—"and controlled a bunch of shadow creatures so that Shadow could get them locked away. I think *I'm* the one who'll be taking care of all of *you.*"

She laughed, a beautiful tinkling sound. At the same time, she sent her wings out to stop the crowds from knocking into us. "Big talk from someone walking at a ninety-degree angle."

"Gods, I would kill for an energy boost of some form," I moaned. "It's weird because I'm exhausted, but it's more than just a physical thing. It feels almost soul deep."

The closer we moved to the Shadow Realm door, the more crowded the area got. Angel eventually had to tuck her wings back in because there was literally no room for them. We started pushing our way forward.

"Tell me everything that happened from when you were captured by the shifters," she said, taking in the scene, tendrils of worry finally seeping into her tone.

Sticking close to Angel, since she was the muscle getting us through, I detailed quickly—and quietly—what had transpired from the moment I'd left the library in the arms of two dumbfuck shifters. Shifters I still had to murder.

I finished up with how I'd called the mists and creatures, which had finally torn through the spell on the realm doorway.

Angel listened to the entire story before speaking. "Do you believe Shadow when he says that Dannie was born in his realm and couldn't have been killed?"

"I have to until proven otherwise. For my own sanity." Most of the pain was dulled now, just a sliver of aching hollowness that would remain until I saw her again.

She nodded. "I haven't known him to be a liar," she admitted. "I mean, he would conceal information if he felt it wasn't relevant, or for other reasons—he's a secretive beast. But I don't know him to outright lie."

"I agree."

And I did. Shadow was a lot of things, most of them annoying as fuck, but he wasn't a liar. Nope, he was more along the lines of a sneaky bastard.

When we got through the last of the onlookers—what was with all the Brolder animal asses taking up all the room in here?—we reached six broad shoulders. The kings of the Solaris System had formed a semi-circle around the door, blocking it completely from view.

Shadow and his merry band of assholes.

As if he'd felt my energy—or scented me—the beast turned, his eyes running across my features. No doubt copping an eyeful of one exhausted, hot mess.

"Sunshine," he said in a tone that brooked no argument. "Get your ass into bed."

Len, the silvery fae, opened his mouth, but a single dark look from Shadow had him backing off, both hands held up in front of him. His expression was all innocent, like he'd never think or say anything untoward or sexual in nature. We all knew better.

I ignored them both, choosing to speak with Reece, whom I felt might actually provide me with accurate information. "What's happening with the door?"

He set those intense blue eyes on me, with their impossibly long eyelashes, and I swallowed hard. Shadow *the second* was too hot for his own good. Just like Shadow *the first*. "The spell is broken, but the door has not been used yet." He shook his head. "How did you manage what the rest of us couldn't in thousands of years?"

I shrugged. "I got pissed off?" Vast, *epically vast*, understatement. "Never fuck with a woman scorned, and all that jazz."

There was a minute of silence, until Len started to laugh, which set a couple of them off. Even Galleli, with his gold wings tucked neatly against his back, cracked a smile. "Remind me never to upset Mera," Lucien said with a chuckle. "Unless I want to find myself turned into a puddle of blood."

Ignoring the idiots in the room, I focused on Shadow. "Are you done with me now?" The laughter died off, and there was no evidence of a smile on any one of their faces. I wondered if they'd misunderstood the intent of my question. "Will you send me back to Earth?" I pushed.

Shadow turned his huge body toward me, crowding closer, and I stood my ground so we were near touching. "Do you *want* to leave?"

I swallowed roughly, my body going haywire at being this close to him. We'd had that one night together in Faerie, and since then, life had been a shitshow, and I'd had no chance to really think about what had happened. But my body remembered. The way he'd buried his head between my thighs, his talented tongue that had brought me to orgasm more times than I could have imagined...

Shadow leaned right down so he could run his nose along my neck—unsurprisingly, this dude had a lot of shifter tendencies. "You smell delicious, Sunshine."

He could scent my arousal; I didn't bother to get embarrassed about it. But I did need him to focus. "Are you sending me back to Earth now that you've achieved your goal of getting into the Shadow Realm?"

My words were clipped and brittle. Maybe it was the reality of leaving hitting me hard, but all of a sudden, I was desperate to stay. I wasn't done; there was so much more here that I had to explore.

He reached out and brushed back a lock of my red hair, his hold on the strands almost possessive. "Answer my question, Sunshine." The low voice vibrated through me, settling somewhere... quite low. "Do you want to leave?"

"No." The absolute truth of that was slamming through me with the force of a bullet. "I have so much more to experience and learn; I've only just gotten started."

The hand holding on to my hair shifted, sliding farther through the long, somewhat tangled strands so he could gently tug my head back. Our gazes met with a searing connection, energy almost visible in the air. He was so much taller than me that immediately my neck ached, but as his strong fingers caressed my scalp, the last thing I would do was complain.

"I need to know what you are, Sunshine," he said softly, and it almost sounded like a threat. "You're not going anywhere until the mystery is unraveled. The fact that you broke a near two-thousand-year-old spell on a door when no one else could, tells me it's in my best interest to unravel your mystery."

"So I'm staying?" I confirmed.

"Yes. You're still mine. For now."

Relief almost crushed me to my knees—not that I'd ever admit that to the beast before me.

"When are you heading into the Shadow Realm?" I asked.

He shook his head. "I'm not sure, but probably not today. I have some preparations to make first."

"What do I do while you're in the realm?"

A perfect smirk appeared on his face. "It's cute that you think I'd leave you here unsupervised." He shook his head. "Nope, Sunshine. You're coming with me. We're going to figure out your connection to my world if it's the last thing we do."

With those ominous words, he stepped aside, and I saw the Shadow Realm doorway for the first time. Gone was the black smoke, and in its place was a solid black door. The only black door in the library.

And apparently, I would soon be exploring this realm. A world that had not been visited by outsiders for thousands of years.

No problem.

Chapter Five

I was done, exhausted to the point of delirium. Shadow saw me swaying on my feet and nudged me toward his lair. "Get some sleep. I need you fully functioning when we make our way into the realm."

I just nodded or shook my head... I might have even been drooling as I mumbled something about Simone, and was assured she would be secured and brought to the library. Then, with the help of Angel, who half-carried me, I made my way to the barrier between the lair and library.

"I'm coming with you to the Shadow Realm," she said shortly, her face set in hard, determined lines. "I don't trust Shadow Beast to put your safety above his own agenda."

Our eyes met, and the magenta in hers was the pinkest I'd ever seen. That color felt like it was penetrating into my damn soul, but in a good way. Warm and fuzzies. "I feel the same way," I said softly. "He's proven more than once that I'm only a means to an end. But I need to know who I am as well, so I'm not going to fight him."

Angel nodded once. "You must discover your truth so that, moving forward, you will be at the strongest you can be."

She pressed her hand to the spot above my breast, where she'd previously bonded us, and I could have sworn I felt her emotions for a brief second. A mix of worry and determination to get us both through this alive.

Following this was a definite boost to my energy that would give me enough juice to make it into the lair and my bed.

"Our bond grows stronger," she said, sounding surprised. "What should take decades appears to be maturing much faster."

I blinked at her but didn't bother to ask why. No one knew what the heck to expect when it came to me and my energy. We were just going with it.

"Get some rest," Angel said softly, a heavier accent slipping through before she tucked her true self away again. Angel was excellent at blending—quite the achievement for a near supermodel-goddess. Occasionally, though, I caught a glimpse of the being she'd been before her family had been lost to her. Before she was alone and broken.

I got a glimpse of the true heart of Angel. And it was so fucking pure.

"I'll see you soon," I promised. "And thank you for taking this journey with me. Together, we will keep an eye on Shadow."

"We certainly will," she promised.

She left and I made my way into the lair. It was warm and welcoming inside, and I felt the oddest urge to run to the fire and give it a hug. Maybe it wouldn't even burn me now that I'd found some unknown source of internal fire that I could produce on my skin.

On a whim, I tried to turn into a fireball again, but there wasn't the faintest ember. My energy might have been too drained, or just like everything else, I could only channel that shit when I was rocking a fury so complete, it was its own entity.

Dannie... She was still on my mind, and just the memory of her "death" had my hands trembling. Every part of me was hoping that Shadow was right, that she was alive and reforming somewhere, and I would see her again. That was the one hope getting me through.

Not wanting to be alone with my messed-up thoughts, I ended up crashing onto one of the couches before the fire, snuggled down until my entire body let out a sigh.

Here, wrapped in the warmth of the fire's embrace, I felt safe. So I let myself rest.

INKY WOKE me some time later, its energy a distinct tingle of power. As it drifted closer to my face, my eyes shot open, the wolf in my chest stirring as a low rumble spilled from my throat. It was instinctive after being woken by a powerful entity, even if I'd known exactly what was here with me.

Blinking, I cleared my throat. "Inky?" I rasped. "What are you doing?"

The smoke swelled larger, and in the same instant, I backed right up on the couch because it looked different. Inky was now more of a midnight purple, swirls of green breaking up the endless darkness. "Did something happen to you when I opened the doorway?" I asked. Stupidly, because I couldn't communicate with Shadow's bonded mist.

Mist. I finally had an idea of what Inky was, and the reason he was bonded to Shadow. The beast had taken a small part of the creation energy of his land and tied his soul to it. Weird, but what an awesome boost to his own powerbase.

"Inky?" I pushed. "You're weirding me out. What do you want?"

Reaching toward it, I let my hand brush across the tendrils flickering around the dark edges. Inky hadn't shocked me in months, so I was taken completely by surprise when a heavy jolt shot up my arm.

With a yelp, I almost fell to the floor as my arm went completely numb. Panic kicked in hard, and at the same time my wolf surged forward pushing us to change. She slammed against an invisible barrier, my body unable to shift with Inky's power surging through us.

There was another pulse in my aching arm, and I tried to lift it to cradle it closer to my body, but I couldn't even move a finger. Whatever Inky had done, my limb was no longer responding, and that was not good news. Especially for a shifter with excellent healing abilities.

There was one of two explanations for its current behavior: Inky had gone rogue or this wasn't Inky. Both options were equally horrifying.

My legs still worked, so I pushed myself up, backing away from the *clearly different-colored* cloud of mist. My useless arm dragged beside me as I growled.

"Stay back," I warned, stupidly because I had zero weapons to use against it.

Mine.

The word filtered through my head and since it was not my thought or internal voice, I quite rightfully had a mini freak-out. A cold blast of foreign energy wrapped around me, and almost in the same instant, my arm started to respond.

I lifted it so I could quickly check it over, pausing at the sight of a shimmery purple mark on my palm. In the exact spot *I'd just touched Inky Two.*

This wasn't good. This was not good.

Mine.

Again! *What the fuck?* "Did... you just talk to me?"

It drifted closer, and while not touching me, I could literally feel the power it wielded. I hadn't been able to do that before I'd been marked with a purple tattoo *scarily close in color to the mist itself.*

You are ours. We belong to the same land. You called me and now we are bonded.

It swelled larger, its sparking synapses flashing in the same way as Inky.

Wait... bonded?

"I don't want to be bonded with you!" My words came out shouty, but it was starting to turn into an epic sort of joke how all of these powerful *things* just bonded to me, or kidnapped me, or rejected me without asking for my damn permission.

You will grow used to our bond. It will be as if you never knew life without this connection.

Yeah, somehow I strongly doubted that.

"I knew Inky could communicate," I bit out, pissed as fuck.

Like I'd summoned Shadow's bonded mist, the original Inky burst into sight from behind some shelves, all swelled up and sparking like crazy. Seeing them together it was clear the purple one needed its own name, so I decided on a whim to go with Midnight. Seemed fitting.

They started to circle each other, and in this close proximity, all but facing off against the other, their differences were so obvious that I wondered how my dumb ass had ever thought Midnight was Inky.

They were both clearly mists, though. Had Midnight been part of the huge mist I'd called in my fury on Earth? Was this a section that had escaped my attempt to return it?

"Stop it!" I shouted when they started sending sparks at each other, clearly not friends. The two mists obeyed almost immediately —to my fucking surprise—moving and drifting apart.

Midnight swelled, starting to shake. I'd always assumed that when Inky did that, it was laughing, and sure enough, there was a weird vibration of sound in my mind.

The mists' version of amusement.

You will come to appreciate me being on your team.

Somehow I doubted that I would ever appreciate having a voice in my head.

"Inky," I said turning to Shadow's minion. "Can you please get your bonded bastar—beast. Your bonded beast. I need to have a quick word with him about Midnight." I jerked my head toward the other smoke cloud.

Inky thankfully didn't "argue" with me, disappearing fast, and I warily watched Midnight, my pillow held in front of me like that would keep it back.

Midnight?

It didn't need to be close or touching me to project thoughts, and I shook my head at the invasive feeling. "You have midnight purple in your colors and Inky doesn't. It helps keep things straight in my head if I name them. I'm sort of human in that way."

It jiggled again, and I felt the connection of thoughts and realities as it sifted through my memories of Earth. Of human television. Of the past and future as we knew or guessed at. In mere minutes, it had the complete and total knowledge of everything I'd taken twenty-three years to learn.

The mists were scarily powerful, and I wasn't sure I was capable of handling this new bond, but there seemed to be very little I could do about it. Maybe Shadow would know a way to sever the bond.

Speaking of, where the fuck was he?

Wait... Why had Inky even needed to leave to get Shadow? Could they not communicate over long distances? Supposed I had the perfect entity to ask...

"Can you talk in my head if I'm far from you?"

It swelled. *The mark on your palm is part of my energy, and through it, I can feel your life force, but for us to communicate, we have to be in close proximity. Especially while the bond is so new. But if you need me, through time and space, I can feel it.*

Then it was similar to the bond Angel thought would eventually grow for us, but with Midnight, it was near instantaneous.

"What exactly are you?"

Midnight rushed forward and wrapped around my arms in a similar manner to how Inky acted with Shadow. There was no pain or numb limbs this time, just a pleasant warmth, my palm tingling hardcore until the bond between us settled. It was the way I imagined owning a snuggly pet would feel... comforting.

Before I could contemplate my new companion, flashes of a world appeared in my head. Memories. But not mine.

The Shadow Realm was created through a collision of two energies, Midnight said, showing me swirling black and purple sparkles. One looked like fairy lights, the other glittering diamonds, and when the two met, it was an atomic bomb in force.

Midnight had been there. At the first creation of its world.

Well, damn.

Way to make a shifter feel somewhat insignificant and infantile.

It took a long time for the dust to settle, and when it did, the mists blanketed the entire land, a living energy that allowed an ecosystem to form below. First came the waters, and then the lands grew above. The creatures, the freilds, who are like humans, and the royals evolved after that. The two mists still war, and it's only in the place of origin that we are bonded. Here, where the creatures are born, is the one place you'll find pure and complete creation.

I was following along with the images and words, the place of origin Midnight showed me, looking like my imagined fantasy of the Garden of Eden. Flush with life and bursting with red and gold colors.

Your Inky is from the leicher mists, those that blanket from below, and technically, we are warring entities.

The images were so vivid as they detailed a brief but complete history of the Shadow Realm. I could see that in lots of ways, it was similar to Earth, but what had taken millions of years of evolution in my world, the mists had done in the realm in much less time.

"Why are we bonded?"

Shadow had implied it was very rare, and considering I was a damn shifter with no obvious origins in their world, well... I had a lot of questions that needed answers.

Midnight swelled larger, lights shooting around it faster than ever.

It is not common, but I was called to you. There will be a reason, but the time has not arrived for us to know it.

Great.

Before I could freak the fuck out—and let's be real, I was overdue—Shadow stormed into the room, his face awash in fury.

I stood and my smoke cloud wrapped around me. Inky did the same to Shadow, and I had to stop and wonder... if they were competing energies, did that mean Shadow and I would be enemies as well?

Were our powers set to fight the other's for eternity?

Chapter Six

"**M**era," Shadow said, his voice as serious as I'd ever heard it. "Step away from the mist."

I snorted, crossing my arms. "I'm afraid you're too late for this lecture. About the same as advising a dude to wear a condom after his chick is already pregnant."

Shadow paused, his head tilting left and then right as he examined us closely, trying to get a look in from every angle. I could have saved him the trouble by telling him that no matter which angle he used to look, Midnight and I were very much bonded, and nothing was changing that.

"It's bonded to me." Impatience was my middle name.

He shook his head. "Impossible."

My smile was definitely not filled with joy. "You keep saying that about me. Maybe at this stage, we can agree that nothing is truly impossible when it comes to my fuckups."

His eyes were flinty as he shook his head again. "Mera, that mist is not from the *leicher* like Inky. It's the antithesis of Inky, and I have no control over its power."

I knew this to some degree, thanks to my own mist.

"Where is Midnight from?"

His brow furrowed as he pinched the bridge of his nose. "Of course you've already named it."

I smiled sweetly. "Don't pretend you're surprised by that."

He shot me a deadpan stare in return. "Your mist is from the ether region. A high-up mist that blankets from above, while the leicher covers from below."

"They join at the point of origin," I reminded him. "So maybe it'll be okay."

He blinked. "That translation is rough, but yes, it works."

I understood then that Midnight had been communicating in English, clearly, because I'd comprehended it. And that some of the realm words had no literal translation. Shadow got it, though, and that was all that mattered.

"The mists of Leicher are much more controllable than the Ether region."

That was a warning.

Inky swelled, growing super large until it was a wall behind Shadow. Midnight apparently didn't like that, bursting to life in a purple haze of *whatthefuckery*.

"It's dick measuring time," I said, somewhat amused. My eyes met Shadow's. "You gonna whip yours out too? You might be the underdog here, but I'd still put some money on you."

His lips twitched. "Anyone ever tell you your smartass mouth is going to get you killed?"

Another snort of laughter. "Old news, my friend. Very old news."

Shadow actually grinned, the first true smile since he'd entered the room to find me once again breaking the laws of his world. Focusing on the plump, perfect planes of his lips, I wondered how, for the love of shifters, I was lusting over the devil?

"Your mist is communicating with Inky," Shadow said suddenly, his eyes locked on the two of them towering above us.

We are reaching a truce to coexist with you both.

I nodded. "It's going well, right? A truce is the best we could hope for."

Shadow looked like he needed a moment to wrap his head around what was happening here. "Your mere existence is upsetting the delicate balance of these worlds, and I have no idea if we'll all survive the fallout when whatever is coming makes itself known."

I took a step closer to him. "What is coming?"

His face gave away no secrets. "I have no idea, but one thing is clear: Nothing will be the same now that you've embraced your destiny. We're about to find out the true shine of your light, Sunshine." His smile was mocking. "Let the games begin."

For some reason, this didn't send me into a tailspin of panic and existential dread. My upbringing in Torma pack had prepared me well for this life, and the thought that I might not make it to the next moonrise had always been my constant.

This was just the next challenge, and I'd deal with whatever terrible shit happened... well, when it happened.

"It'll be fine," I told Shadow. "Let's put our positive thoughts out into the world. We've got this."

His laughter was low and unexpected. "You are delightfully human at times. Naïve, but I enjoy the break from normalcy."

"I aim to please." And at least he didn't have his hand around my throat today, so we were making progress.

Inky and Midnight, having finished their standoff "conversation," shrunk down to small clouds of smoke again, each wrapping around their bonded partner. Despite my misgivings about this bond, there was a facet of comfort in its presence, and I'd only had about ten minutes to get used to it.

Shadow was just staring, those flames in his eyes flickering brightly. "I've never known another to bond to the mists. It's beyond rare. "

"How did you?"

His expression morphed and I almost took a step back. For a brief moment in time, he personified death, a mask of darkness shrouding his features. "I'm the Supreme Being, the true heir." He had told me this before, but not in much detail. "I was betrayed the day I should have received my power, and as I was sent from my world, I dragged Inky with me. We bonded, and he's been with me ever since."

I pointed at myself and then at him. "We're way more similar than I bet you'd like to admit." A horrific thought hit me, one that Angel had touched on, but maybe she'd misread the genetics. "You don't think were related, right?"

Jesus, I didn't have the mental capacity to handle that truth.

Shadow laughed. "We're not. My kin are well known to me, and I plan on killing a decent amount of them."

Phew. "Good to know." A pause. "Also, you're a touch scary."

Shadow shrugged. "I am what I am. If you can't handle me, that's your issue."

That stopped me short, for the pure beauty of his statement. For my entire life, I'd tried to shrink myself to fit in, to make others comfortable and happy and accepting of who I was. But Shadow was unapologetically himself, and if it was too much for me, then *that was my issue.*

Years of blaming myself, when all along... The issue didn't lie with me.

The revelation was breathtaking. And painful. And the best gift Shadow had given me.

"I can handle it," I told him truthfully. "You're not too much for me."

He tilted his head, unsure, but there was a low, simmering ember deep in his eyes.

Midnight pressed into me, and I felt its confusion. *You like him?*
"Yes."

Shadow let Inky twirl around him. "You need to work on your mental communication skills."

"Nah." I shook my head. "I'm cool with it being all one-sided in that regard. There's only so much of this magical shit that I can get used to. So I'll be speaking out loud for the foreseeable future."

He didn't seem to be upset by that. "I want to hear your thoughts. Don't start hiding them from me."

"No plans to," I promised.

I'd never held back from Shadow—well, almost never—from the first moment we'd crossed paths. It had probably brought me close to death a time or two, but now I saw that it had also endeared me to the beast. Over time, he'd come to appreciate my brand of quirkiness, and apparently... I wasn't too much for him, either.

It was odd that what had started as one of the worst days of my life, ended as one of the best. In this second, I felt happy and accepted.

For how long? Well, fate was a nasty bitch. And the sun was often the brightest right before a storm.

Luckily, I was well-equipped with both a raincoat and knee-high galoshes to handle whatever wild weather was thrown my way.

Chapter Seven

I'd been through a lot in the past twenty-four hours, and before I could handle one more situation, I needed a shower, a change of clothing, and food. In that order. Shadow left to finish his preparations for our journey into the realm, and I headed toward my room.

Midnight stayed close, and since I wasn't exactly used to my new companion yet, I asked for a little space.

Space?

I nodded, my shirt half over my head as I stepped into the bathroom. "Yeah, human-type people like privacy when they shower and dress and even at other times. We often need a moment alone to gather our thoughts. Some space between us and the rest of the world."

It seemed to understand then, swelling and sparking lights around its darkness.

Right. I will wait for you outside. I prefer to exist up high anyway. Just call if you need me.

It twirled away, under the bedroom door, and I took a deep,

extended breath, trying to sort out my mental state. The exhaustion that had plagued me before my nap wasn't completely gone; it lingered on the edges of my energy, confirming that I hadn't had enough sleep or food to completely restore my well of power.

One thing at a time, though, and those two would have to wait.

The shower felt amazing, and I sank to the floor, letting the heavy stream beat down on me. Cranking the heat even higher, the chill that had been lingering in my bones eased with each drop of water. I might have even dozed off for a few minutes, allowing an extra boost of healing and restoration to kick in.

Eventually, I had to get out, and after drying off, I did my teeth-brushing and moisturizing routine, feeling a hundred times more myself after. I really needed to spend more time on self-care because I'd been a ragged mess when I'd dragged my ass in here an hour ago. Most of which had been washed away in the shower.

Figuring it probably wasn't long until we made our way into the Shadow Realm, I dressed in the most comfortable outfit I could find. And since the library provided it, it was of course perfect.

Black jeans, with enough stretch that they could have passed as thick leggings. Black leather boots that slid perfectly over the jeans, stopping around my calves. A green tank that brought out the lighter tones in my hazel eyes, and over the top, I threw on a leather jacket for protection and warmth.

I had no idea what sort of weather or temperatures to expect in the Shadow Realm, but there was every chance that parts of it could be as extreme as Earth. At least from what I'd seen in Midnight's memories.

Midnight. It was so weird how I could feel the mist in my energy, the tingling on my palm reminding me that I was now bonded to another powerful entity. One that was at war with Inky.

At least Midnight might be a source of information, and for once, I'd be ahead of the game. *Ether mists...* a blanket from above. It was the oddest concept, and I couldn't quite picture it. In the images from Midnight, I hadn't noticed a black cloud across their world, so maybe... maybe it was hidden from sight. I supposed I'd find out once we stepped foot into the realm.

My stomach churned at the mere thought, and I hoped that whatever happened there, Shadow finally found his revenge. If anyone deserved it, he did. Of course, I still owed some shifters a knife through their chests, but that could wait. Compared to how long Shadow had been waiting to enact his own vengeance, I was a few thousand years behind.

Midnight floated down to me as soon as I stepped out from my bedroom door, and I didn't waste any time. "How many different beings live in the Shadow Realm?" I paused. "Wait, that was rude. Hello, how are you? I have a few questions if you don't mind?"

Midnight swelled and jiggled, and I heard the disembodied laugh in my head. *My knowledge is yours.*

That one line might have been better than an orgasm.

"Tell me as much about the inhabitants of the Shadow Realm as you can."

Midnight swelled into a wall of darkness. *Shadow Beast is Darkor, the Supreme Being. He has power over the mists, mostly leicher, and can command the creatures and other royals.*

He was betrayed on the night he was supposed to accept his position. He was young—taken completely by surprise—and only just managed to escape with his life.

His need for vengeance made more sense every day. I was going to help him the best I could, even if it meant I would risk myself in the meantime. His mission in life was much greater than mine.

"So Darkor is one of the beings of the realm, but he's technically a royal, correct?"

Yes. There are also freilds, who are the regular beings, not born royal. They all exist within one of the five lands of the Concordes.

"Concordes?"

Geography wasn't my strongest suit, and without a map, I was struggling to piece it together in my head.

The Concordes is the main mass of land. There are five kingdoms of royals sharing its territory. Trinity is Shadow's, the strongest of the five. Then there is Holister, second in power, followed by Fraple, Glist'n, and Ashan.

Yeah, no way in fuck was I remembering even one of those kingdoms. But maybe I'd learn on the run while there.

"Are there any other beings there that I should be aware of?"

There are royals, freilds and their many sub-species, shadow creatures, and quite a few other beings who are not able to communicate with you, so there is no need to worry about them.

And yet, I would most definitely worry.

"What are the Shadow Hunters?"

The strongest of the freilds. Not born to be royals, but with a strength and affinity to trap creatures. They trade their 'souls' for the ability to elevate their power. The mists transform them, but the process is quite... dehumanizing.

That had to be why they looked the way they did. No faces. No physical bodies.

Just as I was opening my mouth to ask another of my million questions, Shadow strode into the lair, clearly searching for me.

I met him halfway, and Midnight fell silent in my head, choosing to tag along close by without too much interaction. "Is it time to leave?" I asked, examining Shadow's face.

His neutral expression didn't give anything away, so I just waited for his answer.

"Simone has arrived," he said, and I almost jumped onto him in my excitement.

"Is she okay? What happened to the rest of the pack members?"

Shadow shrugged. "They're alive for now, but I have Torma locked down so those assholes can't cause any further damage until I have time to deal with them."

"*I* will deal with them," I spat out. "It has been a long time coming, and I'm not exactly the forgive-and-forget sort of chick."

He brushed his hand over my cheek, the movement fast and over in a heartbeat, but the heat of his touch lingered. "You will have your vengeance," he told me softly. "As soon as I've had mine."

"Deal."

There was a fissuring of power in the air, and I wondered if we'd literally sealed that deal as something more than mere words and sentiments.

"You want to see your friend before we leave?" Shadow asked, distracting me.

I nodded. "Yes. I need to make sure she's safe. Can she stay in the lair?"

"No."

One word, but it was clear that he would not change his mind. "Why not?"

"Strangers are not welcome here."

"You let me be here," I reminded him. More like *forced* me to live here, but the sentiment was the same.

He shook his head, those thick curls catching my attention before they settled again. "Don't push me, Mera. She'll have a room off the hall and will be perfectly safe."

It didn't make sense, but then again, so much of my relationship with Shadow didn't. And maybe a tiny stupid girlie part of me liked that he'd let me into his private inner sanctum, when as far as I knew, no one other than his five friends—and two mists—had ever crossed that barrier.

I was slowly chipping away at him, and fuck, if that didn't give me a sense of accomplishment I hadn't felt before.

"Who are the two who know your weakness?" I asked him suddenly, and he jerked his head at the rapid change of subject. I didn't take him by surprise a lot, but I had.

He laughed bitterly. "My sister and my mother. One who is my enemy, and the other I assume is dead."

I grabbed his hand. "You will take your sister down. She stole from you, and it's time for her to pay for it."

Shadow's face was darker than I'd ever seen, scarily dark, but he didn't pull away. "She will pay. As will the shifters who hurt your Dannie."

My voice was a shaky mess now. "Will she come back the same?" I asked, voicing a question that had been mentally freaking me out for some time.

Shadow released my hand, draping his arm around my shoulders, dragging me closer. "She'll still be the Dannie you knew, even if she doesn't look quite the same. You'll feel her, though, and it will be comforting."

He started to walk, mostly pulling me along for the ride.

"She's my first priority after the Shadow Realm," I told him. "Hopefully at that point, she'll have had enough time to reform into Dannie again."

He squeezed my shoulders but didn't reply.

Needing to talk or my head would explode, I hurried to ask, "So Simone first and then we head into the Shadow Realm?"

"Food first," he corrected. "You're still too weak, and our journey into the realm isn't going to be an easy one. We will have to go incognito, so minimal energy use. They cannot see us coming and have time to prepare."

"Won't they already be waiting, since the spell on the door has fallen?"

He shook his head. "We checked the door, and there's no one waiting for us. Clearly, their arrogance is still firmly in place. A fact I told my sister would one day get her killed."

He looked positively pleased by this preemptive thought coming to fruition.

This was Shadow's scary face, and since it wasn't directed at me, I could just enjoy the stark beauty of his features.

"Blood will be spilled," he murmured, adding to the sexy serial killer vibe he was rocking.

Hard to believe that probably twenty-four hours ago I'd wanted to kill him, and now I found myself falling into an alliance like we were the best of friends. There was one truth I could never deny: I was stupidly obsessed with this dude. Since we were once again fighting on the same side, I wondered if I might truly fall for the one being I could never have.

Knowing my luck, the answer to that was a resounding *yes*.

Chapter Eight

A tray was already waiting for me when I sat down, courtesy of Shadow, who had disappeared to finalize shit before we left. Or maybe Angel had ordered it, since she dropped into the chair beside me not five minutes after I'd started to eat.

"Good," she said, observing the classy way I shoved food into my mouth like I'd been starved for a month. "You need to fuel up as much as you can for the hard journey ahead."

I chewed a few vegetables before swallowing my mouthful of stew. It was delicious, thick and hearty, and apparently needed for the *hard* journey ahead. "You could sugarcoat it for me," I said with a sigh, stirring more of the dark broth. "Pretend we're heading on vacation to a tropical island, where we'll have cocktails and food brought to our lounger, while we sunbathe and swim in turquoise waters."

Angel side-eyed me. "Been planning that vacation for a while, I see?"

I shrugged. "Yeah, there wasn't much else I could do when I was a prisoner of Torma. Daydreaming about vacation destinations was my mental escape."

She wrapped an arm around me. "Don't worry. We'll make it

through the Shadow Realm, figure out your place in the world, and fit in a vacation to—"

Angel was cut off when someone screamed my name. As a reflex, her huge amber wings sprung to life as she spun to see who was causing the commotion.

I didn't have to look. I knew that voice as well as I knew my own. Pushing to my feet, I was in the aisle, sprinting toward my friend. Simone and I collided, our hug lasting for what felt like days.

"Oh my freaking god," she said, bouncing me in her arms, her thick blue-black hair flying around us. "This place is unbelievable. You must have been in heaven, Miss Book Lover, living in that incredible-as-fuck library." Her words spilled out in a rush. "And there are so many other supernaturals, and worlds, and beings, and Shadow Beast lives here..."

I had to laugh because if she didn't breathe soon, she was going to pass out.

"It's definitely been a journey," I told her when she finally ran out of steam and I could get a word in. "And you have to meet one of my favorite people here. Not that she's a person, of course—Angel is a damn goddess. Which you'll see quite clearly when you see how freaking gorgeous she is."

Turning Simone toward the table, I looked for Angel, only to find the spot where she'd been empty. "Oh, guess she had to take off. But there will be plenty of time to meet her. Shadow said you could stay as long as I was here."

Simone all but fell into Angel's seat, and I had a flicker of worry that maybe I should ask her to move to the other side of me. Angel was pretty particular about this chair, and I sensed she was already upset about the way I'd ditched her mid-conversation to go to Simone.

Fuck. This was complicated, and hopefully my narcissistic ass was just creating drama. Angel was probably off preparing for our journey too.

I scooped up more of my food, knowing I had to finish it. "Are you hungry?" I asked, shoveling another spoonful into my mouth.

She shook her head. "Nope." She popped her *p*. "I'd literally just finished dinner when a dark smoke cloud arrived with a note for me."

Clearly, Shadow had gotten around Inky's inability to communicate, and the mention of dark smoke clouds had me looking for mine. Midnight was still hovering up high, keeping an eye on everything. It swelled when my gaze turned its way, and I just waved my hand to say *hello* and *I'm all good; you don't need to come down to me.*

We couldn't actually communicate at this distance, but when it didn't move, I figured it got the general idea.

I focused on Simone again. "Did Shadow show you to your room?"

I wanted her completely settled in before I left.

She nodded, brown eyes practically sparkling in excitement. "Last door on the left of the hallway before the library. It's really nice, with a little lounge, television, and a marble bathroom! I mean, shit, it's nicer than my parents' house by a lot."

Her parents' house was pretty damn fancy. "Shadow Bastard hasn't let me near a television since he kidnapped my ass," I grumbled. "I'm gonna have words with him about that."

Simone looked around in a panic. "Should you call him that out loud, I mean, especially here? Everyone is so scared and respectful of him."

There was a deep chuckle from behind us, and Simone let out a squeak, spinning in her chair. I sighed, turning slower since I already knew what I'd see. And sure enough, there he was, leaned in his favorite position against the nearby wall. Shadow Basta—Beast.

"Sunshine is about the least respectful being from any of the worlds I've ever met," he said, sounding amused.

Simone's head jerked to me. *Sunshine?* she mouthed, her eyes wide.

She didn't bother waiting for me to reply, her gaze returning to the beast in question. I had no idea if she'd ever really seen Shadow before—in the theater basement there had been so much chaos, especially with my *tiny little fire incident*, that I doubted she'd gotten a decent look.

She was making up for that today.

"Damn," she murmured under her breath, and I hid my laughter in a cough.

"His face might be pretty, but his personality needs a lot of help." I reminded her of the facts while eating another spoonful of stew.

Simone raised an eyebrow at me, panic in their dark depths. "Girl, you did not just insult the fucking Shadow Beast to his pretty face. What is wrong with you?"

I shrugged, chewing and swallowing before I answered. "What's wrong with me? Let's see... My father fucked up my entire life; I was mated to a piece of shit shifter; got kidnapped; got over being kidnapped; decided that if I was going to die, I might as well go out with a bang. Ever since then..."

"She's let whatever random smartass thought she has fall from her mouth," Shadow finished as he took the seat beside me.

Simone's breathing grew heavier, and I couldn't blame her. Shadow was a lot. Like... *a lot lot.* The intensity didn't wear off as time went on, either—in all truth, the tingles that ran across my skin in his presence might actually be getting worse. I'd just learned to hide my reaction better.

And Simone would get there too. One day.

"When you're done with this meal, we need to head into the realm," Shadow said, focusing all of his attention on me, and, if his intense, lingering gaze didn't lift from the side of my face, I was about to join Simone with the labored breathing. "The longer it takes for me to get to my sister, the greater the chance she'll have amassed an army to stand against me."

"What?" Simone leaned forward to see Shadow. The moment he was in her line of sight, a hungry expression pulled at her features, and I would bet good money she wanted to lick him. No judgement from me, even if I did sort of want to kick her ass for looking at him like that. This possessive shit was going to get me into big trouble one day.

"We're heading into the Shadow Realm," I told her. "To hopefully figure out how I'm able to burst into flames and draw creatures into this world. Oh, and yeah, Shadow has some shit to do there too."

He actually laughed, chest rumbling beside me. "Yes, something like that. But rest assured, Sunshine's friend, you'll be safe here. I'm having Lucien stay in the room beside yours to keep an eye on you."

Simone's lips twitched. "The fact that you haven't bothered to learn my name doesn't even bother me because your nickname for Mera is just too damn cute." Her voice went to a much higher pitch at the end.

Shadow got to his feet, his face set in resigned lines. "I'm going to leave now before the girly screaming starts. I'll meet you in the library in five minutes, Mera."

"Yes, sir." I saluted him.

A flicker of his fire ran along my skin, but it didn't burn. It sunk into my body, heating me through to my core, and I was literally panting as he walked away. *Definitely a bastard.*

Simone nudged me. "You okay? Your face is a little flushed." She shot me a knowing look, and I had to sigh.

"I'm good." I fanned my cheeks to try to cool my libido down. "Just Shadow playing hardball and reminding me who has the most power."

If I had a spontaneous orgasm right here in the dining hall, I was going to fucking kill him. Right after I thanked him.

Simone grabbed my arm, her fingers digging in, and for the first time, I felt nails. I blinked. Simone always had the weakest nails, breaking before she could get any length on them—a pain she had more than once complained about. "Do you actually have long nails right now?"

She snorted. "Seriously? You want to talk about the fact that since my change I can't keep my nails down, those bastards growing like weeds? Or should we discuss the beyond-this-world gorgeous, sexy, sexy god who was eye-fucking you the entire time he stood in the room?"

"There's nothing to discuss," I said to her, pushing my tray away —it was swept up by a robot server in seconds. "Shadow and I have to work together until the Shadow Realm situation is under control. There's nothing else to it, really."

She was the one to fan her face now. "I can't tell if you're lying to me or yourself. The heat between you two could set this hall on fire, and I'm not even talking about the fact you can literally burst into flames." Her eyes narrowed on me. "We should add that to the list of things to discuss as well."

"I'm so happy you're here," I said, hugging her as I got to my feet and pulled her up with me. "It's been really hard navigating this new world without my BFF."

She hugged me back just as fiercely. "You'll never have to do that again. We are lifers, babe. For. Fucking. Life."

My tears, once again hovering way too close to the surface, had to be forced down so I could get on with my day. There was no time for waterworks.

I reluctantly pulled away. "Can't believe we have to be separated again," I said sadly.

Her petite face screwed up, the brown in her eyes deeper than ever. Maybe it was the lighting here, or the release of her shifter side, but I was sure she'd never looked as beautiful or regal as she did now. "I think I should come with you. It doesn't sit right that once again you're off to dangerous lands without me."

"I wish you could," I told her truthfully. "But Shadow won't even consider it, and no one goes against him here."

Hence the reason I'd lost our bet. I'd been determined to lose my virginity to someone in the library; Shadow had been determined to stop me. One guess who came out on top in that situation. I was sure he'd inform me of my punishment for that soon enough. No doubt he was ready for me to fall on my knees and worship him as the god he was. Probably wanted me to call him *master* or *lord*...

"You're thinking about him, aren't you?" Simone both looked and sounded amused. "Girl, you got it bad. Thank fuck I'm here now to keep you from making any stupid decisions."

I snorted. "Are you telling me you'd warn me off Shadow?"

Her laughter didn't arrive as expected. "I'd warn you to not get your heart involved. He's the perfect being to give your body to because *girrllll*, we know he has some skills. Did you see the size of his hands?" She bit her knuckle and I almost lost my shit right there in the dining hall, barely holding my laughter back.

She sobered. "Despite his many, *many* positives, I can tell he has the power to destroy you, Mera. I don't trust he wouldn't do just that."

I didn't argue with her because she wasn't wrong. I'd already suffered a fissuring of my soul when Torin, my asshole of a true mate, had rejected me, and I wasn't sure I'd survive another loss like that.

Maybe with Shadow, it would be even worse.

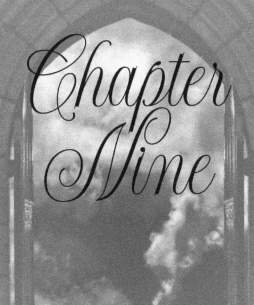

Chapter Nine

Despite a few more arguments, Simone decided not to push her luck, and with reluctance, followed me into the library, knowing we were about to be parted again. Shadow and Lucien were waiting near the realm entrance, and once I'd moved past them, the black door drew all of my attention.

I actually loved the color, so rich and vibrant, filled with energy and life. It made the others look positively boring in comparison, and I wondered if it was the "shadow connection" in my soul that drew me to the color, or... I just liked black. Fuck, not everything had to have a deeper psychological meaning, and I had to stop trying to assign one to all aspects of my personality.

Lucien flashed his signature grin, the tapered points of his fangs barely visible. I knew those babies could extend when he fed or fueled up his power, but in normal times like this, they just looked like slightly sharper teeth.

Simone all but launched herself at him. "Are you a vampire?" she asked, exuberant in a way that might get her killed here if she didn't learn to control it. "Why didn't you show me those babies when we were in Torma? I'm a massive Twihard. Pretty sure I'm the perfect woman for you."

Thankfully, Lucien, *the master vampire who didn't glitter in the sun*, took her enthusiasm in his stride. "Once again," he murmured, "I'm coming to the conclusion that humans are my new favorite beings in the Solaris System." He all but ate up my gorgeous friend with his *darker than normal* green eyes, leaving Simone on the edge of panting.

Pushing between them, I forced the eye contact to break. Lucien glanced down and smiled at me. "Have a nice journey, *ma petite*."

I jabbed him in the chest. "Listen up, smooth talker. While I do love the way you all use your Earth knowledge in conversation—it makes me feel right at home, despite French not being my native language—I'm only going to tell you this once... If a single hair on Simone's head is damaged when I return, I will put a stake through your heart, laugh out loud, and then shove one through your dick as well."

He blinked about a billion times before he slowly turned to Shadow. "Your woman is scary, brother. She's going to laugh out loud as she stabs me."

Simone looked like she was trying not to laugh herself, and I couldn't see Shadow's expression, but he did snake his arm out and pull me away from his friend, positioning me behind him almost... protectively.

"Heed her words," was all he said to Lucien, and I had a brief heart-stopping moment where I wondered why he didn't correct the "your woman" comment.

Lucien clenched his fist and dropped it on his chest. "I will protect Simone of the shifters with all I have. If I'm alive, she will be alive. That's a promise I make, as a Master Vampire of Valdor."

Simone looked a little like she was going to hyperventilate. Her interest in Lucien was concerning, since she had been known to get herself in over her head fast, and I wouldn't be here to reel her back. I just had to hope we wouldn't be gone too long, and in that time, Lucien would keep his promise.

And his dick to himself.

Midnight wrapped around me, comforting me near instantly just from its touch. I finally understood why Inky often drifted around Shadow. The bond between mist and person was one that offered much.

"Thank you," I told Midnight out loud, still not comfortable with a mental connection. I wondered if it could read my thoughts anyway, but so far, I had no indication it could.

"Will you stay here and protect Simone?" I asked my mist.

Midnight reared up, and I knew I'd actually taken it by surprise. I was somewhat surprised myself, having said that without really thinking it through. The desire to keep my friend safe was the strongest I had.

I need to be in Shadow Realm with you.

I shook my head. "I'll have Shadow, Angel, and Inky. Simone needs you."

Midnight's reluctance was strong, burning through our bond.

"Who is she talking to?" Simone whispered, no doubt concerned for my mental health.

Lucien answered her. "The black smoke entity is bonded to her."

Simone just nodded. "Sure, I mean, makes sense."

Midnight settled in somewhere near my shoulder, and I could feel a sense of resignation filter through our bond.

I'll sense if you're in trouble, it reminded me, and my palm tingled. *So I will stay, for now, but if anything happens, I'll come for you.*

That was the best I'd get. "Thank you."

Midnight swelled again, getting a little too close to Shadow. Inky zoomed in, putting itself between Shadow and me. It didn't want its master to touch Midnight.

Shadow waved Inky away. "Unnecessary, old friend," he said.

Before the battle of the smoke blobs could commence, Angel

strode into view, and she was in warrior mode. In all honesty, this mode was my favorite, with her gold and bronze molded armor, multiple weapons, and don't-fuck-with-me expression. Her wings were widespread, and anybody or thing standing nearby got the fuck out of her way in an instant.

"Holy damn hotness," Simone whispered. "I choose her."

It was no secret that my bestie liked to play both fields—she often said she didn't love parts she loved hearts. In my experience, she was a sucker for super-hot beings in any form, and she was definitely going to have fun in this library, with the multitude of unique, beautiful, and powerful beings who visited.

"This is Angel," I said when she reached us, her energy doing its typical thing of slamming everyone in the face. It didn't burn like Shadow's; instead, it felt like a warm summer breeze, powerful and enticing.

"This is your friend?" Simone gasped. "Are you only allowed to have hot friends here? Is that, like, a requirement?"

Lucien grinned broadly before he hastily hid the smile when I narrowed my eyes on him.

"Yeah, they're definitely blessed in the genetics department. Especially Angel." I stated the obvious. "And it's not just her beautiful face, but she's beyond powerful and badass, and I want to be her when I grow up."

The badass herself didn't seem to know what to do with my compliments, her face crumpling briefly, before she recovered enough to school her features. So rarely did she lose composure, that I had clearly struck a chord with her.

Before anyone else could speak, Simone squealed, and all but dove forward, wrapping her arms around Angel. "Thank you for keeping Mera safe," she choked out. "Thank you so much."

I was watching closely, wondering how this was going to play out. Angel's face showed another brief moment of shock, which morphed into something softer, and before my eyes, her icy demeanor thawed. "You're more than welcome." She patted Simone on the back. "I care a great deal about Mera, and... her friends are mine."

She'd fallen into her formal talk and was clearly out of her element, but it felt like less tension lingered after that.

Simone pulled away, wiping at her eyes. "Same for me. If you're in my girl's corner, then I've got your back."

Angel nodded. "We will meet again, and upon this day, we will eat and laugh."

She didn't mean that literally, since she didn't need to eat and hadn't enjoyed her single taste of food. But the sentiment itself was what mattered. We'd made grounds that could spell a true long-lasting friendship between the three of us.

Simone was amused and overwhelmed, rubbing at her face. "I look forward to that day, Lady Warrior."

"We need to leave," Shadow rumbled, clearly sick of this "girly" bullshit. I elbowed him. It was subtle, but Lucien saw. The vampire's face went a little ashen, and he darted toward me with an arm out, like he was going to save me from the beast.

Shadow blocked his friend, wrapping his arm around me, spinning my ass toward the door. Peering around Shadow, I saw the way the vampire paused, his gaze flicking between the two of us. He wore a new expression, and even though he'd joked before about me being Shadow's "woman," he was clearly surprised by what had just happened.

When my gaze met his, I shook my head. *There's nothing to over-think here, dude.*

He replied to my silent statement with something like... *What the fuck have you done with Shadow?*

A shrug. *He needs me to complete his vengeance. End of story. Once he's done, I'll be kicked to the curb.*

Lucien's emerging grin was very smirk-like, and I kind of wanted to slap it off his face. He shouldn't have been stirring this pot; the beast and I had enough issues.

Shadow, once again, stole my attention by nudging me toward the door. When we stood right before it, he leaned over and picked up a backpack that I hadn't even seen sitting there. "Since I'm going to be minimizing my energy use, I packed you some essentials. For your frailties."

Ignoring the urge to elbow him again, I shrugged the reasonably heavy bag on my back. Shadow had one as well, and I wondered what was in his, since there were no "frailties" he needed to stress over.

Angel opened the door in one quick movement, and I knew all of us were anticipating some sort of attack. Holding my breath, I tried not to panic about what would emerge.

"I can't see anything," Simone said softly from behind us. "Should we see something?"

Lucien whispered to her, too low for me to hear, and I didn't bother to chastise him again. All of my focus was on the mysterious Shadow Realm.

Simone's comment was accurate—all I could see were swirls of darkness. Probably because the pathway was waiting for directions from the first being to step through. A skill Shadow and Angel had, but not me. "It smells sweet," I whispered. "Like... nectar."

Shadow closed his eyes for a brief second, and it was only because I was—*once again*—staring at him that I saw his throat move roughly as he pulled himself together. "Home," he breathed.

In my own fear about what we'd find in the realm, it had slipped my mind that Shadow would finally step back into his world. A world that had been blocked from him for near two thousand years. *His home.*

I couldn't help but wonder if on the other side, he'd finally get everything he'd been wanting... or would it spell his downfall?

A surge of protectiveness rose within me.

My fear about what lay beyond paled in comparison to my worry about Shadow's new path.

I was in way too deep, but it seemed there was no other way to be. Sink or swim, I was in for the long haul.

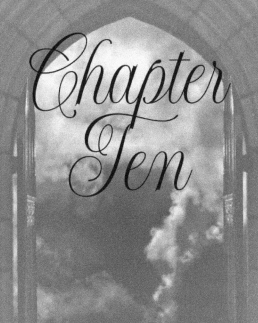

Chapter Ten

Simone pushed through for one more hug. "Promise me you'll stay safe and return to me," she said against my neck, her voice hoarse.

"I promise," I replied, not knowing if I'd just lied to her again. I would do my absolute best, if that made a difference. "Stay close to Lucien and Midnight," I told her as we parted. "They will keep you safe."

Her eyes darted to the vampire, who was without his characteristic smirk for once. "Yeah, I think I can manage that," she said softly.

I leaned in. "Not *too* close, you little hussy."

She lifted her eyebrows at me but didn't reply as she stepped back.

Midnight wrapped around me one more time, and I sucked up the comfort. *Thank you for staying and protecting Simone. She's my family.*

Yeah, maybe I could rock the mental connection at a time like this.

Be safe, my bonded one. I'll come the moment you need me.

That made me feel better, like I had a guardian angel. Well, a second one after Angel.

And don't fear this world. It's different, but you are more than capable of handling it. And it needs you. It hasn't been easy in the realm since the Supreme Being disappeared.

Nodding, I swallowed hard, forcing the fear down. Logically, I knew the realm was a lot like Earth, and it smelled good, and I had already adopted more than one creature born from its energy, but logic had no place when it came to irrational fear.

It was home to Midnight, Inky, and Shadow. I was also fairly certain that Angel had been there before at some point, too. I was the only one about to step into the unknown. The fear of that was far stronger than I'd expected.

Midnight sent one last burst of comforting warmth into me, and I sucked it up, feeling a strange sense of melancholy about being parted from my mist. A mist I'd been bonded to for all of an hour. It was the oddest sensation, the feeling that I'd known Midnight forever, and yet... I hadn't.

I wouldn't be selfish, though. Keeping Simone safe in this unknown world was worth whatever discomfort arose in my separation from the mist.

Shadow caught my eye as he reached down, his hands wrapping around my waist so he could haul me up and over his shoulder. He was so strong that he threw me around with no effort, and the control with which he held me was both terrifying and incredibly sexy. I was into it, no denying, but I preferred to walk.

In this situation, though, he was the one who controlled these doors, so I didn't fight. No point getting my ass dumped off in an in-between spot, leaving me stuck.

It could happen. Literally could happen, according to some of the books I'd read.

These pathways were tricky, and one needed to be very sure of what they were doing before they stepped into them. A fact I hadn't known my first day with Shadow when I'd tried to escape into Faerie.

My wolf howled as we strode into the darkness, but it wasn't from fear. She was excited for this adventure, and that could only mean one thing: she was going to get me into trouble at some point.

Shadow ran a hand along my spine, and almost like he was stroking the wolf in that movement, she calmed. It was growing clearer as time went on that she loved Shadow. Her capitulation toward him was concerning because her moods definitely influenced my own, and I didn't want to completely give ourselves up to him. He was too domineering, and I sensed that if I gave in to him, I'd lose a large part of myself forever.

Try telling that to my wolf, though, who continued treating Shadow like he was our beloved and trusted alpha.

I supposed he was our god, so it made sense... while also being frustrating.

Focusing again on our journey, I noted that the darkness hadn't lifted yet, but the sweeter-than-honey scent grew stronger. Shadow remained calm, no sign of his flames or any surge in his energy, so I remained calm as well.

Still...

Why was there no freaking light?

I'd seen this world through Midnight's memories, and it had been just as bright as Earth, with a sun-like illumination in the sky. So far, the reality was far from that... Shadow Realm was living up to its name.

"It's always the darkest right before the sun shines," Shadow murmured.

I stilled, my pulse the only part of me racing.

"Is there a hidden meaning in that statement?" I shot back, louder than intended.

His hold across my hips tightened. "Just wait for it, Sunshine."

I used to hate that nickname; my chest tightening every time he said it, bringing bad memories to the surface. I'd always been "Sunny" to my dad, and Sunshine was close enough that it had hurt to hear.

It had burned.

At some point, that changed, and now when the rumble of my nickname left his lips, caressing my ears with his deep baritones, the burning I felt was of a completely different nature.

My eyes closed, and then I remembered I was about to see a new world and forced them open again. The darkness slithered away in a similar manner to the first time I'd seen Shadow in Torma. His mere presence had caused all light to fade into misty energy, until Shadow had sucked that darkness back into himself.

It felt like something similar happened here as a whirlwind whipped around us, gathering up the shadows of this world, and then we were in the light.

The "sunshine," so much brighter than I'd expected after such an eternal night, was blinding and warm. For a brief second, I felt my bond with Midnight, my love for Simone and Angel, and the burning ache Shadow caused inside of me.

All the good things in my world burst to life in a single, brilliant drop of light. The scent made sense then, even as it faded once we were here. A scent of home and love.

"Don't let it fool you," Shadow whispered, his voice rebooting my senses into their normal semi-cynical setting. "The darkness of the realm exist above and below the light. In some way, this entire world is an illusion."

I looked to where Inky was drifting along beside us. "Our mists are not the same," he added. "Being bonded changes them. They absorb what makes us exist, and they feel when we do. The leicher and ether mists feel nothing and act only as a pure power. They will not consider your circumstances or hear your pleas. They will take and destroy if that suits their purpose."

Okay then. Only slightly terrifying. Especially considering we were apparently walking across a blanket of these mists and another blanket covered us from above. It reminded me of the disembodied voice that I'd heard when I sent that wall of darkness from Earth. If the mists didn't have a presence like that of Inky and Midnight, then what had that voice been?

Maybe Shadow didn't truly know what the mists were capable of? A fact that might spell our downfall.

Before I could get too worked up, Angel appeared at our side, having found the way through the dark path, all without touching Shadow. I had zero idea how she'd followed, but once again, her kickass power was impressive. To say the very least.

"What part of the realm are we in right now?" I asked them.

We'd arrived on a rocky outcrop, facing what looked like a mass of water. I noted that it was a bright green compared to Earth's bluer oceans—possibly due to the minty vibe of the sky here—and there was no sign of waves or disturbance across the waterline.

The glassy, unbroken surface was almost eerie. And the weather here was very moderate, so I wondered if they had seasons such as we did back home. I'd thought so from Midnight's vision, but there was no sign of any particular season where we stood.

"The Shadow Realm is smaller than Earth," Shadow said, standing beside me as we stared out into the unnatural water. "It has three main landmasses and five outlier islands. The islands themselves are about the size of the current United Kingdom. I've brought us to the mainland: The Concordes. This is where the five families of royals exist, all with their own territory."

Midnight had told me some of this, but I didn't clue Shadow in on this knowledge. I wanted to know everything about this world that had, until this point, been completely off limits to me.

Shadow waved his hand to Inky, and when the mist swirled in front of us, I choked on my next breath as it turned into a map. The synapses inside were a roughly sketched, basic outline of the world. There was one large landmass in the center—The Concordes, clearly —with five much smaller islands scattered below it. The top right and top left corner had other landmasses, and I figured these were the other two of the three lands that made up this world.

"The Concordes," Shadow pointed to the largest land as expected, "and we're currently in the kingdom of Fraple. It's the easternmost territory, which borders on Trinity. That is where my family resides."

Trinity was the largest of the five kingdoms, situated near the center. It seemed to run from the top to the bottom of The Concordes, following a... trench maybe? It was hard to tell in the monochromatic Inky map, but it was clearly some sort of divide.

"The other royal territories aren't of any concern," Shadow added. "We won't cross them on our journey. So for now, we just have to worry about Fraple and Trinity."

I nodded. "What are the five outliers?"

Shadow crossed his arms. "They're the lands that reject the royal way, trying to exist on their own without creatures or mist influence." He pointed to each on the map. "Rodan, Green Isle, Dety, Samsan Grove, and the Isle of Rechest."

I nodded. "The royals don't try to force them back under their control?"

Angel laughed drily while keeping a vigilant watch on our backs, as if an attack were forthcoming. "They tried, but the beings there resisted, and eventually, the royals grew bored. The outliers have no true power without creatures, so the royals let them be."

Shadow nodded. "Yes, but much could have changed in thousands of years. I put nothing past my sister."

"Especially without the Supreme Being," Angel added. "Who should have ruled them all and kept the balance in this world."

Without Shadow.

He laughed, a dry, sardonic chuckle. "I was supposed to be crowned on my twenty-second year here, but that was the day I was betrayed."

Twenty-two. That number had been significant to the Shadow Realm, and that was no doubt the reason he'd incorporated it into shifter law as well.

Finally had my answer.

"So if you could rule them all," I asked, trying to understand, "then would all of The Concordes have been your home?"

"I would have ruled from Trinity. The largest land with the lava chasm, giving me direct access to the mists."

Access to the mists sounded like access to the power. And it seemed I also had my answer about that divide I'd seen. *The lava chasm.*

"What are the two lands up top?"

Shadow reached out and ran his hand over Inky, disrupting the map in the same instant. "One is a land of birth, the other of death."

I paused, waiting for more information, but he was apparently done. I had a weird, ominous feeling about what those two lands were, and I recalled Midnight's story about the place where the two mists joined. *The Grey Lands?* Was that in one of those two?

At least I had the basic idea of how the realm was setup, and hopefully during our adventures, I'd learn even more.

"So, we're walking to Trinity?" I asked.

Shadow nodded, turning away from the view to face into the land. A land we would soon be journeying across. "We must keep our power usage to a minimum. For my attack to be the most effective, I need as much surprise on my side as possible. Until I know for sure I've been found out, it's stealth mode only."

Good times. "Okay, cool. Let's do this then."

His lips twitched; his eyes filled with gold. "It won't quite be that simple—there're many creatures, royals, and freilds scattered across The Concordes. We must avoid them all until it becomes necessary to engage. It's going to be a long, hard journey."

I sighed, already exhausted. "Honestly, with all of your power, Shadow," I said carelessly, "I expected a lot more killing and a lot less sneaking." He'd told me why, but that didn't make it any less annoying.

He moved so fast, I blinked once before he was in my space, his hand around the back of my neck in what I was coming to think of as *his* personal brand of domination. His power forced me to walk toward him until we were touching, our bodies completely aligned.

"Watch it, pup," he warned, breath fanning over me as my nipples—which were firmly planted against the hard planes of his stomach—stood to attention. My legs did the opposite, going quite wobbly. "You have no idea what I'm capable of. No one truly does. The one that holds my position is nothing but a proxy. Power doesn't recognize you just because you try to trick it, and I will take back what's mine."

Fuck, did my vagina just flutter? Like, I should not have been turned on by this display of aggression and arrogance, but I was. My eyes lifted, and tilting my head back to see his face, I got caught on those lips of his. Now all I could think about was kissing him.

"Come on," he said softly. "The longer we stay stationary, the easier we'll be to spot."

"Yes," Angel said from close by. "I can only block our position for so long."

Shadow released me. "Despite Sunshine's doubts about me, the murdering will come soon enough, but until then, I'll do my best to ensure no one finds us."

He took another step away and I inhaled deeply, unsure if I'd breathed at all during the seconds he'd held me. I had to nip this attraction in the bud before Shadow had the power to convince me to stand buck-naked over those lava fields, ready to sacrifice the virgin for his power.

Because we all knew he was gonna try.

Fuck being that chick. Not even for the Shadow Beast.

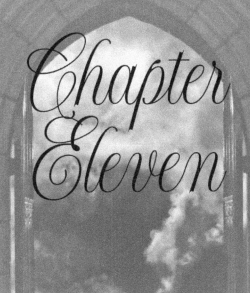

Chapter Eleven

S hadow and Angel started down the path from the hilly outcrop we'd been standing on, and just as I went to follow, an energy stirred behind me and I shot a glance over my shoulder. For a moment, a dark shape moved beneath the water, but it disappeared so quickly that I wondered if I'd imagined it.

Hurrying, I caught up to the others. "Does anything live in the waters here?" I asked.

Shadow glanced back. "The Depths are filled with many creatures you don't want to meet. Best to stay on land."

A trickle of unease traced down my spine. "Roger that, dude. Roger that."

Shadow's chest rumbled. "I'm not a dude, little wolf."

Holding both hands out, I shrugged, the backpack moving with me. "Everything is a dude in my world, just with minor tone changes. You're a dude, Angel's a dude, Simone is a dude. When I stub my toe it's a *fucking hell, dude*. All dudes."

At this point, I'd used the word so much, it now sounded weird.

"I-I don't..." Angel was at a loss for words, while Shadow just shook his head.

I stared between the two of them, truly not understanding what the issue was.

"You're a reader," Shadow bit out. "It's one of your few redeeming features. So how about you use more than six words when having a conversation."

My nose wrinkled. "Aw, come on. That's a little harsh. I have a few more redeeming features. I mean, I'm an excellent dancer and my singing voice has been described as operatic."

"You're a horrendous singer," he told me, deadpan.

I opened my mouth, but Angel got there first. "He's right. It literally hurts my ears when you hum a tune."

Forcing my facial expression into one of fake sadness, I sighed. "My feelings would be very hurt right now, if I wasn't fully aware that I've never been able to carry a tune."

Angel chuckled, the musical sound enough for me to know she probably did have the voice of an angel. I'd stick to singing loudly in the shower and scaring the crap out of anyone in close proximity.

Shadow, seemingly done, picked up the pace, his long legs eating up the distance down the hill. Okay, right! We were doing this, apparently. Time to head into The Concordes.

Oddly enough, I wasn't feeling too uneasy. I trusted the two gods at my side would give us a decent shot at taking out anything that came our way. Plus, being here was still a hundred times better than being in Torma.

I'd take *death* over that any day.

Away from the cliff, we descended along a rocky path, and I was grateful for my wolf's help with keeping balance. She was squirming uneasily in my chest, and I knew that meant it had been too long since I'd released her. "I might have to shift soon," I warned them. "Will the energy for that be detectable?"

"I'll shield you," Shadow said, his gaze running over me, like he was searching for the wolf.

I paused. "You can do that?"

Shadow shook his head, an expression of incredulity on his face.

"You continue to underestimate my control over shifters. Just because I've let you all basically go free to create your own fuckups, doesn't mean I couldn't turn puppeteer at any point. Your freedom is not guaranteed."

There was a low rumble in my chest, and I barely managed to hold on to my wolf. It was truly fascinating how my beast alternated between wanting to roll over for a belly scratch from Shadow and trying to literally tear his face off.

"My freedom better always be guaranteed."

He shot me a cocky smile. "Can't promise anything, Sunshine. Only time will tell how you and I end up. Where our pieces will fall. There's also that little topic of a bet you lost that we need to discuss."

Fuck, I was hoping he'd forgotten about that.

Needing a distraction and taking full advantage of the fact that touching him without his permission didn't shock me any longer, I jabbed him right in the side. "No. Just no, beast. You can't take people's freedoms. It's not okay and you're deliberately missing my entire point."

Angel was staring at us with her jaw slightly unhinged. No doubt she'd never seen anyone treat him with such little reverence, except maybe his friends, and even they still approached him with a certain degree of respect.

"Listen up, wolf—" he rumbled, and then strangely, he cut the rest of his words off.

I was about to jab him again when I focused on his expression. It was the same look he'd worn when we were about to be attacked by a creature.

Something was close by... watching us, and Shadow was on full alert.

Angel, too, twin blades appearing in her hands, the impressively curved weapon her clear favorite. She twirled them, and I tore my gaze away. No point in focusing on the two I knew weren't a danger to me.

My wolf rose up and I used her senses to discern the threat in our vicinity. If I wanted to survive this, I had to start relying on her. My wolf was not to be underestimated; she'd been able to touch the Shadow Hunters, she'd given me boosts of power so I could burst into flames and call on the mists—she'd gotten me through a lot of shit.

There was a hidden strength and destiny tied to my wolf and me, and in a life-or-death situation, I liked having her there as backup. I'd happily shift into a wolf covered in flames who could call the dark mists, if it meant saving my friends.

"Keep moving," Shadow said, and he looked visibly calmer. "The mists are curious about a new power in their lands—it's been so long since that happened that we briefly caught their attention. It's not any concern for now."

The mists... Great. My wolf remained restless in my chest, pacing back and forth, searching for an opening so she could burst out of the human skin.

"Don't release her yet," Shadow warned me, feeling the tension wrapping insidious tendrils around my insides. "We still don't know what will happen the first time your wolf is freed here. In this land that has been calling her. Let's hold off as long as possible."

I heard the rest of what he hadn't said. *Maybe even he couldn't control me here.*

"I don't know how much longer she'll stay in her cage," I warned him.

Shadow stared *into my damn soul,* as was his way. "We'll deal with it when it happens, but I know you're strong enough to lock her down now. Do it."

My chest rumbled again, and I patted my right boob in a comforting gesture for my wolf. It was weird, but fuck, what part of my life wasn't now? *We will be free soon,* I promised her. *We will find out our truth.*

If it was the last thing we did.

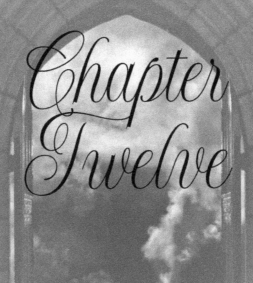

Chapter Twelve

The cliff we'd arrived on had had white wildflowers scattered underfoot, contributing to the sweet scent that filled the wind, but the farther we got from the water, the more desolate the realm became.

The air still smelled clean, a slightly tangy taste on my tongue, but the flowers soon died off, making way for what resembled black tar. "Is this what all of The Concordes looks like?" I asked, grimacing as I lifted my boot to find dark sediment clinging to it.

Shadow, whose jaw was set, brow furrowed, looking down as well. "This is rocky leftover from a lava flow, but... when I was here, it was only around the chasm. I've never seen it so widespread."

"Excellent," I muttered. Shadow didn't have the answers about what was going on in this world, not after being exiled for so long. We'd just have to discover it together.

"How does it feel being back here?" I asked when the endless expanse of the same parched land lost my interest. "I mean, you must have thought of this moment a million times over the years."

My question even had Angel easing up on her warrior focus of the land around us, as she tilted her gaze toward Shadow.

"It's odd," he said slowly. "My energy is returning now that the shackles of my expulsion are fading, but my inherited power is still missing. I worry that without it, this battle against my family will be harder than anticipated."

It was so odd to see him unsure about anything. His confidence basically followed him around like an entourage. Inky and Shadow's ego were his constant companions. Being out of his element was going to take some getting used to, but I thought it was smart of him to be wary about what he was walking into.

Might keep all of us alive.

"You expected that once the spell on the door was broken, you'd be gifted the full range of your power again?" Angel asked.

Shadow's chest rumbled, like the memories were swelling his anger. "Not all of it, since the ceremony bonding me to my position still has to be performed, but I was hoping for a good chunk. Right now, I'm probably at sixty percent of what I expected."

In a flash, he faded out, smoky mists twirling around him. Then he was a few hundred yards away from us. Then he was back at our sides. "I have gained some new gifts." He sounded energized, his voice vibrating with energy. "My ability to move through the shadows of worlds was a power lost. I can't go too far or someone will feel our presence, but it's nice to know it has returned."

I blinked. "So, technically, you could zap into the library right now without a doorway?"

He shook his head. "The library is protected from this power, but I could go straight to Earth or Brolder. I no longer need the Solaris System pathways."

Angel cleared her throat, her brow furrowed. "I finally understand why you created the portals of the Solaris System now. You wanted the ability to world jump again, and that was the closest you could get."

He shot her a sardonic stare. "I shared the power, didn't I? Be grateful."

She wrinkled her nose at him but didn't bother to comment on her "gratitude."

"What other powers have returned?" I asked him.

He shrugged. "A few others, but mostly it's my strength. I've been drawing from my shifters for years, as your *mate* pointed out. But no longer do I need their energy to boost my own."

The way he'd said *mate* was the same way I said fuck when I stubbed my toe. Shadow hated that alpha, and if I was Torin, I'd be sleeping uneasily at night, knowing there was a beast out there stalking my ass. If Shadow hadn't been busy with his few-thousand-year-old revenge right now, Torin would be fucked.

"You definitely don't have the power of a Supreme Being," Angel said, examining him like she could feel his energy.

Shadow growled, a howling rumble that reminded me of my wolf. "Only the death of the one who usurped my position, and the ceremony, will give me my full power."

"They should not have been able to utilize the power," Angel said, shaking her head. "Only the one born to the position can play with the mists."

Shadow's flames appeared, and they were so much stronger than I'd ever seen or felt from him that I had to jump back or risk being barbequed. Inky swelled larger as well, seemingly absorbing the energy from its master.

He wasn't kidding about sixty percent of his true strength reappearing here. His powers had been impressive before, but now... they were scary.

He was scary.

There was no reflection of humanity in his face. Instead, it was pure and unadulterated fury. This was our devil. The god of shifters who had created an entire race of beings—and literal pathways between worlds.

He was lost to the new surge of energy, and I knew that someone had to pull him back, but I wasn't sure I could get any closer. Taking the risk, I stepped into the flames, but the burn was instant, and when

I pulled my hand away it was red and blistering. It healed fine, but it was enough for me to know that I couldn't run in headfirst and take him down.

Shadow was literally untouchable to me.

What about my wolf?

Dropping my heavy backpack, I shed my clothing, knowing I'd need them again since we were on limited supplies. When I was naked, standing with a light breeze blowing my hair all around me, I allowed the chokehold on my wolf to ease—she was more than a little excited to finally have freedom. Just as she started to surge up, Shadow's gaze snapped to meet mine.

I paused, the change hovering on the edge, my fingers rippling into claws, even as the rest of me remained human. Shadow didn't move, neither of us did. One covered in flames, the other naked with flaming red hair dancing around. Both of us locked in his power.

"Shadow," I whispered. There was no way he should have been able to hear me over the noise of his fire—it sounded like a jet engine, the ground near shaking from the decibels, but somehow, he did.

He heard me.

When he took a step forward, I shivered. Not from the cold, but from the sheer force of his stare. Holding me in place. Turning my body into one that would literally die for this beast if he just continued to look at me like that.

"Shadow," I choked out again. "Come back to me."

This was a reversal of what he'd had to do in Torma with me, and the irony wasn't lost on me. I also wondered what would happen if both of us lost it at the same time... who would call us back then?

He took another step toward me, and I was dragged further into his forcefield. My trembling legs drove me toward his fire. The heat was intense, and not only was my body responding, but so was my energy. That connection—*path*—I had to this realm sprang to life.

As flames burst across my skin, rough hands hauled me up and against his body. I wrapped my legs around him, not caring that not only was I naked, but we had a witness in one of my best friends.

"What are you?" Shadow rumbled. "That you make me feel..."

He trailed off, and I was desperate to hear more. Made him feel what?

He said no more, though, and it took me a few moments to understand that what he meant was *feel* in general.

My gaze dropped to his lips and I desperately craved a taste of him. It was a frantic need that had my breath raggedly escaping in huffs. Kissing him was a bad idea. We'd never kissed before, not even when his tongue had been buried deep in my pussy, making me come until I saw stars.

That night, he'd stopped me from touching him in any way, but today... today he wasn't stopping me at all.

His mouth slammed against mine, and an actual rumbling groan spilled from my lips as our tongues tangled together. Shadow took control, angling his head so that he could suck my bottom lip into his mouth, biting against it, as we fought to taste each other.

I was clawing at his back, and it wasn't until I opened my eyes that I saw his were open as well. Burning gazes clashed as we kissed, and that wasn't all that burned. Our flames were a raging inferno around us, and no doubt this sort of power and energy was not the incognito approach he'd hoped to take here.

There was one positive of the fire: no one could see us in the midst of the flames coating our skins, which meant I could let my control go for a moment, vulnerability creeping into my gaze as I pulled away from him.

"What am I, Shadow?" I whispered.

He was still staring at me, as he had done when he'd taken control and completely owned my fucking mouth. That unbreakable gaze dissected my very being, breaking me down into whatever energy formed my soul.

"What are these scars from?" he rumbled, and the rapid change of subject took me by surprise. *Scars?*

It was then that I felt his hand on my back, tracing up my spine, and I was reminded of the day I was held down and branded by Dean

Heathcliffe. I'd been fourteen, it had been a few years after my father's death, and the beta had called me for a meeting to discuss my options of improving my place in the pack.

Looking back, I had a feeling the entire setup had been about Jaxson. Maybe he'd stepped out of line again, or maybe Dean was just a bastard. He'd tortured me for hours in the field. Branding a hot iron down my spine, all the while "interrogating me" for information I didn't have.

I remembered that day well, from screaming until eventually the pain had been so fucking much, I'd passed out, to regaining consciousness a few hours later, alone and in agony.

It had taken me weeks to heal from the wounds, and when it had all been done, I'd still borne the faded circular scars down my spine.

"Scars of my past," I breathed, my demons rearing their heads as memories flashed at me. I'd just kissed Shadow, a soul-destroying kiss, and instead of grinding against him like I wanted, all I could see in my head was Dean *motherfucking* Heathcliffe.

Talk about cockblocking.

Shadow wasn't satisfied with that response, the fire in his eyes surging to greater heights.

With a sigh, I added a little more to the story. "The beta took his interrogation a little too far, and his branding iron left a mark."

Shadow's chest rumbled under my touch, that deep reverberating sound he made when he was truly furious. He'd made it the day he'd killed Alpha Victor, and when he'd faced off against Torin. Both times it had been about me, and no lie, I was into this grouchy, alpha, kill-everything-that-got-in-his-way side of him. Especially when it wasn't directed toward me.

"I have a lot of scars," I told him, forcing the words out, their truth burning my throat. "Both inside and out, but they don't define me."

He still wasn't talking, his breathing harsh, same as mine, our scents mixing together. Needing to lighten the mood, or I'd self-destruct, I said the first thing that came to mind.

"I'm pretty sure we'll get Shadowshine."

His lips twitched; he hadn't forgotten the last time I'd said that, either, and thankfully, my reminder had the desired effect.

"Sundow sounds like a pet's name," I babbled, saying whatever words entered my head.

I was gently set on my feet, and wanting to keep him in sight, I tilted my head back.

"Shadowshine is exactly how I see us," he rumbled. "One too dark, the other too light, and nothing but destructive storms between us."

I swallowed roughly at the tone of his words, almost broken. He didn't really believe we would ever have a couple name because we'd never truly be a couple. "Storms are my favorite," I said fiercely. "I always dance in the rain."

He leaned down, his nose running along my cheek as he scented me. "You forgot the destructive part, little wolf."

I hadn't. I just didn't care.

I shivered as he pulled away, those serious eyes still on me, even as our fires faded to almost nothing. "I won't let you be swept away in the deluge," he warned, and then he was gone, walking away from me, leaving me naked and alone.

Once again.

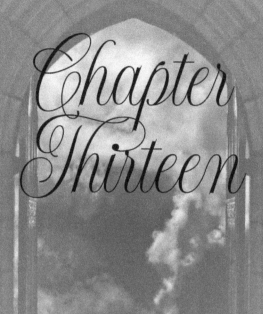

Chapter Thirteen

Angel helped me pull my shit together, dress, and get the backpack onto my shoulders. By the time I was done, Shadow was just a broad-shouldered speck in the distance.

My friend kept glancing at me as we started after him, and I was sure that the shock on my face was a permanent imprint.

"Are you okay?" she finally asked, no doubt hoping to jolt me from my dark thoughts.

"I have no idea what just happened," I breathed, blinking about fifty billion times, like that would clear my head. "My aim was to calm him down, but it appears I might have done the opposite."

Angel shot me a knowing smile. "I've never seen anyone rile Shadow like you do. Or, to be more accurate, it's not the riling that's odd, it's the way he doesn't kill you when it happens. If I know anything about the beast, it's that he doesn't like to come undone. He doesn't want to be out of control."

I snorted. "Isn't he always out of control, bursting into flames, growling and grumbling at everyone?"

She actually laughed out loud. "Firstly, you're probably not going to believe this, but Shadow was rarely out of control before he met you. And secondly, most of the time, even when he's using his power and rumbling his words, it's still controlled. The smoke show is all deliberate to achieve whatever end he's after. But with you, it's an actual loss of control."

"He's not the only one," I admitted. "How can I hate him so desperately one minute, and then the next, feel like I'll die if I don't kiss him?"

My fingers lifted to brush across my lips. "That was my first real kiss," I whispered. That bullshit with Torin didn't count. Fucker. "How pathetic."

Angel ground to a halt. "He kissed you?"

In my surprise, I stumbled forward as well. "Uh, yeah, he did."

She swallowed roughly. "Are you sure?"

What? *Whaaat?*

"Uh, yeah, pretty sure. I mean, I'm inexperienced, but even I know what a kiss is."

She was starting to worry me now as she paced back and forth, her blades finally relaxing in her hands.

"Angel!" I snapped. "What are you trying to tell me? Why are you so shocked about Shadow kissing me?"

I mean, yeah, I got that I wasn't his usual type, but surely, the idea that he might have kissed me wasn't insane enough to merit this reaction.

She stopped moving, meeting my gaze. "Did you know that the royals of Shadow Realm have true mates?"

I shook my head because I was pretty sure that hadn't come up.

"They do," she continued. "Sometimes they are betrothed at birth, and sometimes it happens when they find the perfect match and perform the ceremony. Before they find this *one*, they will be open sexually, but they never..." She swallowed roughly. "And I can't reiterate the *never* enough. They never kiss someone who is not their mate."

"What?" I breathed.

I searched her face to see if she was joking with me, despite knowing it was not her style to joke about something like this.

"Why?"

Her smile was full of secret thoughts. "There's an intimacy in kissing that not even sex can replicate. In the moment of a kiss, you share energy, power, the essence of you. You share a part of your soul, and in the realm, they reserve that for their true mates."

"I'm not his mate."

I wasn't. Torin was my mate. Shadow and I didn't have a bond between us like that of a true mate.

"You aren't," she confirmed, and my chest squeezed at the blunt statement. "As the Darkor, the Supreme Being, he was assigned a true mate at birth. They were set to be bonded on the day he was crowned to his power and position. He hasn't seen her since the door was sealed."

"He never said anything," I whispered, resisting the urge to press a hand to the ache in my chest. "Is this the true reason he was so desperate to get back here? To get to her?"

Angel shrugged. "I'm not privy to Shadow's inner thoughts. I have no idea of his motivations, outside of his obvious need for revenge. That one is the complete truth, but the rest... only he knows."

I wasn't privy to his thoughts, either, but I'd always wondered if there was more pushing him than just the need to destroy his sister. He hid so much from me, a plethora of secrets and intrigue. And the kiss... I had no explanation for that, but now I understood why he'd refused to let me touch him last time.

"He initiated the kiss today."

Not just initiated but *consumed* me. Taking everything and leaving me both horny and broken. Angel didn't say anything, but she was pondering it.

"I can't believe that was Shadow's first kiss too," I said, blinking at the absurdity of it. "Unless he's secretly decided to take up kissing chicks in the last thousand years."

Angel shook her head. "Never. I know females whom Shadow was with, and none of them have gone near his lips. It's just sex—mind-blowing sex, apparently—but no intimacy and definitely no kissing."

A surge of anger rose inside me, and as irrational as it was, I could barely stop myself from demanding more details so I could kill these "females." Since I didn't own the beast, and sadly never would, I forced myself to focus on the situation I'd found myself in. The complete and total insanity of what she was saying.

He'd kissed me. He'd given me a part of himself that no other had ever had.

"Shadow's going to break me," I told her, my throat unexpectedly dry. "Torin almost did, his rejection splintering off a part of my soul that I'm almost certain I haven't gotten back. And Shadow..."

Could I ever let him go? Allow him to return to the true mate who owned his heart and soul? And if I did, would *she* try to murder me for stealing their first kiss?

There was no more time for my current crisis because Inky appeared on the horizon, a huge, black cloud tearing toward us. It was thankfully too far away to have heard our conversation, but it was clear that Shadow had had enough of waiting for us to catch up.

The smoke cloud swept around the pair of us, lifting effortlessly. Angel was having none of that shit, though, her wings sweeping out as she rose out of Inky's embrace. "No one carries me," she fumed. "Tell Shadow to keep his fucking hands to himself."

"Woot," I shouted. "You go, girlfriend."

She shot me a small smile before she floated herself down to the ground.

I patted Inky. "I can walk too, buddy. Please put me down."

And what do you know... it did.

Angel and I didn't delay again, hurrying off along the rocky terrain. Inky stayed with us, directing us toward Shadow. As my boots kicked up the rocks beneath our feet, I noticed that the shiny black had threads of silver and bronze veins bisecting it. A rock bed filled with minerals, which went on as far as I could see.

"It's truly odd for the lava fields to be this far from the main chasm," Angel said, shaking her head as she peered into the horizon. "I mean, there have been geysers that popped up over the years, randomly blasting areas when the mists were acting out of character, but this is weird." Angel was playing tour guide, and I wondered if there was any world she didn't know well.

"So this land is kind of built on a huge volcano?"

"Not the same," she told me. "It's the heat of the mists here that cause the lava flow. But it's a similar concept."

The mists were always spoken about with a combination of fear and reverence, but for me, I was mostly curious about them. Maybe it was my bond with Midnight that made it so I couldn't fear this entity. At least not yet.

It took us what felt like days to catch up to Shadow, who was waiting on another elevated section of rock, a blackened and dead-looking tree beside him. I huffed in a lungful of air, thankful for the light, clean oxygen. I had no idea what the literal chemical composition of the atmosphere here was, but it seemed to be doing the same job as oxygen. Thankfully.

The beast didn't turn as we approached, and since I wasn't sure how he was going to react, I moved cautiously as I got closer. Thankfully, when he finally turned my way, he wore a neutral expression, and it was clear we weren't discussing what happened.

I didn't particularly want to hear about his soulmate, so I didn't push the issue.

"We should rest here for the night," he said shortly. "The light is going to fade soon, and we don't want to cross the rest of the land in the dark. Too easy for us to be ambushed."

I stepped closer to where he stood. "Shadow..." I trailed off as I noticed that he hadn't just been staring off into the distance. There was a village below us, down a jagged side of this outcropping.

"This is your home?"

He shook his head. "No, this is Wenberton, an outer-lying city of the royal compound of Fraple. We're still a few days walk into Trinity, and then it's even farther to the edge of my home: Darkor."

I paused. "That's your name?"

He let out an aggravated sound. "When a Supreme Being is born, we're named after the royal city our family rules from. The heir could be born into any of the royal families. I'm the second chosen heir of Darkor. It's more of a title than a name."

"*Shadow* suits you better anyway," I said, not even joking. "That and *Asshole*. You're both, so it works. "

He didn't bite back, but there was a smile. So brief, but I caught it, and fuck, that was nice.

"How will we get through this town undetected?" I asked, looking across the vast section of land, filled with buildings and no doubt a ton of inhabitants. From what I could see at this distance, the houses weren't like Earth's, most of them a combination of futuristic and ancient. Built of stone and rock, with clear bubbles of glass around the structures, almost protectively guarding each house.

He didn't seem worried. "We should be able to just take the long way around. I'll assess further in the morning. Most villages will be the same, and our true test will come when we reach the great forests that surround Darkor. Then we'll have to plan the attack."

Lots of damn planning.

"With that in mind, I need some sleep," I declared. "Not to mention food, water, and a place to wash up."

Shadow finally looked at me. The first real look since we'd kissed. A lot passed between us in this one look, but no words.

"Come with me," he finally said.

Like I had another choice.

Chapter Fourteen

S hadow was never exactly chatty. Yeah, understatement of the year. But I did have this recurring daydream about the two of us. We'd be sitting back on the couch, the magical fire burning nearby, and I'd ask him all the questions... and he would answer them. Every single one.

Just thinking about all the knowledge he held, it'd be like talking to my own personal library. Did I say daydream? Yeah, I meant wet dream.

Funnily enough, since I'd turned into a fireball myself and busted open his realm, Shadow *had* been more open with me. Even playing tour guide as he led us away from the ridge over the village, and back down into what almost looked like a long-ago dried riverbed. "What truly differentiates Shadow Realm from Earth," he said, "is the age of its inhabitants. The royals, the freilds, creatures, and many other subspecies have been evolving here for millions of years. We're more powerful and we live longer than humans and shifters. The mists give us an advantage Earth does not have, at least not in the short time humans have been on it."

"Earth has a similar energy to the mists?" I asked, reading between the lines. It was there; we just couldn't utilize it.

He nodded. "It does, and there's a possibility that at some point in the next million years, if humans last that long, evolution will bring many more powerful supernaturals to the forefront. For now, you're so young."

I thought back to the other worlds off the Solaris System and had to agree. We weren't even remotely in the same league as those big players.

"Shadow Realm was Earth, just a few million years ago," Angel said softly, her head held high as the light breezes shifted her hair around her face. "And the royals were once near human. Until they figured out how to absorb the mists. How to use them. And then, as evolution does, they grew stronger, and now with the Supreme Being"—she shot a look at Shadow—"they're almost unbeatable in this system." She shrugged. "Well, they were before they kicked him out and shut their doors down."

Shadow smiled at this. "They've weakened themselves, and once I figure out how to claim my power, I'll be able to take advantage of that."

This caught my interest. "How will you find your power?" I asked. "Is it just floating around somewhere, waiting for you to claim it?"

Shadow's smile grew larger. "Sort of. Any who are able to control the power are born with a mist tattoo." He lifted his arm, showing me the dark swirls around the large skull on his biceps. "I've added to this one, but the first mark was there at birth."

I spent far too long staring at the muscled arm, and by the end, I could have redrawn the damn tattoo, I knew it so well. But seriously, it was... nice. Yeah, that was what it was.

Nice.

"Some have tried to fake the mark, right?" Angel asked, thankfully allowing me to tear my gaze away.

Shadow shot me a smug look, always seeing too clearly how he affected me. "Tried and failed," he answered Angel. "They don't usually survive the tattoo, let alone the bonding to the mists that allows the power to transfer."

"So how did your sister do it?" I asked.

"The bloodstone," Angel and Shadow replied at the same time.

I looked between them. "Ohhh, right. The old bloodstone. That was my second guess."

Shadow's eyes were deadset laughing at me. The bastard. "And what was the first?" he asked.

Uhhh. I shrugged. "Fucked her way to the top?"

Yeah, I'd just sent women's rights back a few thousand years, but she was a bitch, and I was too braindead for a better idea.

Angel chuckled. "Knowing her in the short time I did, your guess isn't that farfetched."

Shadow didn't bother to comment on it, and I had no doubt his sister's sex life was the last thing he wanted to think about.

"The bloodstone is passed between the Supreme Beings," he told us. "Its power is nothing much until the bond to its master happens, but my sister must have figured out how to utilize it to some degree. Giving her a little more control of the mists. And that's all she'd need to control the other royals."

I grimaced. "Who thought it was a good idea to give one person ultimate power? I mean, isn't that just asking for corruption from this Supreme Being? A being no one in this land can fight against. What stops them from aiming for complete and total subjugation?"

Still one of my greatest fears. Even if I only lived with the facade of freedom, I needed it to keep my sanity intact.

Shadow shot me a side-eye. "What are you saying, Sunshine? You think I have the capability to destroy worlds once I receive my legacy?"

He expected me to say *yes*, that was clear in his expression, but... once I truly thought about it...

"No."

He paused, stopping our trek across the river plane. "No?"

"You've already had supreme power," I said, thinking it through out loud. "Take Earth, for example—there're very few who would even be able to last ten seconds against you. And as far as I know, you've never abused that power over shifters or humans. You've left shifters to go about their days, let humans continue as they were. So... unless this new energy has the aim to corrupt you, I don't see why you'd change now. But you could be the exception to the rule of total power corrupting."

His lips parted, lips that had kissed me not that long ago, and just like that, I could taste him again. A craving to close the distance between us and lick this delicious beast almost knocked me over. Like, damn. That boy was a magnet dragging me into its field.

And I wasn't even mad about it.

"The power is not evil," he said, and it took me far longer than I'd like to admit to focus on those words. "It will not change me. If anything, it's designed to open my mind. Force me to comprehend every facet of my action before I make it. To my knowledge, throughout our history, there has never been a Supreme Being who was corrupted by the power. Generally, the land is at its most prosperous when the chosen one is at full power."

"My knowledge too," Angel said. "And not that I'm not enjoying this conversation, because I am, but is there any chance we could get to where we are camping for the night? I need to recharge my energy. I anticipate attacks in our future, and I want to be at full strength."

Shadow nodded. "Yes. It's just beyond this meadow."

Meadow... Hmm, I mean, not exactly how I'd describe a field of lava rocks, but to each their own. My expression must have given my thoughts away because Shadow lifted an eyebrow in my direction. "This is unexpectedly widespread, the lava field, but if it's the same as when I was here, there's a trick that will give us some comforts tonight."

He crouched and ran his hands over the ground, moving farther and farther along until he seemed to find what he was looking for. Without a word, he lifted his right hand and punched through the rock. I blinked at the burst of violence, expecting a bloody mess of a hand when he pulled it back, but there was just smooth, bronze skin.

"Show-off," I muttered.

He shook his head, before he started to dig into the hole he'd made, and after a beat, liquid bubbled up from it. He scooped it up, and it was clear. "Looks like we're staying here for the night," he declared, and then he flung the water around.

I felt his energy flow with the liquid, and within seconds, there was a field of grass where rock had previously been. The grass was an odd color, not quite green and not quite brown, but this golden shade of ocher.

When I crouched to touch it, it felt soft and alive, smooth against the palm of my hand. "How did it grow so fast?" I breathed, unsure if it was real or magic.

"The lava spreads across the top of the land, but it doesn't destroy what lies below. Once I find a fertile spot, all I have to do is give a little assistance, and we can return it to what once was."

The grass continued to spread where we stood, as did the water-hole he'd created. A literal grotto of nature in the midst of a field of black rock. "Why did we walk so far if you could have done this anywhere?"

Golden, flaming eyes almost had me forgetting my question as he met my gaze. "Not *anywhere*. I had to find a source of water and energy first, and the farther we are from the villages, the safer we'll be. I will not allow an ambush to take us by surprise while we rest."

Allow. Typical arrogant beast. But I couldn't complain. "Yeah, late-night ambushes are the worst, amiright?"

Deadpan stare. *What?* "I use lame sarcasm to get through scary situations. You're aware of this, so don't act so annoyed."

Shadow just shook his head. "Being aware of something doesn't make it less annoying."

I nodded, wrinkling my forehead, like I was considering this. "Yeah, good point. I'm not going to stop, though."

"Never thought you would."

He turned away, and I couldn't for the life of me figure out why my heart was beating so hard. How unfair was it to finally have this *explosion of chemistry* between us evolving, only for me to find out he was back here to claim his crown and... his mate.

He is not mine. Never was, never will be.

Forcing myself to focus on one thing and one thing only—setting up camp and getting some sleep—I pulled out the contents of my backpack. I had a compressed mattress that inflated as I unrolled and spread it out. Even better, when Shadow pressed his hand to it, the freaking thing doubled in size, giving me a soft surface on which to rest. A broad smile stretched my cheeks, and I was surprised by how excited I was to not sleep directly on the rocky ground. Pretty sure this was adulthood, and I was *here for it.*

Shaking my ass at this unexpected fortune, I did a quick dance to the music in my head, and as I spun on the spot, near combo twerking and flossing, I found Angel and Shadow watching me... closely.

A normal person would have been embarrassed—my dance skills were about as strong as my singing skills. But I wasn't normal. This was the new, improved Mera, who didn't shave off parts of herself to fit into other people's worlds.

"What?" I said, looking between them. "Everyone should dance when they're happy. Promise it's totally worth it."

Shadow's eyes burned into me. "I'll take your word for it," he rumbled, his voice deeper than ever, his accent slightly stronger as he rolled his *r*s. There was a burst of flame flickering deep in his eyes, stirring energy low in my body. If he kept this up, I was going to add squirming to my dance repertoire.

Had he actually enjoyed watching my terrible dance moves? Or was I searching for a deeper connection between us because I was the idiot catching some feels?

Either way, it left me all out of sorts, and I was a little grumpy as I flopped onto my bed and stared up at the sky above. Angel informed us that she needed to recharge her energy, and off she went to meditate with the land or something, and I just focused on breathing in and out and relaxing. Some of my mood shifted as I calmed, and with that, I started to notice more of the world around me.

Like... there were no stars here. Not a single one.

Twisting around to take in the entire midnight black sky, I saw what looked like a slice of golden cheese-shaped moon off in the distance, a few streams of light drifting around it, but other than that, the rest was a heavy blanket across the sky.

"The Ether mists," Shadow said, and I tried not to react when he settled in at my side, our bodies almost touching. We might as well have been, with our energy ping-ponging back and forth between us, near scorching with the intensity. "They're more visible when the light of the day fades."

"Do you actually call it night and day?" I asked, realizing that all of this time, he'd used familiar Earth terms.

"Not in our language," he said, his steady breathing near lulling me to sleep. "But there's no literal translation to most of what exists here, so I'm giving it to you in terms you understand."

I liked that. Shadow wasn't particularly considerate in general, but with me... he had been trying. I had no idea what that meant, but I liked it.

Pretty much why I was a girly mess of feelings.

Shadow continued to tell me about his world, and honestly, the mild accent was enough to drive me both crazy and soothe me to sleep. How he could pull me in such polar opposites, I'd never know, but as I listened to his history, I ended up resting against his arm.

Shadow didn't move me. He didn't shock me. He let me rest against his warmth, and for a brief moment, there was only peace.

That lasted until I closed my eyes, and his chest rumbled, jarring me awake.

"You need to eat," he said.

"You do," Angel added, having finished with her own recharge.

Sitting up, I rubbed at my eyes, wishing I didn't feel like such horseshit. I was not one of those people who could be woken from a few-minute nap and bounce back. Made me and my wolf a little growly.

"You look great," I said to Angel, noticing a visible energy flickering across her skin, almost like she was covered in a blanket of electricity. I hadn't seen that before, but this must have been Angel at full charge.

"The mists are unsteady," she said, brushing her hands along her armor. "There's still power, but the stability is out of balance. I don't know what the royals have been doing since Shadow left, but whatever it is, they're not doing it well."

"Which will soon change," the beast in question said. Before any of us could answer, he reached down and hauled me up. "You're not looking after yourself, Mera," he bit out as he led me to the waterhole he'd created.

We stopped on the side. "This is safe to drink," he added, nudging me forward.

I didn't move, and clearly, my rather epic resting bitch face wasn't doing its job because he just nudged me again. "Shadow," I snapped. "Stop motherfucking manhandling me. I don't need your help with taking care of myself. I will eat... and drink... when I'm ready to eat and drink."

Okay, so I might have been acting a little like a toddler, but I was out of sorts still, and he wasn't helping with his alpha bullshit. Not tonight. Tonight, I knew he had a true mate, a destiny that didn't include me, and I was stuck in this world that might hold a lot of secrets I couldn't handle.

Tonight, I just needed a break.

Another nudge, and it was at this very moment I lost my shit, launching myself at him, tackling the damn devil of shifters. Now, normally, I wouldn't have moved his giant ass, but we'd been balancing right on the edge of his lake, and I took him by surprise, sending both of us into the water.

I coughed and choked, going under as the shock rendered me motionless for a beat. The water was cool but not freezing, and it was surprisingly refreshing as it unexpectedly entered my nose and mouth.

A strong arm hauled me up, and when he slammed his palm against my back to help me get the water up, there was a decent chance he'd just broken a rib or two. But I hadn't drowned, so there was that.

"What the fuck, dude?" I gasped, chasing air to get it into my lungs. "This is all your fault."

He just stared at me, blinking like I was some sort of swamp creature who'd disturbed his swim. "You're always pushing me," I ranted, paddling away from him, because I needed the distance. "Always trying to fit me into your mold, all the while using your alpha command on me—"

His power locked around me, cutting off my words, and I was slowly dragged back through the lake until I reached him. Out here, I couldn't touch the bottom, but it was okay because he held me up with whatever energy he was using to *once again* control me.

Unable to speak, I used my eyes to project how truly pissed off I was.

I am going to kill you when you free me.

Shadow grinned, a not very nice smile, and like the truly pathetic shifter I was, I found myself examining his lips, thinking about our kiss.

Our first kiss. For both of us.

This was just getting sad, an obsession burning through my veins.

Shadow's eyes darkened, with just the flickering embers deep inside. "Your mouth says one thing, Sunshine," he told me softly, "but your scent says another. Not to mention your eyes."

I was drowning again, but this time from the intensity of him. Of his power. Of his presence. Of this tangible connection between us. My body ached, and I tried to arch to ease it, but of course, he was torturing me with a full body hold.

Just when I was about to combust or freak out or hyperventilate— fine line on all three—he finally released me, and I sank into the water, near sobbing as the cool liquid encased me again, soothing my boiling skin.

By the time I resurfaced, Shadow was gone, and I reluctantly followed. I was still horny as fuck, but the simmering annoyance kept it at bay. An annoyance that only grew with each sodden step across the land toward my bedding.

When I got there, Shadow held two bars out to me. "Eat," he told me shortly, dropping them in my hands.

I was tempted to throw them back at him, but that was both juvenile and a waste of food, so I satisfied myself with turning my back and pretending he didn't exist.

If only there hadn't been a constant hot blast of his energy from behind, and those snaking tendrils in my gut, from the Shadow pull.

As I wolfed—pun intended—down the bars he'd packed for me, I felt an easing of the pressing anger that had been riding me for a while. Hmm. Odd.

"She was hangry," Angel said, her voice behind me as well. Sounded like she was standing near Shadow. "I've heard of that with humans, but that was my first time seeing it."

I shot them both a glare over my shoulder. "I was not hangry, you immortal assholes."

Both Shadow and Angel cracked smiles, and I found myself laughing as well, realizing I *had* been a bit of a hungry-angry bitch.

"Sorry about pushing you in the water," I said to Shadow. "I might have overreacted a touch."

That was as much as he was getting from me.

The beast took a step forward, his power blasting into me, and I had to close my eyes at the delicious sensation of his fire. Within seconds, it had dried my clothes and boots. "You feel stronger," I told him.

"It's been a long time since I felt my energy charged up like this." His laugh was dry. "I'd actually forgotten what it was like to partake of the energy of Shadow Realm."

"You were very young when you were kicked out," I reminded him.

He nodded. "Yes, twenty-two is young, but it's also a big milestone here. Especially for a royal. We open our energies to accept the power of the mists, we control our first creature, and we learn how to step into a leadership role."

"You missed it all," I whispered sadly.

His features darkened. "Every milestone was stolen from me. If I hadn't torn at the mists as I was leaving, I wouldn't have had Inky, either, and there is little doubt in my mind that without its energy, I would have perished on my own."

Which had probably been his sister's aim. To send him out so young, defenseless and without energy.

"Now I want to kill your family."

His laughter brushed over me, and I found it hard to remember being mad at him before.

"Killing my sister is my right," Shadow reminded me.

Fair enough. He deserved it more than any, and I would do my best to help him achieve his goal.

It was almost amusing how much our relationship had changed. Would it morph again just as fast? Especially when the true mate came back into the picture?

Chapter Fifteen

At some point, I fell asleep, resting better than I had in a long time. I woke just as the light returned to the sky, sending the blanket of mists into the background.

Rubbing my eyes, I yawned and sat, looking around to figure out where everyone was. Shadow was awake, leaned against a large tree, watching over us. A tree that had not been there yesterday, but clearly, this oasis he'd unlocked by releasing the water was continuing to evolve.

"Oh, hey," I said, pushing myself up. "No drama through the night?"

He leaned forward, his legs slightly bent, and as the heavy muscles in his thighs tensed, I was briefly confused about why I was all the way over here, and not between—

"Outside of your snoring," he drawled, interrupting my horny-girl thoughts, "it was all quiet."

I choked on my next yawn, blinking at him. "Oh my god, dude. You're supposed to politely pretend you didn't hear me breathing like a freight train through the night. Don't you know the rules?"

My outrage was mostly faked, even though no one wanted the

hottest being in the fucking worlds to hear you snore all night. Had I farted, too? Just to get the full range of embarrassing noises in.

Shadow laughed as he pulled to his feet. "I'm just fucking with you. You slept like the dead, and I had to check more than once to make sure you were actually breathing. The water settled well in your system."

"I feel great," I admitted, my body heating at the thought of Shadow touching me throughout the night. How could I have slept through that? Usually, whenever he was in close proximity, every nerve ending came to life, and I was all twitchy, my energy sparking like I'd been plugged into a socket. But instead, I'd *slept like the dead?*

Maybe the water in the realm had some free Valium in it.

"So, what's the plan today?" I asked, needing a subject change. I looked around. "And where's Angel?"

"She's scouting out the landscape from above," Shadow said, "and we're just continuing on toward Trinity. If you want to wash up first, though, the lake is as you left it."

His gaze, which had been on my face, slowly traced down to where my tits heaved as I sucked in a breath. All I could think about was swimming with Shadow again. This time, though, we wouldn't fight.

It took me a split second to make the decision.

This was it, my last chance to give it a shot. If I was losing Shadow to this mate of his, I was going to enjoy every second I had before that happened. It was time for me to step up the plan I'd made with Angel long ago to lose my virginity to him. He was an experience I wanted, and my time was running out.

"I think I will clean up," I said, getting to my feet so I wasn't on the ground, staring up the long length of him. Was it weird that I had the random wish someone would get this guy a pair of grey sweatpants? I needed that experience. Like, bucket list needed.

Once I was standing, I stripped my long-sleeved shirt off, leaving myself in just a black bra. Shadow didn't say anything, but his eyes were warning me not to take this too far. If only I was any good at listening to warnings.

My pants were next, and when I slipped them off, I neatly folded them on my shirt. Turning my back on him, I reached behind and unclipped my bra, sliding it off my arms and letting it fall, leaving me clad in black panties and a fucking smug smile. Not that Shadow could see that since my back was still turned to him. But it was definitely there.

"Are you going to wash up?" I asked, turning my head enough to catch a glimpse of him standing, arms crossed, watching me intently.

He didn't reply, so I just shrugged and stepped out of the panties. Not like he hadn't seen me naked a hundred times, but he hadn't seen me naked since we'd kissed, and that was apparently a big deal to him, so I was curious if anything would change.

The water was warmer than it had been last night, while still feeling refreshing on my skin as I dove in. I glided along for about thirty seconds, before deciding to do some laps. My natural love of water had me forgetting my plan to tempt Shadow into a clandestine sexual encounter, and it wasn't until a dark shape glided by—and I about died of a heart attack—that I surfaced to find he was here. With me.

His hair was slicked back, water dripping along his skin, and from what I could see in the thickly corded muscles, he was at least naked from the waist up.

He glided closer. "You find such joy in the most basic of life's activities," he said, his movements barely even rippling the water. "And after hundreds of jaded years, I find myself strangely desperate to feel what you do."

Unable to help myself, I moved forward as well. Far less gracefully, but who the heck cared about that when I was in here with a naked Shadow. "I've always loved to swim. Odd for a shifter, but the freeing sensation I get from being in the water is greater than I've ever felt on two or four legs."

"You *are* odd for a shifter," he murmured. "Probably because you're not fully a shifter. It took me some time to figure it out, but you're not completely one of mine. I just don't know to whom you belong."

"Here's a crazy-ass concept," I said with a smirk. "Maybe I don't belong to anyone. Maybe I'm a free wolf making my own path without outside influences."

Shadow tilted his head as we all but met in the middle of the lake, circling around, our gazes focused on each other. I couldn't speak for him, but my limbs trembled being naked near him, and... the curiosity of wondering if he was naked too was probably going to kill me.

My eyeline kept drifting into the water, but he was moving too fast for me to be able to see clearly. Fucking hell, could someone just give me a break here and flash some cock my way?

Anyone? I needed a little somethin' somethin' for the long, lonely nights...

"You might be right."

I stopped moving, almost drowning as my legs froze. Right about what? Needing some spank bank material?

"Maybe you *are* a lone wolf," he said. *Oh, right. Yep, yep.* "And the fact that someone chose to place you amongst my shifters is a sure sign that you and I have been on a path to meet. Whether by fate or intervention, our meeting was inevitable."

Water filled my mouth as I sank into the lake. Shadow was right, and the more I thought about it, the more I needed the answers as to why. Why was I the way I was? Why did I have these connections to the realm and to Shadow and the mists?

I was still a shifter, clearly, with a true mate and everything. But I was like no regular shifter. None of it made sense.

"What am I?" I asked him, my flirty eyes dead in the literal water as I focused on the fucked-up truth of my reality. "Should I even exist?"

Shadow was in my face in a heartbeat, and I sucked in a lungful of water, almost drowning this time for real. He wrapped an arm around me, hauling me higher while I coughed up my lungs in an attempt to purge the water from them. History repeating itself. Even if that history had been only last night.

"Jesus, fuck," I snarled, my voice hoarse from the manic coughing session. "That was not planned."

"Nothing with you ever is," Shadow drawled, and now that I wasn't in immediate danger of dying, I noticed the position we were currently in.

He was holding me, and he was most definitely naked. I could feel the long, smooth lines of his body pressed against me, the hardness of his muscles so delicious against my softer curves. I tilted my head back to meet his gaze, and my breath started to burst from me in little pants. My entire vision was filled with Shadow, and once again, his taste was on my lips.

"We need to go," he said softly. "We're both clean, and now we're wasting time."

Neither of us moved.

"Shadow," I breathed.

His eyes darkened. "You keep looking at me like that, Sunshine, and I promise that this fun little swim will end completely different from how it started."

I groaned, trying to climb him, but he held me immobile. He'd done the same thing when he'd devoured my pussy, and it was the only time in my life I would admit to actually wanting to be restrained.

"End it differently," I said with force. "Fucking live up to your reputation."

Apparently, being hungry *and* sexually frustrated made me cranky. It was a flaw... Whatever.

His eyes darkened to something akin to Inky, and I had a brief thought of wondering where that smoke blob even was before Shadow tightened his hold. "You've been fighting me from the start," he rasped near my ear. "No matter how much I push, you push back just as hard."

"I know no other way," I whispered against his neck, my face buried there as I breathed him in, my tongue darting out to trace the water on his skin.

Shadow groaned. "Mera, Sunshine. This is a bad idea. I'm not good for you, and I make no fucking promises. *Ever.*"

I licked him again, sucking against him, salivating at how freaking delicious he tasted. "I don't want your promises," I said truthfully. "I'm a grown-ass woman, and I know the deal. This is nothing more than what it is. Two horny people fucking because we can."

He jerked me out of the water so fast, a scream died in my throat, and when his arms wrapped up under my thighs and around my ass, I found myself sitting right on his face. Like last time, he wasted no time getting straight to my clit, sucking it into his mouth, his teeth biting against the throbbing flesh.

My cry was choked because we were incognito in these parts, and screaming my lungs out was probably a bad idea. No matter how much I wanted to. Threading both of my hands through his hair, I dragged him as hard against me as I could, grinding into his clever mouth.

"Shadow," I cried, jerking into him as the first orgasm hit me. It had been way too long between orgasms, and I fell over the edge so damn easily with this beast.

Arching my back, my tits were all but flapping in the breeze, but I was too far gone to care. Shadow held me in that firm grip, his large hands biting into my thighs, kneading against my ass. The strength of this god should have scared me, but I didn't care.

If he killed me right now, I'd go out one fucking satiated bitch.

He looked up to meet my stare, and his eyes were blazing as he devoured me. When he pulled back a little, tongue stroking up in long, smooth slide, I came again, tightening my thighs and hands to the point that I knew I would have hurt anyone who wasn't as strong as Shadow.

He didn't stop and if the fire in his eyes was any indication, he liked the bite of pain.

Yep, we were the same amount of fucked-up, and that was what made it work with us.

His power zapped along my skin as I choked on my next screams, making me come harder than ever. His fiery electrical strike teetered on the fine line of pleasure and pain, and I craved it.

When the sensations were too much, I threw myself back, and it was only Shadow's hold on me that kept my head above water. He laid me out on the waterline, his tongue's strokes against my pussy slowing as he lapped at the moisture there, devouring everything my body offered. A buildup started again, stronger and with more intensity.

"Stop," I begged. "Let me touch you as well or stop, Shadow."

He paused before sucking my clit into his mouth, running his tongue around it slowly, sweeping it side to side and about killing me. Pulling back a fraction, I was breathing heavily as I watched him. "I'm not sure I can control my energy with you, Sunshine."

It cost him to admit that, and I attempted not to let the fact that I affected Shadow settle in my heart.

"I don't care." Absolute truth. "As you like to remind me, I've risked my life every day since we met. What's one more risk? Especially when it comes with reward."

Using one arm, he slowly lifted me up so that I was vertical again, and as he dragged me closer, he allowed me to sink against his body. A hard cock pressed to my core as I slid farther down him.

"This is not going to happen here," he warned me.

I jerked my head back. "What do you mean?" We were, like, *right fucking there*. He couldn't stop now.

He narrowed his eyes on me, looking too damn gorgeous, all wet and bothered. "You want to lose your virginity in a fucking lake with the chances of Angel or any one of the many creatures roaming these lands to come upon us?"

I had to think about it, like really think about it, before I answered. "You're going to take my virginity, right? If we stop now, you promise we will find a time to finish this?"

His lips tilted up, a wicked smile gracing his face. "Sunshine, I'm going to destroy you before I put you back together. But I don't have the time right now for everything I intend to do, so you're going to have to stop tempting me and let me get on with the rest of my mission."

I tightened my legs around his waist, groaning as the tip of his cock slipped inside, the burning stretch just enough to be fun.

Shadow's chest rumbled as the fire of his power spilled across us. "What if," I panted, "we never get another chance?"

Who knew what could happen after this? He was waging war against his powerful family, without his full powers.

"We will," he said. "I'll find time before we get to Trinity. Before... everything changes."

Before his true mate came into the picture.

Shadow wrapped his arms around me, the sudden movement dislodging me, and I was about to protest until I realized he was hugging me. One of those full-bodied embraces that I felt through my entire soul. A warm blanket encasing me.

"Thank you."

I jerked, wondering if he'd actually whispered those words. I had no idea if I'd heard it right, and even less idea what he was thanking me for, but I was fighting tears. This felt like a goodbye, and I fucking hated it. I wanted to scream and tear my skin off. I wanted to wrap myself around him like this and never let go.

But... if there was one thing I'd learned, it was that holding on as tightly as you could did nothing if the other person was doing everything they could to shove you away. Jaxson had taught me that with the sort of harsh lesson I'd never forget. It was tattooed on my soul the same way Shadow's mists were tattooed on his body.

"We'll have our moment, Sunshine," he said, pulling away. "And then it will be over."

I nodded. "I understand."

And sadly, I did.

Chapter Sixteen

We left the water, and I felt... wrecked. Maybe it was the orgasms; Shadow seemed to be about to wring more than one from me with next to no effort. Or, more likely, it was the fact that whatever this thing was between us, it was on a countdown clock.

"We still need to talk about the bet," Shadow reminded me again as we got dressed, neither of us looking at the other.

I jerked my head up, my shirt half over my arm as I shrugged it all the way on. "Are you finally collecting?"

His smile was smug. "I've thought about it, and you know... I don't think I have to. You've already stopped fighting me. You had long before your time ran out."

I felt super offended by that. "Not true. I've never stopped fighting you!"

Shadow, dressed in black fatigues with desert-brown boots to finish off his hot jungle man look, strode toward me. I tilted my head back in our familiar dance. "You were fighting *with* me in a different way, Mera. Before we were adversaries, but then... it changed."

Jesus, fuck. Did I just die? Because it felt like I'd lost control of my senses as those words left his lips, the stroke of his hand across my face so fast, I wondered if I'd imagined it.

Then he was done, backpack on, all business. This was the Shadow Beast who drove fear into the hearts of all who met him. The Shadow Beast who would kill his family and not lose sleep over it.

The one who would walk away from me and never think my name again.

Hurrying to catch up with him, a figure zoomed over our heads, and I reacted defensively, but Shadow clearly knew it was Angel, since he didn't even turn his head.

"Find anything?" he asked as she landed gracefully, her wings tucking behind her.

Today she wore a rust-colored shift dress, which was covered in pieces of her armor. Her hair was braided down her back, the striking color shiny in the light here, and I had to marvel at how stunning she was. No one existed with such perfection on the earthly realm, and yet I'd never seen Shadow's eyes darken or flames appear in them when he stared at her.

Which made no sense at all to me.

Oh, well. I wasn't about to question the whys of what had happened between us. I was going to enjoy it. Live in the moment.

And mourn tomorrow.

"They have a training session in the field of the village this morning," Angel reported. "A lot of their armed forces are out of the town."

"And the creatures?" Shadow bit out, in soldier mode.

"They're with them."

I knew that the shadow creatures were mostly under the control of royals, with free ones rounded up by hunters.

"There are royals in this village?" I asked.

Shadow shook his head. "No, the royals of Fraple are a few days' walk from here. Their compound is near the border of Trinity because we all like to keep an eye on our royal neighbors."

"So what's with the creatures, then?"

"Every city and village has creatures," Shadow told me, looking out into the horizon. "Descendants of royals can control them, as long as a full-blooded royal has tamed the creature in question."

"Not to mention that those with royal blood are often called into their armed forces," Angel added.

"Okay, yeah, that makes sense."

It did make sense, but every time I learned more about the creatures and how they were treated here, an uneasy feeling swirled in my gut. They were nothing more than possessions. Expendable. They were used and abused to keep the royals and the human-like freilds functioning.

"The creatures I pulled to Earth," I said, "would they have been under the control of a royal?"

"I doubt it," Shadow said. "I couldn't feel the energy of another in theirs, so they were probably pulled from The Grey Lands, where the free beasts roam. The point of origin, where the two mists converge, is there. It was once a place of pure creation and power."

"It used to be known by another name, that land, right?" Angel asked.

Shadow nodded. "Yes. As it changed over the years, parts of it dying inexplicably, it was renamed 'The Grey Lands.' But it was, once upon a time, a very different place. Still, it's where the young royals make their journeys for their first creatures."

This was what had me so riled. The creatures were just out there minding their own business when some punk-ass fucker sauntered in to steal their freedom?

Kind of made me want to kill a few royals.

Shadow smirked. "I know what you're thinking, and trust me, when the unbonded creatures make it to our lands, they carve a path of destruction second to none. You don't understand because you can control their energy, as can I, but for the regular citizen of the realm... there is nothing but blood and guts left by the time the creature is done."

I wasn't convinced. If it was anything like Earth, the reason that land was dying would be totally due to something the royals had done. And of course, as their land died, the creatures would have to search farther afield for nourishment and shelter. It wasn't their fault.

The creatures I'd met over my time with Shadow had held a true intelligence and pure energy, and I'd grown pretty fond of them. Even the creepy ones with poison sap.

"I know some fault lies with the royals here," I said, my disgust seeping out even when I tried to hold it inside. "I know it."

Shadow didn't argue, and I wondered if deep down, his personal thoughts on the creatures were more aligned with mine than with the royals'. In truth, Shadow had lived here for twenty-two years, and out of the realm for a thousand plus. How much of him still thought like the royals?

I sincerely hoped not a lot.

Since this world's issues were not going to be fixed today, we started on our journey. Our path was the same as yesterday, and when we left the slowly growing oasis, we were back on the harsh black rock. I settled into the monotony of walking, feeling thankful that Shadow found a way around the first village, leaving us free and undetected to continue on.

And we did. On and on and on. Thankfully, Angel and Shadow both remembered my frailties, allowing me water, food, and a pee break more than once. Neither of them seemed to require anything, and as the day slipped away again, we had made our way around two more towns that stood between us and the royal compound. I saw quite a few of the inhabitants from a distance, and not all of them looked like Shadow. He was an overly enhanced, super fucking hot, giant version of a human. But some of the regular folk, the freilds, were quite different.

"Blue skin?"

Shadow turned to where I was looking at a small family having... a picnic? "Subspecies of the freilds," he said. "Mixed with water sprites. They call themselves 'fronds.'"

In my head, I was keeping a running tally of what beings I'd learned of here. Creatures, royals, and freilds, which included the

Shadow Hunters, and now fronds. "How many other different races and subspecies are here?"

His lips twitched. "We also have the clordees, who are a mix of shadow creatures and freilds."

I paused. "Uh, are you saying some of the freilds had sex with the creatures?"

Angel and Shadow both laughed, probably at the absurdity of my question, and possibly the look on my face. I hurried on. "I mean, I know that shouldn't be weird to me. I'm a wolf and I've heard of more than a few having a go at fucking in their beast forms, but it feels weird."

Shadow's smile was slow and contemplative. "What did you think of the Brolder inhabitants?"

"Oh, yeah." I nodded. "They didn't seem unusual, but I guess there was some... interspecies breeding going on there?"

I really needed to get my judgy hat off.

"We don't procreate in the exact same way as humans," Shadow told me. "But you're also not wrong. The different creatures all have varying levels of intelligence, and some are on the same par as freilds. Once you learn to communicate with them, it's really not as... depraved as you're thinking."

I held both hands up. "Seriously, no more judgement from me. I can hardly talk when it comes to living an alternative lifestyle."

I mostly hoped to see these clordees at some point so I could experience this particular mesh of two different species. It was an interesting concept, and as long as no creatures were taken advantage of, I was all for diversity.

This strange protectiveness I had for the creatures was growing with time. And now that I was here, seeing the beings of Shadow's world, I could no longer ignore the urge to wrap them all up and keep them safe from those who would hurt them.

As we continued on, there were no more encounters with any of the realm's inhabitants, and Shadow ended up creating another oasis for us to sleep in when night fell. I'd been worried that someone in this world was going to notice these sanctuaries, but Shadow reassured me that it was fairly common to see them pop up from those who crossed the lands. The oases would die over time, without nourishment, until eventually the black rock claimed them again.

None of us rested particularly well, especially not after Shadow told us we were basically on the border of Trinity and would soon be crossing into his family's territory. Our days of moving undetected were numbered.

"Do you ever sleep?" I asked him when he settled in against another new tree.

"Someone has to keep watch," he told me.

The sentiment was very noble, but at least half the times I opened my eyes that night, he was staring at me.

He made me feel safe. Safe and uneasy at the same time, the dual nature of my emotions toward him intense.

It was ironic that the beast who had starred in my nightmares for so long was now the one to bring me safety and peace. Life was funny like that.

"Sleep, Sunshine," he said to me when I tossed and turned for the twentieth time. "Tomorrow we face the royals."

I closed my eyes against his words and wondered if this was the last peaceful night I'd ever have. The thought that Shadow was going to go up against his asshole of a sister, who had thousands of years to amass power, and who'd destroyed his life in the first place, was terrifying and liberating at the same time.

"Do you think she knows you're here now?" I asked him sleepily, keeping my voice low.

He nodded, a single hitch of his chin. "No doubt at all. She'll be ready, but so will we."

He was strong enough. He was not the same young royal who had been kicked out centuries ago. He would destroy them if it was the last thing he ever did, and I had no idea what would come after that.

"Do you think I'll ever learn what I am?" I asked, my eyes

opening again, despite the exhaustion pressing on me. "Will someone in your family know?"

He shifted, and in the low light of the moon above, I couldn't quite tell what expression he wore. Possibly pensive or... worried.

"My sister is the first I have to destroy, but she's not the only one in my family. I'll have to wade through all of them to figure out who was involved in my betrayal, but I expect some will be left standing when it's all over. If there's information among them, I'll find it."

I felt satisfied with that. Shadow would do a thorough job in figuring out what I was, and how I'd come to exist, and when I finally had my answers... well, I'd deal with it once that happened.

Before Shadow had stolen me from Torma, I'd thought I'd had a pretty solid handle on who I was. Shifter; book lover; broken but fighting to stay internally strong; full of sarcastic quips; fan of old action movies and sappy romances; aficionado of flipflops and denim cutoff shorts; unruly hair of indeterminate color; good friend; sometimes terrible friend.

So many facets of me, Mera Callahan.

All the colors of my rainbow spread out before me, visible and vibrant. And I got them, I embraced them. Now, though, there was a new streak of midnight threading it all—kind of ironic, considering I was bonded to a mist called Midnight. I didn't understand this darkness dripping into my colors, and I had no idea how to handle it. Did I embrace it and say this was me now? Or did I fight it so the darkness no longer bled through, muddying the blanket of my being?

"You're overthinking." Shadow broke through my thoughts as he leaned forward. "Whatever we find out about your new abilities, it doesn't change who you are. You've always been you; some of it was just hidden. Like your wolf. You never shifted, but she was always there. It was only that you had knowledge of her existence that you didn't freak out when it first happened."

I nodded, rolling over to use my arms as a pillow, staring up into the starless mists above. "You're saying that this affinity I have with your world, with the mists and creatures, was always part of me? I just wasn't aware until it all rose to the surface?"

"Yes."

Well, okay. That did make me feel a little less like a foreign entity was living inside of me, ready to burst free *Alien*-style at any moment. As cool as Ripley was, I didn't have any ambition to live her life.

"Thanks," I said softly. "I'm sure you didn't sign up for keeping me sane when you already have a lot on your plate."

He chuckled, a deep rumble that filled the night with warmth. "Who said you were sane?"

I laughed too. "Are any of us, really?"

"Fair point, little wolf. Fair point."

After that, I was too tired for further conversation, so I let my eyes close, allowing consciousness to drift away.

Chapter Seventeen

Once we crossed over into Trinity, Shadow grew grim, barely taking a second to converse as he pushed us to quicken our pace.

His dark mood had coincided with a very real security presence around us. His sister was paranoid, and it seemed that all the villages close to her compound were on high alert. It got so bad, that around midday, we found ourselves crouched behind rocks, staring down a long line of guards and creatures completely blocking our way through the next town.

"We can't be detected here," Shadow said shortly, taking in the line of defense. "If my sister knows my exact location, she'll have the upper hand, and will come at me with full force."

"She's clearly expecting someone," Angel noted. "Not really a surprise, since the spell on the door was broken."

"Right," he confirmed, "but as far as my sister knows, I died long ago when she cast me out. The door could have been opened by any, and this show of power might simply be her way of preparing for *whatever* is heading her way. I'm not ready for her to find out it's me."

"So how do we get through the guards?" I asked the most impor-tant question of the day.

Shadow pointed toward the entrance of the city. "It's going to require disguises, and the hope that if I shield our energy, no one will really question us, at least not until we're past the main guard."

Our only plan did not fill me with confidence, as I snuggled further behind the rocks where we hid. There was no black tar this close to the village, the land around us widespread with golden trees, amber grass, and bright red, daisy-like flowers. They were beautiful but reminded me of blood spatter, and that was an ominous vibe as we tried to figure out our next move.

Angel already had her weapons in hand, and while her expres-sion remained calm, it was the look in her eyes that told me she was slipping into a mental place to which all warriors went before they fought. "Need me to scout ahead?" she asked.

Shadow shook his head. "No more flying. They'll spot you from a mile away."

Angel was on her feet in the next instant. "Well, I'm not hiding here in the *shadows*." She arched her eyebrow at him, and it was clear that she had just about had enough of our clandestine journey across the realm.

Shadow rumbled, picking up on her choice of words. "Are you calling me a coward?"

She leaned forward. "You've waited an eternity for this revenge, and I feel like you could have taken us straight into the compound. Only you've chosen *this* route!"

They weren't exactly shouting, but we were going to draw atten-tion soon if they continued.

"Yes, I've had an eternity, and that means I won't barge into a situation and get us all killed. Every day that I'm here, I grow stronger. Not to mention, the element of surprise is what will give us an advantage."

Angel bristled. "Excuses, Shadow. With this attitude, you will not best your family. We need the warrior, not the scholar."

She was being somewhat unfair... Shadow was cautious, and since I was personally not a fan of getting killed before we'd even had a chance to fight, I was all for it. It made sense that with his sister on alert from the doorway opening, he'd be careful in his approach.

"What's your plan then?" he asked her, and I could feel the heat off his skin. I wasn't even that close to him, so that meant he was getting *pissed*. "We just fight our way through? What about Mera? She'll be in danger."

That was the point I realized that he had been extra cautious because of me. The weak link. *Fuck*. Now I was the pissed off one.

My wolf rose, scratching at my chest. I hadn't been prepared for her push this time, though, too focused on their fight. When she surged to the surface, a choked howl spilled from my lips... and I was shifting.

Shadow felt the moment the change took hold; he was the shifter god, after all. His flames burst to life as he dove for me, but he was a second too late for the wolf, who was finally free.

Free to frolic in the mists of *her* land.

I was shoved so far back that I blacked out and lost consciousness for a brief second, giving her complete control in a way that she'd only had for the first few minutes of our first shift.

There was nothing I could do to stop her as she sprinted right for the guards. She tipped our head back, power threaded through us in a blaze of heat, and it was clear our beast form was on fire, scorch marks scarring the land around us. Not just scorch marks, but the grass was alight, and whatever this flora was made of, it liked to burn, a veritable blaze building behind us.

My wolf didn't stop, her power overflowing and spilling into the land, so when she howled, it was the same power-filled ballad that had knocked the Torma wolves down the first time I'd used it. The guard came to attention, but it wasn't me they stared at.

It was their creatures.

My wolf called them, the dozens upon dozens of shadow creatures. In our monochromatic vision, it was hard to tell if we knew what they all were, but we did recognize some of them.

They converged on me, and I braced myself for an attack, but all they did was fall in beside me. The fire burned a few of them, but the others adapted and ran a little ahead of my blaze.

Stop, I begged my wolf, finally regaining some control in this situation.

Free.

She was free, and she was not giving it up. At least not yet.

The line of guards scattered, shouting and screaming in a tongue I did not understand, and it allowed me to leave the grassy field that I'd probably destroyed with my actions. I was almost into the town—one of the closest towns to the compound, according to Shadow.

We had to go through it to get to the royals, and that was apparently what my wolf was doing. As I stepped onto a paved path, there was nothing for me to burn, so I was just a flaming wolf—my hair color made a lot more sense now. I wasn't a sunrise. I was a forest fire.

Stalking into the town, the shadow creatures stayed with me and all I could hear were screams and the sound of running as everyone bailed. My wolf didn't care, stalking through their city like a devil in disguise. Watch out, Shadow, we were coming for your job.

"Mera!"

I heard his roar. My wolf even paused. Shadow stopped her like I hadn't been able to, and that was... curious. Clearly, he was still alpha to us, but despite making her pause, he was too far away to bind her completely. She continued in a fast sprint, dodging through the houses, setting some of them on fire as we went.

Dammit.

This plan of hers was absolute bullshit. I would never destroy homes in this manner, but this was beyond my control. The fire wolf was in charge, and she gave zero fucks.

When we were deep into the village, approaching what felt like the center, a figure stepped out into our path. A tall, brown-skinned male, with no hair visible anywhere, his chest bare, as he wore only leather pants. Across his skin were dancing tattoos. Definitely a royal.

He shouted to me, but it was not in a language I understood. Obviously. Shadow and Angel knew English from their many years on Earth; they spoke about a billion languages. I was the only moron with just one up my sleeve.

Not understanding him, my wolf just plowed on ahead. He shouted again, and this time shot us with an energy that spilled from his long fingers. Our flames surged higher to try burn it off before it hit us, but that didn't work.

His magic slammed into our side, and even though I'd never actually been shot, I could only imagine it felt very similar to what had just hit me. We were catapulted backward, our flames wicking out in an instant.

Whatever had hit us looked like a black tar as it settled against the fur on my side, before starting to spread over the rest of me.

The man shouted again, sounding satisfied. From my current position, sprawled on the ground, it looked like he held more of the dark tar. Not wanting to be attacked again, I struggled to get to my feet, finding the task more difficult than anticipated.

As he got closer, still yelling, the shadow creatures descended on him and attacked. He fought back, but there were too many, and he was taken down almost instantly. My wonderful and protective creatures.

But they were a moment too late. The dark sludge covered over half of me now, and while I had no idea what would happen when it reached my face, something told me it wasn't going to be good.

Shift back, I begged my wolf, but all I got was a whimper in response.

The sludge had cut off our source of power, and very soon, would probably cut off my life as well.

The creatures, finished with the guy, were circling me again, and I felt their protectiveness. They were keeping me as safe as they knew how to, and whatever loyalty they'd felt to the ones who had owned them—the royals I'd stolen them from—was long gone, transferred to my wolf as she'd called them home. Called them to us because we were some sort of damn shadow whisperer.

"Mera!"

It was his voice again, and my wolf struggled, fighting the creeping darkness.

A fruitless fight.

I knew when Shadow arrived, the creatures only parting for him when he used his energy to drag them out of the way. I had no idea how much of me was covered, but I guessed about eighty percent, with just my neck and head free.

The fury on his face was all I could see, and surprisingly, it calmed me. It was insanity to think that my white knight had arrived to save the day. Firstly, I was not a fan of knights—as previously stated. And secondly, Shadow was anything other than a savior; he was the devil in the night—also, previously stated.

But I found that his face being the last one I saw wasn't the worst sight. He'd betrayed me less than most, and that was a fucking achievement. And when Angel appeared over his shoulder looking truly frightened for maybe the first time since I'd known her, I was even more relieved to have a friend by my side.

A howl escaped my wolf because verbal goodbyes were really tough when one didn't have vocal cords. Could they see in my eyes how much they both meant to me? How blessed I felt to have been thrown over a Shadow Bastard's shoulder and dragged into a world of books, magic, and... love.

"No," Shadow snapped. "Get that fucking look off your face, little wolf. You're going nowhere."

He lifted me with ease, and then he was running.

"What are you doing?" Angel shouted, taking to the air above him.

The creatures might have been following—I couldn't tell as the darkness crept over the top of my head toward my eyes. The sound of battle was around us, and I could only assume inhabitants of the village were trying to attack, while the creatures kept them at bay.

Or maybe it was Shadow, deflecting them with barely more than a thought.

His fury was spinning out of control, bursting from him in flames and dark mist, breaking this town to rubble. I'd always wanted a mate who would burn the world down for me, and it looked like I'd get to pretend I had one for a few more minutes.

Inky appeared in my line of sight, and it seemed that it was assisting in burning the town to ash. *Great fucking job, Mera.* No way was Shadow getting into the royal compound undetected now, and I hoped that he'd still manage to achieve his revenge.

He deserved it. Even if I wouldn't be here to hear about it.

Shadow was roaring. I could feel his chest shaking, but there was no sound. My ears were completely blocked now, and as the last of the sludge dripped into my eyes, I opened my mouth and let out another howl.

Felt like a fitting way to go.

Chapter Eighteen

My expected death never arrived.

There was no end once I was encased in a dark cocoon of tar, which held me in stasis, like a coma victim who was still aware but couldn't move.

I wanted to scream. To shift. To push through what held me, but I was lost to the dark magic of my prison. The outside world didn't exist, at least not at first, and then it was freezing cold. So icy it stole my breath, until it was gone, replaced with a heat so intense, I wondered if I was being baked alive.

The hot and cold continued for so long that it could have been days or years or lifetimes. In this waking coma, time had little relevance, and my thoughts were sporadic and scattered, as if oxygen deprivation was getting to me, and I could no longer think in linear lines.

My wolf slipped farther inside as time went on, and at some point, I lost her, returning to my human form.

"*Fight, Mera!* Come on, Sunshine. You are stronger than the *leicher scourge.*"

I heard him. The first outside noise that had penetrated my

prison since I'd been encased, and while I had no idea what leicher scourge was, I liked the concept of fighting it.

I'd been a passive victim for too long.

Clawing out with my energy and hands, I scraped against my cage, the ice and fire of temperature still alternating as I fought. As I pushed more power, my energy near tapped out, I felt a slight crack under my fingers. This boosted my strength as I pressed harder until a gust of fresh air hit me, and I was rolling free of the cage.

Strong hands caught me as I coughed my guts up, air filling my lungs. Wondering why I was being held as I was, I focused on my surroundings, only to find I was dangling over a rolling world of red.

The lava chasm.

Holy fuck.

"Shadow," I choked out as he hauled me up and away from the burning stream below.

I collapsed against him, completely wrecked and unsure how I was even alive. His arms wound tightly around me, and as his chest rumbled, I pulled back to see him half-beast-like, the fire wolf above him and all around us.

He was not in control.

Angel was visible on the outside of Shadow's fire, trying to get closer, but every time she stepped forward, his rumbles increased, the flames growing larger.

Even Inky—and *Midnight?*—were stuck on the outside.

What in the worlds? I must have unknowingly called my mist when I'd been in danger. The mark on my hand started to tingle, as if to remind me that I was bonded to a mist.

Mera. Midnight's familiar voice was in my head, and it was so soothing, I almost cried.

"I'm okay," I choked out, talking to all of them. "But seriously, what the fuck just happened to me?"

Angel tried to answer, but Shadow's power was like standing next to a loudspeaker set on rumble, so I couldn't hear a word she said.

Midnight was the only one able to communicate with me. *Shadow will not let any of us get close to you.*

I wasn't sure how I felt about that, but I wasn't mad.

You were hit with a very rare weapon, built from the mists. It could only have been made from an upper royal, and why they had it in that small town is odd, but whatever the case, you should not have survived. It sucks the life from whomever it encases, but it could not take yours.

And once again, whatever I was had come in freaking handy.

We think it was designed for Shadow; his sister guessed he was coming and when they saw the flaming wolf...

They assumed it was Shadow Beast. Which made perfect sense.

"I'm okay," I repeated, trying to get through to Shadow, who still held me so tightly, it was clear he was not letting go anytime soon. "I don't know how, but I'm okay."

His chest shook beneath me, his features very much wolf man now, with an elongated jaw, more facial hair—I was kind of digging that, to be honest—razor-sharp teeth, and those lethal claws tipping his hands. The fire wolf that formed around us looked just like its master. Scary.

"Shadow," I said softly. No response. "Shadow, come on, dude!" Louder this time. "You're squishing me. I'm fine. Better than fine."

Liar. Midnight sounded like it was laughing at me, and I could see it jiggling.

Yeah, I wasn't better than fine. I felt completely wrung out like an old dishcloth, but I wasn't dead, so anything above that was a bonus.

Finally, the fire and heat around us faded, and like the absolute moron I was, I missed it immediately. "Feels cold when it's gone," I said softly, my face still pressed against Shadow's chest by his big ass hand on the back of my head.

"*You* were almost gone," he thundered. I'd never been so relieved to hear his voice. "You're in so much fucking trouble, Sunshine."

I wiggled against him, naked, of course—that was pretty much my thing at this point. "You going to punish me, Beast?"

His hold on my hair tightened, and I groaned at the painful and arousing tug against my scalp. "If we didn't have a very large audience," he murmured close to my ear, "I would show you exactly what happens when you almost die on my watch."

"Fuck." I groaned again. "Can you get rid of them?"

"I can hear you!" Angel shouted, her words getting through now that Shadow had released some of his power. "Let me at her."

Shadow reluctantly set me on the ground, and I found myself swept up by Midnight and Angel, both of them wrapping around me and holding on for life. "You almost died," Angel said hoarsely, "and I was alone again."

My throat was tight, but I forced the tears to stay put. It was just... the thought of her being alone again, after losing her entire family, was too much for me to handle. I couldn't be so reckless with my life. Angel didn't let a lot of people in; I'd made it into her inner circle, and that meant I had a responsibility to stick around as long as possible.

"I'm so sorry," I choked, holding on to her with everything I had left in me. "I promise I didn't mean to scare you, and I would never want to leave you. We're family, Angel."

I'd never seen her cry, but it felt like she was holding back tears as well.

I should have come with you.

Midnight was distressed too, pressing closer to my spine. I'd scared them, and the fact that I had this much love in my life made me one lucky shifter.

Eventually, I pulled away. "I'm so sorry," I repeated. "I honestly didn't mean for my wolf to escape like that, but once she was free, I had no control. This land... It boosts her energy, and she called all the shadow creatures to her like it was fucking nothing."

Shadow was standing, watching silently, Inky at his back, swelled right up to a huge curtain of black.

"What was I hit with? And how did you get it off me?"

Midnight had already told me it had been a mist weapon, but I wanted to hear the rest.

"It was a weapon built from the leicher mists," Angel said. "I have no idea what the exact translation is, but it roughly works out to be 'scourge' or 'sludge.'"

"It's designed to suck the life from any that it touches," Shadow added. "And then whoever controls the weapons will be powered from it."

"The creatures killed him," I said softly, trying to wrap my head around it.

Shadow shook his head. "No, they just killed the one who was on the frontline. The one who controlled that weapon is safely in the compound. My sister is the only royal nearby who has the power to create such a destructive force."

I sucked in some air. "Did she steal energy from me?"

The last thing I wanted was to assist Shadow's sister in any way, shape, or form. Fuck no. But I was drained... completely wrecked, so it stood to reason she had absorbed my power.

"I don't think so," Shadow said, his gaze tracking across my features. "You're exhausted from fighting against the scourge, but I can't sense that you gave any energy to your attacker, and if anything, you will have stolen their power as they fought to keep you contained."

Good. That was very good.

"And how did I get free?"

"Shadow dumped you into the lava," Angel said shortly, fine lines of stress appearing on her face at the memory, "and then into an icy bath that he created in the rocks." She tilted her head and I saw the pond behind us. I had no idea how he'd made it icy, but apparently, Shadow managed the impossible on the regular.

"How did you know to do that?"

He looked grim. "We learned about creating these weapons when I was young, and thankfully, some of the information came back to me. I knew that to have a hope of disrupting the membrane of the power, I needed extremes. Usually by the time you start the process of breaking the outer shell, the leicher has already stolen their victim's life. Thankfully, this wasn't the case, and I could weaken it enough for you to find your fortitude to fight and break through."

"It should have killed me before you could break it?"

He nodded. "Long before."

His expression was haunted. He'd been fighting for me, but he'd expected that I'd be dead by the time he'd gotten me free. That was...

"The mists are scary," I said softly, trying to catch my breath again after my most recent near-death experience. "I'm finally starting to see that."

Angel shook her wings out, once again looking like her calm and collected self. "Yes, that's why Shadow's position as the Supreme Being was so important. Only he would have the ability to communicate with and somewhat control the power of the mists."

I swallowed hard. "How is the realm still standing if no one has truly had that power for thousands of years?"

Shadow crossed his arms, looking resigned. "The mists for the most part just exist. They don't attack for no reason, but they also can be unpredictable. I have no idea what they've done for the past thousands of years to keep the balance here. I don't know who performed the ceremony to keep leicher and ether from clashing. I don't know why the land is strangely drained and desolate when it never was before."

He clearly hated having so many unanswered questions. An emotional setting I could strongly relate to.

"You'll find your answers when we make it to the compound," Angel reminded him.

Shadow's face settled into dark lines, his frustration leaking through. "They know our location now, and if I can predict my sister's actions, they'll be amassing everything they have to throw at us."

Shit! And it was all, just *maybe a tiny bit*, my fault.

Whoops.

Chapter Nineteen

It wasn't like Shadow and Angel stared accusingly at me, but there was a tension in the air. Everyone knew I was the one who'd thrown this *not so minor* wrench into our plans. I had to say something. "Yeah, so, sorry about that. I swear I never planned for my wolf to escape and cause havoc."

Shadow grumbled in his usual way. Angel patted me on the shoulder. "We know. Your energy is stronger here, and so is the wolf's. Hopefully now that you've let her out, she'll be satisfied until we can figure out what your tie to the realm is and how to counter her strength here."

I nodded. "If any positive could come from this, she is calmer now. I had her locked down for too long. My shifts have been sporadic since I was yanked out of Torma."

Shadow let out another rumble. He was going back to his old grouchy self, and I didn't have the time or energy for it. I was barely standing.

"Do we have any food?" I asked shortly. "Or is my backpack gone?"

Inky swirled forward, swelling up into a large smoke cloud before it birthed a bag again. "You gotta stop doing that," I croaked. "It's creepy."

It grew even larger, jiggling away. Midnight joined in, and despite my exhaustion, they managed to make me smile. "Are you staying now?" I asked Midnight. "Is everything okay back in the library? Simone was fine when you left?"

Everything is peaceful and safe. Simone is in good hands with Shadow's friend.

I narrowed my eyes. "In good hands... with Lucien? Really?" I screwed my face up at the thought. "That's a little worrying."

Lucien was a smooth-talking vampire, and I had never had a reason to worry about a streak of evil in him, but I knew it was there. Deep in his eyes, there was a darkness that lingered. All five of Shadow's powerful friends had it.

It made sense, as Shadow's crew, that they would exhibit the same brutality he did. Birds of a feather and all that. Simone wasn't exactly a naïve little dove, but I still worried she might be out of her depths. I sure as fuck had been, and it was only pure luck that I hadn't gotten into more trouble.

We needed to get this done and get back to the library. "How far are we from your family now?" I asked Shadow.

I knew the compound was near the lava chasm, where the mists were the most accessible. We were at this chasm.

"We're a day's walk," he told me. "I had to take us in the opposite direction so we weren't ambushed while I saved your life."

He was going to hold that against me, maybe forever.

I couldn't really blame him.

"Will we follow the lava chasm?"

He nodded. "Yes, and hopefully, they won't expect us to attack from this direction."

I stared at the red river fifteen feet down, wondering briefly how Shadow had managed to dunk me in and out of it without killing himself. Maybe he'd used the mists, since they could no doubt exist in the heat? Or maybe the mist lava didn't burn him?

I supposed it really didn't matter. Of his many secrets, this one didn't even register in importance; he'd saved me and that was all that mattered.

Bone tired, I sank to my knees, reaching out for the bag Inky had been carrying—I refused to refer to it as anything else—and pulled out clothes, followed by a couple of the energy bars. "Can I drink that water?" I asked, jerking my head toward the icy lake while simultaneously ripping into the bar and eating it in two gulps. "Before we set off."

I could already tell it wasn't going to be enough to give me the energy to continue on. I was so far beyond drained that only a year of sleep, a ton of food, and six orgasms would do the trick. The odds of even one of those things happening was almost impossible, though, let alone the trifecta. No doubt we were about to start a massive hike to get our asses back on track to the compound.

Then Shadow shocked the fuck out of me. "You need a break. You can't continue on like this. We must regroup."

I stared. Was he worried about me? "I'm fine," I said, chewing my second bar.

He shook his head, and I could tell he was determined; I wasn't going to change his mind. "You're not fine, Mera. You're pretty fucking far from fine." I went to argue again, but he cut me off. "It's not just you; I need some intel about this world. I had a friend here once who might help me... if he's still alive. I propose we head in that direction first."

Angel straightened. "For once, I agree. You have lost the element of surprise, and your sister will be prepared. There's no point rushing in for the ambush. We must find a new approach."

This was the opposite of what she'd said before, and it was clear now that both of them were on the *protect poor little Mera* train. I'd have gotten mad about it, except it was clear that I'd almost died today. So, yeah. Best to just shut my mouth and let these powerful, stubborn, gorgeous gods make the decisions for me. It might be nice to regain some energy before we were once again fighting for our lives.

I can carry you.

Reaching out, I brushed my hand through Midnight. "Despite the evidence to the contrary, I actually prefer to walk. On my own, as I've done most of my life."

Midnight blew up, wrapping around me in a hug, just as Angel stepped toward us. Her next words came out gently. "You know independence—*extreme independence*—is a learned response, right?"

I jerked back, those words hitting me harder than they should have. "What are you saying?"

She held both hands up. "I'm not trying to criticize; I just know from my own experiences. It's only natural that when you've had no one to rely on for so long, you start to truly believe you must always do everything yourself. You've learned this response; it's not natural. You're a pack animal and should have always had a community of peers to fall back on."

Heat pricked my eyes as tears choked me. I'd never thought of it that way, just assuming that at the end of the day, you only ever really had yourself to rely on. But had that just been a learned life experience? Resulting in me being overly determined to never rely on anyone?

"Shadow's the same," Angel said, watching me closely, as my face no doubt went through a full range of emotional expressions. "It's our trauma. The three of us all hold on to our independence, as if we'll die if we let go. At times in our lives, we very well could have died if we hadn't cultivated our own strength. But we're not alone here. When you're too weak, let others carry you. There's no weakness in allowing us to help you."

Shadow cut in. "I have no trauma."

Angel and I exchanged a single glance, and I was relieved when my tears faded against my laughter. "Okay, dude." I chuckled. "Whatever you say."

Inky wrapped around Shadow, and they were in their terrifying pose, so I forced myself to stop laughing. But for real, that guy carried more trauma than ten humans put together.

"There's no point denying your trauma," I said with a shrug. "And no one is going to argue that you built yourself up to be strong and scary. A god. A literal creator of races. But when you were twenty-two, expelled from your world and family, alone in a new universe, there had to be struggles."

His jaw clicked. "I survived."

He had, but at what cost?

Forcing myself to stand and get dressed, Midnight drifted under my arms to help, and it seemed that was the moment Shadow realized how weak I truly was. He lost some of his righteous anger and stepped forward to help as well.

Once I was clothed, we started to walk, and he ended up half-carrying me, my feet scraping across the ground.

Tilting my head back to see his face, I smiled sadly. "Surviving takes its toll, Shadow. I know. You did a really excellent job, but it helps no one if we gloss over the struggles. It always leaves a mark, some deeper than others." I rested my head against his arm. "You're not alone. I'm not alone. Angel is not alone. I'm going to keep reminding myself of that. We can lean on each other."

Look at me go. Angel's words had helped me evolve and I was already vibrating at a higher level of consciousness.

Or the exhaustion had me losing my mind.

Shadow didn't look convinced, but now that I'd had a revelation, via my bestie, I was going to keep forcing myself to acknowledge the truth of it.

We could do better.

Chapter Twenty

At some point of Shadow dragging me along on our journey, I took a little nap. Angel's words had hit me harder than almost any advice I'd received in my adult life, and I was legitimately going to try this new thing where I didn't fight every person who tried to help me. Napping on a beast-god while he half-dragged me along was step one in this plan.

Shadow, Angel, Midnight, and Inky—I'd legit found myself a pack without even knowing I'd been looking for one.

When I finally woke from my short power nap, I did feel better, and as I opened my eyes, I found that I'd made it half onto Shadow's shoulder. He was carrying me in his usual fireman-style hold, but since he was so huge, he didn't actually have to throw me all the way over to hold me comfortably.

"Where are we?" I asked, yawning and stretching, relieved that a decent portion of my energy had returned. I actually felt pretty good.

Shadow paused, and then slowly... *so fucking slowly*, he lowered me to the ground. He was strong enough that there was no need for our bodies to be this close as I all but slid down his hard frame. He'd done that deliberately.

And I liked it.

"Are you feeling better?" he asked.

"Much," I told him.

Shadow seemed satisfied by that, finally lifting his hands from me. "We're not far from Kristoff's place. If he still lives there, of course. He was an old royal when I knew him, and so very set in his ways. I imagine that hasn't changed."

"Sounds good," I rasped out before taking another few steps back so I wasn't existing in the energy of his orbit. It was a lot to handle, being this close to him and not jumping his bones. There was only so much to be expected from my self-control.

Backing up farther, I hit Angel, and she shot an arm out to steady me. "Sorry, friend," I said in a rush.

Her smile was knowing as she looked at me before her gaze flicked across to Shadow. "No worries."

"Hurry up," Shadow called to us, and I had no idea what had him so cranky. Knowing him, it was some complex situation that he was running through his head and no one else would have a hope of understanding.

God problems, amiright?

Angel and I caught up, and I reached out to brush my hand against Midnight as it wrapped around me.

Your energy is stronger.

"I feel much better," I confirmed. "No leicher scourge will get this shifter down. I'm made of tougher stuff than that."

I sensed Angel wanted to smack me in the back of the head since I was tempting fate like a true dumbass, but she dug deep into her thousands of years of maturity and refrained. I was still getting the lecture, though.

"Please, no more risks with your life," she cautioned. "Despite recent events that suggest you're tougher to kill than anticipated, we're still fairly certain you're not immortal. You bleed and you can die."

It's hard to love a mortal when you are not, Midnight said unexpectedly.

Its words saddened me.

I was the mortal in this situation.

The one who would die.

I'd never have to mourn them, and that was the best news of my life, but it sucked to know that one day they'd have these adventures without me.

"Shadow can visit me in the dead lands," I said with a little huff. "Maybe you can as well?"

Angel shook her head, her face falling. "The living can't talk to the dead. Not in that way."

"So I've heard," I muttered, noticing the smug look Shadow shot my way. Bastard was listening in, clearly, and he was still completely full of himself. No doubt dying to say *I told you so.*

"No one likes a know-it-all," I snarked.

His smile didn't disappear, but thankfully, before I had to attempt to beat a god to death, we arrived at our destination. A... *cliff?*

Shadow made his way right to the edge, looking down into a large pool of water, capped by a waterfall off in the distance. I wondered for a moment if his friend's house was down in the canyon, or perhaps hidden in the side of the mountain.

"*Kristoff!*" Shadow shouted, cupping his hands and sending power out into the world.

He shouted again, not in English. Instead, a lyrical language spilled from his lips. It was beautiful enough to give me goosebumps, even though I had no idea what he'd said.

He paused, giving his friend a moment to appear, but even as we all stood there, nothing happened.

Shadow turned back, looking worried. "Maybe my sister got to him."

A deep, booming laugh filled the cavernous space, and I heard more of that lyrical language, so loud, it made my ears ache. At first, I wondered if this was an attack, but when Shadow smiled, raising his arms and returning his focus toward the waterfall, I finally understood it was his friend.

Pushing closer, I peered over the edge, wondering if I'd missed something below. A house maybe, hidden on the edge of the water? Before I could find anything, a figure appeared with a near silent pop, standing on... *air?* Directly opposite Shadow.

It was a male, a big booming, larger-than-life male, with red hair that brushed against his shoulders. His red was a strawberry blond, a color close to the ends of mine.

He walked toward Shadow. Or more like floated across the divide, while still taking steps. When the pair of them were near eye to eye, I was surprised that he was the same height as Shadow. A lyrical conversation started up, and Angel sidled closer to translate for me. "He's having trouble believing it's truly Shadow," she whispered. "But apparently, our friend here has some secrets on this guy that no one else knows."

Okay, that was good. It meant that he could prove his identity faster, and then maybe we could find ourselves somewhere to sleep for the night. A place to clean up wouldn't go astray, either.

"The hostility is gone now," Angel continued, "but it was touch and go there for a moment."

It was? I hadn't noticed anything, but since their language was like a lullaby, that wasn't a surprise. "Okay, we're good to approach," Angel said, nudging me toward Shadow.

Kristoff watched us closely as we walked over, his gaze probing.

"Hello," he said in perfect English, without the slightest accent or inflection. "Welcome to my home. Any friends of Darkor's is a friend of mine."

"I go by 'Shadow' now," Shadow told him.

Kristoff nodded his head. "Son, you will always be your appointed position to me; that name is yours by birthright. You can go by whatever you want; it changes none of the truths."

Shadow didn't argue, and I wondered if this was the one of the rare beings in the worlds he truly respected. "Please," Kristoff said, stepping to the side and waving his arm in an arc. "I'm being rude holding you here when I'm sure you are exhausted and require rest and sustenance."

He seemed to be waiting for us to move, but since some of us couldn't walk on air, what was the game plan here?

Shadow strolled straight off the cliff, and I managed to keep my cool and not gasp, but it still shocked me. "It's an illusion," the beast called back. "You are safe to follow."

"Uh..." I looked down. "Illusion or not, my brain is telling me I'll fall to my death, and it's insisting we stay right here on solid ground."

Angel chuckled, the musical sound ringing out and echoing through the gully below, and now I knew how Kristoff threw his voice and made it sound so powerful.

"You got this, Mera," she said, nudging me forward.

"Easy for you to say, chick with wings," I hissed back, dragging my heels as I was continually pushed toward the edge.

She laughed again. "I'll catch you if you fall."

That did make me feel marginally better and confident enough to relax my stiff stance and take a step forward. Forcing myself not to look down, I followed the same path Shadow had, keeping my eyes locked on his enigmatic face. Most of the time I couldn't read the beast, his thoughts shrouded and hidden from view.

Today was no different, but at least his stoic look was comforting in its familiarity, as he became my anchor point to walk toward.

"Not many have taken that first step," Kristoff said, the smallest of smiles gracing his lips. "Especially a mortal."

"She's no normal mortal," Shadow added drily.

Kristoff peered closer. "So I can see."

Angel strolled along behind me, Inky and Midnight nearby. The mists also received a very close inspection from Shadow's friend. "How is it that you have competing mists here?" he asked. "Whom are they bonded to?"

I raised my hand, and Midnight dashed closer, large enough that the purple tones in it shimmered in the light. Inky wrapped around Shadow, both of them answering Kristoff's question.

"A mist bonded to a mortal," he mused. "You, my dear, are a mystery I'd like to unravel."

Flames appeared in Shadow's eyes, and I wasn't sure of the reason, but he did shift to block Kristoff's view of me. "We do need to find out her secrets," he said, "but she's mine. You cannot claim her."

My mouth and throat were dry, unlike other... parts of me. When he went all possessive alpha on me, it fucked me up mentally and physically. Shadow was my trauma and I didn't even care.

"Noted," Kristoff said, eyeing Shadow closer. "What about Ixana?"

Ixana. The mate.

I knew that was whom he'd just referred to, and the white-hot rage I felt didn't surprise me—shifters were possessive, just like the beast who'd created us. Not that I wanted to think too closely about that, since Shadow was about as far from a parent figure to me as one could be.

I also had no right to feel possessive of the beast, and Shadow's mate would probably murder me when she found out my plan of *losing my virginity to the Shadow Beast*.

"I haven't seen her in thousands of years," Shadow said quietly. "For all I know, she's moved on."

I paused. Why hadn't he just explained that we weren't a couple? It would have been easy to tell his friend that I was mostly a possession he'd kept captive for the last year.

"As far as I know, she's never moved on," Kristoff said softly, and I could tell this surprised Shadow.

The silence was awkward then, and without thinking, I moved closer to the beast, wanting to comfort him. As I dropped my forehead against his back, my hand lifted to rest on his firm muscles.

His breath paused for a beat.

I'd taken him by surprise.

He didn't zap or push me away, both of us remaining like that for a moment. A moment of comfort and support. It honestly felt like a hundred years since he used to zap me when I'd accidentally touched him. We'd come so far, and that was all going to be dashed the moment his true mate walked into his life again. I'd felt the bond of a true mate before, and it was strong and all-encompassing.

If Shadow's wasn't a complete cuntosaurus, then I could see no reason why they wouldn't fall back into each other's arms.

From what he'd indicated, they'd liked each other well enough before he'd been exiled. And why the hell would anyone not want to be with Shadow? He was the ultimate prize as a true mate, despite his occasional asshole moments.

Fuck. I couldn't do this. I couldn't lean on him any longer; that time was done, and even if we managed to get that one round of fucking in before we were torn apart, it would change nothing.

I straightened and stepped back, needing to breathe in air that wasn't tainted by his scent and power. I had to get my head on straight.

Or I would not survive what was to come.

Chapter Twenty-One

Kristoff led us to his house, which required a journey down a long, spiraling, invisible road. He warned us to stay behind him because there were gaps where one could fall. Near jumping out of my skin at that knowledge, I basically held on to Angel's wings, forcing her to go first, and even though she laughed at me, she still offered this comfort. And I loved her for it.

As we walked into the base of the mountain, the water was wider spread than it had looked from above, and there was an invisible house resting on a piece of land just above the vast expanse of river. Or so we were told because, of course, with it being invisible, I could see nothing.

At least not until Kristoff pressed his hand to the wall, and then it was there, in all of its glory. Well, not a lot of *glory*, to be honest. His home was a simple structure made of grey and green stones, which I would hazard a guess had been collected from within this mountain range.

It didn't matter to me; I was just grateful to get off this invisible, anxiety-inducing path. Kristoff entered his house first and then both disappeared from sight.

"Anything around this guy real?" I asked.

Shadow shot me an amused look, his eyes filled with fire. "He's the master of illusion, second to none, and it was no doubt the one thing to keep him alive under my sister's reign."

His sister was a fuck of a being, and I hoped there was a slow, drawn-out torture scene in her future. "What's your sister's name?"

Up until now, she'd just been referred to as *his sister*, but honestly, I wanted him to stop claiming that bitch as family.

"Cristell," he said shortly.

I wrinkled my nose. "Sounds like a mean girl name."

He smiled. A genuine smile, and fuck, if it didn't do bad things to me.

"Let's go inside," Angel urged, interrupting as she glanced above, like an attack might be imminent. "I've always thought you could summon her by speaking her name, and now you have."

That explained the use of "sister" all the time.

Focusing on where the stone house had been before it disappeared, I closed my eyes and stepped through the "door." Everything appeared as soon as I crossed that threshold, and I found myself in a surprisingly comfortable room. There was a huge, roaring fire, just like the one in Shadow's library, and I loved how familiar it felt. The main room had stone floors, with half a dozen beanbag-looking chairs scattered near the fire. Literally the most perfect place to sprawl for a nap.

"Make yourselves at home," Kristoff said, waving across the room. "One of my favorite human sayings."

I was curious about that. "How do you know English?"

For the first time since Shadow had gotten between us, the ancient royal was able to look fully at me again. I found myself caught up in his silvery eyes, so striking and unusual. "I'm what you would call a telepath, in your human lore. I can learn from touch."

"He learns impossibly fast from a single touch," Shadow said, cutting in, appearing inside the living area. "Every thought, memory, and all your knowledge will be his the moment he grazes your skin."

Clearly, at some point he'd touched Shadow and now knew everything the beast did. Which was a fucking lot.

"Why didn't you just do that straight up before asking each other questions to determine you were not imposters?"

Kristoff chuckled, crossing his arms over his broad chest, and *how the hell was this dude thousands of years old?* Shadow too. They looked like men in their early thirties, in the prime of life, healthy and powerful. Unnatural.

"Touching him was the last part of my investigation," Kristoff told me, so easy with his knowledge when Shadow was often cagey. "It's always with caution you allow others to touch you. Because if they have more power than you do..."

He trailed off, but I filled the rest in. If they had more power, they could do a lot of damage to you. Looking toward Shadow, an extended moment of understanding passed between us. That was why he didn't allow others to touch him unless he was sure of the risk. My lip trembled at the thought that he trusted me enough to let me in now. From what Kristoff had said, it was a big freaking deal.

"Mera hugs a lot," Angel said. "She doesn't understand the power thing, and it's one of her best qualities."

She sounded annoyed, like she thought they were going to change me with this new knowledge. They weren't.

These ancient creatures needed me in their lives. They needed the spark and joy that only youth could bring. Whether they agreed or not, it was good that I'd stepped—okay, had been dragged, but semantics—into their world.

Kristoff was still staring at me, ancient eyes stripping me to my core, as he worked out all of my idiosyncrasies. *Good luck, buddy.*

His smile broadened, as if he'd heard the silent challenge.

"Come, take a seat," he said. "I'll find some sustenance for the one who requires food as fuel."

I didn't even want to know what he was going to get, but I did sink into one of the thick, golden, puffy chairs. It would be nice to have a decent night's sleep at some point, and real food, and a shower, and...

"What do you eat here?" I asked, needing a distraction. I'd never seen Shadow eat food, and while I knew how Angel got her energy, I wasn't sure about the royals, freilds, creatures, or any other in this realm.

"We don't really have to eat," Shadow said. "Like Angel, we have evolved to take our energy from a transference with the land and mists. But we can eat if we enjoy it."

"Do you ever eat?"

He didn't answer, moving to sit in a chair on the opposite side of me, both of us close to the fire. I'd noticed that the pair of us were naturally drawn to the warmth, sparking embers, and power of the flames.

We were both clearly pyromaniacs—and okay with that.

"I've been known to indulge on occasion," he admitted. "Humans are obsessed with their love of food, and I've craved the same feeling."

And that was all I got out of him. One day, I might figure out what food tempted him to try it, but it was not this day.

"I'll just stick with my way of loving food," Angel said, taking one of the chairs farther back in the room.

I snorted out some laughter. "Your creepy apple-sniffing habit."

She wrinkled her nose at me. "You smell your food too. I've seen it."

I shrugged; she definitely had me there. "Often the smell is better than the taste, which is a fatal flaw in someone's plan."

We relaxed while our host did his thing, and I found myself sinking further into the soft surface—it was hugging me like the best weighted blanket. Midnight drifted closer to me, adding its energy to my own.

Sleep. I will keep watch over you.

"Thank you," I murmured, reaching out to brush through it. This was the sort of sleep I desperately needed: one that was rejuvenating, healing, renewing.

My wolf nosed out from where she'd been since we'd shifted, but I collared her immediately. She'd had her only taste of freedom here, at least until I could figure out what it was that made her go crazy in the realm. *I love you, wolfie,* I told her. *You're part of my soul, and I hate to do this, but we can't let loose like that again. We almost got everyone caught, and you and I almost died.*

She couldn't answer me, but it felt like she understood, and thankfully didn't continue to whine and paw at me. She sank down again, and then I was sleeping.

It was nice that even with a mysterious redhead stranger in our midst, I felt safe enough to go to sleep. Thanks to Midnight, Inky, Shadow, and Angel.

My pack.

Chapter Twenty-Two

When consciousness returned an unknown time later, I shifted in my cushion, loving how relaxed my limbs felt. It took me a few minutes to really wake, and when I did, I opened my eyes to find the fire was the same size it had been when I'd gone to sleep, and the... the room was silent. Unnaturally silent.

Rubbing a hand across my face, I looked around; even Midnight wasn't drifting in its usual spot up high.

"They're hunting for you." His low, deep voice near sent me sprawling from the cushion. How, in the fuck, had I missed the Shadow in the room?

He straightened from the wall where he'd been leaning, silent like a stalking jungle cat. "You're always watching me when I sleep," I said, a touch breathless as I pushed myself higher. "What's up with that?"

He didn't deny it, just strode closer, and when he stood at the edge of my cushion chair, I jerked my head all the way back so I wouldn't miss a single one of his expressions. It was only in his minute facial changes, that I could tell what he was feeling.

He never gave much away, but I occasionally found a gem.

Right now, his eyes were burning, his brows drawn together. "You're a mystery I need to unravel," he told me, and I was surprised when he crouched before me. Shadow never came down to my level, always dragging me to his height. "I'm drawn to your energy. I'm feeling..." He paused. *"I'm feeling, Sunshine.* It's an issue because any sort of weakness could stand between me and my need for revenge."

I sucked in a deep breath, the dryness in my throat annoying. "You give me whiplash," I bit out. "You're so back and forth, up and down, treating me like a pet one second and a friend the next. A person or a possession? What am I to you, Shadow?"

Flames sprang to life in his eyes, and he was closer than ever... *and was it getting super hot in here?*

"Can you not be both a person and a possession?"

I shook my head. "No, I can't."

He reached for me, hauling me up and out of the chair—ah, that was more like it—standing as he did, so I was trapped in his embrace. "Then why do I want to possess the person you are so badly, little wolf?"

Jesus. Fuck. *Fuck!*

"It's the most delicious torture," I choked out. "The desire to submit to you while knowing that I can never let myself. The alpha shifter in my soul rebels against the notion of being owned, no matter the benefits that come from it."

And there would be so many benefits. I already knew that from the small taste I'd had.

Shadow's hold on me tightened, so firm that my ribs ached, which only increased my desire to wrap myself around him and allow him to fuck the life from me.

"How do we resolve our dilemma?" he mused, his hand sliding down my back to cup my ass, and again, his hold was just short of too firm as he massaged each cheek, drawing a low groan from me as I tried to wiggle against his grip.

He didn't let me move an inch, and I wanted to both sob and scream.

"You can't keep torturing me," I begged, finally finding words.

Shadow's laugh was deep and dark. Name and nature were one and the same with him. "From the second you touched the Shadow Realm, you have been a forbidden torment. And I don't think I can let this journey end without having this taste of you."

I tried to suck in a deep breath, but he held me too tight, so it was shallow panting for me. "You already tasted," I choked out.

"Not enough," he said, so low, I could barely hear.

The hand on my ass lifted so he could slide it down under the waistband of my pants, his palm meeting bare flesh, and I swore I could feel that touch deep inside.

Putting those long fingers to use, he slid them down my ass crack, pressing and lingering across nerve endings there, before he moved to stroke his fingers inside my aching pussy.

I was so wet that there was next to no resistance, at least for the first digit, and the second, but the aching burn began as he moved them in and out, with the right amount of force to drive me crazy. "Shadow," I groaned. "Are you going to fuck me or what?"

His lips grazed my cheek, and I was reminded of their "no kissing" thing again. The desire to turn my head and taste him was so strong, it almost killed me.

"Are you going to submit to me?" he breathed against my skin, near my mouth.

I wanted to sob. Was he really going to make me choose between my independence and the pleasure I knew he'd hold in his touch? What sort of fucking asshole was this guy? And why did I still want him so badly?

"I can't." I groaned again. "It would break me. My independence is all I have left."

The stroking fingers slowed, and the hold of his other arm gentled so I was able to move myself to give him more leverage. Just when I was breathing heavy and about to come, he stopped completely and slowly withdrew his hand. His touch disappeared as he set me down to my feet.

"Who is your master?" he asked, his electricity running across my skin, sending my sensitive nerves into overdrive as an orgasm ripped through me with nothing more than his power to stimulate me.

"No," I choked out, "I won't submit."

Where was my wolf now when I really needed her dominant assertiveness? Why was she rolling over ready to show her belly to this beast?

"Sunshine, I'm going to need you to say the words."

I snarled. "What? Why? You want me on my knees too? Are you training me for my true mate? Because he wanted the same bullshit from me."

Shadow's expression darkened. "You will get on your knees for no one but me. Ever."

I shook my head. "The odds of that are slim to none, Shadow. All men are like you, wanting to dominate." I jerked back. "In truth, I think I'd rather be alone than deal with this shit for the rest of my life."

It was then that he realized how serious I was, and that no matter how badly I wanted it, how badly my body was screaming at me to just release my control and let Shadow take me however he wanted me, I couldn't. I'd lose a part of myself that I'd never get back.

Now he was searching for a compromise because he wanted it too. But he was too dominant not to desire complete control of me. That at least made me feel better because twelve months ago, he'd have just thrown my ass to the side and never looked back.

"Let's make a deal," he said, and I was reminded of our bet from long ago. "If you submit to me now, at least eighty percent, I will ensure that you leave this world powerful enough to never have to submit to anyone ever again."

Our eyes locked, and I let his offer simmer in my mind. It was a huge temptation, but could I believe him? "There's no way you can truly ensure that."

He moved his head closer, our lips almost brushing. Goddamn. "I can against shifters," he said, reminding me that he was the god of our kind and could make or break us. "And you're already beyond humans in all ways, so it's basically ensured."

My legs were trembling, and now that he wasn't holding me up, I had to find my own fortitude. "I think... I can agree to that."

I'd do a lot to never be a victim of my pack again, or my true mate, and if the upside of that was having this night with Shadow, I would fucking take it, and rebuild my independence piece by piece if needed.

"I crumbled like a wet house of cards," I muttered, sort of mad at myself, but only for a brief moment because I was too turned on to really care. Maybe I'd care more tomorrow, but right now, I just needed him to touch me.

Shadow's arms were around me again, drawing me up so our lips could meet easily, without him having to lower his height. "I'm going to need you to say it, Sunshine," he murmured, his tongue darting out to slide along the inseam of my lips.

My legs clenched as my pussy all but quivered in response. Fucking hell. This was going to be one hell of a ride.

"I submit to you. For this day, and this day only, you're my master."

Shadow's eyes darkened until the pupil and iris were indistinguishable, and as he threw his head back, an unearthly howl rang from his throat. Control fell away from me, and I welcomed the relief.

One night with the devil. I was taking it, no matter the consequences.

Chapter Twenty-Three

Shadow sealed the room with his power, a fire surging to surround us completely, and we should have been near dying from the barrier of heat, but all I felt was a rush of pleasure. I wanted to dance in the flames and never leave.

He used his power to strip me naked, fire bursting to life across his skin, and my own flames responded. It was his energy causing it, though. I had no control right now, my limbs moving under his command. I'd submitted and he was taking full advantage.

His power drew me up to his height, and when our eyes were level, he smiled. Just this small, knowing smirk. "Are you ready for this, Sunshine?"

"Yes." No hesitation.

He reached out and brushed a hand across my cheek before tracing his thumb down my lips. "I know you're a virgin, but I'm not capable of being soft. And I'm giving you this one last chance to walk away."

Offering that cost him, and I knew on instinct he'd never proposed that to anyone before.

My next words choked out because I was flustered. And so horny that I wondered if I might die from the tension twirling through my stomach. "Just... make it good for me."

No pressure, Beast. But... yeah, a lot of pressure, actually.

The flames faded from our skin, and one of us was way more naked than the other. I reached out for him, and he stopped me with a twitch of his eyebrow, his power holding me in stasis. "You aren't very good at submitting, little wolf." The rumble of his voice filled my head, and I was desperate; he was going to have me begging in a second.

"Shadow," I grumbled.

He released me in the same instant, and I collapsed forward into his arms; he caught me and jerked me up into him so fast that my head spun. I wasn't ready when he crashed his lips to mine, and without thought, I opened my mouth and allowed him entry. We didn't fight like the last time; no dominance struggles. Shadow was the alpha tonight and we both knew it. My wolf wasn't worried, her presence barely even felt in my chest, as she let me have the lead.

This was human shit and she wasn't interested.

As we kissed, Shadow's hands slid across my bare ass, and then he was once again playing with my pussy like he owned it. And today, he kind of did. As he caressed my clit, I was already so wet and aching that barely a tweak had me groaning, and then a second later I was about to come, but he pulled away just as my breathing got noticeably heavy.

"Not yet, Sunshine," he murmured. "You're so sensitive. Let's see how it goes if you have a little buildup."

I wanted to cry. "Shadow, I've been building up for years. You don't need to drag this out."

He shut me up with his mouth, another bruising kiss, and I was grinding against him, seeking release. Only to have his power stop me.

"Let me," he murmured, and then he separated us, using his power to send me across the room, pinning me against the wall. He didn't move a step; his power did all the work. Completely at his mercy, I watched as he stalked forward—I was pinned a couple of feet off the floor, so we were basically eye level—and as he moved closer, he reached over the back of his neck and pulled his shirt off.

Slowly.

Agonizingly slow, giving me an uninterrupted view of what he had going on. I'd seen his body before, but my memory didn't do the ripped, bronze, muscled and tatted form justice. He was a fucking work of art, covered in the most incredible moving images. Perfection, wrapping up a dark soul, that I wanted to possess.

This one night would be worth everything that it cost me.

When his shirt was gone, he was in front of me, and leaning over, he took what he wanted, nipping at my lips before he dragged his mouth across my cheek and then down the edge of my jaw. He licked and sucked across my skin, and I groaned, straining against where his power held me to the wall. My arms and legs were bound with invisible ties, and I could barely even buck my hips, which I desperately wanted to do to relieve the tension building.

He didn't let me touch him, and again, he was the one initiating the pleasure; it was almost too much for my brain and body to handle. When he captured one of my nipples between his teeth, biting gently, and then rougher, my moan was loud as I writhed in the small movement allowed to me.

Shadow moved to the other nipple, and I was so wet, my arousal slid down my thighs.

I was beyond fucking ready for him. "Please," I begged.

He let out a dark chuckle against my tits, capturing my nipple again, and hot damn, this guy knew how to use his tongue.

It should be registered as some sort of weapon.

One orgasm via nipple stimulation was definitely in my near future if he didn't stop.

Please don't stop.

But of course, the bastard did, in his quest to build me to the biggest orgasm of my life. He'd probably be successful, if the tension spiraling in my gut was any indication.

As he kissed his way down my body, my eyes near rolled back into my head, and I was fighting his hold again, desperate to move. "Your words say, 'submit,' but your body doesn't," he rumbled, kissing along my hip bone, his tongue dragging across my overly sensitive skin. "I'm going to need you to try harder, Sunshine."

I sobbed, but I forced myself to remain still, feeling every swipe of his firm, brilliant tongue across my body. He moved down the center of my hips, leaving a wet path, and I was too far gone to really think about anything now. My body jerked as he blew across my clit. Could a clit quiver? Like, this was a life question I needed answers for, because if it couldn't, then what the hell was mine doing? A fucking samba?

A scream built in my chest as he grazed across my pussy, brushing over my clit again, with nothing more than that puff of air. I was so desperate that a moan escaped. This was torture. Literal torture.

But I wouldn't have walked away for all the fucking power in the world right now.

He brushed across me again, and I flexed my hips so that I all but shoved my vagina in his face. He tilted his head back. "Naughty little wolf," he growled.

His power hit me harder, forcing me into the wall so I had literally zero movement. Just when I was about to freak out because this wasn't a comfortable sensation, his fingers parted my folds, and he licked right up the seam of my pussy. The warmth of his tongue as it swirled across my clit had a scream spilling from my lips.

"Jesus, fuck. Jesus."

He stopped. "That's not the god here, Sunshine. Use my name."

"Shadow." I repeated myself, omitting the other name he didn't want to hear, before I added in a breathless rush, "It's just an expression."

His chest rumbled as his growl ripped through the room. "Not fucking here it's not."

I tried to nod, only I couldn't move, and my head was clouded, so I forgot what we were even talking about.

Please just... get back to what you were doing.

He must have seen the desperate yearning in my gaze, and with a low chuckle, he returned to my body, and this time, I wasn't missing the orgasm. He swiped his tongue up through the moisture dripping from me, plunging his tongue into me, over and over, stimulating the sensitive nerve endings as I came screaming, sitting on his face, as was my favorite pastime. Well... almost sitting. Same, same.

My world exploded into a black-and-white, star-filled galaxy, and by the time I was done, my throat was sore, my ears aching.

And I got it.

Finally.

The buildup he'd been trying to achieve was literally the most intense experience I'd ever had in my life, and I was struggling to catch my breath, even as I prayed he would give me another one exactly the same.

He wasn't done, his mouth sucking my clit in, working that ball of nerves. I could *hear* how wet I was, but it didn't seem to bother Shadow. If anything, he settled in between my legs, like he was going to fucking move in and live there.

Yeah, totally okay with that. Price of admission: daily orgasms.

His mouth vibrated, and at the same time, he used his power to send a vibration deep into my pussy. I came again, faster, with a huffed groan as all air expelled from me due to the sheer force of it.

His hold on my body released minutely, and I tried to reach for him, only to find my limbs were still somewhat unresponsive. "My turn now," I huffed, needing to touch him.

He freed me, catching hold of my body as I fell forward. This time when I scrambled to get him undressed, he let me. My fingers fumbled on the button of his pants, and as I finally got it released, he actually groaned.

My hands slipped inside and... screw me sideways, he was completely commando underneath.

Commando and mother*fucking huge.*

I tried to wrap my hand around his hard length, but it must have been the angle because I couldn't manage even half the diameter. Needing to see more, I pushed his pants all the way down, and as I stared, I blinked, wondering if I was going to die tonight.

"I... You're going to have to shrink from your eight-feet height," I said softly. "'Cause that is *not* gonna fit."

I mean, that wasn't even a normal eight-feet-tall man dick. It was so much more than that, and I was a virgin. The math didn't add up here.

Shadow laughed. "First, my natural height is just over seven feet."

So yeah, I'd been guessing his heights and was apparently really fucking shit at that game. "You're giant either way," I shot back.

"And second," he said, ignoring my reply, "it will fit, Sunshine."

Aanndd my pussy was doing the samba again.

His voice got very low. "Submitting means you trust me to take care of you. Have I let you down yet?"

"No." I didn't need time to think about it. There was no letdown. If anything, Shadow only ever took care of me, making sure I got off multiple times. My biggest frustration was that he never let me return the favor.

But I finally had his cock in my hand, and... *why the fuck was I wasting time worrying about vagina damage?*

I'd freak out tomorrow when I couldn't walk.

Shadow stepped out of his pants, and my gaze followed the path from his huge, masculine feet, tipped with a sprinkling of dark hair, up his heavily muscled thighs, which were surprisingly free of ink. Only his torso was marked, and I liked that.

His cock, which was slightly darker than the rest of him, proudly jutted from his body, and when I reached out to touch the silky length, he was so hard that I felt a sense of achievement that I could turn on a god like this. Shadow Beast wanted to fuck me, and that was beyond belief, but I wasn't wasting this opportunity.

"I've never done this," I said, looking up as I leaned forward to lick across the head of his cock. It jerked against my mouth, and I liked that *a lot*.

Shadow groaned. "Virgin mouth, and tonight it belongs to me."

I legitimately had no idea what I was doing, but I went with instinct, needing to taste him. My hand slid up and down as I licked across the tip, sucking in the salty liquid leaking from the slit. Opening wider, I tried to take as much of his length into my mouth as I could—which was sadly not that much, just the tip, really—and groaned at how good he tasted.

Not good like chocolate, but good like male spice and energy. My attraction to Shadow had never been stronger, and I was desperate to make him feel as good as he always made me feel.

As I continued, finding a rhythm with my hand and mouth moving together, Shadow rumbled above me. His hands threaded in my long hair as he held my head firmly, thrusting down my throat. I'd been sort of ready for it, so I didn't choke too much, but his cock slid deeper the next time, and I coughed and spluttered. This wasn't enough of a deterrent to give up, so I just got on board and tried to breathe the best I could between his thrusts.

Why the fuck had I waited so long to do this? I kinda... loved it. The feeling, the taste, the power I felt even as he took control. I was doing this to him, sending him into frenzied thrusts against my mouth as energy zipped between us.

My thighs clenched as my core ached, and I used my free hand to try to slip between my legs, needing some relief. Only Shadow was having none of that, his power stopping me before I could get to the good spot.

"Not on my watch, Sunshine," he rumbled. " I've had to listen to you bring yourself to orgasm too many times in the lair. Today, your pussy belongs to me."

Sucking in a breath, I lifted my head away from his cock. My god, his dirty fucking mouth was perfection. "You heard me make myself come?"

Flickers of darkness brewed in his eyes. "Yes. You're not quiet and I have exceptional hearing."

Embarrassment didn't happen. Honestly, I couldn't find it in myself to care that he'd heard me.

"Guess it's your turn then."

His cock jerked near my face, and I was about to launch myself on it again, when Shadow wrapped both hands around my thighs and lifted me with ease. Like I weighed about two pounds instead of a hundred and thirty.

Tilting my head back, I let my gaze clash with his fire-touched one, and I sort of forgot to breathe for a few seconds.

"Kiss me," he demanded as he started to walk, and before I could lean forward, words spilled from my lips.

"Why did you choose me for your first kiss?"

He stopped, and the flames were mesmerizing as they danced through his eyes, almost spilling out over his cheeks. I found myself as desperate to hear his answer as I had been for my previous orgasms. *Please answer me.*

His expression was destroying me, and when I heard the rasp of his deep voice, I all but clung to him, not wanting to miss a word. "In thousands of years, you're the first being to cross my path and give me a reason to fight for a different future. I never saw you coming, and I never anticipated you would wreak such havoc on both me and my life. There was no one else who was worthy."

He thought *I* was worthy. The mess of a shifter with no pack and a true mate who'd rejected her.

"But you have a true mate," I breathed, knowing I might fuck up everything with this line of conversation, but apparently, my deadass was gonna go there.

Shadow's face was awash in secrets, and as he leaned over, his mouth tasting the tender spot beneath my ear, he murmured, "Her face is a blur, and I have a fantastic memory for almost everything else in this world. Out of duty, I never kissed a single being in the time I was exiled from my world, but then you exploded into my life. Full of sass and fucking questions, with hair of a sunset, and a temper to equal my own. The gods themselves couldn't have stopped me from claiming you."

I felt the truth of that, deep in my chest.

I had a true mate as well, but Torin's face was a faded scene of disappointment, nothing like the brilliance of Shadow.

"I'm glad that I will always have your first," I whispered, knowing that giving him this much of myself was dangerous, but fuck, if I was going to jump, I might as well go all out.

He started to walk again, and then we were out of the main room with the fireplace, and into... a bedroom, maybe. It had what looked like a floating cloud puff in the center, which I had to assume was the bed. It all worked the same: soft surface to sleep on.

Or to do other much more pleasurable activities.

Chapter Twenty-Four

On a normal bed this fluffy, I'd expect Shadow's weight to sink us deep into the depths, but this was no normal bed. It seemed to know the exact firmness required for what we were planning, holding us as I was all but thrown into the center by a beast of a man who prowled across after me, that big body dominating the room and making it feel small.

As he crowded on top of me, he dropped an arm on either side of my shoulders to hold himself just off me. His long limbs made me feel positively tiny, and I really wasn't that small, so it was quite the unusual feeling.

"Missionary position, hey?" I said, but no more words came out of my mouth because Shadow's power had my voice freezing in my throat.

Before I could shoot him a scowl, he scooped up my hands in one of his, and secured them above my head. "This is going to hurt," he said, and instead of the fear a sane person would feel, I was flat-out excited. At some point, I'd been broken, and it appeared there was no chance of repairing the damage now.

His power shot across my skin, that lightning burn I was coming to crave. It hurt, but the pain was also stimulating as my back arched in time to each pulse of his power. A fire built between us, heat pouring off Shadow and engulfing me. When I almost couldn't take the surge any longer, he released his hold, allowing me to catch my breath.

My lungs ached as I sucked in air, struggling against that hand still holding me, but I wasn't strong enough to break his grip.

"Every nerve ending," he said, tracing his free hand across my cheek and then over my throat before he continued down my breasts and over my stomach. He lingered on a few scars, examining them and soothing past pains with his touch. "They're all mine to bring to life."

When his fingers reached the apex of my thighs, he stroked the wetness, moving it over my thighs. When he slipped a finger inside, I arched again, and then he followed it with a second, and I couldn't stop myself from riding his hand.

A feeling of fullness built within me, but it wasn't quite enough. It wouldn't be enough until his cock was seated as deeply inside as was possible for it to go, and I got to fuck Shadow, just as I'd dreamed for so many nights.

His hold was loose enough that I could talk, so I rushed to say, "All those nights you heard me, I was thinking about doing this. With you."

His brows drew together, his expression serious, even as a flicker of something dangerous danced in his eyes. "You're getting the hang of this now, Sunshine," he said in a low voice. "Now come for me."

And I did, jerking against his hand, and as he curled his fingers inside and hit the most pleasurable spot in existence, I was fairly sure my soul left my body for a bit. It took me a long time to calm and relax, and when I sank bonelessly into the bed, he released his hold on me.

"It's your first time," he said, staring down, still sadly holding his full weight up off me. "I should let you go on top, but I want to be the one giving the pleasure today." He growled possessively. "Whom do you belong to, little wolf?"

I groaned, my head still spinning from my orgasm. "You."

"Say my name."

It was a command, and I was helpless to fight it.

"Shadow Beast. I belong to the Shadow Beast."

His chest rumbled and I felt how pleased he was.

"Sorry, Sunshine, *but I am who I am.*"

Reaching up, I latched on to his biceps, pulling him down onto me. "I want that. I told you before and I meant it. I can handle you."

The flames burst to life on his skin, and even though I was once again working through my shock of not burning to death, I reveled in the power... in the pleasant scorch of energy across my body.

Shadow finally closed the space between us, and the fire was forgotten in the feel of his electrical power zapping over my skin. It was just so fucking good, I had to close my eyes briefly, to truly take it all in. Our naked skin was touching, sliding, and catching, and I felt it so much deeper than that.

When I opened my eyes, Shadow wasn't quite as tall as he'd been. He watched me closely, taking in my facial expressions. I raised my eyebrows in question, and the slow pull of his smile pulled at other parts of me as well. "I know you like pleasure-pain play, Sunshine, but the idea of you feeling any pain beyond what's pleasurable, is messing with my head. I don't know why, but I don't want to destroy you. For your first time, this size might be an easier accommodation."

"You don't know why you don't want to destroy me?" I laughed. "Dude, you're a little bit psycho."

He shrugged. "I've never made any concessions for a woman in my bed. They leave satisfied and at times, broken. I don't want the second part for you."

That must have been enough talking for Shadow, as he leaned down and captured my lips. He kissed me like he was making love—a rough, dominating sort of love—and I knew that he was quite enjoying this new addition to his life.

When he nudged my legs apart, I groaned, letting my thighs fall open so he could settle between them. "Protection?" I managed to choke out before losing my head completely. Falling pregnant to the Shadow Beast was not on my ten-year plan. Bunch of little demon babies. I mean, they'd be fucking adorable, but our genetics together would probably destroy worlds.

He didn't pause, leaning down to kiss me. Now that Shadow had finally discovered his love of kissing, he was already near expert level. My head spun and I was certain neither of us breathed for the minutes we kissed.

His hand traced along my body and he slipped it in under my ass so he could hold me up off the bed. That was when I felt the thick head of his cock pressing against my entrance. "We don't need protection," he said. "More than sex is required for children here."

One day I'd find out what that *more* was, but for now, that answer was all I needed.

Shadow was kissing me again, pushing his cock harder into me, and there was a slight burn as I stretched, but I was well lubricated, so there was almost no resistance as he continued to slide inside.

"Shadow, fuck."

"Full sentences, Sunshine," he commanded. "You have to learn to speak in full sentences."

"No."

The fire in his eyes burst to life, and in an asshole move, he plunged the rest of the way inside of me. One long stroke. My gasp was lost in his groan, and I waited for the pain to rip me in two, but outside of a mildly unpleasant burning sensation, which wore off quickly, all I felt was full in the most delicious way.

"Wow," I choked out. "That... It didn't really hurt." It had, but like he'd said, I loved that sort of pain. "Might be because I've fucked myself so many times that whatever virgin entrance I had was long gone."

He actually laughed, his head dropping back slightly so I had the most delicious view of his strong shoulders and neck. "You are never predictable, little wolf. Now shut up and let me fuck you."

A better idea was never had.

Shadow didn't give me another moment to adjust as he lifted himself up, his cock sliding out a touch, before he slammed it back in, and I could have sworn he hit my fucking ovaries, it was so deep.

My pussy, already well warmed up, was purring like its name-sake, and I wondered how I'd managed to survive all these years with just a vibrator. It was like the poor imitation of the real thing, and now that I'd had it...

Dammit.

Shadow kissed me again, and I loved that as he plunged that impressive dick into me, over and over, hard and fast, giving me barely a chance to catch my breath, he kissed me like his life depended on it. We were definitely straddling that line between plea-sure and pain, and even when I ached, I wanted more.

I'd always want more, and while logically, I knew this was just a one-night thing, in my heart, it felt real. Like he was loving me so thoroughly that I might not survive it, and part of me wondered how I'd survive without it.

Just feel it, Mera. Worry about the rest later.

I got out of my head and let myself fall into the sensations of Shadow's body above mine, the curling of my toes as the curling of pleasure built in my stomach.

Opening my eyes, I met his intense stare.

"I'm going to come," I said in a rush, not even sure how it had hit me so quickly.

He didn't stop. If anything, his pace picked up, and I came screaming all over his dick. My hands clawed at him, and he let out a low groan.

When my intense pleasure faded, he picked me up so that my lower half was off the bed, changing the angle as he plunged into me.

Deeper than ever. "Holy fuck," I choked out. "What... What is even happening right now?"

Was he sliding right along my g-spot? Every time the head of his dick brushed over that spot, a moan burst from between my pressed-together lips. He was moving slower, pulling all the way out before plunging back inside in one long stroke. He moved without pause, and I wouldn't have believed it, but I was near coming again in a matter of seconds.

"This angle is my new favorite," I told him breathlessly.

His smile was slow and satisfied. "You haven't seen the half of it yet."

He wasn't kidding. Over the next few hours, he fucked me on every surface in this place, against the wall, on the floor, on the counters, and then finally, he had me bent over one of the beanbag chairs, his fire still right around us as he slammed into me from behind.

I wasn't sore thanks to shifter healing, and the pleasure was so fucking unbelievable that I wondered if I would survive it.

One of his hands was tangled in my hair as he jerked me against him, and the other was on my clit, stroking it in time to his thrusts.

"Dead, Shadow! I'm fucking dead." I cursed as an explosion of pleasure rocked through me. It felt like he was getting bigger as I spasmed around his cock for about my tenth orgasm since we'd started. It seemed a god's capacity for fucking was measured in hours. Unless...

I felt him thicken, and then he groaned above me, jerking inside fast before he slowed right down and rode out his pleasure, all the while sending me into another head-spinning orgasm where I blacked out for a few seconds.

My body was limp, and it was only Shadow's hold on me that kept me from face-planting right into the chair and suffocating in the process. "You. Killed. Me." A weak wheeze left me, and I felt his laughter along my spine as his mouth brushed across my skin there. He was still buried deep inside, still hard, and I wondered if this was normal. Or was Shadow just the exception...?

"Let's get you cleaned up," he said before he lifted me completely, his dick sliding free, with more than a little resistance, like it was reluctant to leave. He set me on my feet, but my legs were way too wobbly to walk, not to mention the spinning head and stars dancing before my eyes.

"I understand now why the women leave you satisfied and broken." I groaned as I almost fell right on my face again.

He scooped me up into his arms, stepping through the house, past the back room with the cloud bed. He dropped the fire perimeter, moving out of the main house and onto what looked like a back deck.

We found the waterfall. Right there, just pouring over the stone deck. I'd heard none of its thunderous roar from inside Kristoff's home, but out here, it was loud and glorious.

"Outdoor shower," I said, figuring it out as I wiggled to get down. Feeling had returned to my legs, so I assumed I could make it on my own now.

And as much as I didn't want to be away from him, I already knew I had to start the distancing process. Getting attached was no plan. It was a one-way ticket to heartbreak, and fuck, at some point, I had to do the intelligent thing and protect myself.

The water was an icy splash across my skin, and I gasped at the first blast, but in a few moments adjusted to the refreshing shower. Shadow joined me, and he didn't seem to be having the same worries about distancing, crowding into my personal space.

And... dammit, I really liked it.

He was still at his slightly smaller than seven feet height, and we fit together well. I went up on my toes, wrapping my arms around his neck, and... he let me. For a moment, we just existed under the water as it washed away our mammoth sex session.

Shadow dipped his head, tracing his lips across mine, and I had to open my mouth, needing his taste. His cock jerked against my stomach, and I pulled back to laugh. "You have *some* stamina."

His gaze moved over my face. "Apparently."

Just as he was about to kiss me again, we both felt a new burst of power coming from off to the right of Kristoff's house. *A burst of power that was foreign* in nature, belonging to none of our friends.

Shadow jerked me behind him in an instant, reacting faster than I could have. He stood between me and whatever was coming for us, and while we were naked, weaponless, and somewhat vulnerable, having Shadow on my side gave me confidence I wouldn't normally have.

"Spies," he spat. "They tracked me faster than I expected."

"Royal spies?" I asked, trying to lean around him.

"I assume so." Short, clipped words, and the somewhat gentle beast was gone. In his place was the demon of shifter nightmares. Our moment was over, long before I was ready, but this was for the best.

Another taste and there was almost no way I'd ever be able to walk away.

Chapter Twenty-Five

Are you okay?

Midnight's voice was loud and clear in my head again, so whatever Shadow had been doing to block us, he'd dropped it in the face of the danger around us.

Royal spy, I shot back quickly. It was a relief to know our mists were close.

"What is it?" I asked Shadow, trying to peer around him, but he kept shifting his position, stubbornly blocking me from view.

We're on our way, Midnight said in a rush.

Best news ever. *We're kind of naked out near the waterfall.*

They're spinning energy around the place, and we're attempting to get through. They may be planning something huge. Be on guard.

With that ominous statement, Midnight cut off from me, and while I was panicked, I also loved that we had mists on our side. I'd seen the look on Kristoff's face when he'd learned they were bonded to us, and since he appeared to be both ancient and powerful in his own right, that told me it was a big deal.

A threat many wouldn't see coming. Maybe the threat that saved us.

Can you see if it's royal spies or something else?

There was a long pause, and if I hadn't been able to feel the bond to Midnight, I might have worried that we'd been cut off again.

Three beings that are cloaked in darkness, adept at camouflage and subterfuge. Kristoff has disappeared as well. No idea what happened to him.

Wow, that sounded a lot like a James Bond movie, and that could only mean one thing: It was my time to Bond girl the situation and sort this shit out.

Placing my hand on Shadow's back, I wasn't surprised to find his skin boiling hot, despite the chilled water still pouring over us. "Midnight said that Kristoff is gone. Do you think he betrayed us?"

Shadow was furious, if the flames licking across his body were any indication. "A lot could have changed in the past two thousand years. So maybe."

"Are they shadow creatures?" I wondered, mostly to myself. "I could try to command them," I added louder.

His muscles rippled under my palm. "They're not like anything I've ever seen before, but their power is different from a regular creature's. I won't risk you."

Midnight had said the same thing about them being odd, or outside its knowledge, but I still thought it was worth trying my ability to call and control them.

"Get inside. Now!" Shadow snapped. "I will take care of them."

I shook my head, even though he couldn't see me.

"Sunshine, you will get your fucking ass inside, or the next time I have you naked, the punishment will be so much worse."

Punishment? I hadn't even realized I'd been punished, but maybe he meant when I was pinned spread-eagle against the wall while he'd eaten me out? Did I maybe *want to find out what the next punishment would be?* I mean... for research purposes, of course.

"Don't push me," he growled.

"I'm not leaving you to battle alone," I said stubbornly. "At least not until the mists arrive."

"They're not going to make it in time," he said quietly. Then he launched forward, leaving me squinting through the waterfall, trying to assess the situation.

For fuck's sake. Shadow was off the edge of the cliff, wrestling with *Mr. Invisible* in the air. Pushing myself as far forward as I could on the outdoor deck, I tried to figure out a way to help. For all my talk about not leaving him alone, I was literally useless when I couldn't fly out into the middle of an open space.

If I stepped off, I'd plummet straight into the water below.

I briefly considered if it would be worth doing that, simply to distract them and give Shadow a chance... The water looked hectic, but I'd survive. That could be Plan B.

I just needed an A now.

The urge to shift into my wolf flooded my veins, pulsing along with her howls in my chest. She'd been quiet during the entire sex session, but now she was chomping at her leash, trying to take control.

We'll follow, Midnight said, but the words were breaking up and staticky, like our connection was being interfered with. *They've transported you, and we keep losing your location.*

Sorry, what?

Transported us? No, we're in the same spot. At the treehouse.

There was no reply this time, just white noise in our connection. Were we actually moving? That would explain why the mists, who had been close enough to communicate, hadn't reached us yet. They were chasing a moving target, and if the current lack of connection was any indication, we were racing ahead.

Shadow was still fighting one of the beings, and it looked like he had another one torn to pieces, a few visible fragments floating around them.

"Shadow," I shouted, over the raging winds. "We're not at Kristoff's any longer."

"I know!" he roared back. "They're moving the entire fucking structure, and I can't figure out what energy they're using."

I could barely see Shadow, and my wolf had had enough, forcing the shift on me. It was scary how easily she could do that. *Super freaking scary.* I had no weapons to fight the change, so I didn't. Nothing worse than being attacked between shifts.

Once I was in my wolf form, we shook off the lingering pain, a nice little surge of energy filling us. We were stronger here, like the wolf was plugged into a Shadow Realm power outlet, getting a boost directly from the source.

Not only that, but I could see the spy through her eyes. It was a ghostly specter, exactly how I imagined a poltergeist would look, with a large, swirling hole where the face should have been. Not to mention the multiple arms around its body. Arms that were filled with deadly silver weapons.

There were no visible legs, just trailing cloth as it flew around. It continued to try to slice at Shadow with the blades, but he was adept at avoiding the attack. The beast transformed his hands into the long-clawed version, swiping at the specter, tearing into it like he'd done with the other.

My wolf, over waiting, leapt off the edge of the stone. I had no idea what would happen once I made the jump, considering a lot of what lay out here might be an illusion. It still looked like there was water below, but we were apparently moving, so what was real?

My wolf sailed through the air for a long time, far too long for the force of my jump, and somehow, I landed on the back of the third creature. I expected to sink through it, but it was solid, and my claws wasted no time tearing into it. My jaws clamped down as well, as we'd done with the hunter back in the library, slicing through cloak and body.

Between Shadow and my wolf, we got this one torn into pieces in seconds. When the final sliver of it fell beneath us, Shadow caught my wolf around the center, hauling us both back to the stone pathway. The water was still streaming across it, but the house we'd walked out of—Kristoff's—was no longer in sight.

That part of the illusion was gone, leaving behind just the stone we stood on.

I shifted back, my bones screaming at me briefly before the pain faded, but at least my wolf didn't fight. I sensed that she was trying to play nice because she knew she'd fucked up forcing the change on me again. We were going to have words soon, but it would have to wait since today was already fully booked with drama.

When I was standing on two shaky legs, I moved toward Shadow. "Where are we?" I asked, hoping he might have figured it out.

He arched an eyebrow, his gaze drifting out toward the misty surroundings. "I'd thought they were taking us to the royal compound, but... I was wrong."

"Did you just say you were wrong?" I coughed. "Uh, did you hit your head? Maybe get scratched and infected?"

He growled at me, turning away from the fake view. "We killed the mist-driven energy that set this in motion, but from what I can tell, the current course we're on is set. I can't change it; we're heading for The Grey Lands."

I grabbed at his arm, holding on because I needed the fucking fortification. "The land with all the creatures? Where the mists used to converge?"

He nodded. "Yes, and I have limited knowledge of that area, which will make it harder for me to protect you when we arrive."

"The birthplace of creatures?"

He nodded. "Yes, of much of the realm, really. It's only here that the remaining creatures freely roam. Wild and untamed. Dangerous."

I wrinkled my nose. "Creatures are kind of my jam. Maybe I'll be the one to protect you. Are you looking for a knight in shining armor?"

His expression could have melted the polar ice caps, and I didn't blame him. It probably wasn't the best time for joking, but once again, it was laugh or cry.

Story of my life.

Chapter Twenty-Six

Shadow and I backed away from the edge, the platform rumbling beneath us—the only evidence we were even moving, since the view around us was nothing but swirls of mist, obscuring whatever lay beyond.

"Not being naked would be really great," I said ruefully. "You know, before I have to go all kung fu on whoever is on the other side of this spell."

There was no place to procure clothing, that was for sure, but then Shadow just clapped his hands together, and when he opened them a folded pile of clothing sat atop of them.

"What...?" I narrowed my eyes on him before looking back to the clothes.

He laughed at my confusion. "How did you think your clothing appeared in your wardrobe in the lair?"

"Seriously?" I pressed a hand to my naked chest. "That was you? But I loved my wardrobe; it always has the best clothing selection."

Shadow's eyes darkened. "It was more enjoyable than I antici-pated, dressing you in exactly what I wanted."

Now that time I'd had no underwear made perfect sense. *Moth-erfucker.*

"Fuck, dude. You're lucky that you have decent taste in outfits."

His grin was slow and predatory. "That red dress... I threw it in the options on a whim, not expecting you'd choose it."

"I almost didn't," I admitted with a laugh.

Shadow didn't laugh with me. "Seeing you in it nearly destroyed my long held control. I've never felt like killing my friends more than I did that night."

I was completely knocked on my ass by that—not literally, but emotionally. "You did seem a little extra ornery that night."

Now he laughed, a rich deep sound that echoed through our current transportation system, and as much as it was a shitty, scary situation we were in, this moment felt like a gift. "Ornery... yeah, I guess that's one way to look at it."

He held the bundle of clothing out and I took it. "How come you didn't create clothing and such for me when we were in Faerie?" I asked.

His eyes flashed, the flames brighter. "Magic is tricky there, and I couldn't be bothered dealing with the fallout. It was easier to let Inky handle it since it can portal directly without any ripple effect."

I nodded. "Well, thank you."

His gaze was scorching me, and I was almost tempted to hand this pile of clothes back and walk my naked ass under the waterfall again. I'd been a virgin only a few hours ago, not to mention we were currently on a one-way trip to the notorious Grey Lands, and all I could think about was climbing all over Shadow and letting him hold me hostage for a few days or weeks.

His nostrils flared, pupils dilating. "Sunshine, you know I can smell your arousal. And now is not the time."

I briefly considered begging for one more orgasm, for both of us, before I reminded myself that this was for the best. It was always supposed to be a one-night thing. A taste of perfection, a moment in time to give myself over to him.

Submitting again was not good for either of us, and that meant no more Shadow for me.

Not in this lifetime.

"I better get dressed," I choked out, stumbling away.

Just as I turned from him, melancholy pressing to my chest, a firm grip wrapped around my hair and back of my neck. I gasped as he jerked me back toward him, the pile of clothing flying out of my hands in an arc.

I didn't give a single fuck, though, because he was kissing me. His hold on my neck possessive as he slid his other hand between my thighs, parting the folds to find the dampness at my center. I groaned and arched, giving him better access. He stroked a thumb over my clit, sending sparks of pleasure through me to the point my legs almost buckled.

One finger entered me, while his thumb continued a relentless assault on the ball of nerves. Almost immediately, a second finger pushed inside to join the first, and I cried out, swirls of pleasure already attacking me with relentless assault.

"Shadow," I gasped.

His throaty groan sent me over the edge, and as I cried out, clawing and scratching his arms, his mouth found mine again. My moans were lost in the kiss as he relentlessly drew out my pleasure. Those damn expert fingers moved over sensitive nerve endings, and I was thoroughly wrecked by the time he was done.

It took me so long to get my breathing under control, Shadow's hold keeping me upright. I leaned into him. "You want me to return the favor?" I was all but face to cock with his massive friend, and I wanted nothing more than to run my tongue over the moisture beading on the end.

"There's no time," he said, sounding disappointed as fuck by this.

I tilted my head back to see his face. "We're almost there?"

He nodded, and the softer side of him was shelved again. I'd never met a man who reveled so much in giving pleasure, without just taking it for himself. Shadow's mate was one fucking lucky lady.

If she could just put up with the dominant side of him, she'd certainly never want for anything in the bedroom.

I really hoped the bitch was dead. Such a terrible thing to say, but my possessiveness of Shadow had reached new heights.

And I couldn't fight a true mate bond, if that was what he wanted.

"I'll get dressed," I said shortly, my head filled with thoughts of him and another woman. It was enough to quench any lingering need to continue this fun foreplay.

My clothes were scattered across the stone, thankfully not near the water, so they were fine to wear. Moving away to give myself a little space, I found black lace underwear, which fit perfectly of course, a pair of jeans, and a plain black shirt.

When I padded back to Shadow, he was dressed as well, his fitted black shirt that matched mine—cute couple alert—showcasing the distracting perfection of his body.

"Boots," he said, handing a pair across to me.

I was already wearing socks, so I slipped on the black biker boots, zipping them up my calf. Shadow had similar black shitkicker boots on, and since he was over *seven* feet tall again, they just added to the height towering above me.

He was vibing badass demon god today, his face grim as he stared out into the mists again. Maybe he was seeing something I couldn't, or maybe he was just waiting for the inevitable end when we landed?

Meanwhile, my legs were still weak, the new magic panties no doubt damp, and that was all I could think about while I stared at him.

"Sunshine," he warned, not turning to me.

"I'm stopping," I said with a laugh. "But it's almost cruel to show me everything I've been missing and then tell me I can't have it again. A girl has needs."

His lips twitched, and some of the stoic calm faded from his face. "We'll take care of those needs later. For now, we're about to reach the end of this road and find out exactly who decided to commit suicide today."

Take care of those needs later... Hot. Damn.

More and more, it seemed that this *thing* between us was not going to be just a single night. Maybe I'd squeeze in a dozen or more orgasms before our inevitable parting. Could I sacrifice my will to fight for that long? If it was just in the "bedroom," then, yeah... I probably could.

The thought that we weren't quite done yet was enough to allow me to focus on the current situation.

The mists finally started to clear in the distance, and I stepped right to the edge of the stone with Shadow.

"How dangerous is it in The Grey Lands?"

His grim expression was answer enough.

I swallowed roughly. "Wow, well, when you put it like that, I am filled with so much hope for the future."

When he didn't say anything again, I shut my mouth, trying to mentally prepare for a possible forthcoming attack. The whirring under our feet halted, and I felt the moment we touched down to our new destination. The misty swirls faded like they'd never been there, and I swallowed a gasp at what lay beyond.

The Grey Lands evoked a certain mental image, one I'd already assigned to the name. I'd expected it would be a broken, barren, possibly desert terrain world.

But I was so far off, I wondered if Shadow had made a mistake in his estimate of where we'd been heading. "These are The... Grey Lands?"

From what we could see, our platform stopped somewhere close to the large front gates. The village that lay beyond was a winter wonderland, filled with snow-topped trees and picturesque lakes— frozen over and perfect for skating. There were many scattered buildings made from a shiny silver material, and it was almost Christmassy, even though there was no tradition or holiday like that here.

Basically, the view before me was about as far from a "grey" land as a place could be...

Shadow didn't answer, just wrapped an arm around my shoulders, jerking me to the side. The projectile that had been shot our way narrowly slid past, and I looked down to see that it was a blue, crystallized net. A net that had been heading right for me.

"They want you," Shadow bit out. "Of course they fucking do."

Reacting faster than eyes could track, he slid behind me, grasping on to the side of the silvery netting and yanking on it hard. There was a brief moment of struggle, but Shadow won—shocker, right?—and a creature was hurled into sight. It scrambled back, and when it got to its feet, it was almost as tall as Shadow... not to mention built like a linebacker. Kind of explained how there was any struggle at all.

"What do you want?" Shadow roared, hauling the being up in his hands.

The face that stared back was not like Shadow's or mine. It was not like any of the others I'd seen in this world, either. I was struggling to categorize it accurately, but at best guess, some sort of mix between animal and human? Not how I expected a clordee would look, but more like a... *Dr. Seuss* character.

Big yellow eyes blinked at us, the blue fur rippling beneath Shadow's grip. The body was humanoid in shape, wearing natural hessian-type clothing, over the top of its... fur. Similar blue fur to what lined its face, only a little shorter.

And there were ears. Cat-like, point-tipped ears.

He opened his mouth, this man-cat, and spat out some words I didn't understand. I had no fucking idea how I was supposed to react. Should I pet him...? Maybe throw some catnip his way?

Was I being super ignorant here thinking of this being as a cat-man? Probably, but it was the only way I could categorize him in my head, and that was how my brain functioned best. When shit was labeled.

Shadow answered it, switching from English to his melodic language, and Cat-man reacted, a scowl crumpling his feline face. Human expressions on a cat face freaked me out, but at least I could somewhat read what he was feeling. Since I still hadn't learned to speak Shadow Realm.

Cat-man replied to Shadow in a rush of melodic words and the beast paused in his attempt to shake a fur-ball free from our attacker. "Their queen wants to see us," he said, sounding surprised. I pressed closer to the heat pouring from Shadow's skin.

"See us or me?" I asked.

The cat's eyes shot to me, and he stared almost... hungrily. It was more than a little disconcerting.

Shadow shook it again, a harsh jerk that had a cat head snapping loudly. "Eyes off her," Shadow warned before switching to their native language, and despite the melodic words, it was clear that he was still ripping this cat a new asshole.

"So what do we do?" I asked. "I'm less inclined to want to meet with a queen when she forcibly brought us here. Not to mention that little net that was just sent our way."

It felt a lot like she'd attempted to make us her prisoners, and that was not cool with me. Not cool at all. As I'd told Shadow many a time, if you wanted to capture me, you had to buy me dinner first. It was only polite.

Shadow's chest shook as his darker side tried to break free, and I knew the fire was only moments from appearing. Singed fur was in this Cat-man's future if he didn't come up with a way to appease the beast.

He must have figured that out as well, his feline features calming as he said something else, looking between Shadow and me. There was a gleam in his large yellow eyes I didn't like.

"They will assure our safety for this initial meeting," Shadow translated, "and from what I'm sensing around us, there are a lot of its kind close by. Could be easier to save the fighting until we know for sure they're a threat. Our mists are on their way here, so we have backup coming."

I nodded, feeling better about that.

"Okay, yeah. Let's do it."

Chapter Twenty-Seven

Cat-man was set on his feet, and Shadow made sure to stand between me and the creature. Maybe he'd seen that look the cat had bestowed on me before, or maybe he was remembering all the times I'd been the target. Either way, I didn't mind having a buffer.

A possessive, shifter god of a buffer. Could do worse.

Shadow barked out some words at Cat-man, and while I couldn't tell what they were, I knew it was a command. The cat's claws briefly appeared on blue-pawed hands. Baby claws compared to Shadow's, and the cat seemed to know that, choosing the smarter route and not attacking.

When we stepped off the side of the stone platform onto snowy ground, I was surprised at the sudden bite of cold in the air. The Concordes had rocked a moderate temperature, not too hot or cold, so this new chill was almost refreshing in its intensity. My energy buzzed beneath my skin, and as astonishing as it was—fire and ice shouldn't exist together, right?—there was a part of me that felt complete. Like another piece of my puzzle was slipping into place, and maybe, just maybe, one day soon, I'd have the entire image.

Shadow must have felt me slow as I looked around, relishing in the energy flowing up through the soles of my booted feet to the top of my head.

"I feel strengthened by this land," I said quietly when he slowed near me. "I don't understand why, though. *Fire* should be my thing, right?"

Cat-man turned as well, and even though I was fairly certain he hadn't heard me, and most probably didn't speak English, I shut up. There was already too much going on here that scared me, and I didn't want to add to that by giving these *beings* additional ammunition to use against me.

"It might be the mist connection," Shadow murmured. "It's strongest here where they converge."

I nodded. "Yeah, that makes sense. But why are we here? What does this queen want with us?"

His lips thinned as his face darkened. "I have no idea, and that rarely happens to me. This entire situation is sending my warning systems into overdrive."

"Mine too," I whispered back.

It wasn't that Shadow looked rattled, because he didn't, but the knowledge that he was uneasy was enough to have my stress levels sky high.

The chill in the air became more pronounced as we moved further into the winter wonderland looking city. The beauty here was awe-inspiring. Every house and dwelling was shaped like a snowflake, and just like a snowflake, each of them had a unique pattern that spanned the exterior of its icy structure. I had no idea how the interior worked with such odd structural shape, but the outside was nothing short of spectacular.

Inhabitants soon started to make themselves known, appearing on the street and peeking out of their snowflakes, and every single one of them was like Cat-man. Well, not a cat, exactly, but some sort of animal-humanoid hybrid, a near seamless blend of the two.

Cats, wolves, lots of reptiles, a few birdy sorts with unusual beak-mouths, and many others who had absolutely zero comparison to Earth's animals.

"Did you know this village existed?"

The vibe he'd always given about The Grey Lands was a desolate place, dystopian even, where creatures roamed, and there was nothing but war and fighting. Not a fairytale city with perfect snowflake houses.

"I was only in the realm for twenty-two years," he said, leaning toward me while his eyes took stock of every being surrounding us, "and while I did venture through many lands, I didn't make it here. But none of my research ever indicated a village like this existed within The Grey Lands."

Seemed it was a mystery we would unravel together.

When we were quite deep in the city, many gazes were focused on us. Their animalistic features scrunched in what I could only assume was suspicion. I mean, who could blame them?

Shadow was a huge man, and he was a royal. I had a feeling they didn't like those here, since there was no sign of anyone else like the beast man beside me. It was eerily quiet as well, not a word spoken to us, or even amongst themselves.

Just a tingle of unease floating on the breeze that sent my senses into high alert.

Cat-man continued to lead us along snow-covered, rocky streets, and I was just wondering at the end destination, when we turned a corner to face the "castle." Like the other buildings, it was made of snowflakes—a ton of them. I actually paused to take in the true artistic beauty of it, with "falling flakes" starting high in the sky and cascading down to form the front of the building.

Cat-man spoke up, saying something to Shadow.

"This is where their queen lives," he passed on to me. "She's the one who wants to see us and is guaranteeing our safety for the day."

I nodded. "Okay, not like we have much choice. I just wish I could understand the language."

Shadow looked at me thoughtfully. "I might be able to help with that. I've never tried it on a shifter before, but there's a chance the same energy that I used on the universal translator in the library, would work on you as well."

I almost jumped on Shadow in my enthusiasm, throwing my arms around him, which startled Cat-man, who stumbled back with a hiss and scowl. Way to be a cat cliché.

"Yes, thank you so much, dude!" I gushed at Shadow. "I've been so worried that we'd get separated, and I'd be completely fucked without anyone to translate. I know Midnight is on its way, but until then..."

Shadow rumbled, his hands wrapping around me with just enough bite that I felt *other* parts of my body respond. Damn him and his too-sexy-for-his-own-good nature.

"Firstly, don't call me 'dude,' Sunshine. I am not your dude."

I swallowed roughly, trying hard to bring my temperature back to regular levels. "As I've told you, everything is a dude."

His arms wrapped around me tighter, and I realized just how often he did this now. He used to push, push, push, always keeping me away from him, but now... He drew me closer to his heat. It was freezing deep in snow town, but standing in Shadow's embrace, I could have closed my eyes and fallen asleep, warm and secure.

"This is an experiment," he rumbled, his breath washing over my skin—goosebumps following the sensation. Shadow's hands came up to cup my cheeks, trapping me in place so he could inflict his torture on me. The pain was sharp and immediate, clawing through my skin and into my brain. I fought back a scream, not wanting to alert everyone in the vicinity, and have a bunch of furry beings rushing into our personal space.

"Hold on, Mera," he said, his eyes locked on mine, no doubt seeing the pain reflected there. "I'm rearranging some of your brain chemistry and it's not without its challenges."

He was doing *what the fuck now?*

Gritting my teeth, I glared murder at him, and while I tried to cuss him out because *rearranging someone's brain chemistry was sort of an act you asked permission for*, I couldn't get the words to emerge through the searing brand of pain.

Cat-man, looking curious and worried, moved forward. He said something in his musical language that I couldn't understand, and Shadow snapped something back at him, and then...

"Our most supreme leader... be kept waiting!"

Holy fuck, it was... working! The words were fuzzy, but I understood Cat-man for the first time. The pain faded in the same instant, and as Shadow stepped away, I shook off the last lingering sensation of being violated.

The disorientation remained, so I closed my eyes and shook my head again.

"Mera, look at me," Shadow commanded.

My eyes shot open, and he nodded and smiled. "That wasn't English, but you understood me?"

Well, fuck me sideways. "I understood you perfectly."

His eyebrows shot up. "You just replied in Greek."

I tilted my head, my eyes narrowing. "Are you sure?"

He smirked, but not in humor. "Are you questioning me, Sunshine?"

I knew better than to answer him.

"Your energy has adapted," he continued, "and for now, you should be able to both understand and reply in the native language of whoever you're conversing with. Not bad work, if I do say so myself."

Arrogant beast.

"Here's hoping there are no weird side effects," I said shortly, "since you just jumped right in and rearranged my brain. I already had enough problems with the weirdness in there, thank you very much, and now I have to be on alert for all its new shenanigans."

Shadow shot me a deadpan stare. "You'll be fine."

Resisting the urge to punch him because I still knew there was a limit to how far I could go with Shadow, I just rolled my eyes at his not-so-subtle way of calling me a drama queen. And even if he wasn't wrong about that, it was rude to point it out.

"Are you able to leave now?" Cat-man was done waiting, his hands on his hips, tufts of blue fur peeking through where his shirt had lifted. I had a sudden thought that maybe the beings here were furred and feathered to protect them from the icy temperatures. What we were seeing here, might all be a form of evolution.

"You will shut the fuck up and not question us again," Shadow rumbled at the cat-man. "We'll move when we're ready to move."

I heard it in English, but the lyrical words told me it was a language from the realm.

"I'll just be over here," Cat-man said, spinning on a furred foot and taking off toward the snowflakes castle.

It was a nice change to have Shadow's annoyance directed elsewhere. I could get used to that, and as long as this ruler we were off to meet didn't try to kill us, I was interested to see what we'd find when we arrived inside the castle.

Chapter Twenty-Eight

Since I had to be careful with my translated words, I refrained from asking Shadow if the mists were close. I did reach out through the mental connection for Midnight, but there was no answer; it was too far away still for us to chat. Shadow and Inky's bond, though, was way more established, and I really hoped he had an updated timeline for their arrival.

I'd just have to wait for a private moment to ask for an update.

Shadow whistled as he walked beside me, and I shook my head at how damn calm he looked.

Did nothing bother this dude?

I mean, since today he was on my side, I couldn't really complain. It was a comfort to have Shadow here, not to mention Angel and the mists on the way.

Our backup. Who I really hoped we didn't need.

The coldest section of the land so far was right at the front entrance of this palace, or at least where I thought the entrance was. There was no visible doorway, and as icy winds whipped through us, I rubbed my hands on my arms and bounced up and down to keep warm.

My wolf whined lightly in my chest, but she wasn't pushing for freedom. She was happy to settle in and be my backup if needed.

"Follow in my exact steps," Cat-man said and then he was moving.

I had a moment of déjà vu, remembering Kristoff saying the same thing. Kristoff, who was missing, and might have possibly been the one who'd directed this queen toward us. Was it an illusion here as well, just as it had been with Shadow's friend?

Cat-man approached the first huge snowflake, which stood twenty feet in the air, and as he slipped around the side, I knew this place was no different. A trick of the mind, a façade to cover the truth within.

When I reached the spot at which he'd disappeared, I was briefly mesmerized by the beauty of the building. The walls were so glittery and silver up close, and I loved the multifaceted pigments of their material.

By the time I tore my eyes away, it was to find myself alone, with no actual idea where the entrance was. Running my hands along the icy wall, I couldn't feel an opening, and all I could see was a distorted view of my own reflection splashed back at me.

Speaking of, my hair actually hadn't fared too badly considering I'd been thoroughly fucked, had washed up under a waterfall, and then had been attacked while shifting back and forth—

"Mera!"

Shadow's head appeared, and my focus was once again back where it should have been. But for reals, anyone with even mildly curly hair would have understood. A good hair day was worth celebrating.

"Come on," he said, reaching out for me, and when I placed my hand in his, he dragged me a few steps to the right, where I could finally see the indent of the hidden entrance.

Sneaky, but also a brilliant defense to prevent outsiders just walking into your home. It would be near impossible to find the front door unless you knew the exact spot to stand.

Shadow didn't release my hand as he dragged me through the twisting path inside the snowflake, and my stomach swirled in a weird dance of emotions.

I paid zero attention to where we were going, my entire focus on the beast before me, thinking of how much I'd miss the tingles of his power. Tingles that were so familiar to me now, I'd almost feel empty without them.

And yeah, I'd just turned into that chick who couldn't live without her man. But these were straight-up facts. My energy liked his, and there was no point pretending otherwise.

At the end of this maze entrance, we stepped out into a massive room, about the size of a Regency era ballroom. I had to shake off the weird sensation of being out in the open and exposed after trekking through the tight turns of the front entrance.

Shadow straightened, tugging me against his side, his grip not easing at all. My thighs clenched at the sensation of his strong hold. It reminded me of a hold that had not very long ago been on the back of my neck...

"Wait right here," Cat-man demanded. "I will ensure the leader is ready to see you." His little black nose quivered in the middle of his blue-furred face, and I had this sudden urge to reach out and pat his head, just to see if it was as fluffy as it looked.

My hand lifted, and it was only Shadow capturing it—he now held both my hands—that stopped me from petting the being. "Don't keep us waiting long," he snarled at Cat-man, who swallowed hard, spinning to run away.

When he was gone, Shadow relaxed, releasing his hold on me. "Were you really going to try to pat that being like it was a literal cat?"

I shrugged. "What can I say? It's been 'Cat-man' in my head since we first saw him, and... it's really fluffy."

Shadow's stare was expressionless until he eventually shook his head. "I cannot leave you alone for a second or you'll most definitely get yourself killed."

"Maybe not," I replied. "Weird creatures seem to love me, so it might have worked out okay."

There was nothing expressionless in his face now—it was filled with fire and darkness and shadowy intrigue, as he considered what I'd just said. Shadow might not have been a creature who loved me, but he certainly held a fascination toward me that was unexpected.

I always hated those stories where everyone just fell for the main character, and there was legitimately zero reason for it to happen. And while there was a little of that going on here, with my power being such a mystery, I did somewhat understand the connection between the beast and me.

We were not a "love at first sight" or "fated mate" situation, but we did have energies that meshed and connected. Drawing us together, like moths to a flame.

Just like the shadow creatures fascination with me, Shadow Beast's was definitely due to whatever I was. No point denying it after everything that had happened, and until I knew where this *other* energy I rocked came from, I couldn't really trust my feelings for him.

And I definitely couldn't trust his for me.

Didn't mean I wouldn't enjoy it while I had it, though. The sex was just too fucking good. I'd be a smarter person next week, after a few more orgasms.

If we lived that long, of course.

"Can you tell if the mists are still on the way?" I asked, lowering my voice. "I can only converse with Midnight when we're close, and while I can feel it in my energy, I can't figure out how far away it is."

He tilted his head back, strong throat muscles contracting as he communicated with Inky. A look of frustration dragged on the sides of his face as he let out a huff. "I can't sense their exact location." He lowered his gaze to meet mine. "I could before, and they were following our path, but now we're being blocked."

He looked around at the silvery hall. "The design of these dwellings... it's deliberate so that the shape of the snowflake interferes with natural energy waves. When our mists get closer, our bonds will be strong enough to overcome these barriers, but until then, only the one who created this mess of a maze knows how to manipulate it."

"Yeah, I got that," I said. "They weren't exactly subtle in their endeavor to control their security this way, and... one day I might just do the same thing. Fuck strangers wandering in without warning."

Shadow let out a low laugh, and as rare as his real laughs were, I craved to hear another. "Not a bad idea, Sunshine. You require a fortress to keep you safe."

There was so much I read into that statement, and so many things I wanted to say, but thankfully, we were interrupted before I could make a fool out of myself by falling into my feels.

"Follow me," Cat-man called, waving from the far-off opening in the wall he had exited through earlier. Shadow remained close to my side as we crossed the empty room, and it was scary how right this was starting to feel. I was making a mistake letting this get into my head, but I couldn't seem to stop myself.

"Pack," I murmured. Shadow felt like pack, now more than ever.

His eyes drifted from where they'd been focused ahead, meeting mine—I'd been staring at him without even realizing it. "Sunshine?"

I shook my head. "No, nothing. Just... It's weird, but I feel like we're a pack. A team."

The flames roared to life in his eyes, a sure sign his emotions were getting involved. "They're going to wish they never put you in danger, little wolf," he whispered ominously. "Whatever diplomacy I felt was dashed the moment you got involved. Now, it just might be a bloodbath."

He released me by turning away, and I sucked in a few short, panting breaths, trying to get myself under control. Had I just heard him correctly? Was I important enough now that he would kill them all to protect me?

And why was there a fucked up part of me that liked this side of him the most?

"Come on," Cat-man called again, voice impatient.

Shadow and I countered that by walking slower than ever. I

might have even gone backward at one point, but eventually we couldn't piss off the scowling cat any longer, reaching the doorway it stood in.

"You will show her respect," the furred being said, looking at Shadow, since he didn't know I could understand their language.

Flames shot up around us, and the pungent scent of singed hair filled the room. When the fire had finally cleared, I bit my lip to stop the burst of laughter from escaping. One side of Cat-man's head was now completely bald, and with his mouth slightly ajar, he was clearly trying to figure out what the hell had just happened.

Shadow wasn't amused as he reached out and wrapped his huge hand around the throat of the feline being. *Signature move there if he had one.* "If you don't want me to destroy the fucking foundation of your world, you will do well to remember who I am."

The cat nodded, a wide-eyed look on his face. Shadow held on a beat longer before he released him. Cat-man dashed from the room without another look in our direction. We followed to find that on the other side of the doorway was a corridor. We walked over white floors, so shiny I could see a perfect reflection of Shadow and me; he was still surrounded in flames, and for a second, I thought I was as well, only to realize it was my hair, floating around my body, longer and thicker than I'd ever seen before. It was almost past my waist and a cut wouldn't have gone astray, but then again, from this view, it was actually pretty cool.

Like having a permanent flame surrounding me at all times.

Once I pulled my attention from the floor, I looked ahead to see what was at the end of this pathway between rooms. Only there was nothing but shiny white walls ahead, and this place was reminding me of...

"This is like the Earth hallway," I said, looking around. There were no doors, but everything else was almost the exact same.

He didn't get a chance to reply, as a white-haired woman who clearly held no animal side, stepped into view. She wore a long, silver robe and had an absolutely stunning blue-and-silver crown perched on her head. *Whoa.* This lady was six and half feet of perfect ice queen.

"Ixana," Shadow breathed, and my heart about dropped out of my chest.

Holy fuck. It all made sense now; why we'd been pulled from Kristoff's.

And we'd been very wrong about one thing: the queen didn't want me at all.

She wanted Shadow.

Her true mate.

Chapter Twenty-Nine

Shadow and Ixana took what felt like sixty hours to stare at each other, both of them seemingly stunned and *broken* at finally finding the other. Meanwhile, I was standing there like the awkward third wheel.

An awkward third wheel who was possibly having a minor heart attack because why was my chest hurting so badly?

Ixana stepped closer, breaking the silent stare-off. "I have waited ten lifetimes to see you again," she said, her voice light and musical to match the cadence of their language. "Darkor. You... haven't changed a bit."

Shadow's face darkened as he crossed his arms and made no move to close the gap between them. "Ixana. You... have changed a lot." He appeared to have recovered from his initial shock. "Why am I here? Why did you drag me from my set path?"

Ixana didn't take offense, and I was surprised because I had the urge to punch Shadow on her behalf. No doubt this was a trigger for me, true mate rejection. Shadow was stepping into dangerous territory with his current tone and demeanor.

He clearly wasn't excited to see her. Why, though?

"I think we need to have a discussion," she finally said, her movements slowing. I took another long second to really look at her, noting that not only was she tall and willowy, her white hair was almost to her ankles, tied back in a thick and intricate braid that she wore down one shoulder. Her eyes were an icy blue, her skin so pale, she was almost blue as well, and in her hand she carried a long, slender staff that looked to be made of crystal, with a navy pigment through the carved, translucent handle. Atop this was a deep, almost ruby red stone. A color that was super out of place in this setting.

"Come," Ixana said, turning and waving us over. Her white robe trailed out behind her, showcasing what looked like a million glittering crystals sewn into its length.

Looking all regal and queenly and shit. But she wasn't wearing clothes specifically chosen by the Shadow Beast, and it showed.

We followed her out of the white hall and into what looked like a receiving chamber, with a platform and ornate throne chair perched upon it. On either side of the room were her guards, all animal-people hybrids. They bowed as she crossed through the middle of them, and she was most definitely the queen here.

Two burly guards in black pants, furred chests on display, waited near her throne. They approached her as she walked, falling in on either side of their queen. They were huge and looked a little like bulls, with dark, thick, and coarse fur. The humanoid mix in their facial features was odd, especially with the tusks on either side of their mouths, but somehow it worked for them. The spear-like weapons they carried, were the same ivory color as the two huge horns out the top of their furred heads.

It seemed that these two were her personal guard and I totally understood why; they were scary motherfuckers.

Shadow moved, jolting me from my observation of everything in the room. Forcing me to once again focus on the fact that he had a mate.

Sure, I'd known in theory, but seeing it in person was a new kind of hell. And even with their first meeting more awkward than either might have expected, I knew it was only a matter of time before the magic of that bond eased the tension and got them back where they'd once been.

"Mera," Shadow snapped. My heart clenched because there was no 'Sunshine' from him today. His face was blank, his eyes gold and without flames, and I had absolutely no idea what he was thinking.

"What?"

"We have to follow," he said shortly.

A spark of defiance made itself known, pushing through my pride and hurt feelings. "We do? Or what?"

Shadow closed the distance between us, and his eyes were pleading with me to understand, but his words were as short as mine had been. "She carries my stone. Without it, I can't best my family. I need to hear her out."

His stone? The red stone was... the bloodstone? No wonder it had looked out of place... But how in the fuck had she gotten her hands on it? And why hadn't he just snatched it away from the ice bitch the first second he saw it?

I crossed my arms. "You might have to hear her out, but I don't. Dragging us in here, being all freaking cryptic, and then wandering her ass off with a 'come.' What? Am I just supposed to obey?"

Shadow's rigid jaw twitched. "You usually obey that command."

I narrowed my eyes on him, my lips pressing together as I fought the combination of fury and arousal. How dare he remind me of that in the house of his mate?!

Reaching out, I grasped on to his shirt, pulling him closer. Or at least attempting to because he was an immovable object when he wanted to be. There were gasps and animal calls around us, and I wondered if it was because I'd touched their queen's mate, or were they aware of what usually happened when people touched him without his permission?

Only we were past that. I was one of the six beings who—

Shadow's power zapped me, sending me away from him.

"Learn your place, wolf," he rumbled, his cold expression telling me I'd pushed my defiance too far. Especially in the presence of another royal and leader.

Shadow could not lose face, but in that second, my heart broke a little.

He turned and walked off, leaving me all but sprawled against a nearby pillar, and I wondered what the hell I should do now.

I wanted to leave. Storm from this place and find my way back to the library. If I could meet up with Midnight or Angel, I knew they'd show me the way.

But there was this tiny part of me that wasn't ready to just walk away. Not yet, not without answers. I still didn't know who or what I was. So many unanswered questions, and maybe... I'd learn something here.

As a bonus, me staying might just make Shadow's life a little uncomfortable. Worth it after that shit he'd just pulled. The animal guards crowded in around me, and while none of them touched me, they were definitely urging me to start moving, to follow Shadow and the queen.

Shadow and his *mate*.

My wolf rose to the surface, ready to fight our way out if needed. She'd been quiet recently, but there was a rage in her soul as she scraped along the surface of her cage. She wanted to battle. Take them all on, one by one, and prove that we were no longer a prisoner.

I felt the bones and muscles in my face start to morph, pushing against the restraints of my human skin, and I was so tempted to do my worst. The *pissed off* rattling around deep in my soul, had caution falling to the side.

Whatever loyalty I owed to Shadow was gone, and I was ready to fuck shit up. Our pack life was dead before it even truly begun.

Fuck. It hurt.

It hurt so much, but anger was easier to deal with, so I grasped on to it. Straightening with all the dignity I had left, I marched along the white floor, my boots clicking with each step, and I took pleasure in the sound because I wanted them to know I was coming.

The plethora of guards followed, and I spent the short walk into the next room examining each and every one so I could commit to memory the range of creatures that were part of this world.

Lots of feline beasts, like Cat-man. Cat-man, who was nowhere in sight, having disappeared after Shadow singed its fur. I'd feel sorry for it, only... nah.

There were other cats with its blue fur in the guard, also a few with greyish gold, and a very dark magenta one, with piercing emerald eyes. Next to the cats were half a dozen birds, similar to the ones I'd seen on the way here, with sharp, pointed faces and beak-like mouths. The beak itself looked quite lethal, with an intense point on the end.

The rest weren't really like any Earth animals, but if I had to liken them, it would be to something prehistoric. Dark green and browns in color, with boney shield plates around their heads and along their arms.

They were kind of scarily hardcore, and I wondered how long it would be before I found myself tangling with one of these creatures. And who would come out on top when it inevitably happened.

Chapter Thirty

The next room in this never-ending labyrinth of chambers appeared to be a gathering area. There was a colossal table, spanning from one end to the other, and it was made of— you guessed it—crystal that shimmered in the twinkling lights from above. The ceilings themselves were up so high that I had no idea what was being used for illumination, but from what I could tell, it appeared to be gaps in the design of the building that allowed light from outside to filter through specifically designated spots.

And, yes, I was examining every single other aspect of this room so I didn't have to look at the pair already seated. The true mates. Bleh.

The guard pushed up on me in a bid to hurry me along, so I went slower than ever.

"Wow, really love what you've done with the place," I said, chatting to a bird-girl like we were old friends. "I mean, the color scheme alone must have taken *weeks* to perfect."

Everything was white. Stark, stuck-in-a-snowstorm white.

A few of the guards started to mutter, pressing even closer as my steps slowed dramatically. I wanted to look at Shadow. I wanted to look at him so badly my eyeballs hurt from the effort to stop them moving, but I was on a mission, and would be stronger than the need he created in me. *I had to be.*

When one of the dinosaur people got fed up with my game of *walk as slow as possible without going backwards,* he did what no other had until this point.

He grabbed me.

The move took me by surprise. They'd been so careful up until this point to not even graze my skin with theirs, and that made me slower than usual to react. By the time I swung my elbow back to jab Dino-boy, who still held me, a rumbling roar filled the room.

Everyone in the damn place froze. I mean *everyone.* Shadow's power swept ahead of him as he got to his feet. I couldn't look away any longer, my eyes on the raging beast as he stalked across the room to where we stood. Around me, the animal-people cowered and a part of me almost felt sorry for them.

His flames slapped out first, followed by smoky darkness seeping from his skin. "Better put me down, triceratops," I said cheerily. "Shadow doesn't like people touching his possessions." I lowered my voice. "And that's all I am, so don't stress on the behalf of your poor little queen."

I was dropped, and Shadow went at us. Well, at me because everyone else bailed. His power wrapped around my body and I was lifted to my feet. When I was eye level with his furious, flame-filled gaze, I forced a smile on my face. One of those fake, *we're strangers and I'm gonna pretend shit is fine* sorts of smile.

"Oh, hey, fancy meeting you here. Can I help you with something?"

Shadow's eyes traced across my face and down to my arm where Dino-boy had grabbed me. I blinked at the visible bruising, already fading out as my healing kicked in. Not fast enough for Shadow, though.

His flames snapped out and there was a bellow as Dino-boy was dragged back to sprawl on the ground between us. Shadow, who hadn't touched me yet—I was dangling in the air from his power alone—stepped closer to me.

"He hurt you?"

I shrugged. "You know, it's kind of a theme with me today. Dudes getting a little rough, *shoving* me around. I wouldn't worry your pretty head about it."

His expression was fucking furious, and I felt nothing but a sense of satisfaction. Part of me knew I was acting like a child. Shadow had a true mate; that was not new information. I should have been accepting and happy for him; this was what he'd wanted for the last few thousand years.

In the great scheme of his life, I'd been around for fuck-all time, and it was stupid to expect anything from him outside of what we'd already shared. It was just... when his power had zapped me, it had zapped my ability to take this graciously.

Now, Shadow got to deal with the same angry-ass bitch he'd thrown over his shoulder that first day back in Torma.

Dino-boy was begging on the ground now, whimpering and crying—in a dinosaur way, which didn't seem to include literal tears, but there was a lot of slobber. It was sad and gross, and I honestly didn't need him to suffer any longer.

Drawing on my anger, I slammed my energy back into Shadow. I'd learned this move when I'd figured out how to trace the pathway into the realm. I couldn't do the flame thing on command yet, but I could definitely use my energy aggressively.

My power slapped against Shadow's, and I felt a sense of surprise from him, but he didn't drop me. If anything, his hold tightened and it wasn't until his *mate* called out across the room that he stopped dragging me forward.

"Darkor, please. Leave the guard alone. They know they're not supposed to touch you or *your wolf.*"

She said that the same way someone would say *your pet.* This woman, for all her light and bright smiles, was a secret cunt in disguise. Call it women's intuition; I already knew she was a complete and total psycho. All the damn white had been the first giveaway.

"Good luck with that one, *Darkor*," I whispered sweetly. "You're going to fucking need it."

Shadow's lips twitched, and finally, he released me from his hold. I landed easily on my feet before *accidentally on purpose* kicking Dino-boy, sending him sliding across the floor. "Don't ever fucking grab me again."

Strolling over to the table, I sat right in the seat Shadow had occupied before.

"Oh, uh, excuse me, that's Darkor's seat."

I tilted my head at the queen bitch before I leaned back in the crystal chair and lifted my boots to drop them on her table. "Plenty of other seats," I said sweetly, pretending to clean my nails as I stared at her. "He'll figure it out."

She looked horrified, and then furious, and then completely calm. If I hadn't been staring at her over my pointer fingernail, I'd have missed the full range of her emotions. As it was, the rage lingered long after she covered it up with a smile.

"Very true."

Shadow made his way back to the table, dropping into the chair on the opposite side of me. We were both beside her, since she sat at the head of the table. Only now, he got to stare at me as well, and hopefully that made him just a little squirmy.

Though judging by his cool-as-a-cucumber expression, he wasn't bothered at all.

"Ixana, this is Mera Callahan, one of the shifters I created."

She eyed me like I'd just been shit out of Dino-boy's ass, her petite little nose wrinkling. Up close, her skin was quite blue, not like the fronds, but it was noticeable. And her eyes, those icy-blue eyes, were freaking me out with their laser intensity. She didn't feel powerful like Shadow, but there was a frosty crush in the air whenever she moved, the scent of freshly fallen snow following her around.

"It's, uh, nice to meet you," she said.

I'd figured out pretty quickly that Shadow's translation spell was rewording everything into the sort of colloquialism I would understand. Because there was no way this formal bitch talked like that.

Shadow and Ixana were watching me, so I loudly dropped my boots to the floor, pleased to see mud and debris remained on the pristine crystal table. "Wish I could say the same."

Shadow's chest rumbled and I narrowed my eyes on him. "What? She kidnapped my ass and you know how I feel about that. A simple invitation would have me feeling much more gracious, and since she isn't my true mate, I'm not going to just forgive and forget."

Fuck, the amount of unsaid shit in that petty ass statement could have filled a 747 jumbo jet, but before we could really throw down, the ice queen fell back on diplomacy.

"Yes, sorry. I do owe you both an apology for the way I brought you here, but I was afraid to miss my chance, and if you ended up in the royal compound, you would have been beyond my reach."

Dammit. Why was she not snapping back? Right now, I looked like the childish, petty asshole in the room. And even though I was sensing undercurrents of evil from this lady, there was not a shred of evidence that she was anything other than the gracious and kindly benevolent leader before us.

I had to dial it back. Until such a time I had evidence of her underhanded ways.

"What did you want to tell me, Ixana?" Shadow asked, diverting attention from me before I could say something else horrible. Bastard knew me too well. "You obviously brought me here for a reason."

"I mean..." She blinked, looking a little shell-shocked. "Were you not here to find me? I have been waiting, building our army, all for the moment I knew you'd return to this world and take back what was ours."

Shadow didn't say anything, his face unreadable. "Shadow," I pushed, my fake smile firmly in place. "Why don't you answer the nice lady?"

Ixana flashed me a glare before re-fixing her affable expression. "Would you like to freshen up? I can have someone show you to a guest room and bring some food. You must be exhausted."

"No," Shadow rumbled. "She stays here. She can hear all of this, and I don't trust your guards yet."

Ixana didn't like that, but she didn't argue. I wondered if she'd been the deferential type when they'd been together. "I'm definitely staying," I said with faked enthusiasm. "Shadow and his mate taking back what is theirs is totally my jam. Super excited."

If looks could kill, they'd both be having a shot at it. Luckily, I had thicker skin that that.

Ixana released a long breath. "Okay, well, I guess I best start with my side of this story." Another deep breath. "The day of your crowning, Darkor, I was waiting in the wings to congratulate you. I wanted to see you before the moment we reaffirmed the bonds we felt at birth."

Nice, they'd been true mates since fucking birth. How sweet—cough, cough, gross cough.

I was really proud of how well I was handling this situation so far.

"I saw your sister give you the cup. I didn't know it held a stasis spell until you took a drink and fell." There were tears in her eyes, and I found myself somewhat moved by the stupid tale. Did she have to be an excellent storyteller as well? With just the right touch of emotion in her voice?

Fuck her and her perfection.

"I had your stone," she continued.

Shadow sat straighter. "Why did you have my stone?"

Her big, blue eyes did a lot of blinking at that one. "Well, I was going to be the one to bond it to your mist mark. Right?"

Shadow didn't look convinced of that, but he also didn't argue.

"And when it was clear you were in trouble," Ixana hurried to add, "I rushed off with the stone so Cristell wouldn't get it as well."

What the fuck had she been doing running like a coward when her mate was in danger? If I'd held any respect for her, it would be gone now. I mean, there was a decent chance that the rules here were protect-the-power-first or some shit.

I'd never be that person.

Shadow looked around. "And you ended up here? Creating... your new world?"

If he was angry about her story, he wasn't showing it.

"I've gathered a lot of power over the years," she said, and her smile was a touch creepy as it tilted up her pale-ass lips. "Experimented where I should not have, using power from the creatures that walk this land, and the few followers I managed to take with me. I was determined to build an army that all would fear."

All the while her mate had been locked out of this realm and she'd done fucking nothing to try to get to him. Bullshit if you asked me.

Clearly the ice queen was not worthy of the beast.

Chapter Thirty-One

"Tell me what my family have been up to."

Not a surprising question. Shadow had been waiting a long time to destroy his sister and information from Ixana might give him an advantage.

She straightened even further if that were possible. It was either a steel rod down her spine or a stick up her as—

"That is why I pulled you out so suddenly," she said in a rush, interrupting my super important *petty as fuck* thoughts. "Cristell has ruled with complete control and fear since you left, and in that time, your family has amassed a lot of power in their corner. The other kingdoms are so weak comparatively, giving yours the ultimate control. There's no fairness or justice any longer, and since your sister has been on the throne, they have gathered so many creatures that it would be next to impossible to defeat them without help."

Shadow shot to his feet, the solid table shifting with the movement. "Return my stone to me, and the power I should have always had is what I'll use to defeat Cristell."

I had no idea where the staff—and Shadow's stone more importantly—even was. It had disappeared from sight the moment we'd followed her into this room. Ixana was a smart little witch, concealing her one reason to hold the beast here. I mean, outside of their true mate thing.

Yeah, whatever.

"Here's the truth," Ixana said, her voice softer than ever. "I can't give you the stone."

Shadow's flames filled the room, so red against the white landscape. "You are very good with illusion, Ixana, I remember well, and I can't take it from you without you showing it to me, but I can destroy the foundation of the world you've built here. Don't test me." She was getting the same warning as Cat-man, and it was not an empty threat.

Ixana swallowed but didn't back down. "It's the only power I have right now to keep my people safe from The Grey Lands," she got out in a rush. "And honestly, as much as I've prayed for this moment with you, I cannot sacrifice them all for our bond. Not yet at least."

"So... what is the plan?" Shadow bit out. "How do we amass this power you think I need to best my sister?"

Wishful thinking that she had one. Well, one that didn't involve Shadow moving in here, lots of boning, and a bunch of fire-ice babies.

"We must gather even more creatures," she said.

Well, color me fucking surprised. She did have a plan.

"If we gather enough, combined with your power and the bloodstone, you will have the means to take them on. Once the royal family falls, I have nothing more to worry about, and the stone is useless to me. Your family has hunted me since you were taken, and only here do they not touch me. Once they're gone, I can return to The Concordes."

Shadow's face was calm. His eyes were not. I wondered if she knew the signs since it had been a damn long time since they'd been together, and I would have bet everything I owned—except my library—Shadow had been a hell of a lot kinder before he'd been booted out into the universe and forced to survive.

She didn't know this version of him, one that was a rotten bastard, with enough power to be considered a fucking god in multiple worlds. He didn't like to be denied shit, and he sure as hell didn't like to put a halt to his plans again.

"Okay," he said, retaking his seat.

Sorry, what? I shook my head, like I could clear my ears out. Had he just said *okay?*

"How many creatures do we need?"

He had! He'd fucking said okay, and now they were discussing their plans like a married couple.

"You will need at least a thousand," she replied, excitement finally crossing her face. "I've built a paradise here, but beyond my village, the rest of The Grey Lands is as you remember. Barren and dangerous. We will find our creatures out there."

Shadow's jaw was twitching. "A thousand? What's your plan to bond that many to us?"

Before she could answer, I got to my feet, drawing their attention. "I think I'll take you up on that offer of freshening up," I said saltily. "There's a lot of bullshit in the air, and I think a bit landed on me."

Ixana looked confused, so there was maybe not a great translation available for that little dig. Shame. Shadow, on the other hand, understood me perfectly.

"Mera," he growled.

I smiled sweetly at him. "Yes, Darkor?"

He didn't like me using his name, not at all, as his fingers tapped a hole into the side of the table, and if I'd been closer, the heat on his body would have had me positively sweating.

"Don't push me, little wolf," he murmured, and my stupid heart clenched for a beat.

"Wouldn't think of it," I replied, managing to keep my tone even.

Ixana, clearly done with our verbal foreplay, waved her guard over. "Please show the shifter to her room, and if anyone touches her without her permission, I will personally send them out beyond the fence."

The bird-girl she'd called over to guide me actually paled. Her yellow-feathered face turned into a peach color, and that was the weirdest shit I'd seen today. "I will guard her with my life," Birdy said.

Ixana nodded before turning to Shadow. "Does that work for you?"

He wanted to argue, it was so fucking clear on his face, but he just nodded. Letting me go.

He. Let. Me. Go. All so he could go back to playing happily married family with the ice queen, discussing their plans.

I could not stay here and watch this relationship rekindle. I wasn't a strong enough, gracious enough, or good enough person for that. Nope, I had to escape, and then hold out long enough for Midnight and Angel to arrive.

There was a second reason I was leaving as well. If either of them thought they could use my power to gather the creatures they needed...

It was a big fat hell no.

My sole aim was to figure out what I was, what my power was, and how both had come to be. The moment I knew that, I was hauling my ass out of this world and heading back to my library.

Shadow wouldn't need either library here, shacked up with his ice queen.

"Are you okay?" Birdy asked as I stormed along after her.

"Yes, totally okay. Ready to find my room."

Some of the color had returned to her feathers now, and she had quite the bright... plume? Her hair, instead of being like mine, was this fancy-ass crest that started on top of her head and then trailed down her spine. It was wickedly cool, and the fact that she wore clothing over her feathers amused me to no end. Did they have something to cover that their feathers didn't? Or was it part of making them more humanoid?

I'd probably never know and at this stage was just going to accept it without questioning everything. One day soon, this world and its inhabitants would no longer be my problem.

The halls Birdy led me along were as white and winding as the first entrance, and I knew there was not a fuck in hell I'd find my way out of this maze. "You can actually ask for guidance at any time," Birdy said when I made a comment about it. She reached out and placed a hand on the wall, long claws tapping on the white panel. "Exit to main street," she said.

The spot under her palm lit up, and then the light started to move along the wall, fast enough that it was gone in a few minutes. "If you followed the light, it would lead you out. I'm not supposed to tell anyone about that little secret, but honestly, I don't have time to keep babysitting you, so it's best if you can get around on your own."

What. An. Idiot.

Birdy had just handed me an absolute weapon—my freedom—and she didn't even realize what she'd done. Which was totally okay with me.

"Your secret is safe with me," I said, genuinely happy.

We headed upstairs after that, and when we hit the second floor, the space opened dramatically. "This is where the guests stay," Birdy told me, stopping at a blank wall.

I looked around, my eyes taking in the full expanse of the area I could see. "You've lost me."

A tweeting sort of huff escaped her beaked mouth. "Place your hand on the wall."

I did that, and beneath my palm lit up like it had for Birdy.

"Say, 'Room.'"

"Room." See, I could do as I was told.

The light exploded, and I stepped back, wrenching my hand free on instinct. The doorway formed a moment later, and I was shoved from behind and sent stumbling inside. Disregarding the fact that Birdy had touched me without my permission—someone was in trouble—I attempted to figure out what the heck I was staring at.

It was an... igloo. Basically the only thing I could compare it to. Curved icy walls, with white floors, and a ton of thick pelts in the middle of the area. It was not as cold as I'd expected as I walked farther inside to examine the space. Looking back once, I realized that the door behind me had closed without a sound, and Birdy was nowhere to be seen.

I was finally alone with my messy thoughts. Great.

The pelts were amazingly soft and warm when I dug my hands into them, and I was super tempted to bury deep and have a nap. But I wanted to check out the rest of my room before I relaxed.

What if there were threats in here I wasn't aware of?

The main area in this round room held only those thick pelts, at least five in total, so I wouldn't be sleeping on the cold ground thankfully. At first, it appeared to just be the one round room until I ran my hands across the wall and found another opening. Should have guessed there'd be more optical illusions. *Queen of Illusions* was Ixana's middle name.

The second room held the *bathroom?* It had a huge hole in the icy floor, and the water in there was hot and inviting. On the other side of this room was another hole, and I couldn't be sure, but I had a feeling that was the toilet... maybe? That was what I'd be using it for, so hopefully it wasn't actually a laundry chute.

Awkward.

I had no other clothing to change into, so I decided to wait on the bath situation, in lieu of having a nap first. It had been exhausting dealing with my emotions since they'd decided to explode inside of me and drip acid through my soul in painful dribbles.

Yeah, I was being super dramatic, but there was real hurt inside of me that I wasn't mentally or emotionally able to deal with today. It was just too much. The last ten years had been bad enough, but now there was this, and maybe... just maybe, I'd finally learned what it was like to truly be broken by someone I trusted.

I could still feel the zap of Shadow's power, the cold burn in his eyes, and the way his name for me had turned from 'Sunshine' into 'Mera.'

It all hurt, and if a nap helped me escape, I was taking it. Hopefully by the time I woke up, Midnight would be here, and I could figure out my next move. Without a beast by my side.

Chapter Thirty-Two

Despite how comfortable and warm the pelts were, I was somehow still cold. And I slept like shit.

At one point, I woke, tears on my cheeks, and that just made me even angrier with myself because I wasn't supposed to let my emotions get in the way. Yeah, Shadow had given me my first kiss... had been my first lover... and he was the first male I'd let myself be vulnerable with in a very long time. But I'd known all along it wasn't going to last. I mean, that had been the one constant in our relationship, so why was I taking this so hard?

Was it just how perfect his mate was? Was it the thought that while I was sleeping my day away here, mourning what could have been, he was probably fucking her against an ice wall right now?

I mean, maybe not fucking—she really didn't look like the type to enjoy a royal fuck. Gentle lovemaking in the moonlight?

Ugh, whatever. Screw him and her, and not in the fun way they were probably enjoying.

Mera.

I jumped at the sound of Midnight's voice in my head, and there was a strange flutter in my chest that followed. The flutter felt cool and calm... Angel was close too. I wondered if maybe there had been a new evolution of my bond with her.

Either way, I was beyond ecstatic to feel both of them closing in.

How far away are you?

Midnight's reply came a moment later. *We've arrived in The Grey Lands and are now following Shadow's energy through an ice city.*

Yes. Fuck yes. I wouldn't be alone here, and that gave me options.

Angel is with you? It was best to confirm, even if I already knew the answer.

Yes.

Can you pass messages to her?

I didn't think it was possible for any normal being from the Solaris System, but Angel was special.

I can. Through your bond with her.

Great. Tell her that the queen here is Shadow's true mate! She has his stone and is using that to get what she wants from him. I don't know for sure what that is, but she wants us to gather shadow creatures to use to take on his family. It's all weird and messy and I don't even know what's the truth or not, but she needs to be careful.

There were a few moments' pause before it got back to me. *She said she's prepared for anything, and Ixana is no match for her.*

I had to laugh. In some ways, Angel's confidence was almost equal or superior to Shadow's, but I loved her strength and fire so much that it didn't even remotely bother me. I mean, some might call her arrogant, but was it arrogant to own your badassness? Not in my books.

Great. Let me know when you arrive at the largest snowflake building.

See you soon.

Getting to my feet, I made my way into the second room and used the facilities. The bath still looked amazingly enticing, and since the chill in my bones had settled in during my nap, making me feel a touch drained, I decided to have a quick bath. Just as I had my boots off, shirt over my head, and was about to slide my pants down, there was a tinkling sound in the air.

The energy in here felt disturbed for the first time, so I pressed myself back to the wall, right near the entrance to the bathroom door. Allowing my wolf to rise up, we waited silently, and when a figure slid around the corner, I wrapped my arms around their shoulders, managing to knock their feet out from under them before slamming the intruder down onto their back.

Clothes went flying, as did a bunch of feathers while Birdy cursed and squawked in her weird way.

"Shit, sorry," I said, straightening. "I thought you were someone about to attack me."

She coughed and wheezed before awkwardly getting to her taloned feet. "You're a psycho."

I shrugged. "Yeah, and...?"

Birdy just blinked at me, and I wondered if my translation thing had broken or something. Did she not understand?

She shook her feathered head. "You're so confident. Just owning all of your flaws..."

Oh, right, that was what had Birdy all confused. "You see flaws... I see character. No one is perfect, and if they're pretending to be, it's only to hide a fuck-ton of damage. No one deserves to exist like that, and in the end, it will drive them a little cray cray. So, for me, it's all about embracing the quirks that make up Mera. Got me?"

She didn't *got me*, but she did nod. I wondered if Birdy was thinking of her boss in that moment, because if anyone was making a strong effort to "appear perfect," it was the queen. No doubt the ice bitch expected the same perfection from the beings she surrounded herself with. I mean, it made sense wanting to control everything in the inner circle of your life, especially when it was chaotic in the outside world. But I'd bet living with it was no fun at all.

"I brought clothes," Birdy said, sounding sullen as she indicated the articles of clothing scattered around. "Master Shadow said you'd find these comfortable."

She spun and disappeared out of the bathroom before I could say thanks or apologize for slamming her ass into the floor. Whoopsie.

Gathering up the clothing, I noted they were basically the same sort of outfit I was wearing right now, but with a red shirt and blue jeans. I had no idea if there was any significance with the red shirt, being that it was Shadow's color, but since I was trying not to think about him at all, I just placed everything on a shelf carved into the white walls and finished undressing.

As I dropped one foot into the deliciously warm water, another tinkle sounded through the room, and this time an aggravated huff escaped me. Turning my back on the enticing water *that I was clearly not going to get into*, I waited for this intruder. Naked, because I was about done with today.

Shadow appeared in the doorway and when he saw me, his eyes flared. "Sunshine?"

As his gaze drifted down the long, bare length of my body, his expression darkened. He then looked around the room, but there was no place to hide anything here. "Are you alone?"

I snorted. "No, not even remotely. I just threw the cat-dude I fucked down the piss hole. He should be fine though; cats always land on their feet."

Shadow's nostril's flared. "You better be kidding."

My hands ended up on my hips because I needed to get this point across with a serious show of body language. "What's the issue?"

Shadow, who looked stupid huge with his heavy soled leather boots, stepped toward me. One fucking step and he was in my space. There was no way I could back up, or I'd end in the bath, so I just had to hold my breath and hope I didn't cave. Easier said than done with his fire power running over my skin, and that spicy, darkly tempting scent of him invading my senses.

"Because. Little wolf. *You belong to me.*"

He said every word with a little pause between them, really cementing his statement.

"But you don't belong to me?" I choked out. "You belong to Ice Queen Ixana, and she's probably going to be super unhappy about you standing here while I'm naked." My voice lowered to a whisper. "Better run home before she finds out."

Shadow's arm snaked around my waist, and like he had so many times, he brought me smack bang into his body. There was no pain this time, but I remembered it all too well from our arrival here.

As he slowly dragged me up, using just that one arm, I forced my face to remain impassive, even though my hormones were doing a fucking happy dance on the inside.

"Who said I don't belong to you, Mera?"

It took me way too long to register what he'd just said, and I kept running it through my head, wondering if I'd misheard or misunderstood. Or was this one of those mean trick questions...?

His lips tilted, so obviously, my expression was amusing him. Nice, since I felt like I was about to self-destruct inside. Shadow leaned over me, running his nose along my throat, and up my cheek. My head dropped back before I even knew what I was doing, giving him more access.

"We are irrevocably linked, Mera Callahan," he rumbled against my skin. "A bond built in fire and shadows."

Fuck. This was everything I'd wanted to hear, but at the same time it wasn't.

He still owned me, and I was still the possession.

And he still had a true mate.

Shadow's lips pressed against my throat, and I groaned before reality slammed back in and I fought him. "Don't fucking touch my skin with lips that have kissed her."

He growled, shaking me so my head jerked up and our eyes met. "These lips have touched nothing and no one but you."

I snorted, not sure whether to believe him or not. "What about oral sex? Surely, you've had your mouth on *those lips*."

The thought of him touching another woman like he had me, made me want to claw some bitch's eyes out, but I was also realistic.

He'd known me like one millionth of his life, and in those other years, he'd clearly not been celibate.

He growled close to my face. "Never. We don't kiss any who are not our true mate.... anywhere. I've had more sex than you'll know in ten lifetimes, but never have I used my mouth to fuck a pussy like I did yours. Never have I tasted such sweetness, and I'm starting to think you put a fucking spell on me because I can't even remember my life before you came into it."

Holy shit. I was so fucking turned on, I felt like I was about to self-destruct. My body was like jelly as I tried to wrap my head around what he was saying. He'd never had his mouth on a woman. Except me.

I mean, I'd seen his face that night in Faerie, and he'd been super torn about what he could do. He'd been determined not to let me lose my virginity, so he'd had only that choice.

He could have used his hand.

Involuntarily, I moved against him, the memory of my multiple orgasms thanks to his talented tongue all I could think about.

Shadow laughed, a darkly seductive sound. "You're lucky I have somewhere to be, or I would tie your naked ass to my bed and make you come a thousand times on my face."

He licked across my skin, tasting me with kisses and nips, and I jerked my hips against him.

"Wait." I gasped. "Somewhere to be?"

He rumbled again, and I wasn't sure he was going to answer, but apparently, the bastard had more control than me as he lifted his head with a sigh. "Angel and our mists are here. It's time to head to the wall with Ixana. She wants to show us where we will be traveling to gather the shadow creatures."

Just her name made me see red, some of my arousal fading. "Why should I help her?"

He knew I was dead serious, and as he set me on my feet, I tried not to mourn. My vagina was crying, though. Pretty much literally at this point.

"Ixana has answers to what we need to know," he told me, and it was my old Shadow back for a moment. "She might even know what it is that draws you to this world, and if she doesn't, something tells me the answers will be in these lands. Where the wild creatures roam."

I went to grab him before I remembered the last time I'd done that in the hall. Holding my hands a few inches from his chest, I lifted my gaze to meet his. "Are you going to zap me again?"

Some of his blasé attitude fell. "Mera, fuck, that was... I'm keeping our secrets."

He was keeping *his* secret, anyway... His dirty little secret.

"Whatever, Shadow." With a huff, I turned and made my way into the water.

I would hear Ixana out because there might be knowledge here about me, and in that case, I was invested. I was going to be clean first, though.

As I sank down into the hot water, I sighed at how fucking good it felt. My muscles finally relaxed. Shadow was watching me, his eyes filled with flames, but he was managing his self-control, one arm lodged against the wall as he observed.

Since he hadn't left yet, I decided to ask more questions. "Did you always expect answers for me would be in this land?"

He nodded. "I had a feeling that whatever information we got from my family would only point us here. The land where the mists converge. I sense your power originated here."

This didn't surprise me. The connection I had was strongest with the creatures. A facet of this land was part of me, and I wanted to figure out how that was possible.

"Fine," I said, sinking a little deeper. "I'll get cleaned up and meet you... where?"

He crossed his arms, and I tried very hard not to look at how broad his jacket made his shoulders look. It was one of those long, wool coats in a style businessmen often wore, and with black pants and shirt under it, he was more than a little devilishly handsome. "I'll wait here for you."

I nailed him with a glare of my own. "Actually, I'd like a little privacy."

"Tough. Luck."

I growled. "Shadow, for fuck's sake. I won't try to run. Just piss off and let me have my bath in peace."

There was a decent chance I would need to come before my unsatisfied vagina let me go exploring.

The bastard didn't argue again, just stayed where he was, his eyes on me. The possessive alpha thing that he naturally possessed, was jacked up tenfold here. Almost with its own energy, drifting in the air between us.

"Fine," I snapped. "Suit yourself. You get to see the show now."

Shadow thought he could get me all worked up and not follow through, then this was what happened.

Chapter Thirty-Three

My hands slipped under the water, tracing over my body, and I threw my head back as a moan fell from my lips. My skin was overly sensitive, and as much as I wished it was Shadow touching me, any caress was working for me today.

"Sunshine," he cautioned, his voice disappearing into the beast territory, deep and rumbly.

Ignoring him, I slipped my fingers into my pussy—not wasting time since we didn't have any—going straight for what I knew would get me off first. Another moan escaped, and at this point, I really enjoyed Shadow watching me. Under his dark pants, I could see his dick swelling, not to mention the fire in his eyes and the tension in his muscles. He wanted me, and I wasn't the only one suffering in this current situation.

Opening my eyes as my fingers slipped inside again, I met his gaze, and there was no need to act defiant because I was hovering closer to my orgasm.

"You are going to be the death of me, Sunshine," he said through gritted teeth. His power froze me, and I was lifted from the water.

"Don't ever touch yourself like that again." Now I was completely fucking locked in by his hypnotic voice. "Your orgasms belong to me."

I would have writhed if he wasn't holding me still.

"*Mine*, Sunshine."

"Shadow," I choked out. "If I'm yours, then fucking prove it."

His power jerked me forward, and by the time he caught me, the heat he was throwing off had dried me completely. I arched as he held me tightly, and when he turned us, my back hit the wall. His hard length pressed into my nakedness. He was still fully dressed, but somehow his pants were open, the velvety tip of his cock edging inside of me.

"You want this, little wolf?" he rumbled, and I cried out, jerking my pussy to slide down his cock further.

"Dude, you better dick me right now before I lose my brains."

Shadow's chest shook with his laughter, but he did as he was told for once. A choked gasp escaped as he thrust up into me, and he was still in his seven-foot height, which meant I was about to get my vagina annihilated. And I couldn't find it in myself to care. I was a wolf shifter, and it would heal.

Shadow went hard and fast, holding me immobile as he fucked me, slamming into me like he was determined to ruin me for all other cocks. And, unfortunately, I was starting to think he had.

"Fucking hell," I screamed, clawing at him when the orgasm slammed into me. It was one of those hard and fast jolts, and it started another buildup, so quickly, I couldn't catch my breath.

He was relentless, his eyes locked on me, one hand holding my neck and shoulder blade while the other was under my ass as he drilled me so intensely, I saw stars.

"Come, Sunshine," he ordered.

I did, jerking against him. "Gods." I was sobbing now. "Shadow god."

"Correct, baby," he whispered, and fuck me, if that endearment didn't tether my pussy to him just a little more. This was like the possessive attitude he threw around. It did it for me. Outside of the bedroom, I would hate his attitude, but inside it... I was hooked.

For some reason, he slowed, his thrusts no softer, but he drew each one out, his cock almost completely out of me before he slammed it back in, over and over again, and this time, the buildup was slower. I could already tell the intensity was possibly going to kill me.

"Don't come yet," Shadow warned, and I didn't, even if my head was spinning, the pleasure in my stomach spiraling from my toes up to my gut. His fire burst to life across the both of us, bringing more energy and pleasure.

I tried so hard not to come, but it was too much. I wouldn't survive it.

Thankfully, just when I was about to explode, Shadow let out a low groan. "Come now, Sunshine. Come with me. Together."

I screamed. A guttural, beyond-my-control sound, and it was so much that when the dark spots danced before my eyes, I embraced them and might have passed out for a few minutes. Shadow didn't stop even as he came, each thrust continuing to draw out the pleasure for both of us.

What felt like hours later, he stopped moving, his weight solid and comforting against me, as we both breathed heavily. I was pretty sure the wall at my back was the only thing holding us up.

"Fuck," he rumbled. "That shouldn't have happened here."

Like an ice-cold bucket of water had been thrown over me, clarity returned with force, and I wanted to scratch his face off. Somehow, I managed to keep my shit together.

"Let me down, Shadow," I said softly, not releasing my fury yet.

For once, he didn't argue, and when I was set on my feet, I swallowed another groan at the pain in my body. Pleasure and pain mingled together. My freaking jam, apparently.

As I slipped out from under him, Shadow dropped his head toward the wall for a second, like he was pulling himself together. He straightened not a few seconds later, so maybe it had been something else.

"Meet me in the dining hall in ten minutes," he bit out before he left the room in a flurry of energy, his coat flying out behind him, and for all I knew, his dick flapping in the icy breeze. Stupidly impressive dick.

On weak legs, I made my way back into the bath, and as I sank down, my body continued trembling from the aftershocks of the sex. I wondered if maybe that was the actual last time we'd ever be together like that.

He hadn't even gotten naked, so desperate, he'd only had his cock out and nothing else. There had been an urgency in his actions, like he couldn't help himself.

A darker thought followed.

At no point did he kiss me.

Not like he had the last time when he'd devoured my mouth, unable to get enough. There was a void between us that hadn't been there yesterday. A void I feared would only grow with time.

We've arrived and wait with Shadow.

I felt Midnight's presence the moment before it spoke, and that jolted me from the bath.

Meet you there. Give me five minutes to dress.

There was nothing to dry myself with, but that was proven redundant when I stepped into the center of the room, and a whirl of icy air all but spun me around. I hadn't been prepared for it, but the moment it hit me, the moisture on my skin and hair faded, leaving me feeling refreshed and clean, if not a touch frozen. And again, that drain on my power hit me briefly before I regrouped and got shit done.

Once I was dressed in the newly provided clothing, I noticed a small bag of toiletries that must have gone flying with Birdy. I was relieved to be able to brush my teeth and hair, which I then braided back to keep it out of the way.

I felt better approaching this day clean and ready for battle.

Walking through the solid wall, which was as weird as it sounded, I used the wall guides to find my way back to the main dining room. Shadow and Ixana were the first people I saw, in deep discussion, and what do you know... there was food between them.

Looked like they did eat on occasion.

My view was cut off by Angel, half-running and half-gliding across the wide space. She'd clearly been waiting on me, zooming over the moment I'd appeared. When her arms wrapped around me in a tight hold, I found more of my natural quirky disposition returning.

"I'll kill him," she murmured in my ear, her hold almost to the point of painful. "How dare he parade her in front of you!"

I had to chuckle at her ferocious nature. Since my father's death, I hadn't been able to trust new people, but Angel had blown through those barriers, and now I couldn't imagine my life without her.

This friendship might be the true love story here.

"It's fine," I said, not quietly, because why the hell was I protecting anyone else in this situation? "It's no secret that I was always just a side-chick until the frontrunner showed up."

I had no idea if Ixana heard me—she didn't stop chatting animatedly to Shadow—but *he* sure as fuck heard. The fire in his gaze drilled into me as he watched every step I took across the room, Angel at my side, and my confidence exactly where it should have been yesterday.

I'd had a moment of weakness in my room, fucking him again, but that was all it would ever be. A moment. I could never settle for the mistress position, while someone else held his heart and soul. I deserved better.

For the first time, I didn't let my eyes remain locked with his. I turned away.

Angel, the smartest and most observant being I knew, wrapped one arm around me as we walked toward the table.

"Never let him see he's getting to you," she murmured.

"Never," I parroted.

And in that moment, I meant it. Shadow hadn't been exactly warm with his "true mate" since our arrival, and he was clearly playing some sort of game. Until I knew my part in it, I had to be cautious with my approach. For my future sanity.

When we took our seats at the table, I looked toward the food, which was in a long line down the center of the crystal. There was absolutely nothing I recognized, but with the help of Angel and Midnight, who popped down from the ceiling long enough to wrap around me in a welcoming hug, I managed to find some food I would have eaten on Earth. Mostly the realm's equivalent of fruit and crackers. "They don't always eat, but when they do, it's definitely the good stuff," Angel told me. She, of course, still wasn't eating, but she did move a plate of food around.

Just like old times.

While eating, I drank about ten gallons of fresh water, my body needing replenishment in more ways than one, and the entire time I chatted to Angel, who told me about their dash across the realm to find us. "We had days over the water," she said with a huff, "and I would have been more than a little drained if Midnight hadn't allowed me to regenerate some energy through their network."

Thank you.

Midnight responded immediately. *Your family is my family.*

I honestly couldn't thank it enough. And while this unexpected bond had freaked me out at first, I felt differently now.

I'm so honored that you're part of my life. That we are bonded.

Midnight swelled larger and did a jiggling move with lots of sparks of its synapses.

The honor is mine.

We would work this bond out over time, and even in the short days we'd been together, I was growing used to the feel of its energy within mine.

Speaking of... "I felt you when you got closer," I told Angel, eating a soft "cheese" spread on a cracker. I hadn't bothered to ask what it really was because that would probably gross me out. I preferred to just enjoy the new experiences.

"You felt me how?"

I tapped my chest, swallowing the last bite. "In here, like a warmth that flared harder as you arrived in The Grey Lands."

Her smile was near-blinding. "I mean, we were warned about never bonding to any being not from Honor Meadows, but... I had a gut feeling, as your humans would say, and I went with it. The fast evolution of our bond is quite exciting for me; I think it speaks of a connection truly destined to exist between us."

"What warning did they give?"

She hesitated, reaching out to pick up a round, purple fruit that tasted like a melon but with large, passionfruit-like seeds. "Bonding allows our energies to intertwine, and over time, there's no telling what might result from that. It was a risk worth taking for me because there's another bonus of this bond. When I die, you will inherit my power, and since I have no line left to pass it on, it's imperative the power goes to one who is worthy. One I want to have my family's protection."

Tears sprang to my eyes, even though there was no reason to think Angel wouldn't be around for another few thousand years.

"I don't want your power," I whispered, my voice choked. "I just want you to always be alive."

She smiled. "I have no plans of going anywhere, but I like to be prepared. We always bond within our family, from birth actually, so no power is ever lost in our passing. I now have a millennia of family members' power, and it cannot die with me."

The odds of my immortal bestie dying before me was slim to none, but the fact that she considered me worthy of this honor, absolutely destroyed me.

"I love you," I said, throwing my arms around her. "But if you do ever die, I'm going to be pissed as fuck. I'll figure out a way to find your afterlife and kick your ass."

She laughed, returning my hug with the skill of someone who'd been hugging her entire life, when I knew for a fact, she was brand new to the experience.

"I love you too, Mera. You're the friend I never even knew I was missing in my life. You're my ride or die, and I will bury every body for you."

She was mixing Earth sayings like a pro there, and as a laugh of pure joy escaped me, I wondered why I even gave a fuck about Shadow.

This shit right here was what life was all about, and I was one lucky bitch to have it.

Chapter Thirty-Four

"**S**hould we head to the wall now?" Ixana was all business, her white robe trailing down her body as she stood before us. Her hair was out of the braid, styled up today, with a different silver crown.

She looked very put-together and I would have guessed she'd made a true effort to dress up for her mate. Couldn't blame a chick for that. Shadow was a catch, that was for sure, but no one would "catch" him with fancy clothes or hair. That wasn't how he rolled.

Not to mention, girlfriend had the most advantage of all, being his true mate. Fucking fate wanted to push those two together, and they would feel a bond and craving for the other, based just on a quirk in nature.

It was kind of a no-brainer, and yet, there was a distance between the pair that she hadn't managed to lessen. At least not yet.

No one answered her, but we all moved closer, which was an answer in itself. Angel and Midnight remained right at my side, and while Inky was with Shadow, the pair didn't walk with Ixana. She was out front with her two main guards.

Once we left the room, it was again into the mindfuck of a house.

"It's ingenious," Angel said, her eyes alight as she catalogued every twist and turn.

"Ingenious or insane," I muttered. "Jury is still out."

She just shook her head at me but couldn't answer because *the queen* was talking. "Once we reach the highest point in my castle," she called back, having just stepped onto a rather steep and winding marble staircase, "we will have to fly across to the wall. My guards can arrange transport for those..." She paused. "*Lacking the skills* to get themselves there."

In this group, that was probably only me. But if she thought I was allowing Birdy to fly me anywhere, she was out of her mind. I'd argue at the top, though, because I was currently busy trying to walk up the longest, trippiest—literally—set of stairs in the worlds. There was no handrail, and they were shiny with zero traction, and a very narrow lip on the upward curve. It was the sort of stairwell that could have been the end of me if Midnight and Angel weren't there to keep me on my feet. For a shifter who was not usually clumsy, it was an odd experience to be unable to gracefully ascend.

"Step closer to this side," Ixana said, appearing in front of me so fast, I was fairly sure she'd instantly transported. She leaned over to point to the side closer to the spiral, which looked way too small for my feet to fit. I mean, surely she knew that, since she was near a foot taller than me and had bigger feet. "It's another illusion to make the journey harder," she explained as I narrowed my eyes on her.

She then let out a nervous chuckle, turning and hurrying away. Staring after her, I really wanted to disregard her advice and move to the farthest spot from where she'd told me to step, but I also knew the value of not cutting my nose off to spite my face.

With that in mind, I decided to swallow my anger and pride, pretend I was the bigger person, and try what she suggested.

Almost immediately, it was easier. She'd been right about the illusion, which hid small grooves, allowing me to find the traction previously missing.

Damn her.

I had no idea what her game was, but she was playing well.

"Almost there," she called back a moment later. "You're doing great."

She might as well have given me a pat on the back and a "*Nice work, honey.*" I could hear the condescension in her tone, but since I was being a bigger person, I didn't reply with equal sarcasm. My wolf let out a howl of annoyance in my chest, and I had to remind her we were above such things.

All class, baby. We were all class.

By the time we reached the top, I was almost convinced this was a devious plot to kill us through hours of stairclimbing, but apparently, it was just how high the damn snowflake was.

When we exited onto a platform, the views were beyond spectacular. Or at least the initial view was, with Ixana's snow-touched kingdom spanning out around us, white and wintery, with snowflake houses, furred beings milling in the streets, and what looked like a... garden in the center. It was huge, and the entire setup reminded me of the images I'd seen of Central Park in New York City.

"This is Landor," she said, waving her hands around, and the icy breezes that had been buffeting us faded. Everything here obeyed her command, and I wondered if it was the power of Shadow's stone that allowed that. He'd said it was fairly useless until it bonded to the Supreme Being, but somehow, she'd figured it out.

I hadn't seen the stone again since that first time. She knew that keeping her leverage hidden away was her best chance of getting what she wanted. That in itself, was triggering all of my red-flag warnings about the queen, and her end game here.

"I have about five thousand of my *Clangors* here," she said proudly. "The beings made of my creation. It has taken more than a thousand years, but they're perfect now."

I held a hand up, and everyone looked at me like I was a fucking bug. Ignoring this, I said, "I have a question."

Shadow's lips twitched, and he shook his head, like he'd been expecting that all along. "Uh, yes," Ixana said.

"Is everyone in the Shadow Realm immortal?"

Why I'd waited so long to ask this, I had no idea. Maybe I'd just assumed because of Shadow that they were, but it had been well established he was a special snowflake—ha, ironic, considering what surrounded us—so it stood to reason that maybe there were those who died of old age here.

"It varies depending on the being," Shadow said, the rumble of his voice doing downright sinful things to me. "Many of the creatures are, and they pass this on to the royals who bind them. But the freilds, fronds, and other races all age and die."

Ixana nodded. "Oh, yes, the rest of the realm's inhabitants have a lifespan of maybe five hundred cycles."

"About five hundred years," Shadow translated her translation.

"So, you're immortal because of what?"

He met my gaze, and his eyes were actually sparkling in a way that told me he was amused as fuck. "Combination of Inky, the Solaris System, and... yeah, even shifters help boost my energy. Your power recharges my own."

Torin had picked up on that weakness. Warning him that he knew how to best the beast. What had his plan been, though? Kill all the shifters?

Knowing that stupid fuck, I probably wasn't far off.

"Okay, cool," I said, nodding at Ixana. "Proceed."

She blinked at me before turning back to her "perfect creation."

"As I said, this land is mine and I control every aspect of it, from the weather to the protective fences that keep my residents safe from the outside."

"Illusions," Shadow muttered.

Her lips twitched, and she nodded. "It protects us. You can't blame me for that."

There was a history there, but neither of them delved any deeper.

We shifted our view from the white landscape, moving on to what lay beyond. Now the barrier itself was actually super impressive —until this moment, I hadn't really seen the full effect of the snowflake fence. It was at least fifty feet high, with interlocked points on the flakes, the swirling patterns separating her land from the darker world beyond it.

A world we were about to step into.

"This is the birthplace of the shadow creatures in their purest form," Ixana said, "and I will take you to the center point from which they emerge. The point the two mists converge. Once we reach that place, we will have gathered our army.

Shadow cleared his throat. "And how do you propose we make it to that point without being torn to shreds? Not even I can take on the wild lands alone."

She grinned, a creepy sort of smile that made me think of a predator. "You can't, but *she* can..."

Her gaze turned to me, and when it did, so did everyone else's.

"No," I said. "No way in fucking hell. Why would I help you two take over the world here? I'm basically ready to head back to the Solaris System."

Shadow didn't look happy with my statement, but he wasn't the first to argue.

Ixana stepped toward me. "You're in my kingdom and will obey my rule."

Shadow cleared his throat, and ten to one, if he'd had a chance, he'd have been giving her the signal to shut up now. He knew better than any how well I took orders.

Ixana moved even closer, but Angel was between us in a flash, with her wicked curved blades in hand. Ixana was a smart little cookie, backing up immediately.

"Yeah. See, that shit doesn't fly with us," I told her conversationally. "I bow to no queen, and I obey no orders blindly. So unless you can give me a very good reason for why I should help you, I won't be."

Ixana, who had looked highly offended at those words, somehow managed to school her expression. "What if I told you that the answers you all seek to what and who you are can be discovered in this land? That, by heading to the original source of the creatures, you will unlock the part of you that's been hidden from sight? The part that allows you to control the creatures?"

Peering around Angel so I could assess Ixana's expression fully, I narrowed my eyes. "If you know, then just fucking tell me."

It was Ixana's turn to smile. "And why would I do that? As you've just said, what's in it for me?"

Well, fuck. "Touché, and with that in mind, I still won't be helping you."

"Sunshine."

He'd used my nickname in front of her, and even more than my need to know what this mysterious part of me was, was my need to help Shadow. Help him achieve a plan two thousand years in the making. Dammit. That was a truth I couldn't ignore or walk away from.

I looked at Angel, who had relaxed a little, her blades gone. She tilted her head, shooting me a sad smile. "Whatever you decide, I have your back. If you want to leave right now, we will..."

That would be the smart thing to do. Leave, never look back, and forget about the near perfect year spent with the shifter god. Only, this part of me screaming louder than the rest, wouldn't let me walk away.

"I promise nothing. But for now, I'll stay and see what's up."

"'See what's up...'" Ixana repeated. "How gracious of you."

"I know, right?" I smiled sweetly.

She had no fucking idea how gracious it really was.

Chapter Thirty-Five

Once we had our share of viewing the landscape from her tower, it was time to head to the wall for a more in-depth look. She went to call Birdy for me, but I shook my head. "I'll pass on the lift, thanks."

Midnight swelled up larger. *I can take you.*

Thank you! I appreciate you.

"My bonded mist is going to take me."

Her smile was brittle. "Great idea."

When Midnight swelled out, wrapping around me, it was like a warm hug and weighted blanket in one, and I felt secure and loved.

We should travel like this more, I thought as we soared over the landscape, many curious, furry faces looking up from below.

Our bond would like that. I would like that.

The mists were not sentient, literal beings, but the longer I was bonded to Midnight, the more it seemed to form its own identity. No wonder Inky always felt like a person in mist form. It'd had thousands of years to develop a strong sense of self.

When we reached the wall, my view was blocked at first by Midnight as it drifted down toward the path woven between the top tiers of the snowflake fence. This was where we landed, and as I stepped out to the edge, I found an uninterrupted view of the landscape beyond. "Fuck," I breathed.

Shadow's chest rumbled behind me, and I hadn't realized he was that close. I'd been too caught up with the view of The Grey Lands. Turning to see him, I shook my head. "Was it always like this?"

"I never made it here," he reminded me, "but I don't think it was." He faced Ixana. "What caused this destruction?"

It was a wasteland, with not a scrap of grass, or tree, or visible source of water. There was nothing except parched grey dirt. A deep, dirty grey that I would guess was a mixture of the elements of this land and decay. *The Grey Lands.*

This part at least, was exactly the way I'd imagined it.

"It's been on the decline for many years," Ixana said, her eyes focused on the landscape beyond us. "Even when you were still here. But it has continued to deteriorate, especially with Cristell abusing her power, taking more creatures, stripping the energy, and then... there's her."

And now she was looking at me.

"How do you figure?" I had my hands on my hips. "I've never even been to your world until now, so you're going to need to point fingers somewhere else."

Her face darkened, her next words coming out as a hiss. "Your energy. It was an energy that used to be in this land, and ever since it disappeared, the creatures have been out of control. The structure disappearing, their society falling, and it's one constant war against each other. Abervoqs rule the top of the power structure, and they are fine with killing everything." Her eyes flashed to Shadow. "You know how they get."

Meanwhile, I was over here having a minor freak out because I did not want any part in the destruction of this world or the creatures. Creatures I was drawn to protect.

"How do we fix this?" Angel asked, her ancient eyes heavier than ever.

Ixana's laugh was bitter. "We could kill this one and see if that works."

"This one" was definitely me, but fuck, it was a slow day when I didn't get at least one death threat, so I wasn't going to panic. Besides, I doubted anyone else here would support that plan.

Case in point. Angel's blades were against Ixana's throat. "You ever touch her, and I will kill you and every single being you control." She delivered these words with a cold, clinical promise.

I waited for Shadow to step in and save his mate—there were no guards here since Ixana had chosen to travel alone—but he didn't even twitch, choosing instead to watch it play out.

The ice queen had been looking to him for a save, judging by the way her pupils shifted between Shadow and Angel, and when no rescue appeared, her lips trembled. "I am no threat to the wolf," she choked out. "I was just offering a suggestion for the most likely way to fix the situation."

Shadow growled. "No one touches Mera. Ever. If her death is required, then this world will continue to fall. It's as simple as that."

Well, fuck. It was hard to hate someone who was willing to sacrifice worlds for me.

Angel took her time withdrawing the weapons, and when they finally disappeared into her magical pockets, Ixana rubbed at her throat. There wasn't a mark on it, due to the sheer skill and control of Angel.

"Then we have no choice but to journey to the original source," Ixana finally said, sounding bitter. "To find out for ourselves where the destruction is originating. I've never been to *The Nexus,* the spot of convergence, but it has to hold answers. Maybe here we will find our army and figure out how to heal this land."

The Nexus. All of a sudden, I was desperate to go there.

"And you think I can do this?" I asked. "Bond the creatures and form an army?"

She didn't want to look at me; it obviously cost her something to turn my way. "Yes. I think you're the missing link, and even if you're not willing to sacrifice yourself to save this land, there could be another solution. I just won't know what it is until we get there."

I didn't miss the digs. The not-so-subtle way of calling me selfish. I think we all knew she just wanted my death to get me out of the way, though, and there was one seven-foot-tall reason for that.

"Let's do it!" I said with fake excitement. "I live to save worlds. It's my calling, and I so appreciate you making this happen for me."

Ixana didn't know what to do with that, staring blankly at me like I was crazy. A tried and tested response to a bully was to confuse them with your enthusiasm for their bullshit.

"Okay, well, I will call for supplies," Ixana choked out, "and once we have that at our disposal, we should head straight out."

"How will we travel?" Shadow asked.

She sidled closer to him, her eyes focused with laser intensity on his face. "We cannot use any sort of energy near the Nexus. Our aim is to go in slow and secretive, gather the creatures who cross our path on the way, and by the time we reach the place of their birth, we'll have an army at our disposal to deal with whatever we encounter there. I have only watched the chaos from the outside; all of my power used to keep my world safe here. I've been waiting for you to return so that we could face this together."

How. Fucking. Sweet.

She placed her hand on his arm, and my wolf growled so deeply in my chest that a little of the sound escaped my mouth. Both of their heads swung toward me, but I was already looking out to the depressing landscape, my face devoid of any emotion.

I would never let either of them know how much this was affecting me. Never.

If it fucking killed me, I would get through this trial with a smile on my face.

And hopefully answers about myself would be my reward.

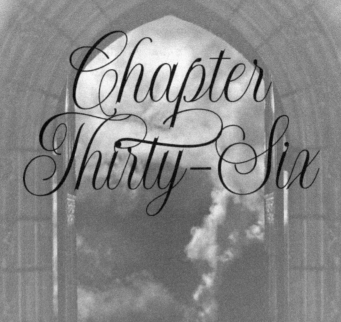

Chapter Thirty-Six

Ixana's guards arrived soon after, weighed down with dark brown crossbody bags. The design looked awkward until it was on, and then the evenly distributed weight had it resting comfortably. The outside of the bag was thick and coarse, made from what appeared to be dried plant, and they felt strong and durable. Easily able to carry the supplies inside.

"There is food," she said. "Mainly for those who are a little weaker." *Dig, dig.* "And some padded rugs, for those who require extra rest." *Dig, dig, dig.* "Hopefully, it won't be too heavy."

"Oh, you are just the sweetest soul to ever live," I said with a broad smile. "Bless your heart."

I'd never lived in the south, but I watched television, and I enjoyed using hidden digs against her too.

"Oh, okay," she said, moving herself to perch on the wall. "Shall we leave then?"

"We shall," I replied grandly.

She smiled, a slow, devious bullshit sort of smile, and then she stepped off the side, landing smoothly, even though it had been a quarter of a mile drop at least. No way I could top that, and frankly, I was growing exhausted by this imaginary rivalry I'd created with her.

"Would you like help down?" Shadow drew my attention, and as I tilted my head back to see him, I was surprised to notice the fatigue just visible around his eyes. Shadow always seemed larger than life, and as an immortal, he'd never look old, but he was weighed down.

I wasn't helping the situation acting like a child.

"Midnight can take me," I said softly, shooting him a small smile. "I'll see you at the bottom."

He reached out and brushed his thumb across my cheek, before he leaned in closer. "Ixana is up to something," he murmured in his low rumble, "and I'm sorry that I screwed up when we first arrived here. In not wanting to tip her off, I hurt you, and that's not okay. I promise I won't do it again."

Before I could reply... or catch my damn breath, he turned and stepped off the side. I watched him all the way, and when he landed as smoothly as Ixana, I turned to Angel, blinking rapidly. "Holy shit, did he just say that?"

He'd been so open and honest. The secretive side that was so much a part of his personality fading out briefly as he shared a truth with me. And he'd apologized. Two guesses how often that usually happened.

"Despite our differences, I have a lot of respect for Shadow," Angel said, her gaze drifting over the side to look below. "It's worth trusting him to do the right thing. He knows how to handle Ixana."

She wasn't wrong, but a part of me still wondered if he might be a little blinded by the true mate bond. It was a strong connection, as I knew all too well. But at least I hadn't completely lost him to her, and that was worth taking the next step forward. Worth having a little faith. Even if there was still one rather large issue in our midst... Ixana.

"Hopefully this entire journey isn't a trap set by the Queen of Illusions," I said wearily, feeling as ancient as Shadow.

Angel considered my words. "She's definitely up to something, but it feels a lot like that *something* is about Shadow and their mate bond."

"I agree, and truth be told, I really do want to know if my weird-ass power is from this Nexus."

Angel nudged me. "You're not weird. And you are worthy of Shadow. Don't lose sight of either of those facts in this quest you're on."

She took off along the side of the wall, gliding down even more gracefully than the other two. Inky had gone after Shadow, so all that was left was Midnight and me. As the mist swirled around me, brushing our energies together, I let out a sigh to rival Shadow's.

I've acted like an idiot, I told the mist, *and Angel hit the damn nail on the head. It was my insecurities causing me to act so defensively and childish. And for what? I wouldn't want a man because I got him through underhanded vindictive means. If Shadow was meant for me, he would be with me.*

Midnight's reply was immediate. *You are too hard on yourself. Angel uses her millennia of knowledge to form these conclusions, and she is not in love. Love is neither rational nor calm. You have acted completely in character, and it was nice for Shadow to see someone fighting for him, even in your roundabout way of doing it. He appreciates that.*

That gave me pause. *Have you been talking to Inky?*

Where else would its insight into what Shadow might appreciate have come from?

There was an almost indignant huff. *We converse when required.*

That made me laugh. *You'll be old friends before long and maybe that's step one to lessening the divide between the two mists.*

Another huff told me everything I needed to know about Midnight's thoughts on that.

"Come on," I said out loud. "They'll be waiting for me."

Midnight wrapped its warmth around me, hugging me tightly, before it picked me up and carried me right over the edge. As we soared up and then out from the wall, all I could see was the grey landscape, and far off in the distance was a glut of creatures. So many that my nerves soared to the same height as Midnight. They were vastly overestimating my abilities if they thought I could control that many creatures.

You have done it before, and you will again.

It had required me to lose control of my wolf, though, and the difficulty of hauling her back after that incident still frightened me.

When we finally landed, Ixana glared at me. "Took you long enough! We don't have time to sightsee. This is extremely important, and you're treating the entire venture like you're on vacation."

My first reaction was to remind her that she needed me more than I needed her, but since I was trying out this *not being a jealous hag* thing, I just smiled. "Sorry about that. Midnight and I had a chat and then it took me on the scenic route. Hopefully, that few-minutes delay won't cause too much issue."

Ixana huffed. "I'm sure it will be fine. We're losing daylight hours, but a few minutes is okay."

I didn't argue, just tightened my side-bag. In all honesty, an excited buzz had started between my wolf and me at the thought we might finally have some answers. Like, how did we control the flames? How did we control the shadow creatures? Why did we feel a bond to a land we'd never been to until now?

If there were answers here, then I wanted them. I needed them.

"Are you not bringing any guards?" Angel asked Ixana. "They can't be happy about you venturing beyond the wall without them."

Frustration was the defining emotion on the royal's face. "I'm their queen. Sometimes they need a little reminder of that. Besides"— her smile grew larger, smug even—"I'm not alone. I have my true mate, and no one can protect me better than the one who was born to that position."

It hurt. It really fucking hurt. But I didn't snap back with something smartass. I just remained silent, my gaze outward as I examined the world we were about to step into.

Being a bigger person sucked. The end.

From above, The Grey Lands had looked barren, and down here was no better. Unlike in the lava fields, there was no current of power beneath the surface here, either. Something was sapping this particular land of its power, and eventually, it would kill the creatures. Why didn't the royals care about that? If the creatures fell, so would their power and immortality.

Frustrated with everything I was learning, I marched forward with Midnight at my side. I didn't bother to wait for the others, instinct driving me into this land.

When I was half a dozen steps in, I felt Shadow at my back. "Where are you going?" he asked. "You don't know the way to the Nexus."

"I feel it," I said softly. "In the same place the path to this world originates within my own energy. So, yeah, I do know the way... I just don't know why I know the way."

My path must have been the right one because Ixana didn't argue, falling in behind us. She tried at first to engage Shadow in conversation, but he was not in the mood. She didn't know that about him yet, of course, but when he was like this, you might as well chat with a brick wall. All you'd get were some annoyed grunts and rumbles. The big fucker did not handle inane chatter at the best of times. Let alone when he was mulling shit over in his head.

Of course, usually I took that on as a challenge, but today, Ixana was the one with incessant questions and comments. I kept waiting for Shadow to demand she shut up, like he did with me, but that moment never came. He even fucking answered her on occasion, and once again, I was battling stupid jealousy.

After some time, I started to pray for creatures to appear, anything to break up the bonding that Shadow and his mate appeared to be doing. Despite his earlier words, if he was playing a part, he was doing it all too well.

Maybe I can call the creatures to me.

Midnight brushed over my shoulder, hearing that thought

through our connection. It wasn't exactly mind reading, but when I projected something loud enough, it traveled along our bond.

You can definitely call them. Might be a good experiment.

Drawing from the energy guiding me on this journey, I closed my eyes briefly, tugging on the power, like one would with a dog leash, pulling them closer. At first, I thought it failed, because we were still just trudging through a land without a single creature in sight, until...

"Oh, no!" Ixana exclaimed. "They're never this close to my city. My repelling spell is designed to detract them."

Oh, whoops.

A line of shadow creatures appeared in the distance, all the same species, and it was one I knew very well. *Abervoq.* One of the most dangerous creatures that could exist. Apparently.

The one I'd met on Earth had been the same height as Shadow, but the group approaching us now was more varied. All of them had the same general look, with their top halves like bulls'—horns, snouts, large eyes—and their bottom halves akin to shaggy bears. Their fur, for the most part, was dark like the abervoq from Earth, but there was a huge variation in the shades. Some falling more toward brown, and others almost blue-black.

Ixana had stopped walking, and I was fairly certain she was hiding behind Shadow. "There are too many abervoqs to best without having first gathered other creatures," she whimpered.

Shadow didn't answer her, but his flames had appeared, so he wasn't completely comfortable with this, either. "Mera, get behind me," he said.

Yeah, that wasn't going to happen. I'd called these damn creatures for a reason, and while I hadn't been aiming for the highest echelons of the creature chain here, this was what I had to deal with. Time to see if I could put my power to actual use.

My energy flowed from me as I drew them forward, having not a fucking clue what I was supposed to do, but working on instinct anyway. Seemed instinct was all I had these days.

"Mera!" he snapped. "What the hell are you doing?"

I couldn't tear my eyes from the line of abervoqs, but I did manage to answer him. "We want this dealt with as quickly as possible, right? Well, if I can control them, then we'll have the strongest at our disposal for the rest of the journey."

Maybe this was a blessing in disguise—if these guys were the baddest of the bunch, might as well start with them. I didn't like the thought of bonding them when I wanted their freedom above all else, but for now, there was no other option. This was step one in securing their freedom. I sensed it deep inside, in the energy of the realm.

"You have no idea what you're doing," Shadow bit out, trying to grab hold of me. Midnight got in his way, swelling up into a massive cloud of mist. I heard more curses, but I could no longer see the beast.

Midnight remained at my back as I strolled forward alone—the others blocked by my mist, which was sparking like crazy in its huge cloud form. Angel wasn't happy about it, if her shouting was any indication, but I was already on this path, instinct still pushing me forward.

My wolf surged to the surface, and as we dropped our head back and howled, I felt a partial shift come over me. The howl continued, even as my jaw elongated, and when that happened, the tone of my cry changed. Power flowed with it, and I remembered clearly howling this exact same way back in Torma... when I knocked the wolves down.

The creatures cowered before me, and it was a powerful, heady feeling to stand above such strong beings who feared me. Caught up in the power, I didn't flinch as they knelt before me; instead, I walked between them, pressing my hands to each of their bull heads.

The moment I touched them, there was a zap between us, and I knew they were mine. Mine to control. Mine to protect. Mine to save. I just had to figure out how to restore what had been lost in this land. And how to stop the royals from using the creatures for their own gains. Ironic, yes, when I had to use them at this minute, but I would not hold them forever.

They would walk free here again, if it was the last thing I did.

It felt like a mission I'd never known existed, but now that this realization had hit me, it was clear and strong: there was no other destiny for me. My mind was consumed in a way I'd only felt once before, when I'd touched the spelled door to the Shadow Realm. When the darkness had crept into my being, and while I'd expunged most of it, it had left this small crack in my soul—the only way I could think to describe it. Like a sliver of space, waiting to be filled so I would once again be complete.

This was what had to take its place, my destiny as protector of the shadow creatures.

Protector. Guardian. *Mother.*

The abervoqs brayed before me, and I threw my head back and joined them, my wolf still riding across my skin in our partial shift. Nothing was going to interrupt this bonding session, or so I thought until a flaming beast smashed through Midnight's shield and landed snarling on the ground before me.

"Holy fuck," I breathed, the words garbled around my wolf jaw.

I'd waited what felt like an eternity to see Shadow's true form, and now that I had, there was so much, I almost couldn't take him all in.

A monster shrouded in darkness.

He had a huge wolf head, humanoid-shaped body, with thick, curved legs beneath him, and the entirety of his being was on fire. A flaming wolf, but like the ancient god version of it, and when those black orbs of eyes met mine, he stalked forward.

He stood at least six feet taller than I did, at the largest size I'd ever seen from him, but even when he moved closer, I felt no fear.

A connection sprang to life between us, like it had been waiting for us to meet in these forms. Shadow and I were alike, in so many ways, and only now, as his power reached for mine and he attempted to wrest me back from what he believed was the darkness here, did I truly see our similarities.

The abervoqs rose, ready to defend me against a beast whom I knew could destroy them all. Shadow was still the ultimate power and had very little to fear here, except for his true mate. Now that I was connected to the power of this land, I saw her darkness. She had been stealing from the land and creatures for years to power her own world, and whatever her game was now, I was going to figure it out.

This army was not hers. And I would be using it to ensure that no creatures ever had to be prisoners again. Shit was going to change around here.

I was the reckoning the royals had never seen coming.

Chapter Thirty-Seven

"Mera," Shadow rumbled, his voice even deeper in this form. His accent was slightly stronger too.

I examined the wolf god, finally realizing whom he reminded me of. The most epic version of Anubis, the Egyptian god, and I wondered if maybe Shadow had been rocking around Ancient Egypt to spread some rumors back in the day. *God of Death* would be kind of appropriate for Shadow, especially before he invented shifters and technically became a god of life.

"Mera!" he snapped this time, since I had spaced.

"Shadow!" I shot back. Dude better find some more words if he wanted me to understand.

"What are you doing? Why did you block me out?"

It felt a little like hurt threaded his anger; I'd shut him out and he'd not reacted well to it. He'd had to delve into his deepest energy to break through Midnight, and for me, he'd done that.

He also changed into the true beast form when you were hit with the scourge, Midnight told me. *You missed it.*

I wasn't actually surprised by that, even if I was a touch sad to have missed it.

It's okay, I told my mist then, noticing it was still blocking the others. *Let them through.*

It did, and at the same time, the energy binding me to my wolf and creatures eased, and I was able to return to my human form. The bond between me *and all the things* remained, though.

Angel rushed through first, her gaze darting briefly toward Shadow, and I saw her sharp look at his Anubis form. Shadow didn't give her much of a chance to see it, releasing the fire and returning to his gorgeous man version. It happened so quickly, I was fairly certain only Angel even saw anything.

Ixana, who arrived a few seconds later, rushed straight to his side, glaring at me all the way. "Are you okay?" she burst out, running her hands across his chest.

Shadow, eyes like burning fields, didn't acknowledge her. He just stared at me over her head, and there was a chokehold of emotion in his expression that I didn't understand.

"Mera! I should beat the crap out of you!" Angel shook me, and I gave her the attention she rightfully deserved.

"I'm so sorry," I got out in a rush. "Instinct kind of took over."

She shook me again, with a little less force, and the abervoqs reared up behind us, clearly not liking her handling of me.

"It's okay," I said to them, sending soothing energy along our connection. "This is my family. *Tresorana.*"

This was a word from Honor Meadows, but it apparently translated. The creatures calmed almost immediately, and when I returned my focus to Angel, she looked taken aback. Her face... The depth of feeling there tore through me, and I hugged her tightly. "Please don't die," she whispered to me. "I can't lose another member of my family."

Jesus. Fuck. I wasn't strong enough to stop the single tear from escaping, and I felt her sorrow. "I promise to do everything in my power to never leave you."

It was a promise I had to keep. No matter what.

Shadow finally brushed his fussing mate off, after way too long in my opinion, and crossed to me. This got the abervoqs riled up again, clearly none of them forgetting what he'd been a few moments ago.

"Calm," I said, and like freaking magic, they all just settled. Although they did move closer to my back, forming a very tall line of defense.

"You are exactly what I expected," Ixana said, looking at me with something akin to satisfaction before she examined the creatures. "The moment I felt your power enter the realm, I knew you were the one who could tame the creatures."

How fucking convenient that she would just feel and know me. My *evil bitch* radar was in overdrive, and even though she was Shadow's mate, it was time for me to remind her that no longer would she be able to spread her malignancy in this land.

My wolf broke free briefly, her howl aimed directly at the ice queen. Ixana saw me coming and her energy snapped out at me, an attack of sorts, but it slid off my skin like I was covered in magic-repelling oil.

"What is wrong with you?" she snarled, panic crossing her features when it was clear she had nothing to stop me. "We're on the same side. Have you lost your damn mind?"

Another snarl and howl. "You have built your world on the blood of these creatures," I said coldly, my words echoing like I had a megaphone. "I will no longer let their sacrifices fuel your success. No more."

Ixana spluttered. "I had no choice. If I didn't create my world here, the royals would have killed me."

I snapped out with a burst of energy, but Shadow intercepted it, and when he winced, I knew that would have really hurt Ixana. Still, why the fuck had he gotten involved? Trying to save his damn mate.

"You should have died rather than use and abuse creatures just trying to survive."

Ixana opened and closed her mouth. "I don't... I promise if you help us build the army to best the royals, we will no longer use their power."

Easy promise to make since she expected to be ruling The Concordes with Shadow.

Shadow side-eyed her, and he was lucky I still wanted his ass around, or I would have blasted him again. "Royals need the creatures," he reminded her.

Ixana, fear still pulling at her features, choked out a reply. "We don't. The way you have bonded with the mists is how we will continue to rule. That was the old way, at least according to all the research I've done over the years. The royal's bond to the creatures became a quicker way to achieve it, since they are born directly from the Nexus. But it doesn't have to be that way."

I released my power, and she started to splutter. "This is my mission now," I said. "To help you rebuild the power structure of this world, so there's no need for the use and abuse of the shadow creatures. The Grey Lands will one day flourish again."

And I would be keeping a very close eye on her until that came to fruition.

Wrapping my hand around Angel's, I walked off, bringing a dozen creatures with us. "You were born to change this world," my friend said with conviction. "It was that odd energy I felt about you from the start. It's creation energy. Mist born." She shook her head, like she couldn't believe it. "If I hadn't thought it impossible, as no one has been to this world for thousands of years, I would have seen it immediately."

This time, I didn't bother to argue with her. "Now that I'm here, I feel a potential that has been locked away. Waiting for me to become what I was always meant to."

I didn't understand how it all worked, or how I could still be a shifter and have a true mate in Torma pack. Two worlds had collided in a way that had formed *whatever* I was. And yeah, I didn't know how, but maybe the Nexus would hold answers.

Shadow was quiet, but he never took his eyes off me as we continued on through the land. It was a depressing journey, and I was furious when I saw the abervoqs near starving, having to dig into the dead ground to try to find sustenance. How many of them had perished this way?

"Can they die from starvation?" I asked quietly when we stopped to let them forage. "Like, a lack of nutrition or water?"

"No," Ixana said. "They will be weakened, but it's not going to kill them."

Even better, they got eternal suffering.

"We need to find sustenance for them," I said with enough force in my tone that they knew I would not be swayed. "Is it blood they need?"

Shadow looked between the creatures and me again. "They're sustained now through you," he said slowly, his gaze drifting along my body before he followed the ground between me and the creatures. "It's a clear connection." There was a flash of fire in his eyes. "You must not let them take too much and drain you."

I was feeling a little exhausted, but I'd thought that was a normal part of this journey. It had been lingering on and off since I'd made it to The Grey Lands.

Ixana scoffed. "She won't. It's a relationship that goes both ways, a circular bond. Mera will gain as much as she loses."

"She should lose nothing," Shadow snapped, and Ixana was taken aback. Pretty sure he hadn't shown her his more growly side yet, and if her expression was any indication, this was an unwelcome introduction.

I didn't care about some loss, if my creatures were okay. And sure enough, as time went on, their color started to darken up until they were all in shades of blue-black. It was then that I understood that the browner tones had been weakness.

When we finally reached our campground for the night, we rolled out small padded mats on the ground. It felt good to rest, and I spent my time snacking on a few cocoa flavored energy bars, drinking water, and watching as the others did their "absorb energy" thing.

In a land already dying, it wasn't ideal, but they had no choice.

Maybe by the time I was done with them, they'd find themselves a lot closer to humans in how they recharged their energy. Unless all of them could bond to the mists, like Shadow had.

Which made me think... *Are you helping sustain me and the creatures?*

Midnight drifted down from where it had been up high. Always floating above the land, which made sense for an ether mist. *Of course. I finally understand why we're bonded. You called me because you needed my strength. And now it is yours.*

Thank you. I've taken your strength for granted, but I am so grateful for you and our bond.

Warmth traveled along to me, and I knew that was the closest a mist could get to human emotions... It made me feel loved.

Sleep came quickly, and since Ixana felt fairly certain we wouldn't be accosted by creatures here—still too close to her city—I slept solidly. At least I did until I felt a hand brush across my body. It was a familiar touch, one that had woken me in a garden in Faerie what felt like a million years ago.

This time, I opened my eyes in an instant, looking for Shadow. Pushing myself up, I saw Angel in her stasis-like sleep beside me as she recharged. Other than Angel, I was surrounded by a circle of abervoqs, who slept in a wall of protectiveness between me and the outside world.

They hadn't been like that when I'd gone to sleep, and to see it made me a little emotional. Once I moved past my new buddies, with their bullish snores, I found myself searching for him again. It took more than a minute, probing the semi-darkness that had fallen across The Grey Lands. Not a true night, but some sort of twilight, which I'd been told would last a few hours.

Finally, I found the beast himself, standing in a mist of shadows. It wasn't Inky. It was the literal smoky energy that formed Shadow. Carefully stepping over the creatures, I crossed to where he was, and even though his true mate was sleeping nearby, I couldn't help but meet him in the middle when his mouth descended to mine.

He swallowed my moan as he jerked me up against him, my legs wrapped around his body, and we kissed like it was the last fucking time.

Again.

It was dangerous, kissing near his true mate, and I'd feel bad about it, but he'd been mine when he'd gotten here, and that hadn't seemed to lessen yet. There was one thing I had to know first...

I wrenched my mouth away, my lips feeling bruised. "Have you fucked her?"

"No," he murmured, his lips on mine again. "I told you, this time with Ixana is so I can figure out what her game is, and more importantly how to get my fucking stone back." His smile was brief as it curved the corner of his lips. "Even if it wasn't, there's no room for her in my head when a certain redhead is dominating every damn thought."

My pussy spasmed. Like legit tried to jump out of my clothing and onto Shadow's cock.

But there was apparently one more thing I had to know. "Will you help me save the creatures?"

"I will," he murmured, and that was all I needed.

Shadow moved, with me still wrapped around him, and we faded back into the darkness, Inky swelling up around us as a protective shield. "It will block noise from the others," he told me, his tone a normal rumble. "Don't hold back."

I had zero plans to do that.

Shadow stripped our clothes off in a rush of magic, and when I reached for his cock, the beast stopped me before I could get a good hold. "You first," he said against my skin, his lips kissing a path down my throat. "I need to taste you first."

I was panting. One would be embarrassed by that if one wasn't too fucking horny to see straight.

"I knew you touched me in the garden in Faerie," I huffed as he slowly lowered my feet to the ground, his lips following the path of his hands.

"You looked so perfect, sleeping," he murmured against my skin, "surrounded by Len's plants. I couldn't *not* touch you."

I moaned as he kissed my stomach, on his knees before me. He was so close to my aching center that I started to rock my hips, needing some relief. Just as Shadow's lips skimmed my clit, he lifted his head and stood again.

"Wait, what?" I complained, but the rest of my words were cut off as he wrapped one arm around me and jerked me higher. He kept a tight hold on me, and using his free hand, parted my folds, finding the moisture already pooling there. Sliding one finger inside, followed by another, he curled them up in the most delicious move that allowed him to rub right along my g-spot.

I'd never felt that particular angle before; it was not one I could really reach myself, and as he started to slide his fingers in and out, slowly, over and over in a relentless assault, my arousal near covered his hand.

And I was about to scream.

Over and over, the buildup achingly slow, but the intensity was beyond anything I'd felt before. It was almost too much, my thigh muscles quivering so badly that if I'd been holding my own weight, I would have collapsed.

"Shadow, please," I begged.

He just kissed me, devouring my lips, while his fingers destroyed my pussy. The quivering in my thighs increased, and as a whimpering scream escaped, he slowed his assault and removed his fingers.

Breathing was hard as I struggled to fill my lungs, and as he gracefully dropped to his knees, one hand went under me to keep me standing, the other returned to my pussy, those long fingers finding my g-spot once more.

As I cried out, his mouth landing on my clit. He was always a fucking genius with that tongue, but this time, he had a new move. He sucked that ball of pleasure into his mouth, and without allowing any break in pressure, worked me with his tongue, while his fingers stroked inside.

Low, sobbing cries fell from my mouth as I lost all ability to stand or control myself. The buildup was powerful, so different to anything I'd ever felt before, and I had the weirdest thought that I was about to do something embarrassing. Shadow sucked my clit even harder, stroking his fingers inside, and in the same moment, the ball of intensity building in my body detonated.

I came.

But it was like no orgasm I'd ever had before.

Cum literally shot out of me in a gushing load, and I was about to freak out, but Shadow's chest rumbled, a pleased tone emerging from him as he removed his fingers so he could bury his face in my pussy, licking and cleaning up every fucking last ounce of my pleasure. In that time, I managed to orgasm again, and it was nothing short of spectacular.

"Holy fuck," I said when he got off his knees, one hand remaining on me—the only thing keeping me standing. "I didn't know I could come like that."

His smile was predatory. "You will come like that every fucking time now, Sunshine."

For once, this was a command I was more than willing to obey.

Chapter Thirty-Eight

What was it about orgasms that rendered a person all soft and gooey? Shadow and I were hardly the cuddly types... we'd never cuddled once in all our time together. But after that soul-destroying orgasm, I felt like I could wrap myself around him and go to sleep.

Well, at least that was what I thought before he fisted a handful of my hair, holding my head still so he could kiss me long and hard, and I could taste my pleasure on his lips. Fuck if that didn't make this kiss way more intense.

"You ready, Sunshine?"

I gasped, choking out some words that sounded a lot like *oh, my fucking yes, yes, yes*. Shadow's smile was wicked, and again he kissed me with the sort of intense passion that I'd only ever dreamt of experiencing. Shadow's brutality tempered with just enough gentleness apparently did it for me, and I would forever compare other men to him. No doubt always finding them wanting.

"Stop thinking," he ordered, and as his grip in my hair tightened, he used his other hand to spin me around. I gasped as he slowly pushed me over, inch by inch, until my ass was exposed in the air before him.

Shadow's power lifted me so he could fuck me this way, and I felt the head of his cock push against my still-pulsing pussy. "Please," I gasped, trying to wiggle back on him.

He chuckled, a deep rumble, and I moaned. He held me still, and the force was enough to have my stomach clenching and toes curling as air huffed in and out of me. He pushed inside another inch, so he only had a billion more to go, and I wanted to feel the full freaking length. I needed it.

"Your pussy is the best fucking thing I've ever felt or tasted." Shadow growled. "And it belongs to me."

"Yes," I gasped. "It's yours. Just fuck me."

The hand that had been firmly pressed to my back started to move, sliding down my spine, bringing with it the burn of his power, and as it mingled with my own, I was about a moment from coming again. Shadow leaned over and another inch entered me; this was torture, but I was *definitely not* going to complain.

Another inch, and another, until I was panting over his dick like a bitch in heat. This was what I'd always promised myself I'd never do, but who had known it was going to be like this? Definitely not me.

"Our demons match, Sunshine," he murmured, and I could have sworn he leaned over to press a kiss along my spine, just as he plunged the last of his length inside. The stretching burn had me choking on my next breath, and when he pulled out and slammed into me again, I started to moan and couldn't stop.

He was relentless, slamming into me, his power keeping me from flying forward with each forceful thrust. The orgasm building was just as intense as before, but different. This time it was fast and earth-shattering. When I came screaming around his cock, he just let out a satisfied laugh, not stopping for a moment.

Fucking demon. But fuck, he was good at what he did.

By the time he finally came with me, I was basically dead. "Just roll me over and throw a towel on me," I moaned, barely able to open my eyes. "I'm done-ski."

His power turned me so he could hold me close, and in a brief moment of sweetness, his energy cleaned me up, redressed me, and then I was once again on my mat beside Angel surrounded by my creatures.

Sleep claimed me in seconds, but just before I was unconscious, I could have sworn I felt lips press to mine. *"Our souls match, Sunshine."*

It was a whisper on the winds, and when I woke the next morning, I knew I'd imagined it. Because souls matching was so much more than our demons matching. It was the building of true mates, and one thing I knew for certain was Shadow and I might have sexual compatibility, but our true mates were other beings.

Fate was fucked sometimes.

"WE'LL SOON BE COMING along the main territory of multiple species of creatures," Ixana said the next morning. She'd been particularly snarky since we'd gotten up, and I wondered if somehow she knew about Shadow and me. I mean, Inky had been blocking us, and I doubted that she was able to get around its power, but there was a chill in her already icy eyes that was much more pronounced than usual.

And I gave zero fucks. She didn't own Shadow. Until they had an actual relationship, *she* was the other woman. *Mine first.*

"I should be able to handle whatever comes our way," I said, "especially with the abervoqs on my side."

They all brayed and there was a strength and vitality about them now that had been missing yesterday when I'd found them. My energy was powering theirs, and Midnight was powering all of us—this was what I'd lacked back in Torma when I'd called the mists and creatures. I hadn't had Midnight.

This is why we bonded, it repeated.

I agreed completely. Midnight had come to me because I'd needed the strength of the mists to complete my life task. There was no going back now; in truth, there had been no going back from the first moment I'd lost my mind and touched the shadow world.

As Ixana had predicted, we started to run into more creatures. The intensity picked up the farther we got from her land, and I was absolutely disgusted by the state of them. Weak and tired. Broken and weary.

It took next to no effort to bond them to me, and even though many of them were mortal enemies of each other, they didn't fight when they were connected in my net of power. Each time it took some power from Midnight and me, but we were also getting energy back from the healed beings, until eventually there was a veritable hum in the air.

By the time we were starting to slow for the day, I had a hundred or so various creatures following in a long line across the dead land. I had not eaten or drunk a single thing all day, either, and it was the weirdest sensation, since I felt no need for sustenance. I was exhausted but satisfied.

"You're starting to self-sustain," Angel said, sounding impressed. "It's usually a sign of an increase in power and immortality. In your situation, I don't know for sure what it means."

I nodded. "I have no idea. I mean, I'm not even hungry! What the fuck is up with that? So trippy."

Angel shot me an amused look. "The trippiest."

She was pretty good with my random Earth slang, but it still made her laugh. I liked making her laugh.

"We should stop for a rest," Ixana called, shutting down any further conversation. "There are more than enough creatures in our army now to keep us safe."

Our army? Not even in her wildest dreams. But I'd play the game until such a time it wasn't convenient for me to do so.

We set up camp, and Angel was once again at my side, along with my original abervoqs. I kind of liked the safety and security that came from this new life; not even once had I been overwhelmed with all the energy or noise. If anything, I'd feel desperately alone without it.

But there was a sense of loss already creeping into my being, the knowledge that it was all temporary. I was living someone else's life at the moment and eventually reality would come crashing right back in.

Chapter Thirty-Nine

The next day continued on the same way. We walked and I collected creatures—I had to be near the back now so the army could spread out behind me. Shadow and Ixana stayed close to me, which was frustrating, since I had been trying to avoid the pair of them since Shadow had fucked me within an inch of my life.

Today I was "lucky" enough to hear their conversation.

"Remember when we were kids?" Ixana said with a laugh, warm to him when she iced everyone else out. "Your sister used to torment us both and we'd hide in that massive maze near your family's home."

Shadow's rumbling laugh had a familiarity in it, as he too got caught up in past memories. "I should have known Cristell was an evil bitch even back then. She would take any opportunity to hurt me. Or get me into trouble. Her favorite pastime was calling me the 'little maggot heir.'"

Ixana didn't laugh. "Yes, she was always horrible. Jealous and spiteful about the fact you were born to inherit the ultimate power, while she'd always exist under her younger sibling in power. It was what drove her crazy in the end."

I couldn't see Shadow's face, but I knew that tense set to his muscles. "My mother was the only one I could trust," he said. "It's been the hardest part of being locked from the realm. Not so much the loss of my destined power, but the loss of her."

Ixana placed her hand on his shoulder, and I forced myself to look at my feet, watching the small splatters of dust kick up under my boots. Shadow had been procuring me new clothes throughout the days, but the boots were a staple.

"Your mother was the one who helped me escape," she said softly. "Because she knew one day you'd return and with me at your side, we would take Cristell down."

And that, ladies and gentlemen, was how a soul shattered.

I mean, not mine, of course, because I was made of tougher stuff than that. But all the ladies who thought they could tame the beast god were currently sobbing into their pillows.

"How long since you've seen her?" Shadow asked.

Ixana finally removed her hand, shaking her head at the same time. "Not since that day, so thousands of cycles ago. I heard rumors that she went missing, and I wondered if maybe your sister managed to get rid of the rest of your family who felt any sort of connection to you."

Shadow's flames burst to life, a fierce burn that sent heat shooting out around us. Ixana leapt away, clearly not enjoying his fiery side. Meanwhile, I just wanted to climb that damn flame-filled giant and absorb every last iota of his power.

"Cristell will suffer." He growled. "That's a given. But if she hurt my mother, then I will make it so much worse."

"We'll have enough power to best them very soon," Ixana said, and she sounded far too pleased. "Between the stone and your creature army, there is no chance for any of the royals."

I'd be using this army to defeat them only so we could free the creatures and restore their land. And yeah, it was a bonus if Shadow could take his place as his family's rightful leader, but it was also a double-edged sword. After he took on the mantle of Supreme Being, he'd be gone from my reach forever.

"Excuse me," I said, interrupting, and for some reason, the moment I spoke, Shadow's flames died off. Our eyes met, and just like always, the buzz of awareness between us was enough to have me stumble on the completely flat ground. "How far until we reach the Nexus?"

Ixana scowled. Did she not like me interrupting her little bonding time with Shadow? Tough shit, cupcake.

"One more day of walking, I estimate," she said stiffly. "If you can keep up the pace, of course."

"You mean, the pace I've been maintaining while carting along hundreds of shadow creatures who are protecting us?"

No need for her to forget who was doing all the heavy lifting here. There was a cacophony of noise behind me as the creatures screeched and bellowed and called to the sky, and I felt a small sense of satisfaction as her gaze darted about, her expression drawn in fear.

"Of course. You've been doing amazing." She actually reached out to touch me. She'd been doing that a lot over the last few days, trying to be reassuring, but it was mostly creepy. Fighting the urge to shake her icy touch off, I was thankful when she removed her hand. "We're grateful for your assistance in reestablishing us on the throne, right, lover?"

She turned to Shadow, missing the fucked-off expression descending over my face. I had no idea what the literal word she'd used was, but the translation had clearly gone with *lover*, and that made me want to use my creatures for evil. I didn't, because they were not actually my personal army to destroy my enemies, but it was certainly tempting.

"It's my throne," Shadow said gruffly, and he had my attention now. "My power and stone that you've been withholding from me."

She shook her head. "No, I told you I needed to keep it to maintain my land. Without the stone, every being there would fall victim to the rogue creatures of The Grey Lands. You wouldn't want that on your conscience, right?"

Shadow spun on her, one of those rapid, scary moves that I recognized from my early days with him. "I cannot accept my birthright without the stone. I've been patient; we've done it your way. But I refuse to leave The Grey Lands without the bloodstone. Understood?"

She swallowed hard. "Yes, and it will be okay by then with the creatures under the rule of Mera. The stone's protection will no longer be required, and my people will make their way to the royal compound when we do."

She had it all worked out. Oh, boy, did she have it worked out. I could tell that Ixana had been planning this for many years. Dreaming about being the "princess" in the Shadow Beast fairytale. What she didn't realize, though, was that this was not that sort of tale.

This was one streaked in darkness, with a broken beast both feared and revered by beings that lived in worlds far from here. Shadow, who had powerful friends and two libraries. He was so much more than just being the Supreme Being of the realm.

When they'd kicked him from his home, they'd changed the course of his destiny, and now they had no idea what they were dealing with. He was super independent, and I was almost positive— I'd have bet my favorite dragon shifter series on it—that he didn't want to share the crown with anyone. He'd waited centuries to claim his throne... his destiny.

She's his destiny too.

I couldn't really argue with true mates, but these two were the oddest I'd ever seen. Did it work the exact same way here as it did with shifters? I assumed the reason we had true mates was because the royals of this land did.

Shadow had created what he'd known.

Right?

"HOW DOES someone find their true mate?" I asked later that night when we were getting ready to go to sleep. I couldn't take the unanswered questions any longer. "In Shadow Realm?"

Ixana's icy gaze warmed up. "It's a promise at birth. Usually between two royal families. Mine is from Holister, to the northwest of Trinity. I was completely honored to have such a strong and powerful mate."

Wait a freaking minute...

"Are you telling me there's no magical connection" I confirmed? "It's just an arranged marriage?"

Okay, now everything made a lot more sense, especially Shadow's general lack of interest in her. It gave strength to his assurance that he was only sticking around for reasons that had nothing to do with their bond.

And fuck if I wasn't secretly doing a little happy dance about that.

"The initial connection is formed by our parents," Shadow said, and the blaze simmering in his eyes told me this was not his favourite topic of conversation. "Then there's a bonding between the two children. Like a promise ceremony. Which holds until we come of power-age, and the final bond is cemented at twenty-two."

"We were robbed," Ixana said bitterly. "It was supposed to happen the night of Shadow's ascension to his destiny. We were so close to our final bond."

"It's different for shifters," I said softly. "We find ours at first shift if they're in close proximity. Our wolves know each other straight away, and you feel this... like shock of lightning in your chest. An awareness of the other. They're supposed to be your match in all ways: power, strength, soul."

Shadow's hands flexed on the piece of rock he'd been tossing from palm to palm, and it was now dust.

Ixana didn't seem to notice as she leaned forward. "And do you have a true mate?"

I snorted. "A selfish fuck of an alpha. I don't know what that says about me, but I really haven't spent much time with him since we recognized our bond." I jerked my head toward a silently glowering Shadow. "Beast over here kidnapped me just after that, and my life has been in his hands ever since."

His expression was reminding me that it hadn't just been my life in his hands. He had all but owned every fucking part of me, and I was a prisoner to the desire he sparked to life within me.

"Why did you take her?" Ixana asked Shadow, and as he finally, *finally*, tore his gaze from me, I shivered, feeling naked after that penetrating stare.

"She touched the Shadow Realm. I'd been trying to find a way around Cristell's spell for most of my time on the outside, and finally there was this small hope of another way."

"He pretended he needed my help to round up the shadow creatures that had escaped," I said, cutting in. "When really he just needed me to open the doorway between our worlds."

And I had done that when no one else could. I could claim that as a victory, even if I still wasn't sure if it was good news or not that we were here. With his damn mate.

Shadow's lips curled up. "Turned out you could have been an even bigger help, had I known everything you were capable of."

I shrugged. "Surprised us both. But in the end you got what you wanted from me."

His shoulder's lifted as he chuckled. A dark, smoky sound. "So much more than I ever expected."

Only a moron would miss that innuendo, but apparently Ixana did not want to hear the truth in what he was saying. "I'm very happy Shadow had your help. That in the end, you figured out how to bypass the power of Cristell's spell. She used a never-ending rotation of creatures, one of the greatest losses in our history of their energy. It near bankrupted our lands, and it contributed to the drought-like conditions across the realm."

"The spell itself was the issue," Shadow said. "It was so clever and adaptive. No matter what I did to try to best it, the power would anticipate my next attack. Cristell was good with spell work, but the illusions it created never felt like her work."

Ixana jumped in quickly. "Cristell is a royal of many hidden strengths. Truthfully, her skill in spell weaving is second to none; it's been the one thing that has kept her on the throne all these years. The royals and freilds in your area didn't want to accept an interloper, at least not at first, but she eventually silenced any who stood against her."

"This spell weaving," Angel interjected, and as always, everyone paid attention when she spoke, "is going to be the biggest issue we face in taking her out. No doubt she has woven some intense and complex securities over the years."

"Inky told me you learned a little from Kristoff about what we're up against?" Shadow said to her. It had been some time since he'd mentioned his friend who was possibly missing... and had possibly betrayed us.

Angel shook her head. "He didn't have a lot to offer, since it's been a long time since he visited her compound. His one warning was to expect the unexpected. Cristell has an ever-changing security around her, and you never know what you'll come up against. His best advice was to interrupt her power source; cut her off from the creatures she controls."

Well, if there was one thing I was good at, it was stealing creatures from megalomaniac royals. Speaking of...

I turned to Ixana. "What happened to Kristoff after your goons snatched us up?"

She cleared her throat, but Shadow answered instead. "She assures me that he's still safe where we left him." He'd clearly already asked her that question, in one of their private chats, but he wasn't satisfied with her answer. My clever beast knew she was full of shit, and it was only a matter of time before he uncovered all of her secrets.

I couldn't wait.

Chapter Forty

We were a silent group the next day. The strain from the creatures I'd gathered was getting to me, and I lagged at the back of our group. It was a weird exhaustion, not the same as I'd felt holding the creatures back on Earth, but enough that my legs were heavier than usual.

"We'll reach the Nexus very soon," Ixana said. "I've never been here, obviously, since I would have been destroyed by the mists and creatures long before making it this far, and I'm just as interested as you all to see what we will find."

"To my knowledge, no one has been to this sacred place, correct?" Shadow rumbled.

"As far as I know, there has been none strong enough," Ixana confirmed.

"I can feel its energy," Angel said, her head tilted back, wings expanding like they too were scenting the air for power. "It's a spot of life in a land of death."

It was calling me. It had been the entire time, really, and this close, I was a magnet dragged toward its polar opposite.

"Mera?" Shadow asked.

I shook my head in an attempt to reorient myself. "It's calling me." I breathed. "I felt the same pull the first time I touched the realm. The first time I saw you. The first time a creature appeared in my life."

Shadow's pull was the strongest of all, and I'd tried ignoring it, hating him, even fucking him, but nothing had changed that feeling deep in my body.

Our demons matched.

Our souls matched.

It was an absolute truth that was set to destroy me any day.

"I can see the Nexus," Angel said, lifting herself up to fly above us.

I gestured to one of the abervoqs that were rarely far from my side. It knew without me having to say a word exactly what I wanted. Pawing at me with his bear-like claws, I was lucky not to be disemboweled as it started to lift me.

"No!" Shadow raged, cutting its movements off.

Ixana put her hands on him in an attempt to stop him from striding forward. "Lover, she has her army to help. You're not needed any longer."

Shadow and I did our thing, a long, drawn-out stare-off, where a fuck-ton of shit went unsaid, and I was mentally begging him to insist. For some reason, this felt like the moment where he had to choose sides. Mine or Ixana's. Words were all well and good, but it was actions that said everything.

"Mine," he rumbled softly. My heart lurched. "Until such a time I say she's not, Mera Callahan belongs to me."

Two steps and he stole me from the grip of the abervoq, and like any quasi-intelligent creature, it didn't fight. Especially since it knew I was more than a little okay with this arrangement. I'd take as many of these moments with Shadow as I could. Even if eventually life tore us apart.

Shadow's grip around my waist softened as he lifted me like I weighed nothing, hoisting me up to sit on his shoulder. I was perched on one side, awkward at first, but as he walked, his size grew. Bigger and bigger, until he was massive, and I could comfortably sit, able to see for miles.

Angel drifted in at my side, and the creatures let out their calls below. "Wow." I gasped as the Nexus came into view. It was an oasis in the center of a desert. Not green as it would be back home, but bright yellows and reds. Like a plume of fire had sprung up, only the fire was built behind an impressive stone fence, with just an arched red stone entrance.

"The last of the power," Shadow said, able to see it as well.

"We have to restore this land," I told him. "It must have been beautiful at one point, all wild and untamed with creatures roaming. When the two mists were strong and intertwined."

Midnight had shown me bits and pieces of this world, and now I was seeing that the images had been from here. A lot of them must have been from before the greed of the royals had stripped it bare.

"It used to be called *Paldeena*. The land of plenty," Shadow said sadly. "Long before my time, of course. I've only known it as 'The Grey Lands,' but once upon a time, this was our haven."

It could be that again. I sensed the truth of that deep inside. This could be the *land of plenty* again. In my moment of realization, envisioning the potential here, I felt better. My creatures would have paradise once again.

I'd be so focused on looking ahead that I hadn't noticed just how freaking tall Shadow had grown until I looked down. "Holy shit," I exclaimed, staring at the ground at least twenty feet below us. "Do you have a height limit?"

Shadow laughed, but I was seated so comfortably on his massive shoulder that I barely moved. "I've gone a hundred before."

"A hundred feet?" I screeched.

Another laugh.

"I really can't picture that, and please don't decide to show me right now."

"I've never seen anyone shape change like Shadow," Angel said, still flying beside us, her stunning and powerful wings flapping between glides. "It's definitely a unique power."

He shrugged, lifting me momentarily even higher before his shoulders settled. "I developed the ability when I was thrust from the realm. Inky and I surmise that when I was scrambling to stay here, I gathered energy into myself that I should never have had. Like Inky itself, whom I drew with me, these other gifts were not mine by birthright."

"They're yours now," Angel said. "Power is funny like that. Once it has been commanded, it adapts to the commander. You've become so much more than you would have if you'd stayed here and taken your mantle. You'll be the most powerful Supreme Being to ever rule the realm."

I expected Shadow to be pleased by this observation, but there was no smug twist of his lips. No acknowledgement or sign of excitement. He almost looked... resigned.

Was this one of those the *grass isn't always greener* on the other side things? Shadow had wanted this for so long that I expected some aspect of being so close to his goals was overwhelming. But once it was all said and done, and he sat on his throne, the ground below decorated with chunks of his sister, he'd finally feel content. Right?

Since this might be my last chance to speak to Shadow without his mate hanging on to us, I had to ask. "Was getting back to Ixana always part of your plan?"

Even Angel was watching him closely, waiting to hear his response. "At first, yes," he finally said. His eyes drifting to where his mate marched along below us, his face set in cold lines, looking fierce and very...

"She's beautiful," I said because she was. Beautiful and evil.

He didn't acknowledge that. "Ixana has not been a priority of mine for a long time." He lifted his gaze from her. "We knew each other for a few scattered years, lifetimes ago. We did have a bond, but as more time passed, the less I thought of her. I'm not really onboard with the way we're assigned mates here. It's why I didn't plan for the same with shifters. A soul connection is always going to be stronger." He trailed off, muttering something that sounded like *at least I used to prefer it* before he changed the subject.

"We should reach the Nexus soon. Are you ready to find out where your power comes from?"

I snorted. "Good try, dude. But I'm not done with my last topic. If you weren't waiting for your true mate, wanting to return to her and cement the final bond, then why didn't you kiss anyone before me?"

He released a deep breath. "For some reason, it was the one thing I held on to, until..."

Me. "Why?" I breathed.

Shadow was tense, his shoulders hardening under my ass. "You know why, Sunshine."

Now I was tense, but I did know why.

Our demons matched.

Our souls matched.

We were more than just a random hookup. We'd been more the first moment I'd touched the Shadow Realm and drawn him into my world. But why were we more?

Why did we match?

And what did it mean for our future?

Chapter Forty-One

Shadow set me on my feet eventually, and I was a little sad to see him return to his regular height. There was a commanding and captivating presence about him when he really let loose with his power.

Ixana appeared much happier when we were apart, as she sidled toward him, and I had to look away because I apparently wasn't quite ready to handle that sight. Not when I was a tiny bit in love with my devilish beast.

My creatures perked up when we reached the start of an incline, the first real elevation in The Grey Lands so far. It appeared the Nexus was at the top of a small hill, but due to the color of the landscape, none of us knew that until we were basically right on top of it.

I wondered if there used to be mountains and valleys and other unique landscape here before the royals had sapped this land of its energy. What else had been lost due to the royal's greed?

As we ascended toward the stone arches, the connection circling between my creatures and me increased. It was a fascinating view, looking back down the massive line of gangly, burly, occasionally scary creatures. There was no way this many of them would fit on the top of the hill, unless the size of the Nexus was also deceptive from where we stood, but they were going to get as close as possible.

"Feel that original magic," Ixana said, shaking her hair out. It whirled around her, and I remembered my own doing something similar when I'd first shifted. Had that been my connection to this land coming through even then?

Shadow's skin was dancing with flames, and I knew it was a response to the magic. I felt the whoosh of energy coat me as well, my own flames that matched his, rising across my body.

Angel grinned broadly. "You look like an immortal goddess," she said, her eyes locked on me. "It's the most powerful form I've ever seen you take."

She hadn't seen me on Earth, but somehow I already knew that here, I was more.

Shadow reached out and brushed his hand along my side, our flames dancing and twining together, like lovers, and I had to close my eyes at the sensation of him stroking more than my skin.

"Darkor!" Ixana said. "What are you doing? Why does she have your power?" Her words were angry, but the tone was not. It was odd. But it almost felt like she wasn't actually surprised by this.

Shadow ignored her. He was going to kiss me, and as much as I wanted him to, I knew it would lead to drama we didn't have time for.

I pulled away. "We're out of time," I rumbled, sounding like the female version of my grumbly beast.

He chuckled. "You can't escape me for long, Sunshine."

"I don't want to, Shadow."

Shadowshine. We were going to rock that couple name... if we ever sorted our shit out.

Ixana let out a low scoff, sending icy power surging up between us. Unfortunately for her, our fire was beyond the reach of her snowy spell. She didn't even dent our flames, but again, choosing not to deal with the *Shadow and Ixana* thing, I made the choice to walk away. My speed picked up as I headed toward the red-arched entrance I'd seen from afar.

Midnight floated ahead, keeping an eye out for any dangers. *All clear so far.*

Excellent news.

Angel also took the opportunity to fly ahead, and I wished I could call her back to my side, where I felt she was safer. No doubt that would be insulting to the formidable warrior; she didn't take well to anyone fussing over her like a worried mom.

Even if it was my instinct to try.

When I reached the arch, I only had a few of the abervoqs by my side; the rest were scattered down the hill. They'd be fine there, so I decided to step inside and see what exactly this Nexus was. What had been calling me for days, dragging me across the desolate Grey Lands.

"Wait!" Shadow called, but it was too late for me to do that.

A wash of frigid power sent bumps over my skin as I crossed the threshold into a land of red and gold. Shadow's colors. The color of the mists in their rawest form. It made sense, since Shadow had been born to do what no other could in the realm.

Nothing else happened as I took another step forward, tilting my head back to take it all in. Power trailed along my spine, and it wasn't until I turned that I noticed that no one else had made it through the archway.

Something was holding them out.

What...?

Thankfully Midnight could still communicate with me. *We're being blocked for some reason. They want you in there without the rest of us. Be careful.*

I didn't even have the time to contemplate that before another being walked into view. At first, the burst of light that followed their path was too bright for me to make out who it was, and even though it would have been smarter to run back to Shadow, I didn't.

I stepped forward, into the light.

As it engulfed me, I was surprised by the sense of familiarity dotted throughout the energy. The land was familiar too, this pocket of paradise with waterholes and nature—mostly of the gold and red variety— scattered about.

But my main focus was on the figure.

Like she hadn't wanted me to see her until the absolute last moment, we were mere feet apart when the light finally eased. I stared into beautiful and *familiar* eyes.

My heart slammed against my chest as I tried to figure out if I was hallucinating.

Could this place cause you to hallucinate? To see loved ones?

"Dannie?" I whispered.

She didn't look exactly the same as she had on Earth. This version was a little taller and slimmer, a lot younger, with a mass of messy blonde curls trailing down her spine. She wore brilliant red robes that both blended in and contrasted with the Nexus.

Here she was, looking like a sun goddess. A very alive goddess, right down to the scolding look on her face. "My little Mera. You had no idea if I was friend or foe, and you just walked right into my orbit."

My lips trembled, my throat tight as my eyes burned. "How?" I said hoarsely. "How are you here?"

She took my hand, and the tears I'd been trying desperately to keep at bay broke through their barrier. "We have a lot to discuss, Mera." Her voice was calm and warm. "I just wanted a moment to see you first before I allowed the others in."

I swallowed hard, painfully, my desire to curl up and bawl my eyes out so strong even as I fought against it. "Please let them in," I choked out, "and promise not to disappear on me again."

"I'm not going anywhere, sweetheart."

Tears slipped free, and she brushed a hand over my cheek before she crossed to the archway. She did something to the energy barrier, and as it dropped, Shadow—furious and covered in flames—stormed through. He didn't give Dannie a second look, his focus all on me. "Are you okay?" he demanded.

I nodded, lifting my face toward him, the moisture I hadn't bothered to wipe away still on my cheeks. "They're happy tears."

This finally seemed to penetrate his worry, and I had a feeling we'd been minutes from seeing him all Anubis-a-fied again. Sweeping me closer to him, he positioned himself in front of me as he finally turned to acknowledge Dannie.

She was walking toward us, her long, red robes trailing behind her. He tensed further, and I was confused. "It's Dannie," I said, pressing my hand to his back.

I felt a spark of his power, but it didn't hurt me, so that was not a warning. Shadow was reacting to something else. Dannie's face softened as she stared at him, and I hated not knowing what the fuck was going on here.

"Your energy did not feel like this on Earth," Shadow rasped, and I had never heard him sound so... sad. "I felt flashes of the realm and the royals. I figured you were from one of the kingdoms. I didn't know it was you."

She reached up toward him, and just as I was about to warn her of the dangers of touching him without his permission, he met her hand with his own, wrapping that huge palm around her much smaller one.

"I have missed you," she said.

Just as I was about to freak the fuck out and start demanding answers, Shadow replied. "I missed you too, Mother. So fucking much."

Mother?

The world spun and for a brief moment, I wondered if I was about to embarrass myself and faint. Dannie was Shadow's mother?

Who and how and why and what the fuck was happening here?

Chapter Forty-Two

Angel must have seen my confusion, reaching my side in an instant. Her support was given freely, an arm wrapped around me, which I was a touch ashamed to admit, I needed. The truth of what I'd just heard had knocked me over, and I wasn't sure which part was the hardest to handle.

Shadow's focus was on his *mother*—the fuck?—but I sensed that he was aware of me as well. Dude was very good at multi-tasking.

"We should sit down," Dannie said, sweeping her arm wide like she wanted to take in the beautiful land of the Nexus. Unlike the rest of The Grey Lands, here there was a plethora of energy and life. A taste of what used to span out across all of this land when it had been Paldeena.

No one said a word, not even Ixana, as we followed Dannie. She moved through what I would compare to a field, but there was no grass. The golden matter beneath our feet was soft, cushioning my boots, and as I leaned over to run my hands across the velvety, cloud-like substance, I wondered what it was.

It wasn't sticky or weird to touch... It felt nice. Like I could comfortably curl up in a ball and sleep on this field that morphed from gold to red and back again with careless abandon. It was so much like Shadow's eyes that I felt an odd pang in my chest.

Pushing that aside, I fell into the back of the group. Shadow and Dannie were up front, talking to each other, but I couldn't hear what was being said.

As she led us deeper into the Nexus, I started to wonder why she'd wanted to see me first, before her own son. Had she known how destroyed I'd been over her "death?" Or was there another reason? Either way, I really hoped she had some answers to my many, *many* questions.

Deep down, I wasn't actually handling the truth of who she was very well. She no longer felt like my Dannie; instead, she was the being who quite possibly knew all along what I was, and had kept it from me.

I felt betrayed. Was nothing the way I believed it to be? Was my father's death connected to this as well? Did I truly know anything about myself?

"This spot will work," Dannie called back for all of us to hear.

The "spot" was beside what looked like a creek, but the water was red and thick. Dannie pulled her brown leather sandals off and dropped her feet into it, sighing as she did.

"It's a lot like a river back on Earth," Angel whispered in my ear. "One made from gelatin."

As I crouched and ran my hand through it, I was surprised by the cool liquid suctioning onto my skin. The deeper I went, the more icy and intense it was. After a few seconds, I enjoyed the sensation of it swirling against me.

"This is mist born, and the purest form of the original energy," Dannie explained. "You should all partake in some, restore your energy. I believe you're going to need it."

Shadow and Ixana both scooped up a handful and drank it down. I hadn't seen Shadow ever truly eat anything until this point, but he clearly was all over this.

"It's safe for you, Mera," Dannie told me.

As I pulled my hand free, it made a small popping sound emerging completely clean. Crossing my arms, I glared at her. "And why should I believe a word out of your mouth?"

I was gonna yell at Shadow's mom, and honestly, I didn't even care if it pissed him off.

Dannie got to her feet again, two pops as she pulled them from the Jell-O creek.

She approached me slowly. "I owe you an apology and explanation, and I promise both are coming your way. Energy first, though, since you're carrying the burden of all the creatures. You feel a little... worn down."

Shadow's gaze snapped to mine, and he was looking me over like he was checking for broken bones. The exhaustion had been coming and going in waves, but I'd felt like I had been doing a fairly good job keeping it hidden from the world. All of the world except Dannie, apparently. Never could hide anything from that woman.

"How long have you been here?" Ixana asked Dannie, clearly giving zero fucks about my state of being.

Dannie's eyes shifted color, gold bleeding into the familiar blue. I'd never seen that before... Had the gold in Shadow's eyes come from her?

"I've been here since the day my son was stolen from me."

I had the sense then that she didn't really like Ixana, and I was stupidly pleased by that. Why had she helped her escape from Cristell, then? Out of loyalty to her son?

Dannie sighed. "It's time for me to explain everything, and it's going to be difficult for some to understand their role in all of this, but I would appreciate it if everyone could just wait until the end to yell at me."

My lips twitched. That last part was definitely directed at me.

"I was not born a royal." Her first statement was a fucking doozy. "I'm not even from The Concordes." Shadow's chest rumbled, but he remained quiet, as she'd requested. "I was born in this land. Right here, actually."

Shadow jerked back, his face wreathed in confusion. "Only shadow creatures are born here."

Dannie smiled, her expression much darker and fierier than I'd ever seen before. Shadow clicked on first, shaking his head in disbelief. "It's not possible," he shot at her. "The Danamain is a myth, and your energy is that of a royal's."

Those flames in her eyes spilled out onto her skin, and she lit up like Shadow. The heat was intense, buffeting against us, pushing all of us back. I wondered if these flames would burn me or not. They felt the same as Shadow's, but also different somehow.

"I'm like nothing that any of you have known," she said, her voice deeper than I'd ever heard. And then, like a snake shedding its skin, she tilted her head back and spread her arms to the side as her body melted away.

In the place where Dannie had stood, there was a very different being. *A creature?* She was bird-like, with a long, flame-colored plume, and tail feathers that had to measure six feet in length. She was also covered in very real red and gold flames.

From the ashes, the phoenix will rise.

Dannie was a freaking phoenix, or at least as close an equivalent as I could think to a mythical creature who didn't actually exist. But every image I'd seen back home of a phoenix was so close to Dannie, it was almost scary.

While I was having my freak out about what I was seeing, the others were as well, but once again, they had more information than me.

"It is the Danamain," Angel breathed before she shook her head like she couldn't believe she'd just said that. "No. Seriously. You're a myth."

Ixana breathed heavily. "You're the original creature, Mainey? *How?* The literal Mother of Creatures?"

They knew her as Mainey. I knew her as Dannie. Between all of us, she'd been the Danamain. We just hadn't had all the puzzle pieces to put it together.

Unable to stop myself, I stepped closer to my old friend, running my hands through her flames. As always, anything fire dragged me in and never let go.

The burn was pleasantly warm, and comforting, like I was the one coming home to my own mother. Once again, I panicked at the thought that Shadow and I were somehow related, and apparently only one person had the answer to that.

The Mother of Creatures.

Chapter Forty-Three

Dannie, having proven her point, shifted back. Unlike me, her red robes appeared the moment she returned to her humanoid form.

"I'm sorry," she said, and she was talking directly to her son. "For keeping this from you. But you were so young when they stole you from me, and I could not escape this realm until I figured out how to release Mera into your world."

"Excuse me," I cut in, blinking near a million times as I tried to figure out what she'd just said. "You released me into... *What the actual fuck, Dannie?*"

Now it was my turn to get an apology. "I have a lot to tell you, my sweet little wolf. And I'm sorry for the many years that you didn't know your true self, but you are exactly the magnificent creature I expected when I sent your energy into a shifter pup."

I shook my head, waving both hands in front of me as I refused to believe what she was saying. Shadow's nearby rumbles were ominous; he was absolutely unhappy with his mother. "You better tell us everything from the start," he said. "Leave nothing out."

Dannie nodded, and then she directed us to sit at the water again.

"The mists will restore your energy," she said, "and this is a long tale. Take the restoration, trust me."

Nobody was trusting her, that was for sure, but in this regard, they complied, sitting. I placed my feet into the Jell-O water and almost instantly felt better. Dannie and her freaking remedies.

"I was the first to emerge from the Nexus," Dannie said, getting right to the point. "The first creature. The firebird. My place here was one of guidance. I brought the creatures into the world, a mother of sorts, and every single one has some of my energy in it. Only a sliver, though; most is the raw power of the mists. Here they do not fight or battle, they are not opposites."

She waved her hand. "Once upon a time, everything in this land looked like this, but then the leicher mists in the chasm created the royals and all the beings under them, and after that, we have known no peace. The royals stole my children, controlling and using their pure energy, and there was little I could do to stop it. I was duty bound to stay near the Nexus and maintain the balance."

I mean, we all knew that wasn't strictly true. She'd been in The Concordes when Shadow had been born, and she'd been on Earth. Clearly, we weren't up to that part of her story, but it better get there soon.

No one interrupted her as she continued. "Eventually, I grew strong enough to leave the Nexus for short periods of time while still maintaining the power balance. When I saw the way the royals treated my creatures, I had to figure out a plan to save them. Only, there was so many being controlled that it would have destroyed the entire balance of the mists if I just took out the royals." She looked between all of us. "The balance is so important."

She'd mentioned it enough times by now, that I was sure we'd all gotten the point.

"So you decided to take them out from the inside?" Shadow finally spoke up, his voice a dark mist of anger and confusion. "Change them by taking your place among them?"

Dannie's face crumpled as she forced a sad smile. "I did. And here's another truth you're owed: Cristell is not my child. She was adopted from another royal family, after they were killed in a lava blast."

Shadow's expression didn't shift. If anything, that was probably welcome news, after what his sister had done to him.

"How did I come to be born?"

Solid question from the beast himself.

Dannie cleared her throat. "I fell in love with your father. I got to know the royals and figured out pretty quickly that a lot of them weren't the monsters I'd expected. They also didn't treat my creatures badly, for the most part."

She'd been Stockholmed. Couldn't blame her. Shadow had basically gotten me in the exact same way.

"So you eventually wanted a royal child of your own?" I asked, unable to swallow down my worry that I was about to find myself in the same family tree as Shadow. "Please tell me Shadow and I are not related."

"You're not related," she said without hesitation.

Thank. Fuck.

"You are what I am, which is a creature born of the Nexus."

I blinked at her. "I'm sorry. What did you just say?"

A creature born of the Nexus.

She continued on like she hadn't just dropped a fucking bomb on my head. "It took me near two thousand Earth years to figure out how to do it; I had to come close enough to death that the Nexus believed it needed to create another mother. You appeared right when I was giving up hope." She smiled at me. "You can call yourself Mother Junior of the Creatures. You and I are born of pure creation."

I was on my feet, and I wanted to scream. I wanted to tear my skin off, turn into a firebird and leave, never to have to see these beings who were ripping at the foundation of who I was.

"How?" Shadow bit out. "How did Mera come to be on Earth then? In my shifters?"

This distracted me from the volcano of emotion about to explode from me because I needed that question answered.

Dannie sighed. "There's no easy way to say this, but... I kind of destroyed her first form, which freed her from the confines of having to stay at the Nexus. I sent the remaining energy into the shifters, through my connection to you, Darkor. It's complex, but basically my bond to you and your bond to the shifters allowed me to bypass the spell on the door, and then I could place Mera where I needed her. She was always going to be the one who would open the Shadow Realm door, since her energy was destined to return home. This Nexus would call her until she returned."

"Did you make Shadow and me have feelings for each other?" I choked out. Nothing I hated more than being manipulated, and it appeared she had done it with every part of who I was.

Ixana lost it at that point and tried to push me into the river. "I knew you were trying to steal my mate," she screamed, only to be stopped by Shadow's huge-ass hand shoving her away.

"Do not touch Mera," he warned the ice bitch.

Dannie got between us, her half-smile reminding me of her knowing look I'd seen a hundred times. "I did not manipulate any emotions. You and Shadow are both powerful beings, with the mists of creation in your veins. It makes sense that if they didn't kill each other, you'd do something else..."

Ixana stormed off in the direction of the gate, and for a brief moment I thought I caught sight of a smile on her face, but I must have been mistaken.

Shadow didn't bother to follow, his focus on Dannie. "How did you get to Earth then?" he snapped. "Since Mera had to bypass the spelled door in energy form."

"Mera called me the day her father died," she said softly. "She allowed me to leave this world, and in our absence from the Nexus and mists, the land perished to what you see now."

I'd called her...?

"Not literally of course," Dannie assured me, "but your pain was so strong that I believe it was the first doorway you opened between the worlds. I took advantage and stepped through." She eyed me closely. "Thankfully, because you needed someone on your side in the years that followed."

"I am still part shifter, then?"

She nodded. "Of course. That's the reason you have a shifter mate and can turn into a wolf. The reason you can be without the Nexus and not fade, like I would eventually. I'd been growing weaker on Earth, hence why your pack mates were able to hurt me. You have a true dual soul, and one day these two sides will collide in a spectacular manner. You'll be reborn into the Supreme Being with the power to rule both worlds."

Her words were too much for me to truly comprehend. I would need a few hundred years, and some serious alcoholic beverages, before I could touch that statement.

She paused briefly. "I am truly sorry I destroyed the first vessel, Mera, but I promise, your energy is still as pure and beautiful as the first time I held it in my hands."

This was a lot. It was more than a lot, it was near unbelievable, but it also made sense. It explained away all my stupid shit, and the reason I could call and control the creatures. I was apparently a Mother of Creatures, like this spectacular woman before me, and I supposed I knew now why my hair was the color it was. *Like a sunset.* Exactly like Dannie's phoenix, and my fire touched wolf.

Like the mists.

Midnight drifted down and wrapped around me, comforting. *Do not fear your power. We are creation, but we are also more than that. Sentient in a way the pure mists are not. You have nothing to fear.*

"This is why the mists bonded to Shadow and me," I said softly. "Both of us are partly the same as they are."

Dannie beamed. "You always were clever, my girl. It's also why Shadow could create shifters. Because he's born of my energy. We are all connected, but not related," she added with a sharp smile at me.

It was a fine line, I was honest enough to admit that, but hopefully Dannie was right. There was no literal blood or direct energy connection between Shadow and me. Therefore, no need to scrape all the sex we'd had from my brain, and that actually made me feel a lot better.

It also explained why Shadow and I fit together. We were a match, an even bigger match than the one I had with Torin, and that gave me this stupid sense of hope I had no right to have.

Was there actually a future where Shadow and I could truly be together?

Chapter Forty-Four

I had to look away or I was going to jump the beast, and now was not the time. Not after being near-floored by all the truth bombs dropped on me today.

"Do you understand, Darkor?" Dannie asked her son. Her expression one of a mother desperate to connect with the child who had been out of her reach for an eternity. A son she had spent thousands of years trying to save.

"I go by 'Shadow' now," he told her, less bite in his words than before. "And I do understand. I'm not sure I'm happy about it, but I'm old enough now to see the sacrifice you've made. And I might actually owe you..." He looked at me but didn't finish the sentence. I was desperate to know if it was about me, but there was no way to ask and not sound completely narcissistic.

Dannie stepped closer to him, and it was almost painful how awkward they were. It must have hit them at the same time that this was their chance for healing. He wrapped his arms around her, and it was the sort of hug that usually destroyed me on the rare occasions he handed them out.

His hugs were A-game material.

"Two questions," he said when they pulled apart. "How come you couldn't break the spell on the door, being as powerful as you are?"

Dannie didn't like this, her brow furrowing as a dark expression crossed her features. "I was weakened when I had you, Shadow. My power is yours now, and I'm nothing more than a figurehead, still here trying to keep the balance."

I sensed that she hadn't expected to lose part of herself to a child.

She reached up and touched his cheek. "I don't regret any of it, I promise. But I definitely don't command the power I used to."

He thought on this, his expression unreadable.

"What's your second question?" she pushed.

This time, there was a chink in his armor. "If you were on Earth for years, why did you never try to find me? I thought the entire aim was to get me home. To see me again."

He'd missed his mother, and fuck, if that vulnerability didn't make him seem—for a moment in time—like someone much less jaded and alphahole-ish.

She swallowed roughly. "I'm weakened in the human realm, away from the Nexus. It's why Mera's much stronger than me. She doesn't have my limitations, in either land."

Shadow focused on me, looking for a moment longer than was polite. "She *is* extraordinary."

Slaying me as always. "*She* is sitting right here," I added, forcing normalcy to return. I didn't want to think about being a mist-born creature of power. I just wanted to be Mera. Me. That was enough.

They both just smiled at me and I wondered how the fuck I'd ever missed the similarities between them. "How exactly do royals have children?"

The question was out before I thought about the intricacies of it. Was I about to get the Shadow Realm's equivalent of the birds and bees talk?

Dannie's grin was knowing. "It's a joining of body and power. It requires you to exist in the head of your mate, and it's intense to the degree that many can't handle. Pleasure beyond what you can imagine, but it's also how I lost energy to give to Shadow. So be aware of this."

That part didn't bother me as much as the thought of allowing anyone to exist in my head. My messy, messy head.

"What is our next step then?" Angel asked. She'd been quiet, taking in all the new information. There was nothing she loved more than discovering new facts about the worlds. She took her role as the quiet observer very seriously, cataloguing it all away, her super-brain never forgetting a thing.

"Now we must correct the power balance in this world," Dannie said, dusting her robes off. "Mera and Shadow are the two able to return the royal rule to its correct position. Cristell, I've been trying to keep an eye on her, but her energy keeps morphing and changing. I don't know what you'll find when you return to the compound."

It was clear she hadn't been back there since the day her son had been stolen, too weak to do much more than search for a way to return him. She'd said it had taken near two thousand years to get the Nexus to produce my energy, and honestly... that was dedication. A true mother's love for a child.

"Where the fuck is Ixana?" Shadow asked suddenly. "She's disappeared and she has my bloodstone."

Dannie's eyes turned murky, which was always a bad sign. "She is gone. And..." She focused on me. "Can you feel your creatures, Mera?"

Flames licked across Shadow's arms, his face set in angry lines. Ignoring this, I tried to feel the creatures in my bond, and... they were still there, but it was weak. Much weaker than I'd expected. "The connection is fading," I choked out. The power of this Nexus had hidden it, but now that I was focusing my attention on the bonds, it was obvious.

Shadow rumbled. "Wait here," he said to me. "I'll look into it." He disappeared into a blur of shadows, and I tried not to freak out.

"Can you ever forgive me, Mera?" Dannie asked, her voice flat. "I dragged you into this war. Without your permission."

"You did it to save Shadow," I said, keeping my true feelings hidden away. I got it, but it stung that the one adult I'd thought had given a shit about me had only been interested in what she could use me for.

"At first, yes." She surprised me with her honesty. "But all too quickly, I loved you. I even contemplated figuring out a way to stop you from taking this journey. Risking you didn't feel worth it, even to save the realm from its ultimate end."

"It's dying?" Angel cut in, surprised. "There has been no talk of that."

Dannie snorted, and it was so ungoddess-like that she once again reminded me of Earth Dannie. My weird, eccentric friend. "Since the door was barred, all of the realm's drama has remained internal. No one would know, and it's only those who live here who see the suffering. The balance is so far skewed, I'm not sure it can ever be righted." She gestured out to the dead lands again. "This is not only happening here. It's happening everywhere."

We'd seen it in the lava fields, where the decay had been so much more widespread than Shadow and Angel had expected.

"They need Shadow to take his place," Angel mused. "It has to be one of the biggest factors in this imbalance. Cristell not only sucked up ten times her share of power to fill his role, but that much again to keep the spell on the door. She's killing this world."

"She is," Dannie confirmed. "But her power, or the balance of power as you've noted, is so far tilted her way, I'm afraid it might be too late."

"And what happens if this world falls?"

Maybe it wouldn't be that bad. We could evacuate as many as we could and then let the assholes suffer in the destruction of their own creation.

"It's an essential part of the Solaris System," Angel told me. "To lose one could result in the loss of all. There would be a long-reaching impact that we have no idea of."

Dannie nodded. "Oh yes, not to mention that any creature born of the energy here, including you and your mists, would perish. We cannot survive without this realm."

"Okay, we must do this," I said, slumping as more energy seeped from me.

Something was going on with my creatures; I needed to get to them and figure out what was wrong, but I would wait for Shadow to return.

Dannie clapped her hands. "My child deserves his birthright. I lost so much when we were betrayed, and my mate..."

My chest tightened as I finally figured out why she'd bailed on the compound and never returned. "Shadow's father is dead?"

She nodded. "Yes. Cristell forged the bloodstone into a weapon, this long staff. She used it to destroy any who stood in her way. None of us were ready."

A staff? Angel and I exchanged a glance. Ixana had said she'd taken the stone as soon as Shadow had been betrayed, so how had Cristell used it as a weapon?

I was about to ask Dannie more about the day Shadow was betrayed, but before I could, the beast himself burst into the clearing. "She's gone," he roared. "And she took the creatures."

It had been what I feared, even as I'd held onto a weak hope that there was another explanation. Dannie was on her feet in an instant, and as her fury grew to match her son's, flames spun out of control from them both. "I knew it," she seethed. "I never liked or agreed with their pairing, but my mate insisted that it was a solid match. A strong union between royal families."

Shadow didn't seem surprised by this. "She's no match for me. I saw that from the first moment we reconnected here."

"What is she doing with my creatures?" I snapped, needing them to get to the point.

"She betrayed us," Shadow said softly. "She's either working for

Cristell or planning to use the creatures to take her down. Either way, she used our power to get what she wanted, and now she's gone."

I took off, sprinting toward the entrance, crossing that soft meadow before I skidded out of the stone archway. I stared across the barren, empty land, my knees near-buckling under me.

They were gone. The desert lands empty.

My scream was long and guttural, and I called the creatures to me, but there was no response. "How?" I sobbed. "How did she command them?"

Shadow was there, as he always was. "She's been siphoning your energy. I've been so focused on you that I missed the obvious signs. She kept touching you, and I thought she was trying to break the ice, but it was betrayal." He was pissed. So fucking pissed that I wouldn't have been surprised to see a forest fire of his making rage across this land. If there was anything left to burn, that was. "They're too far away for you to reach them. We have to follow."

Siphoning. My. Energy.

That was why I'd felt so drained the closer we'd gotten to the Nexus. Fuck that bitch. I was going to rip her hair out when I caught up with her.

Dannie appeared in the archway but didn't step out into The Grey Lands. "You must go after her. If she destroys the last of the creatures here, the Nexus will fall."

Shadow spat out. "Bet that was Cristell's plan all along. She is so narrow-minded, thinking that she'll be the strongest once this land is gone."

"We have to follow her!" I demanded. "I won't let my creatures be used to win this war." I took a step forward, but my legs crumbled under me. I almost hit the ground, but Shadow was too fast for that; he caught me, hauling me up into his arms.

"What's happening?" I asked, the weakness in my legs extending to the rest of me as I hung limply against him.

"You have bonded thousands of creatures to you," Dannie said in a rush. "And now they're being stolen away. Stolen away to destroy. Which will destroy you. You must catch up to her now."

Shadow threw his head back and roared, his expression a combination of fury and fear. I'd never seen that look on his face before, and as much as I hated to see it now because it meant I was dying, there was something about seeing the man you loved lose his shit like this.

I'd have been turned on if I wasn't actively dying.

Wasn't that always the way.

Chapter Forty-Five

S hadow held me tightly, and with my avenging Angel above, her weapons out as she flapped those powerful wings, we were racing across the land. Just the three of us and our mists.

Dannie had to stay with the Nexus, keeping it powered as long as possible. Once again, we would be on our own, trying to save the damn world.

"Mera!" Shadow snapped, attempting to keep me conscious.

At some point, it registered that I was actively dying. After all of the years expecting it, this was the moment it happened, and I found... I was not ready to go. Not when I'd finally discovered my true purpose. I also needed more orgasms with this sexy beast of a god.

"I have to save my creatures," I managed to choke out.

They were already hurting them. There was no other explanation, and it was slowly killing me. That was the risk when one bonded a few thousand beings to their energy.

"Stay with me, Sunshine," Shadow growled. "And I promise we'll save your pets."

"Shadowshine," I slurred, my head cloudy as the exhaustion

pressed down on me like a cloying material designed to snuff my life out. "Told you we'd have a couple..." I coughed a few times, my lungs seizing. "Name."

"Quiet. You are ordered to keep breathing and nothing else."

When we arrived at the ice city, it was to find it completely empty. Not just empty, but as dead and desolate as the rest of the land.

"Illusion," Shadow raged. "That was always her specialty."

"That bitch had it all planned," Angel spat out, and she was as furious as the rest of us. "We have to catch her."

"We will," Shadow rumbled.

He was moving again, knowing exactly where Ixana was heading. Using his powers, he jumped all of us in a burst of misty smoke, straight into The Concordes.

The time for stealth was apparently long gone.

We ended up over Trinity, and from here, Midnight and Inky carried us toward the royal compound. My bond to the mist was basically the only thing keeping me alive. Well that and the way Shadow was losing his shit, shouting orders at me to *keep fucking breathing*.

As we closed in on my creatures, a small surge of my energy returned, allowing me to lift my head. "They're here, but how did she move them all so fast?" I asked in a breathless whisper.

Shadow's flaming face, a very Anubis-looking face, twisted toward me. Now that I'd seen his beast side, he appeared to be much more relaxed about letting it free.

"I have no idea," he bit out, "but it's clear her plan all along was to usurp the creatures from us. Whether it's to join forces with Cristell, or to try to best her so that Ixana is the next queen, I don't know."

My anger bloomed as more of my strength returned. "I think she's working with her. That's why she had the staff and stone. And my creatures..." My chest tightened. "She's destroying them. We have to hurry."

I was just managing to function, but as my creatures were killed off, I would be too. The smart thing would be to release them, but I honestly didn't know how to.

And even if I did know, it was my duty to save them; I had promises to keep.

As we crossed above Trinity, the mists concealed our position. From this bird's eye view, I could see how widespread the lava fields were, not to mention the lava chasm that nearly divided the land in half.

"We're almost to the royal compound," Shadow said, his hand grasping mine. "And I expect you to be alive and functioning when we get there, or I *will* release the lava and let it wash this world clean."

He'd do it too; the truth was written across his face.

"You'd burn The Concordes down for me?" I swallowed roughly.

"I'd burn the entire world down for you, Sunshine."

It hurt in the best way to hear him say that. In my pack, everyone outside of Simone had turned their backs on me out of fear of being shunned. No one supported me, not my alpha, or Jaxson, or my true mate, or my mom. But Shadow, he would literally let it all burn.

"I lov—" I started, needing him to know how I felt if this was our last moment together, but before I could get more than half a word out, a massive explosion from below rocked into us.

Shadow shot me a look, and I had no idea if he'd heard me or not because there was no more time to delve into our softer emotions. The world he'd just threatened to burn down was already on fire.

Inky and Midnight slowed their journey since we'd clearly arrived. I leaned over the side, trying to take it all in, only turning away when flapping wings brought Angel to our side.

Her magenta eyes were burning as they clashed with mine. She would have known I was alive through our bond, but she looked relieved to see me somewhat awake and functioning.

"What's the plan?" she asked as we stared at the chaos below.

"I have to get to Cristell," Shadow said. "We need to break her bond to the creatures and find my damn bloodstone. Without both, she should be rendered weak enough to destroy."

"As easy as that," I joked, knowing that it was going to be anything but.

Shadow shot me a look, his eyes hooded as he stared for a beat longer than I'd expected.

"Can you see Ixana?" Angel asked, drawing our attention back to what was happening below.

There were beings everywhere, running and shouting, while a huge wall of flames burned. It looked like chaos, but it might actually have all been planned.

"I can't see her," I said, having another decent look. "But I feel my creatures are here somewhere."

Here and being slaughtered. My hand pressed to my chest as another was stolen from me, and the urge to scream filled me so strongly that I barely managed to keep it down.

"Royal guards below—she's prepared for us," Shadow observed. "We're going to have to fight our way into the compound, and as soon as I enter her securities, she'll hit us with everything she has."

Angel flapped her wings, blades spinning around her hands. "I'm more than ready to fight my way through. Sheer numbers won't keep us from that bitch."

"I need to get my creatures back," I said suddenly. "If Cristell's main focus is on Shadow, maybe I can sneak in and find where she's hiding them. If I get close enough, I'll separate them from her and she'll be weakened."

Ixana or Cristell. We were about to find out who was the true queen of illusion, playing her war games.

"Not a fucking chance," Shadow said shortly. He didn't even sound mad; it was just a matter-of-fact response.

"You know that if you're the target, it will be easier for me to sneak in," I reminded him. "You'll be the one in danger."

He set his jaw, shaking his head, not giving me a chance to reply before he was ordering the mists to take us down. "Stay with me, Mera. Keeping you safe is all I have to worry about."

We all knew that was a lie, but I couldn't leave now even if I'd wanted to. This was my world too. My energy. And my creatures being slaughtered.

I wasn't leaving without making it right.

Chapter Forty-Six

Inky and Midnight descended toward the guarded entrance, and it seemed that everyone was on board with Shadow being a total dominating asshole, keeping me locked down.

Everyone except me. And thankfully, my bonded mist.

I'm bailing as soon as we hit the ground. It will be chaos. Shadow can't keep track of me at all times.

I sent that message through in a rush since we were losing sky and would soon be on the ground.

I will watch your back. Keep you safe as we track the creatures.

Do you have any insight into where they are?

The mist was silent for a beat. *Their exact location is hidden, but I believe we'll find them underground.* Another pause. *Below with the leicher mists. I cannot follow you there.*

Dammit. I would be on my own, but that was okay. I could do this, and I'd figure out how to save my creatures.

When we landed a moment later, the guards came straight for us, the noise intense enough that my ears rang for a moment before they adjusted.

Angel was already fighting, her blades slashing through the air, taking out guards. She sliced across the throats of two black-shrouded figures who looked a lot like hunters. They weren't, because I could see their faces—faces that were grey and crumbly, like they'd sat out in the sun for too long.

Once Angel was done with them, they were nothing more than dust on the breeze, and I was officially freaking out.

"You need weapons from here," Shadow reminded her, and Angel shot him a tense smile.

"The moment I stepped into these lands, I infused realm energy into my blades. They'll kill with ease now."

Shadow returned her grin, his lips tilting up evilly. He held weapons now too, lifted from the ones Angel had just killed, and be still my heart, the man moved like a ninja, all stealth and grace as he brutally tore heads from shoulders and limbs from torsos.

Yeah, okay, our romance was not the conventional sort, but that was what made us work so well.

Shadow and Angel didn't mess around, killing whoever got in their way as we tried to move closer to the entrance. Between the two of them, there were bodies scattered across the ground and it hadn't escaped my notice that they made a real effort to keep me between them so I wouldn't be ambushed.

They couldn't stop the pain in my body, though, as my creatures were obliterated.

Soon I'd be unable to move—and if we continued this way, we would be too late to save the creatures. To save the world.

I had to get to them. Maybe I could take Inky with me. Would Shadow agree to that...?

"Shadow," I said, and he turned my way while still ripping through guards. "I'm going after my creatures, with or without your support. But I'm hoping to have it. Midnight said they're under the leicher mists, and it can't go down there."

Shadow's flames were roaring now, which had many of our attackers flying back to avoid his power.

"But I can take Inky," I finished.

He was already shaking his head, ferocity painting his features, along with the various colors of liquid and blood from the guards he'd killed.

"Please," I begged. "If they destroy all the creatures, I'll die. The Nexus will die. The damn world will die. This is so much bigger than the two of us!"

He couldn't answer because a raging *thing* was barreling through the crowds heading straight for us. I had no idea what it was—it didn't look like a creature—but it also didn't look like one of the royals.

"They have rocksburt?" Angel bit out, annoyed and surprised. "I thought they were extinct."

"Clearly not." Shadow growled, and then he was grappling with it. It looked like a rock-being, its skin a combination of lava stone and gems. It was about ten feet tall and wide, and when Shadow tried to punch his fist through its stomach, there was almost no reaction at all.

The beast barely made a dent.

"Go, Sunshine," Shadow growled, no doubt realizing I was in as much danger here as anywhere else. "We will distract, and Inky can get you through this chaos. Don't engage Cristell—just get your creatures and get your ass back to me."

Our eyes met briefly, and I wondered if this was the last time I'd ever look into those red and gold depths, the flames burning deep in his irises a comfort to me now.

"I'll be back soon," I promised.

Stay and help Shadow, I said to Midnight, and my mist wrapped around me before Inky took its place.

"You and me again, buddy," I said to it, and as it grew larger, I ran my hand over the sparking synapses.

It lifted me up, moving us over the ground level, and we were missed in the chaos of rock-beings and Shadow's attacks, and all the crazy. When we closed in on the wall of fire, my energy responded, loving the burn, and I knew on instinct these flames were from the lava chasm. Mist born.

I had no idea if I would be burned or not, but there was no other way to follow the call of my creatures, except to plunge through the flames. Inky didn't try to stop me, so Shadow must have thought the risk was minimal, but just in case, I called up my own flames, and what do you know? They responded.

We easily passed through the fire, and the other side was much quieter.

As Inky drifted down toward the ground, since we knew we had to go underground, an ear-piercing scream rang out around me. Looking to see who it was, I found there was not a single soul nearby. It was only when a second scream rang out, equally as painful on the eardrums, that I pinpointed the location as coming from the flames.

Cristell... or Ixana. Whoever was in charge here had felt me cross her spelled wall, and she was fucking pissed about it.

Well, good. Maybe the twat-tastic bitch would save me the trouble of tracking her down. I owed her for thousands... tens of thousands... hundreds of thousands of deaths of my creatures. And she would pay.

For them. And for Shadow.

Inky nudged me along, and we took off. On this side of the flames was a somewhat impressive compound. Everything was well-maintained, with maze-like gardens and scattered outer buildings, made from rock and stone. They looked like accommodation houses for grounds staff, and beyond them was a truly spectacular castle.

This wasn't Earth, but the castle wouldn't have looked out of place in Europe, as part of a royal estate, with its stunning combination of porous grey stone and a smooth white slate. Even in the fading light of night, I could clearly see all the details in the multiple gothic turrets, towers, and vast wings. The appeal was instant, and I wondered if this was exactly as it had been when Shadow had grown up here.

I wanted it to still be his childhood home, as he remembered it, so when he took his throne back, there'd be a comfort and familiarity.

My chance to observe was cut short as a huge group descended on us. The bitch in charge had retaliated to my appearance, and I wondered if she thought it was Shadow. Our power was linked in more ways than one, and I had no doubt we would appear very similar if you were only reading energy signals.

Inky took out the front line without an issue, and I was able to use my flames to destroy a couple of others. That was about all I had in me, since I was drained as fuck, the tie to my slaughtered creatures dragging me down to my death. As each one was destroyed to power this war, I lost another piece of my life force.

Swiping up some weapons, I held the two blades somewhat awkwardly, hoping they'd be better than nothing. Swinging the heavy object, the first soldier I met deflected it easily, but I'd learned a few things from Angel and was already following through with the second.

I could see the surprise in the face of the blue-skinned frond, who had not expected me to move so quickly. Probably because I was half-hobbling like a two-hundred-year-old shifter. My wolf rose up and loaned me some speed and dexterity, and when I cut across the frond's throat, the look of surprise it wore would probably stay in my head for a long time.

Being prepared to kill and actually doing it were apparently two vastly differently things. The next attacker didn't allow me to dwell for long, but I'd probably revisit that first kill another time. In my nightmares.

Swinging both blades again, I was able to keep them away long enough for Inky to take control and rip the shit out of the guards. "Thanks, buddy," I shouted as we ran again.

Another creature's death tore through me and I stumbled, but Inky was there just as Shadow would have been, scooping me up. My legs were weak, and since more guards were heading our way, I let it take me along. We didn't share a mind, so I relied on pointing Inky in the direction I felt the pull—toward the castle, on the side closest to the lava chasm.

Their energy was so strong here, along with that of the mists, royals, and many other beings. It was a huge jumble of power, literally buffeting at me as we closed in. When Inky got us right near the side of the castle, I patted it gently.

"I can walk from here," I said quickly. My legs buckled for a beat as I hit the ground, but Inky stayed with me until I found my strength to stand. It then formed a wall of protection behind me so I could lift my head and search for my creatures.

The bond was strong here, thrumming in my chest, and I tried to call them to me, tugging on the invisible cords that tethered us all together. *Come to me.*

They wanted to, these poor beings in pain, confused about what was happening. They were weak and hurt, but wherever they were, their path back to me was blocked. They couldn't return to me without my help.

Dammit. Shadow was going to murder me if I actually descended into her evil lair, but there was no other choice. I would sacrifice myself to save them; I would expect the same from him.

I'd join Shadow in burning this fucking place to the ground if it meant one more creature would not be hurt.

Chapter Forty-Seven

Guards were still coming after me, but they were far away thanks to Inky and its speedy flight process, so I was able to walk around to find the entrance I needed. It didn't take long, the literal oozing energy coming from it the first giveaway.

The only issue was the door appeared to be embedded into the wall of the castle, and there was no obvious handle or way to push through. Just the outline of a door, and the sense that I needed to get down there. Shoving the stone didn't help, kicking the stone didn't help, screaming and calling it a *dumb fucking fuck* didn't help, and when I slumped against the castle, knowing my time was almost up, and we were about to once again be ass-deep in guards, I let out a long sigh.

My wolf pushed up to the surface, and I let her come. There was no other option, and honestly, what could it hurt? She'd always been much more adept at calling the creatures, and she was stronger, able to attack beings that would destroy me.

It was her time to shine.

Inky intercepted the guards, as I shifted in a swift, semi-painful moment. My clothes were destroyed, as always when I didn't take them off first—a combination of magic and heat literally disintegrated them to nothing more than some scraps and buttons. It was all good, since my fur would do the job of keeping me covered, at least until we finished our quest.

As soon as I was in my wolf form, we picked up so many things I hadn't had a hope of seeing with human eyes. The monochromatic vision was able to detect a gap in the corner of the door, and I could taste the breeze coming from there.

This was the key here.

Inky!

It must have sensed that I needed it, and as it zoomed to my side, I nosed the small opening, jerking my head to indicate that it needed to go through there and see if the mechanism to open this door was on the other side.

Inky didn't want to at first, as it shot more energy toward the guards. My wolf growled, pawing at the ground, and our flames shimmered across the red and white of our fur. We could handle the guards; Inky just had to hurry.

Thankful my energy was stronger in this form; I attacked the front line, and like before, I needed no training to know how to fight as a wolf. She was brutal, using flames, claws, and teeth to bounce across them, ripping throats out. She held none of that human hesitance about taking life. It was *them versus us*, and in that situation, she was without mercy. Without morality questions.

She was death, relishing in the power.

As we bit into one of the freilds, she started to drain their life, stealing it and sucking it deep into the well that was sustaining us and our creatures. I'd done this before, even if I hadn't quite known it at the time.

Whatever Dannie had created when she'd bonded a mist born with a shifter had formed a being that no one had ever seen before. A being with the potential to destroy worlds.

If it hadn't been me, I would have feared that being, and I knew that one day someone would come after me. Worried I'd go rogue and be a true threat. I'd deal with that then; for now, I was fighting, all the while hoping that Inky had figured out how to open the door—

I heard the whoosh of air behind me, and that *beautiful amazing cloud of fucking smoke* had done exactly what I'd needed. It had gotten me into the passage that would lead me down under the mists. Down to my creatures.

Now we just had to get there before an entire fucking army descended on us. Even a mist and a fire wolf would be screwed if that happened.

Ripping out my last throat—the bitter taste of the blood had the human side of us gagging until it cleared from our mouth—we bounced away from the guards and toward the open doorway.

Inky was waiting for me on the inside, and when I leapt in, it slammed the door closed again, shutting off the dying light from outside. My flames were still sprinkled across my fur, brighter in some places, giving us enough illumination to see the stairs that we had to descend.

Another creature death hit me, and then another, and whoever was killing them was going for gold now, sensing I was on my way. Fucking fuck. Inky swept my wolf up and we tried to rip it to pieces— don't startle the wolf, apparently—but there was no way to hurt the mist. Thankfully.

We settled a moment later, since this was the fastest way down the stairs, all the while trying not to howl at the agony of losing more of my creatures.

The curve of the stairs widened as we zoomed toward the bottom, round and round, until I was dizzy and wondering how fucking deep this chamber went.

Another death hit me. *One of my abervoqs.*

My howl split the air, and even Inky flinched at the guttural sound, ripped from the center of my being; from my own pain and loss; from my power.

We flew wonky for a beat, but we'd finally reached the lowest level, so I was able to jump off, running toward my creatures.

The heat down here was intense, and it was only when I rounded a stone corner that I understood why. The lava was everywhere, spilling in rivers down the walls, across the floor, and puddling into a huge lava pit. It was also in a curtain separating me from the thousands of creatures, and that was why they hadn't been able to get to me.

They couldn't cross the lava barrier.

As I closed in, another one was thrown into the large pool of red, burning lava below, and a cry tore from me. I was a mother losing her children, a part of me dying with each of their deaths.

Stalking across the stone, I had to walk a fine line between lava and rock to make it closer to the massive platform where all the creatures gathered. Only pausing when the bitch of the day stepped into view.

I felt not a single flicker of surprise when Ixana appeared, part of me knowing all along that she was more than Shadow's poor broken true mate. She had an evil streak, and now we were going to know exactly what her game was.

"If it isn't the whore who stole my true mate," she said with a raspy laugh. Truth be told, she did actually look a little pissed off by that.

Wanting to speak, I drew on my human side, and my wolf let me change back. When I was naked and on two legs, I felt my hair fall in long strands to my thighs. Each shift near the mists was giving me vitality and life.

Hopefully it would be enough to get me, and the beings I loved, through this.

"Where is Cristell?" I asked.

Ixana laughed. "Dead."

Hmm, okay. "When did she die?"

If Shadow was watching this through Inky, then this was important information for him to have.

"She died the day I barred Shadow from the realm."

This truth did take me by surprise.

It had been her all along.

From the first betrayal, when she must have created an illusion to make Shadow think it was his sister who'd given him the spelled cup. To the spell on the doorway, her energy powering it all.

I held a finger up, furrowing my brow. "You're gonna have to bad guy monologue for me here because I'm confused about why you'd tear your true mate from this world. You could have just ruled with him."

Ixana didn't answer, but she did attack, her power barreling across the lava and into my chest, sending me flying into a nearby wall. She was beyond strong, and the simpering annoying ice queen was nowhere to be seen, her true form blossoming to life. This was the being who had ruled for thousands of years, stealing energy and destroying my creatures.

Inky rushed to help me up, and by the time I got back to the divide, Ixana managed to toss a bunch of my creatures into the lava pool below her. As each died an agonizing death, my stomach swirled, and I turned my head to the side to throw up. There was nothing solid in there, so I got the fun of gagging and choking on bile.

"Stop!" I screamed. "If you kill them all, the Nexus will fall!"

Ixana laughed, blasting more power my way, like a wall of bullets raining across Inky and me. "I *want* the damn Nexus to fall. No power can stand against mine then, and I've built enough down here to sustain us all."

What? She was freaking insane.

"The Nexus falls, so does Shadow Realm."

Inky was trying to get me closer to Ixana and the creatures, but her power was too great. I was about to wolf out again and hope that made a difference, when I felt Angel closing in through our bond.

Relief smashed through me when she burst into the underground, Shadow right behind her, covered in flames. He didn't stop for a beat, tearing through the lava and crashing into Ixana. The pair disappeared behind another flowing wall of lava, gone from sight.

Inky took off after its bonded master, and I sent a quick hope and wish into the universe that I wouldn't lose both of them to this insane bitch.

There was nothing I could do to help him. Well, not directly, but indirectly... if I freed the creatures, some of her power would be voided.

Angel reached my side, and without words, she knew what I needed. I needed my creatures. Even as Ixana had destroyed so many, there were thousands still trapped. "We can't get through that," Angel shouted, her gaze darting down the fall of lava. "It's lava born of the mists. And Ixana has been powering it for years."

She had, by throwing living, breathing beings into her fucking sacrifice pool.

"She said she had the power to keep this world running even if the Nexus fell," I told her in an angry snarl of words. "How? How could she possibly manage that?"

Angel paused, and I could tell that she was running her computer brain through every possible scenario of how that would work, cataloguing the most likely scenario. Before she could spit out her results, a new energy filtered through the space. More than one, actually, and the only reason we didn't panic at power like that racing toward us, was that I recognized it.

Shadow had called in extra backup; we just had to pray they weren't too late to save their best friend. "Let's get you some clothing," Angel said, her energy weaving together a shirt and pants. They were different to what Shadow created, the clothing rougher, as if they'd been pulled from the raw materials that existed here, but at least my ass was covered.

"Mera!" Len shouted, the first one to appear just as I finished getting dressed. His skin glowed silver as power surrounded him in the same manner as his cloak. "Where is Shadow?"

He stopped at my side, and right behind him were Alstair, bringing a sense of calm with him. He wore a full armored outfit this time, brandishing deadly gold-and-bronze, long-bladed knives. Then there was Reece, the dry winds of change coming with him, and the desert deity had never looked larger or angrier as he did storming forward, literal dust flying around him. Gallilei was last, silent and deadly as always, and I felt the caress of his energy in my mind as he greeted me.

No Lucien, and I was grateful that not only had they arrived to help us, but they were still taking my request to protect Simone seriously.

"Shadow is fighting his mate," I said in a rush, pointing to where they'd disappeared. "In the lavafalls."

Alstair placed his hand on my shoulder, and against my will, I calmed. "He's alive, and he's fighting strongly like the warrior he is. You do not need to panic."

Thank fuck.

I was about to say something else when Len froze. It was noticeable because he always moved fluidly, with the sort of grace that only the fae had, but this had been a jagged, jarring movement.

"What is it?" Reece snapped, picking up on the distress on his friend's face.

"My stone," he breathed, his skin ashen. "It's here, and it's brimming with power."

"Fuck."

We all looked at Angel as she breathed out a human curse, her eyes wide and shiny. She met my gaze and in that second, I knew exactly what Ixana had that gave her confidence to keep this world running even without the Nexus.

The sunburst stone.

She had the sunburst and the bloodstone, and between the two, she was going to take all the power for herself. She wanted to be the next Nexus. The next goddess of all.

Len grabbed at me, and I could have sworn that Shadow let out a raging bellow from somewhere in the depths. It was so nice to hear that sound. "What do you know?" Len demanded, uncaring that his friend was going to beat his ass for throwing me around like this.

"Ixana has your stone," I confirmed, hurrying to explain what I'd learned from Dannie about Shadow and me, and the ice queen herself.

"Ixana had this entire elaborate illusion set up to trick Shadow and... well, me. Once she felt us return to her realm, she knew she could use our power to fulfill the goal she'd been working toward for thousands of years. Destroy the Nexus and become the only true power here."

"That's why the land is so drained," Angel said, her voice shaking. "She's been gathering as much power, sacrificing as many as she can, all on this quest."

Len lifted his hands then, his eyes closed as he called power to his being, and my mouth went dry at the wash of energy that felt as ancient as the worlds themselves. A high-pitched, ringing sound started low before picking up intensity.

A beat later, the stone came into view. It was suspended over the lava pit, above the sacrifice pool, and it was the most brilliant gem I'd ever seen. About the size of two fists, the bright yellow orb twinkled and spun, visible energy trailing up to it from the sacrifice pool.

Len took a step forward, his arm shaking as he lifted it, twirling his hand like he was feeling for an energy in the air. "She's been hiding it; the stone's natural energy has been meshing to the mists so no one could tell it was here." He sucked in a deep breath. "It's so powerful. Enough power to destroy this world... even create new worlds. The mists are the power of creation, and this stone is now that as well."

I placed my hand on his arm, both of us needing the fortification. "This is why you never found any information," I breathed. "This world was blocked from the Library of Knowledge, making the realm the perfect place to contain it in secret."

He shook his head, squeezing his eyes closed. "But it was stolen by fae. By a family friend who tricked us all into thinking they were on our side."

"Ixana," I growled, "is the queen of deception. Of illusion. And she alone has controlled the spell on the door that kept the realm barred from the other worlds."

There was a decent chance, that even Kristoff was part of her elaborate scheme to get us exactly where she needed us, to ensure all of this would happen. He was probably dead, despite what the others had seen.

"Why didn't she just collect all the creatures herself?" I wondered out loud. "She obviously had the time and power to get it done."

Angel's wings shot out behind her as her face darkened into furious lines. "She was trying to, but even with her considerable power, there was one part always off limits to her. The land and creatures near the Nexus."

And I'd come along and just handed them all to her on a silver platter.

Flames of my fury licked around me, and it took concerted effort not to rage and kill everything in this room. That would be a little counterproductive to what I wanted to achieve here today.

"How do we stop her?" Reece bit out, his hands clenched at his sides. He was watching for Shadow, that much was clear as he scanned that unbroken lavafall through which the beast and the bitch had disappeared.

At this point, I was done waiting. Shadow hadn't been destroyed by the fire, so I had a shot. A shot was enough today.

Chapter Forty-Eight

I didn't ask permission because I knew they'd stop me, especially Angel. None of them had been born of the mists like me, so there was no way they could cross the threshold. I had to do this alone, without my mist, because down here, Midnight was the enemy.

Sidling away from the group, I found they were thankfully occupied with the intensely bright sunburst stone, trying to calculate if touching it would kill them all.

Calling my flames, I felt the singing in my blood as more heat filled the air. My wolf leant me her strength as well as I literally stepped through a barrier of boiling lava. It burned at first, and I screamed at the unexpected jolt of agonizing pain. In the same instant, my flames surged to the surface, cutting that pain off so I could finish crossing unscathed.

My flames counteracted the burn of this lava. Protecting me. Healing the few burns I had received.

On the other side, my creatures howled and brayed at me, the noise near deafening. Angel and the guys were calling to me as well, and while I couldn't hear them through the lava barrier, I recognized their body language, and could lip read well enough to know they were not happy about my rash decision to go lava diving.

Eh, we could deal with that later.

Drawing on my bond to the creatures, I filtered through their energies, my heart hurting at how scared they were. These were intelligent, feeling beings, and they had been standing in line waiting to be slaughtered. Even worse, watching as their brethren were killed in front of them.

Death was not good enough for Ixana. She needed to suffer for an eternity.

Ten fucking eternities.

I was surprised to find a lot of the creatures here weren't bonded to me, so as Angel had surmised, Ixana had been gathering them on her own as well. The ones she could get to anyway.

Before I could figure out how to bond the rest to me, I was jolted by another creature death, and since Ixana was still occupied with Shadow, I had no idea how the creatures were still dying.

It wasn't until I pushed through the abervoqs to get to the edge that I saw about five of her furred people throwing my creatures off the cliff.

"NO!" I screamed, my energy rippling from me as I sent Ixana's minions freefalling straight off the side and into the lava below. Now it was Ixana's turn to scream and rage, and I heard her from in the depths of the lavafalls. Shadow's rumble followed, and at least I knew he was alive.

Now to save everyone else.

Knowing that all of this was tied to the stone, I decided that was the key. I needed to break the connection it had to Ixana and the mists, removing her true advantage.

But how to do that and survive?

Len would probably know if grabbing the stone would destroy me, but since he wasn't here, and I couldn't hear them through the lava, I'd have to do what I did best: wing it.

What could possibly go wrong?

"Lift me, please," I said to an abervoq, one of the largest of the creatures.

It understood me, reaching down to haul me up, holding my body above its head. I had to wiggle myself around, but after climbing up its arm and standing on that large, meaty paw, I was just about the right height to jump for the stone.

Crouching, preparing myself mentally for what pain might come from this, I shot one last look at my friends, finding all of them staring at me in horror.

No, wait... They weren't looking at me. They were looking *behind* me...

I spun in time to find Ixana right there, smashing into my side, knocking me down off the creature. As we hit the ground, my flames and wolf surged up, shredding through my clothes as we tore into her without thought of consequence.

My attack took her by surprise; she was already visibly beaten, no doubt thanks to Shadow, who also appeared a moment later, yanking her off me.

"Whoa," I groaned, jumping to my feet. "You are one heavy bitch."

She snarled again, hands out as she looked between Shadow and me. He had already backed up closer to me, and I felt a moment of satisfaction that he still chose me. I mean, sure, his mate was a complete psychopath with delusions of grandeur, but... technically, I'd still won the beast.

Score.

"She plans on using the sunburst stone from Len's family to turn herself into the next Nexus," I murmured to him in a rush, feeling the vibrating surge of his power across my skin.

"I know," he bit out.

"I invited Shadow to join me," Ixana said. "I mean, he started as a means to an end. My family wanted to take over Trinity, so they ensured I'd be in the perfect position to do so. But when I learned I would be their puppet, I decided that no longer would I fall victim to cruel, powerful rulers. I would take the power into my own hands."

There was a dark story there, one that had left scars littered on her psyche, but we didn't have time for it today. Today we just had to stop her before this plan came to fruition.

Shadow growled. "Cristell never betrayed me. It was Ixana all along. She killed my sister, used the illusion of her to throw everyone off, and orchestrated it all herself."

The cunt in question laughed. "I mean, everyone thought illusion was such a weak skill. 'Oh, you can make pretty pictures with your mind. How nice, Ixxy.'" Her voice grew stronger. "Little did they know, illusion is the closest power to the mists. I did what no other royal has been able to, I tamed them. And I was content to rule as I was, slowly building power into this stone, all the while keeping Cristell as the public enemy. An easy task since she was an evil little bitch, who probably was planning on taking over, only I beat her to it." Her eyes flashed with an insanity she'd done well to hide up until now. "When I felt Shadow's energy return, I knew I could finalize my original plans. It was time to turn myself into the next Nexus, using a Nexus born shifter to gather the thousands of creatures beyond my reach." Her gaze smashed into mine. "Thanks for all your help with that, *Mera*."

Shadow's chest was rumbling, his muscles tense and visible through the many tears in his shirt. They'd been fighting, but at least no physical injuries remained on his body.

"You were my true mate," she said randomly, and at this point it was fairly obvious she was completely bonkers. "But I could never break through to you. Why?" For the first time, she was genuinely curious.

"You're not worthy," he said without inflection... or hesitation.

She reached for the stone's energy. I felt it as she used whatever bonded her to the gem, and when it gathered in her hands, I knew that it was going to be too much for us to handle. "*You* are not worthy," she snarled back.

In my panic, I reached for the deepest recesses of my energy, drawing up from *the Nexus*. Or at least that was what it felt like. The spell she'd created from the sunburst stone shot our way, and I released the power I'd gathered as well. Just as our two powers were about to slam into each other, a bright light burst up between us, intercepting them both.

No! Not a light... a phoenix.

Dannie's phoenix.

"Mother!" Shadow dove toward her, but the goddess was here to save her son, and she wasn't waiting for a rescue.

Visibly hurt from the energy that had hit her, she swiped out with her flaming tail feathers and smashed Ixana in the face, sending her spinning and cartwheeling into a wall off the side of the platform.

Before she could right herself, Dannie was soaring high, her flaming bird strong and regal, so incredibly beautiful as it went for the sunburst stone.

Ixana shot more energy, but it was too late to stop Dannie from swallowing the stone whole.

Shadow's painful howl was lost in the beat of silence, like the world held its breath, and then a light so bright that it blinded me instantly filled the room. I blinked and tried to shield my eyes, but there was no hope of getting around the power of that stone. Especially combined with a magical Nexus phoenix.

Shadow's hands were on me, holding me close as he crouched protectively across my body, neither of us sure about what was happening in the room. Eventually, the power fell, the light faded, and I was wrapped around my beast, holding on for dear fucking life.

He ran his hands over me, checking that everything was in its right spot, and I took that extra beat of comfort by hugging him, my nails digging into his back.

"Sunshine?" he rumbled.

"Dannie?" I choked out in answer, hoping he would have more information.

There was a heavy pause. "Gone."

Apparently, we could only speak in single-word answers, but I heard the grim tone in that one word. She was gone as far as he could tell, with no idea if she was dead or alive.

When he finally let me stand on my own, the first thing I noticed was that the lava barrier had dried up, allowing the creatures to cross to freedom. First thing first, though. Shadow found Ixana huddled on the floor, her hands over her face.

When she finally lifted them away, I choked on my gasp. Her eyes were gone, completely burned to nothing more than black embers, as she shook her head frantically.

"I can't see," she choked out. "Why can't I see? My stone. Where is my stone?"

The loss of power would be hitting her now, too much for her brain to handle after so many years tied to the stone.

Shadow reached for her. "You're done, Ixana," he said softly. "Where is the bloodstone?"

She was rattled enough not to fight, turning one of her coat buttons, clearly an illusion, into the ruby red stone. It fell into Shadow's palm, and I waited with bated breath, wondering if it was another trick.

The beast's head dropped back, a howl spilling from his lips as the power settled in his bones.

"Shadow," I said hesitantly.

His head snapped toward me. "Mine," he rumbled.

Was he talking about the stone or me? His friends converged on the scene before I could ask him to clarify. Reece went straight for Ixana, securing her with bindings that looked like they'd come right from the desert themselves, as a barbed cactus-type plant twisted around her.

"Shadow's mother should not have been able to do that," Len said, staring up at the spot where his stone had been. "That stone is too powerful."

There was no sign of Dannie at all. No feel of her power. No sense of what had happened to her.

"Let's get the creatures back and then we can search for her," I suggested, knowing Shadow would not rest until he found his mom. Or learned of her fate.

I felt the same way. She'd saved us when I'd had not a clue what to do. We owed Dannie a lot. I would not let her down.

Shadow, seemingly adapted to the new influx of power from his stone, stepped forward, just as Reece asked him if he was okay.

"Yes," the beast rumbled. "It'll be easier when the bonding ceremony is complete, but for now, we're meshing our energy without too much issue."

"Can you help me return the creatures?" I asked. "Before the Nexus falls completely without Dannie's energy."

"How did she leave it in the first place?" Angel asked.

Shadow's flaming irises met mine. "Sunshine called her. She's connected to Mera."

"She knew we were in trouble," I said sadly. "But before we can deal with that, we have to save the world."

Everyone nodded, falling into a circle around me as I drew the creatures toward me, before directing them to cross toward the exit. Shadow dropped his hand on my shoulder.

"I have a quicker way."

His energy surged up, and I blinked at how strong it was. The stone was already making a huge difference to his base power. A portal formed, The Grey Lands visible on the other side. "Thanks, Shadow," I said softly, sending my creatures through the six-feet-wide opening.

It was clearly going to take a few hours to get them all through, so I shooed the others away. "I'll stay here and make sure they get back safely," I said. "You all need to deal with the fallout upstairs."

Angel gave me a hug as she left, as did the other guys. Reece bound Ixana to him, dragging her up the stairs, since she was clearly their new prisoner, and would be dealt with later.

Shadow, the last to leave, hesitated. His eyes burned as his new stronger power hit me like a lightning bolt. One huge hand wrapped around the back of my head, and he lifted me so our lips could meet.

Desperation had me pulling him closer, and the fear I'd been holding deep inside during the entire battle turned up the intensity of the kiss. "We need to talk, Sunshine," he told me.

I nodded, my head spinning. "Yes, talk. Yes."

His laugh was a low, deep rumble. "Flustered Sunshine is one of my favorites."

He released me.

"Go," I whispered, not really meaning it. "You're the Supreme Being and you need to sort out the world of royals, guards, and freilds. Save your people."

He kissed me again, one more hard, perfect press of our lips. "I'll send any creatures I find down here," he murmured against my mouth. "Keeping my promise to you."

He brushed his fingers across my face, leaving behind a spark of power that had my knees buckling. I caught myself, possibly drooling a little as he left the room, his broad shoulders and perfect ass the last thing I saw before he disappeared up the stairs.

Chapter Forty-Nine

A sense of accomplishment settled deep in my chest as my creatures found their freedom. More joined the ones who had been down here, stolen from the royals above, and sent into my protective embrace by Shadow and our friends.

He was absolutely honoring his promise to me.

As the adrenaline wore off, I expected to feel exhausted, but I didn't. Whatever Ixana had been doing, draining the energy from the mists and land, had been hurting me. Hurting every being here.

But now I had a new lease on life. A new surge of energy.

Angel popped her head in a few times to check on me, and apparently, it was going well upstairs. It was going well down here as well, and when the last of the creatures had finally filed through Shadow's doorway some hours later, I knew my work was only beginning.

Shadow Realm had been screwed over for thousands of years, and it would take more than a minute to fix that.

Knowing his doorway would remain open until Shadow was done, I decided to step through myself, following the last of the tiny grekins, their chattering comforting now, when it had at one time been terrifying.

Not that I didn't miss "fuck ours," but it was nice to feel the real essence of their character. My heart overflowing at the bond I felt to them all. Just call me "Crazy Creature Lady" because I was ready to have a dozen or more of them in my life. My new pack.

Family.

The chick with no family suddenly had thousands.

Shadow's doorway had dropped the creatures near the Nexus, and as I stepped closer, I was relieved to feel the strong thrum of that power there. Not only that, but already I could see signs of life spreading across the land, and I felt like that would only be possible if...

"Dannie?" I called.

My creatures brayed at the sound of my voice, the thousands of them setting off into the land. This was their goodbye, and I loved that, but my focus was on the Nexus.

Is the phoenix there?

Running up the hill, I dodged creatures, keeping my eyes locked on the stone entrance. It seemed like the Nexus itself was growing in size, the mountaintop spreading to make room for it. Life was returning and Dannie was here, I knew it.

When I hit the entrance, I stepped through the energy, and it wrapped around me like an old friend. There was no immediate sign of the phoenix, so I began to search. "Dannie!" I shouted as I went. "Are you here?"

Please be here.

I wasn't sure how to deal with her sacrifice for the second time. It was too much for my mind to wrap around, and it was much easier to pretend she was still alive, returning power to this land and the realm with the help of the sunburst stone.

Only there was no sign.

Just when I was about to give up, a figure stepped into view.

It was Dannie. Only a Dannie like I'd never seen before, with her cascading red and gold skin, eyes a burst of fire, and feathers covering parts of her body, like she'd crossed between a phoenix and a human.

If there was ever a *rise from the ashes* scenario, it was this one because the evolution of Dannie was nothing short of spectacular. Rushing forward, I threw myself at her, and she caught me with ease, the warmth of her chuckle both familiar and powerful enough to have my blood fizzing.

"Whoa," I said. "You're powerful, my friend."

Her energy felt a little scary, far beyond her own son's, or any being I'd ever met.

"Mera, born of my mists," she trilled, her voice like a rainbow of sound and texture. "We saved our Nexus and this world."

I nodded, pulling back to see her. "I know! I can't believe it. The realm will be restored, and Shadow will take his place as the Supreme Being."

Dannie's face morphed as she looked pleased by that statement. "Yes. My son will rule the land, and I will rule the mists." Some of her benevolent happiness faded and now she wore a dark mask, making her near unrecognizable. "But what is Mera's place?"

Warning bells rung in my head, and like a blinding flash of light, or a smack in the face, I saw that this evolution of Dannie had done more than change her skin color. It had stolen some of her humanity.

"What do you mean? I'm not planning on taking any place here, Dan. It's just me. Mera."

Could I remind her of the pup she'd taken under her wing when I'd been a broken child?

She regarded me. "Yes. You are Mera, and I don't want to destroy you, but I also fear that you might take my power. My position. There should be one guardian of the Nexus and I lost sight of that when I joined the royals."

More alarm bells, and I attempted to back away, but she had me locked down. "Shadow won't let you do whatever you have planned," I warned her.

Her smile no longer held any kindness, no warmth in her eyes. Just a cold calculation. "You might be right. You're the first chink in his armor in his lifetime, and maybe you will be a distraction that prevents him from being the best ruler he can be."

It was like she had to reason it out in her head, whatever she was planning. "This is all my fault," she muttered. "I altered this world by having a royal child, by throwing off the balance. Then to make it even worse, I brought you to life."

She continued on and on, a fractured mind, a broken goddess. One who wasn't solely evil, but I sensed she was about to do something that could destroy me forever. And no matter how I struggled, I couldn't break free of her power.

Eventually, her face brightened, and any unease plaguing her vanished. "I think this can all work out," she trilled. "You already have a destiny that your other side craves. If I make sure that you can never reach your full potential, you will live the life of the shifters, leaving the balance of the realm alone."

I shook my head. "Dannie, no. What are you saying?" I fought harder, my limbs straining as fire built in my center.

When her hands come up to rest on my head, she smiled, and for the first time in minutes, it was almost kind. A sense of caring emanated from her. "My sweet little wolf. Do not worry. You will not miss what you don't know, and Torin has the potential to be a wonderful mate for you."

Torin? The asshole who'd fucked another woman in front of me? *That Torin?*

My head was racing as I tried to think through a possible scenario to get myself out of this situation. What could I say to convince her to let me go long enough so I could get to my friends?

"Dannie, you love me, remember?"

"Yes." She nodded, her face brighter than ever. She was beautiful in her insanity, the power rebuilding her into this incredible being. "I do, and I will ensure your happiness, I promise. This will work. Memories are such a fickle thing, you know. One year of life, so easily erased. I can do that. For you and Shadow, and then I will right what I wronged."

I opened my mouth to scream, reaching for Shadow, Angel, Midnight... anyone whom I had a connection to. Before a single squeak could emerge, Dannie flicked her fingers and everything went dark.

Chapter Fifty

A hand tracing along my spine woke me first, and in my sleepy state, I felt the fuzzy nature of my mind. Had I gone drinking with Simone last night? Why the hell did I feel like I was hungover?

Wait? Who the fuck was touching me?

Spinning over in bed, I dislodged the hand, finding myself facing a naked chest. Broad and bronze, I had no idea it was Torin until I lifted my head and met his wide-eyed gaze.

"What the fuck?" I snarled, looking down to see I was thankfully dressed. Well, dressed in underwear, but that was better than the alternative.

Torin seemed super confused by my reaction, and if he didn't start speaking soon, he was going to get a kick in the face. "What are you doing in my bed, Torin?" I snapped.

He lifted both hands in front of him. "This is our bed, Meers. We're mated."

I wracked my brain for understanding of what he'd just said. "Mated?"

He nodded. "Yeah. True mates. For like a couple of months now."

His voice was low and gentle, trying to calm me. "We're the alphas of the Torma pack."

I shook my head a few times, but I stopped backing away from him because there was a truth in what he'd just said. Torin was my true mate, our connection thrumming in my chest. His words made sense, but...

"I can't remember it," I whispered, rubbing at my aching temples.

He was concerned, his handsome face drifting closer. "Did you hit your head, love? What's the last thing you remember?"

He tried to touch me, but I flinched back. "I remember you torturing me for years. I remember..."

What was the last thing?

"My first shift," I breathed. "You rejected me."

Torin, still looking worried, shot me a wonky smile. "You forgave me for that, babe. Remember? I did reject you initially, but I've reclaimed you every day since."

Reclaimed.

Was it true? Could I really be mated to the alpha of the Torma pack?

I did feel claimed, but... not by him. If not him, though, who else could there be?

Torin crowded closer, and it was clear he was naked as the sheets moved, giving me more than a glimpse of his body. Once upon a time, before I'd hated him and Jaxson, I'd have loved to have a mate as strong and sexy as Torin, but... he'd been my tormentor.

His hands landed on me, and my wolf arched her spine, enjoying the sensation of our mate touching us. I swallowed again, my throat bone dry. "Maybe I had a bad dream," I told him. "My head is aching."

"Sleep, my mate," he said soothingly. "I will take care of you."

As I settled against the pillows, my eyes drifted closed, and I decided that I'd deal with the weird gaps in my memory tomorrow.

Simone would have answers.

Jaxson too, even if I had to beat them out of him.

Maybe it would be as Torin had said, and in that case, I might enjoy being the alpha of Torma. Torin as my mate.

That was my destiny, after all.

READY FOR THE final chapter in this story? Don't forget to pre-order Reborn here: smarturl.it/ShadowBeast3

STAY CONNECTED

The best way to stay up to date with the Shadow Beast Shifters world and all new releases, is to join my Facebook group here:

www.facebook/groups/jayminevenerdherd

We share lots of book releases, fun posts, sexy dudes, and generally it's a happy place to exist.

Next best place is my newsletter at www.jaymineve.com and

www.facebook.com/JayminEve.Author

And lastly, if you're looking for more delicious demon type guys and bookish babes, this is the group for you:

facebook.com/groups/bookbabesandlordsofdarkness

So many amazing authors to read!

AFTERWORD

So, look, I'm going to be straight up honest here. I really thought this was a better cliffy than book one. I promise, I did. I was all proud of myself for ending a complete story arc and making sure that it wasn't left mid-scene.

Apparently, I was wrong. Apparently, this cliffhanger is way fucking worse, and I did not do anything other than enrage you all.

This was not my intention. I'm definitely... almost certainly... quite possibly (there's a decent chance, okay?) that I will fix this, and we can all go back to being friends.

Cool?

Cool.

p.s moving house if anyone is looking for me. Address unknown.

ALSO BY JAYMIN EVE

JAYMIN EVE

Shadow Beast Shifters (Urban Fantasy/ PNR)

Book One: Rejected

Book Two: Reclaimed

Book Three: Reborn (March 31st 2021)

Royals of Arbon Academy (Dark, complete Contemporary Romance)

Book One: Princess Ballot

Book Two: Playboy Princes

Book Three: Poison Throne

Titan's Saga (PNR/UF. Sexy and humorous)

Book One: Releasing the Gods

Book Two: Wrath of the Gods

Book Three: Revenge of the Gods

Supernatural Academy (Complete Urban Fantasy/PNR)

Year One

Year Two

Year Three

Dark Legacy (Complete Dark Contemporary high school romance)

Book One: Broken Wings

Book Two: Broken Trust

Book Three: Broken Legacy

Secret Keepers Series (Complete PNR/Urban Fantasy)

Book One: House of Darken

Book Two: House of Imperial

Book Three: House of Leights

Book Four: House of Royale

Storm Princess Saga (Complete High Fantasy)

Book One: The Princess Must Die

Book Two: The Princess Must Strike

Book Three: The Princess Must Reign

Curse of the Gods Series (Complete Reverse Harem Fantasy)

Book One: Trickery

Book Two: Persuasion

Book Three: Seduction

Book Four: Strength

Novella: Neutral

Book Five: Pain

NYC Mecca Series (Complete - UF series)

Book One: Queen Heir

Book Two: Queen Alpha

Book Three: Queen Fae

Book Four: Queen Mecca

A Walker Saga (Complete - YA Fantasy)

Book One: First World

Book Two: Spurn

Book Three: Crais

Book Four: Regali

Book Five: Nephilius

Book Six: Dronish

Book Seven: Earth

Supernatural Prison Trilogy (Complete UF series)

Book One: Dragon Marked

Book Two: Dragon Mystics

Book Three: Dragon Mated

Book Four: Broken Compass

Book Five: Magical Compass

Book Six: Louis

Book Seven: Elemental Compass

Hive Trilogy (Complete UF/PNR series)

Book One: Ash

Book Two: Anarchy

Book Three: Annihilate

Sinclair Stories (Standalone Contemporary Romance)

Songbird

9 781925 876239